A King's Trade

Also by Dewey Lambdin

The King's Coat

The French Admiral

The King's Commission

The King's Privateer

The Gun Ketch

HMS Cockerel

A King's Commander

Jester's Fortune

King's Captain

Sea of Grey

Havoc's Sword

The Captain's Vengeance

A King's Trade

An Alan Lewrie Naval Adventure

Dewey Lambdin

THOMAS DUNNE BOOKS
ST. MARTIN'S GRIFFIN
NEW YORK

This is a work of fiction. All of the characters, organizations, and events portrayed in this novel are either products of the author's imagination or are used fictitiously.

THOMAS DUNNE BOOKS.
An imprint of St. Martin's Press.

www.thomasdunnebooks.com
www.stmartins.com

Library of Congress Cataloging-in-Publication Data

Lambdin, Dewey.
A King's trade : an Alan Lewrie naval adventure / Dewey Lambdin.
p. cm.
ISBN-13: 978-0-312-37864-6
ISBN-10: 0-312-37864-5
1. Lewrie, Alan (Fictitious character)—Fiction. 2. Great Britain—History, Naval—18th century—Fiction. 3. Naval convoys—Fiction. 4. Derelicts—Fiction. 5. Sea stories. I. Title.

PS3562.A435 K58 2006
813'.54—dc22

2006043875

First St. Martin's Griffin Edition: January 2008

10 9 8 7 6 5 4 3 2 1

This is for all those chameleons and inflated rubber palominos I brought back from Ringling Brothers, Barnum & Bailey over the years, that went "tits-up" within a week.

And, for Clarabelle the Clown on *Howdy Doody*, Bozo, of course, Krusty on *The Simpsons*, the late, great Emmett Kelly, and Marcel Marceau.

"Honk!"

"Honk Honk!"

"Honk Honk Honk!"

"———!!"

He always had to have the last word.

Quem res plus nimio delectavere secundae,
mutatae quatient.

One whom Fortune's smiles have delighted
overmuch, will reel under the shock of change.

HORACE, *EPISTLES* I, x, 30-31

Full-Rigged Ship: Starboard (right) side view

1. Mizen Topgallant
2. Mizen Topsail
3. Spanker
4. Main Royal
5. Main Topgallant
6. Mizen T'gallant Staysail
7. Main Topsail
8. Main Course
9. Main T'gallant Staysail
10. Middle Staysail
11. Main Topmast Staysail
12. Fore Royal
13. Fore Topgallant
14. Fore Topsail
15. Fore Course
16. Fore Topmast Staysail
17. Inner Jib
18. Outer Flying Jib
19. Spritsail

A. Taffrail & Lanterns
B. Stern & Quarter-galleries
C. Poop Deck/Great Cabins Under
D. Rudder & Transom Post
E. Quarterdeck
F. Mizen Chains & Stays
G. Main Chains & Stays
H. Boarding Battens/Entry Port
I. Cargo Loading Skids
J. Shrouds & Ratlines
K. Fore Chains & Stays
L. Waist
M. Gripe & Cutwater
N. Figurehead & Beakhead Rails
O. Bow Sprit
P. Jib Boom
Q. Foc's'le & Anchor Cat-heads
R. Cro'jack Yard (no sail fitted)
S. Top Platforms
T. Cross-Trees
U. Spanker Gaff

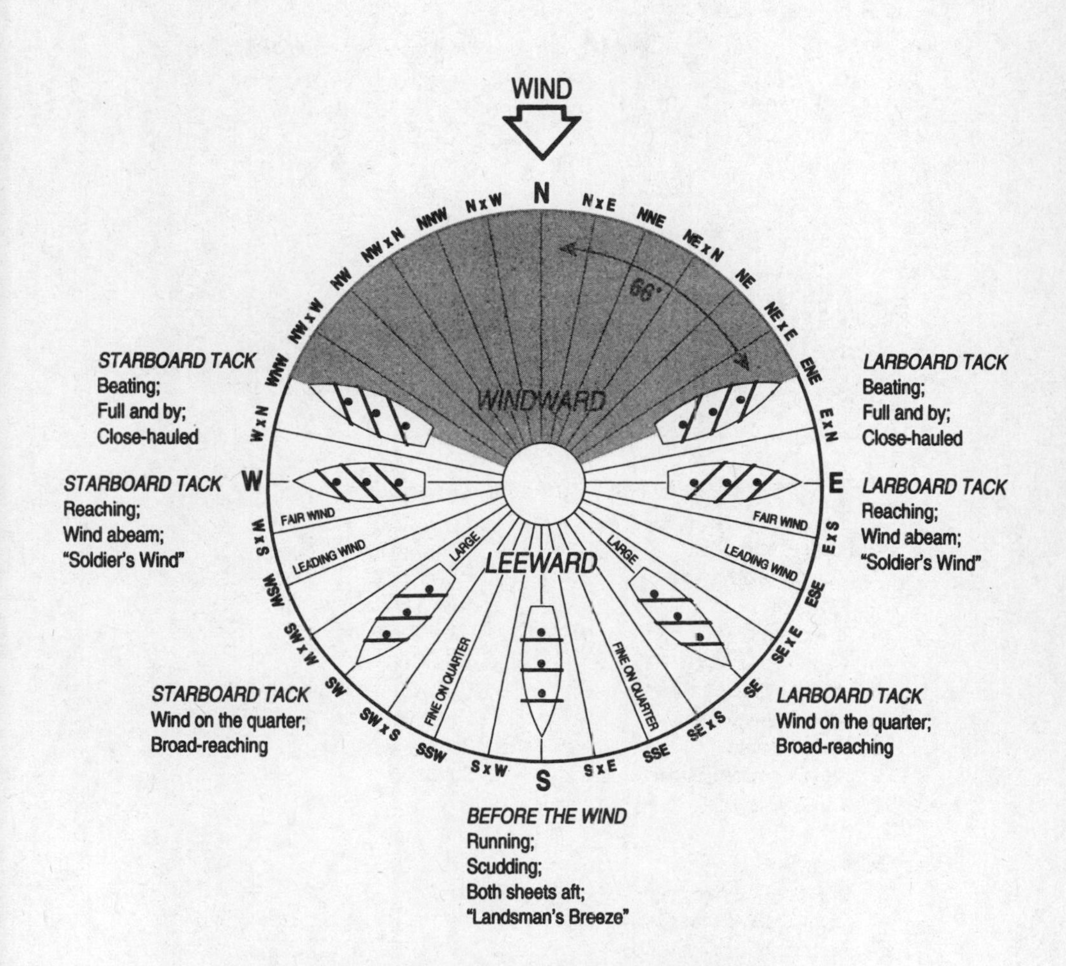

POINTS OF SAIL AND 32-POINT WIND-ROSE

A King's
Trade

PROLOGUE

"Vir bonus," omne forum quem spectat et omne tribunal . . .
"Iane, pater!" clare, clare cum dixit "Apollo!";
*labra movet metuens audiri: "Pulchra Laverna,**
da mihi fallere, da iusto sanctoque videri!
Noctem peccatis et fraudibus obice nubem!"

This "good man," for forum and tribunal, the cynosure of every eye...cries with loud voice, "Father Janus!," with loud voice, "Apollo!," then moves his lips, fearing to be heard; "Fair Laverna, grant me to escape detection, grant me to pass as just and upright, shroud my sins in night, my lies in clouds!"

HORACE, *EPISTLES* I, XVI, 57-62

*Laverna, the ancient goddess of thieves

CHAPTER ONE

Bleakness . . . bleakness on every hand. The North Atlantic was as vast, and grey, and desolate as it was the morning before the Lord said, "Let there be land." A slow, chill rain sullenly fell, pattering as light as cat-feet on the fresh-scrubbed decks, a rain so light that it could be mistaken for heavy dew shaken off the masts and sails, and the miles of rope rigging by a listless West-Sou'west wind, a wind that had a definite late autumn nip to it.

The seas had moderated from a half-gale past midnight, and were now only slowly heaving, the wave-sets between crests now nearly twice the overall length of the frigate that lay fetched-to into that wind, her bows aimed at Halifax, from which she had departed three weeks before.

The sun was up there in the overcast . . . somewhere, smothered by a drab pall that hung like an oxided pewter bowl above the frigate, stretching from one horizon to the other, with darker banks of clouds to the East, where last night's gale had gone. There were, here and there, promising thinner, lighter patches to North and South, definitely to the Westward. Perhaps by the next sunrise, there would be clear weather. It had been a week since they had seen a clear sky for the noonday reckoning by sextant. Their position had been guessed by the miles run from noon to noon, the compass course steered, with an educated guess of the magnetic deviation rate, the farther they had sailed East'rd, perhaps even a dabble in the arcane arts.

For all Capt. Alan Lewrie, RN, knew, his Sailing Master, Mr. Winwood, that humourlessly dour, prim, and ponderously long-suffering fellow, had been taking the auspicious auguries of seagull guts down in the dark of the orlop. However he did it, Winwood had lifted his nose just after sunrise, and had requested that the ship be fetched-to for trial casts of the deep-sea lead line.

After the insistent icy fury of the half gale they'd suffered, fetching-to to relative stillness had sounded like a fine idea, and an opportunity to dry things out below, relight the galley fires, and cook a hot breakfast for the weary, banged-about, and chilblained crew for the first time in days. And brew coffee . . . most *especially* coffee!

Mr. Winwood now stood on the starboard gangway amidships, with two of his Quartermasters, Motte and Austen, amid a horde of curious, expectant sailors who had no duties to perform while HMS *Proteus* was cocked up to windward and only making a slight half-knot sternway; men of the duty watch, off-duty men wakened by the sudden stillness and the sounds and slack motion of an idling hull, found cause to gather round below in the waist and watch, or help with the hoisting winch; on-duty men on the gangway itself casually joshed and japed in soft tones with those poor fellows selected to go overside to tend the deep-sea plumb, who had to wear the chest-deep harsh canvas hawse-breeches and leggings with the cork-soled feet on them, and work on the main-chains platform just feet from the curling, chilly sea, tend the safety lines that kept their mates from being plucked away or drenched by an errant roll or a rogue wave.

Even so, the men overside had to be changed every quarter-hour, or they'd be frozen stiff, and be hauled back in-board drenched to the skin, their hands numb and fish-belly white from guiding the lead-line and counting the knots as it was retrieved from the icy waters.

Think I can hear their teeth chatterin' from here, Lewrie told himself as he took off his cocked hat, his battered second-best, with the gilt lace gone mouldy green, and tucked it under his left arm. He gave his scalp a good fingernail scrubbing, ran spread fingers through his thick, slightly curling mid-brown hair as a "Welsh comb," and took another look about.

Long-practiced, long-trained eyes swept over the sails, weather braces, and rigging, finding nothing amiss. The wind on his cheeks as he cocked his head left and right . . . steady, and the ship's head was in no danger of falling off to leeward of a sudden, for the two hands tending the large double-wheel helm were studiously alert, oblivious to anything outside their duties. Grey-blue eyes swept aloft, again; the commissioning pendant pointed aft and nearly East'rd, curling lazy, sinuous snake-crawls; the lookouts posted at the cross-trees of upper masts were keeping their eyes out-board on the horizon; on their feet, not slouching, and would sing out if they had anything to report. But, they didn't, of course. This patch of the North Atlantic—and just *which* part of it they still had to discover—was yawningly empty of anything. Not a rock, not a wave-breaking shoal, not even a lone seabird that might have presaged their awaited landfall. Surprisingly, given the longitude they estimated their frigate had attained, there wasn't even a hint of another vessel's sail, either. As close as they supposed they'd come to the British Isles, there should have been dozens of merchantmen, fishing boats, by now. Unless, Capt. Alan Lewrie cynically imagined, they'd missed it altogether, and were somewhere to the West of Scandinavia, South of the Shetlands or Orkneys! For it was certainly cold enough for those climes.

Closer-to, Lewrie was pleased to note the steel-greyness of the sea, the milk-white curlings of the wavetops. The sea was scending no more than five or six feet, now, was no longer green with disturbance, and didn't smell like fresh fish any longer. Craning over the ship's larboard, windward, bulwarks near the shrouds of the mizen-mast, Lewrie took a moment to be satisfied, even a bit pleased, as the longish-set waves' troughs sank beneath his frigate's waterline and bared a bright glint of spanking-new coppering on her quickwork. The Halifax yard had done them proud, with so many naval stores warehoused, and too few of His Majesty's ships now based at Newfoundland and Nova Scotia in need of them. The North American Station's labourers only got seasonal work these days, when the two-deckers from the Caribbean fled north to avoid hurricane season, and had seemed happy to have work. There was no drydock at Halifax, but there had been strong tides and good beaches on which to careen *Proteus* high-and-dry, then fire and scrape the weed and marine growths off her bottom, replace rotten or sea-wormed outerplanking that even the Bosun or the Ship's Carpenter, Mr. Garroway, had not suspected, then paper, felt, linseed, paint, and copper her, afresh.

Flight from the threat of prosecution, it seemed, could have its beneficial moments!

"Top up yer coffee, sir?" Lewrie's cabin-servant, Aspinall, intruded from his inboard side. The tow-headed fellow had mounted to the quarterdeck from the galley up forward, holding a black, battered two-gallon pot by its bail, with a towel-wrapped hand beneath. His breath steamed in the chilly air nigh as lustily as the pot's spout . . . though nowhere near as enticing a scent as the hot coffee's, Lewrie cynically thought.

"Aye, that'd be handsome," Lewrie quickly rejoined with a faint smile of pleasure, holding out his empty mug.

"A right nippy mornin', sir, fer certain," Aspinall said, with a long-established and casual familiarity. There were no secrets 'twixt employer and servant, master or slave, mighty captain or the fellow who quietly managed his life belowdecks, and any brusque, stand-offish, and aloof "dignity" on Lewrie's part would have been pointless, by then, and pretentiously cruel, to boot.

"Mmm, good and hot!" Lewrie happily exclaimed after one sip.

It was a continual disappointment to go ashore, even to the best establishments in London where the coffee-house had been king for years on end, and get a tepid (tiny but expensive!) cup of semi-opaque gnat's piss. Aboard ship, it came from the galley stove still half-boiling, as stout and black as the strongest Irish brew.

Captain's second but to God at sea, Lewrie wryly told himself as he took another welcome sip; *and I ordain coffee fit t'wake the dead!*

"Nothin' yet, sir?" Aspinall felt fit to ask, casting a glance at the activity on the starboard gangway.

"No, not yet," Lewrie told him, grinning once more a trifle. "I assure you, when it happens, you can't miss hearing it. I see Mister Catterall licking his chops. Best top up the others, too, lad."

"Aye, sir," Aspinall cheerfully replied, then turned and walked forward to the others gathered near the cross-deck hammock nettings by the break of the quarterdeck overlooking the ship's waist, forward of the helm, and the compass binnacle cabinet and traverse board. He held out the pot in silent offering, gaining glad looks from the rest; the First Officer, Lt. Anthony Langlie, a handsome young man with what women *said* was romantically dark and curly hair. With a month or more between shearings, or washings, though, and with a week's worth of whiskers, those ladies might not *exactly* swoon over him, any longer.

Lt. Catterall, the Second Officer, their wryly waggish and sarcastic bear of a fellow, *was* licking his lips in avid expectation, his battered tin mug held out in two mittened hands like a dockside mendicant whining for alms. Wiry and slim Lt. Adair, long-ago a Midshipman when *Proteus* had first commissioned at Chatham, a less-demonstrative and better-educated young Scottish gentleman, waited his turn with a good grace, taking the time to thank Aspinall for his services. With Mr. Winwood and Midshipman Grace busy on the gangway, there was more than plenty for their resident lout, the thatch-haired and permanently unkempt little Bog-Irish Midshipman Larkin, and their new-come but much more salted "gift," Midshipman D'arcy Gamble, who had come aboard at the behest of Vice-Adm. Sir Hyde Parker back in the early spring after Lewrie, and *Proteus,* had gotten him a pot of Spanish silver from those French Creole pirates in Barataria Bay on the wild coast of Spanish Louisiana.

Lewrie hooked his left arm through the larboard mizen shrouds and cupped his everyday mug in both bare hands, sticking his snout into the rising steam, sniffing deep before sipping. Did he gulp down the scalding coffee quick enough, he might temporarily dispel the chill he felt. Even with his undress uniform coat doubled over his chest, and the nine gilt buttons done up, even with his heavy grogram boat cloak draped over his shoulders and clasped at his throat, he shivered, for he had spent too much time in warmer climes, and had yet to be inured to North Atlantic, or British, weather. Even three months of a Nova Scotian late summer and early autumn hadn't quite done the trick.

Not for inuring, anyway, he silently scoffed, recalling long weeks spent swinging at anchor at Halifax, awaiting the yard's attentions after coming in with despatches. The boresome nature of a naval "village" of fewer than five thousand residents, the unending diet of *cod,* and *moose . . . !*

"One, and two, and three, and . . . away!" the Bosun cried as the deep-sea lead, the heavy 25-pound hollow-bottomed cone, was "armed" with tallow, at last, swung out, and dropped into the sea with a loud splash, and the two-cable line went thrumming out through the main-yard block, the sheave keening, and the long flakes of the line laid out atop the starboard gangway twitching back and forth, one end to the other.

"Watch yer fackin' feet, boys," an Irish sailor cautioned, "or Davy Jones'll swig yer rum ration 'is fair mairnin'!"

Whip-whip-whip went the flakes, racing in pursuit of the plummet as it dove for the stygian depths. One hundred fathoms of it gone, already, the ten-fathom sets of knots passing in a blur, and the Bosun and his Mate, Mr. Towpenny, already looking towards the "bitter end" on the light, horizontal barrel-winch to assure themselves that it would not go overboard. Yet . . . !

The whip-whipping *slowed,* one last flake lazily shortening from bow-to-stern on the gangway, then *stood* upright to the block, its long-stored kinks no longer being stretched out, then the *out-board* length kinking; then, went limp and *still,* feeding out mere inches more with each slow roll or toss of the ship's hull!

"A hun'erd an' twenty . . . hun'erd an' twenty-*five,* an' a quarter less, t'this line!" one of the freezing hands hung in the hawse-breeches shrilled, able to count the dozen spaced knots just below the water, and the single halfway knot bobbing just above the mean surge. "Soundin's! In-Soundin's, at a hun'erd an' twenty-five fathom!"

The cheer that that news elicited could have split the heavens, nearly equalled the volume of a well-controlled, simultaneous broadside from the starboard-side guns, or shivered the main course!

"Hoist, and haul away!" Mr. Winwood roared as the din died off. "Note carefully the *time,* Mister Grace," he told his assisting middle, to whom he had already loaned his large pocket watch.

Long minutes, it took, to winch up the length of sodden manila line, for the pair of sailors on the main-chain platform to guide the line, and the heavy plummet, to the surface, then up the ship's flanks and tumblehome to the entry-port, where Mr. Winwood, Mr. Pendarves, and Mr. Towpenny knelt down, and looked at the muck caught in the tallow in its hollow bottom.

In-Soundings of somewhere, Lewrie thought as he finished off a last cool sip of black coffee. He drifted forward to the binnacle to join his officers, who were already intently poring over the sea-chart pinned to the traverse board, tracing mittened fingers over the "iffy" contours of the 120-fathom line. Which line bespoke an *host* of possibilities, from Danish Iceland to French Ushant.

Somewhere there are law courts, bailiffs, accusin' letters . . . court-martials and nooses! Lewrie quietly despaired. And it had been *such* a promising career he'd had, too, twenty bloody years of his life "press-ganged" into the Navy with nothing better open to a gentleman of his station . . . well, there always had been Pimp and Captain Sharp, and gaggles of the gullible to fleece, but nothing quiet so certain . . . so *boresomely* certain, as the life of a King's Commission Sea-Officer. Dammit!

Aye, though, he felt like groaning aloud; *make one little mistake, try t'do just one good turn, an' see where it gets you! And, it was in the cause of keepin' this ship manned an' efficient, too! Ye'd think that'd earn a man a pat on the back, or someth . . . !*

"Ah, hmm," the Sailing Master announced, after a long, furrowed-brow study, and a peer at his sea-charts once he'd attained the quarterdeck without Lewrie noticing. "A blue-grey ooze, sirs, a clay-ey *muck,* at that, I am bound. Stap me if I do not believe we're within twenty leagues of Cape Clear, on Ireland. Sixty or so sea-miles Sou'west of Cape Clear, to be more exact, ah ha."

"The Sou'wester gale blew us further North than we had thought," Lt. Langlie gayly opined, nodding his head sagaciously. "If we wish to round the Lizard, not put into the Bristol Channel . . ."

"Captain, sir," Mr. Winwood ponderously stated, drawing himself fully erect, "in my humble opinion, we should shape a course abeam the Westerlies, 'til we may take a second sounding, towards evening."

"*Due* South," Lewrie replied, nodding himself. "So there's not a risk of grounding either on the Scillies *or* the Lizard. Who knows? By dawn, and a clearer sky, your tables will give us the time of sunrise t' go by. With any luck at all, the weather will clear enough for the sun's height at Noon Sights!"

"Just so, Captain," Winwood agreed, with a slight bow.

"Then we won't have to embarrass ourselves by speaking the very first ship we see," Lewrie japed, "and hoisting 'Hold Church Service,' 'Location,' and 'Interrogative' flags."

"Sir?" Mr. Midshipman Gamble dared ask, at last, with a look of a young man ready to be amused by his captain's wit, willing to be the goat who supplied the rhetorical question if the others wouldn't, but not exactly sure where his superior's jest was going.

"Stands for 'Oh God, Where Am I?,' Mister Gamble," Lewrie quipped with a wry chuckle. "Very well, Mister Langlie. Secure the sounding gear, get our frozen sailors in-board, and Aspinall?" he bade the lad, who still hovered nearby in his heavy wool-frieze boat, with his white apron dangling below its hem. "A cup o' hot coffee for all who assisted the Sailing Master. Hands to the braces, and make her course Due South, Mister Langlie. Wear her about."

"Aye aye, sir!"

Lewrie paced aft to the taffrails to get out of the way while the cross-cocked jibs and foresails were eased over to starboard, and the helm was put over, the hard-angled set of the principal sails was eased from trying to go "full and by" too close to the winds, to loose-cupping what wind there was, as *Proteus*'s bows swung leeward, the wind came more abeam, then from astern. At the precise proper moment, and with the efficiency of a well-drilled crew with enough experience for two ships, by now, the yards were hauled about, the courses, tops'ls, and t'gallants began to draw, and HMS *Proteus* began to cleave her way through steel-grey seas, her clean quickwork slipping through the icy waters and gaining speed rapidly.

He left the taffrails and paced up the starboard side of the quarterdeck, which was now the windward side, and a captain's rightful station alone, 'til he was by the mizen shrouds, hooked an arm through them, and oversaw without interfering in such a wonderous display of seamanship from all officers and hands, 'til the last brace, halliard, or jear was coiled, flaked down, and belayed on the pin-rails, and Mr. Langlie released all but the sailors in the Forenoon Watch from their stations. A quick cast of the knot-log proved that even on this light wind, *Proteus* was loping along at a decent seven knots, easily riding the quartering seas, slow-rocking more than hobby-horsing, and heeled no more than ten degrees according to the new-fangled clinometer, with the winds nearly full abeam.

The next mid-day might prove them level with the Lizard; half a day's sailing after that might, if the winds remained out of the West or Sou'west, move them far enough below England's westernmost headland to turn East, and scud up the Channel to Portsmouth, there to deliver despatches from Halifax to the Port Admiral.

There to be stripped of his sword of honour and bound in irons, then hauled off to an ignominious Fate?

Liam Desmond on his uillean lap-pipes, the ship's fiddler, and a Marine fifer began to play a semi-lively old hymn. Unfortunately for Lewrie's already-fretful nerves, he recognised the title as "I Want a Principle." Damned if he didn't, though he might have left it a tad late!

He pursed his lips, frowned heavily, and headed below and aft. Aspinall was still tending to those in need of his coffee-pot; Lewrie tossed off his own boat cloak, hat, and undid his coat, then sat down at his desk and dug his personal log out of the centre drawer, dipped one of his precious steel-nibbed (captured) French pens in the ink, and noted the time and date of Soundings, of shaping a new course; catching up on what the half-a-gale had carried away, what sails had split, and had to be replaced, which Mr. Rayne, their Sailmaker, thought he could repair, and what the cost in materials would be when the time came to pay *Proteus* off in a home dockyard, the war with France ended. . . .

". . . that saved a wretch like me!
I once was lost, but now am found,
'twas blind, but now, I see!"

Mister Winwood has a sense of humour? Lewrie was forced to gawp. Two years or more, and the Sailing Master couldn't seem to catch even the *broadest* jape . . . now this waggish witticism? For the suggestion for a thanksgiving hymn surely had been his. Lewrie knew the words as a poem written by a former Liverpool slave-ship captain, John Newton, who had been shipwrecked and enslaved himself on the African coast; the tune, though, sounded suspiciously close to "Nottingham Ale," not a ditty he'd think popular with the fervently religious.*

Apt, though, he decided; *now we know where we are.* He could understand British tars singing so lustily, this close to home, but his "Free Black volunteers," too?

The root of his troubles, those "volunteers," a round dozen of them, who'd really been encouraged to meet his ship's boats one night in Portland Bight on

*"Amazing Grace," also known in hymn books as "New Britain," was not set to the tune we know, "Virginia Harmony," until 1831.

Jamaica's south coast, and escape a lifetime of slavery, chains, whips, and cruel misery, to join the Royal Navy under new aliases as "free men." *Seemed* like a great idea, then, when his ship had been so short of hands after so many of his British tars had died of Yellow Jack, but now, though . . .

> ". . . *many dangers, toils, and snares,*
> *I have al-ready come!*
> *'Tis Grace hath bro't me safe, thus far,*
> *and Grace will lead me home!*"

"*Something* should," Lewrie muttered; "lead 'em home, very far from me," he added under his breath. Listening to the harmonies of his Black sailors, no matter how loyally and stoutly they had served, he could not help but add a fretful "Damn 'em!"

CHAPTER TWO

In retrospect, perhaps—and one could safely assume that retrospection was an activity at which Alan Lewrie had come to excel over the course of a few months (and just *might* have been acclaimed as the champion retro-spector of the age . . . were prizes given for such, of course)—he really should have twigged to the fact that something was "rotten in Denmark" when he received that extremely odd, dare we say *outré,* invitation from Capt. Nicely, back in the summer when he was still based out of Kingston, Jamaica, to wit: Capt. Nicely requested that *he* be dined-in aboard *Proteus* by Capt. Lewrie, not the other way round.

Well, Nicely was a kindly sort, though a bit of a bull in the china shop, an aggressive, "but me not buts" sort, so Lewrie had thought little odd about it, at the time. Capt. Nicely had played "Dutch Uncle" to him since their first meeting at Port-au-Prince in 1797 and had supported his activities, dismissing the vituperative charges that the dyspeptic Capt. Blaylock had tried to lay against Lewrie for not breaking off his bombardment of the rebel-slave army besieging the port of Mole St. Nicholas and giving Blaylock his mooring to try *his* hand at it. Nicely's dislike for Blaylock might have had a hand in it, for they'd heartily despised each other as hotly as the Devil hates Holy Water since their Midshipmen days.

Ever the encouraging and supportive sort was Nicely, even when he'd as good as "press-ganged" Lewrie into a knight-errant's crusade against those French Creole pirates who'd stolen one of Lewrie's prizes from the anchorage at Dominica, even when he'd usurped *Proteus* right out from under him to be Nicely's "squadron of one" to chase them into Spanish Louisiana, *then* sending Lewrie up the Mississippi in civilian guise to hunt them on their home ground, shivering and farting with dread, and . . .

But, no . . . Lewrie had blithely shrugged it off as just one more quirk of a neck-or-nothing man. After all, he'd *survived* it, barely, and the expedition had fetched them all £200,000 to share, gained all participants—the leaders most especially—plaudits in London papers, and the gratitude of their superiors for a job well done. As for Capt. Nicely, it had gotten him out of the dry and thankless post of Staff Captain, *ashore* in Admiralty House on Kingston Harbour's Palisades, and gotten him back afloat in command of a mighty 44-gun frigate. *And*, let Nicely hoist a broad pendant as commander of a wee squadron—even if said broad pendant still bore a white ball to show Nicely was not *yet* a Commodore, due a Flag-Captain to run her.

Better yet, HMS *Proteus* had received orders assigning her, and her suddenly moderately-wealthy captain, to be part of that squadron of two frigates, a sloop of war, and two armed brigs, which would soon sail off on a new expedition to prowl the coasts of French Guiana and the Dutch isles off the shoulder of South America and the Spanish Main.

And, as captain of the only other frigate in the squadron, was not Lewrie second-in-command to Nicely, no matter that he had not yet attained the right to wear a second epaulet on his shoulders, and was still a Post-Captain of Less than Three Years' Seniority?

Given Capt. Nicely's knacky wits, and his bellicosity when it came to trouncing the King's enemies, it had promised to be a fruitful cruise . . . so long as Nicely didn't order Lewrie to sneak ashore as a Spanish grandee or muleskinner and play spy one more time, that is.

Little wonder, then, that Lewrie had cocked his head over that invitation, had muttered something akin to "Hmmpf, well o' course," and had tossed it into the scrap drawer, and didn't give the matter a second thought, except for what he should serve for a working dinner, and for how many. And, given how badly Capt. Nicely had fared aboard *Proteus* with Toulon and Chalky whilst Lewrie was away in New Orleans, what he should do with his cats.

It *did* strike Lewrie as odd that Capt. Nicely came aboard alone, with nary a one of the squadron's other captains in tow, not even his own First Officer, which had prompted two thoughts in Lewrie's head: first, *Oh, good . . . more leftovers for tonight's supper*, followed by *Oh, shit, he's got some harum-scarum plan in his head, again!* A plan which might, indeed, require Lewrie to swot up on his Spanish, Dutch, or French, and quickly master plausible skills at donkey-tending!

Capt. Nicely had proved to be popular with the crew, his recent exploits earning every Man Jack a pretty penny, so it was with happy smiles and waving hats that *Proteus*'s hands had turned out to welcome Nicely aboard, beyond the formality of the side-party, the shrilling bosuns' calls, and the stamping of Marines in full kit.

"Hallo, lads!" Capt. Nicely had joyfully cried, waving his own hat back at them. "Spent your prize-money, yet, you rogues, ha ha? Or, did you owe your Purser too much for tobacco, what?"

That had gotten him a laugh, and a jeer or two at their "Nip-Cheese," Mr. Coote, as all Pursers were termed.

"Seeing as how 'tis just *before* Seven Bells of the Forenoon," Nicely had further said, "and *Proteus* is well-anchored, with none but the harbour watch to stand, with your captain's permission . . . ?" he had looked over at Lewrie, cocking a brow 'til Lewrie nodded his agreement, "I propose that you 'Splice the Main Brace'!" Nicely had cried down to the waist, giving leave for every man and boy to have a full rum issue, with no sips or gulps owed among them to lower the brimming measure.

"And, do you come this way, sir," Lewrie had offered, gesturing aft, "we'll 'splice' our own. I've a case of fine French claret."

"Delighted!" Nicely had cried; though his eyes *had* been shifty.

Once below, with Aspinall and Andrews, Lewrie's long-time Black Cox'n, to take charge of hats, swords, and such, Capt. Nicely shied a bit, peering about intently, though managing to hide most of his nervousness deuced well.

"It, ahh . . . you've re-painted lately, have ye, Lewrie?"

"Nossir, not in some time, why?" Lewrie said as he did honours with the first ready-opened and breathing bottle with his own hands.

"It smells . . . fresher than I recall," Nicely tentatively allowed, accepting a semi-conical, low-stemmed, and footed glass from him.

"Oh, the cats, d'ye mean, sir," Lewrie replied with a well-hid simper. "Don't know quite *what* got into 'em, when you were aboard. A tribe that don't brook 'change' all that well, I've discovered. A new person where their master usually is . . . pining for me, as well, sir? My apologies, again, for what harm they did your things."

Far aft in the bed-space, Lewrie could espy two pairs of ears, two sets of hard-slit and wary eyes, perhaps even two noses, one with pink nostrils, the other grey, lurking over the top of his extra pillow and the folded-up coverlet, in his wide-enough-for-two hanging bed. Where, he fervently hoped at that moment, they would be content to stay . . . muttering only the *faintest* spiteful "Mrrrs," scheming nothing.

"Delightful creatures," Nicely intoned without even attempting to sound convincing.

"And didn't they take to you, just, sir!" Lewrie couldn't help saying as he led Nicely to the dining-coach and a seat at the table.

"Ummm . . . yayss," Nicely rejoined, "and aren't you so fortunate?"

High summer in Jamaica, even with wind scoops erected at every hatchway, the awnings rigged tautly over the quarterdeck against direct sunlight, and all the transom or coach-top windows of the great-cabins opened, mitigated against a heavy repast. They'd begun with a thin but spicy chicken broth, which was followed by freshly-caught red snapper with lemon and clarified butter sauce, and boiled carrots. Green salad with shredded bacon and oil-and-vinegar cleansed the palate for a main course of de-boned pork chops served with fried potato wedges and middling dollops of mushy peas, which repast required the opening of some hock with the fish, soup, and salad, and a second bottle of claret with the chops.

Not a single word was said about their coming mission far to the South'rd, of French and Spanish foes sheltered at Aruba or Curaçao, at Caracas or Cartagena, nor what dangers lurked in the port of Cayenne, or the marshy inlets of French Giuana, and Lewrie *had* begun to squirm a bit, waiting for a particularly ugly, but "inspired," shoe to drop.

It was expected, of course, that naval officers never discussed Politics, Religion, Women, or "Work" in the mess, so . . . perhaps *after*?

It was only once the tablecloth had been whisked away, the sweet biscuits and mixed nuts, and the port bottle, had been set out, that a nigh-broody Capt. Nicely had appeared to wince, or steel himself for a secret discussion, requesting that Aspinall make himself scarce.

Secret doings? Lewrie had wondered; *Or . . . look out, here comes another of his brain storms, with me up t'my neck in the quag, again.*

"So . . . what is it to be, sir?" Lewrie had prompted, scooting up closer to the table, expecting to hear Capt. Nicely whisper revelations about secret sailing times, sealed orders for *rendezvous* out at sea, so the French, who still had informers on Jamaica despite efforts to root them out, would hear nothing of the squadron's destination, or its formation, 'til it was much too late.

That, or another miserable spell of dirty-work for Lewrie.

"These . . . walnuts?" Nicely had grumpily asked, instead, with his face screwed up like a hanged spaniel as he nibbled on one.

"Uh . . . no, sir," Lewrie said, topping off his glass of port and passing it down-table. "American pecans," he informed Nicely, saying it the way he'd heard it from Capt. Randolph of the USS *Oglethorpe* from whom he'd obtained them. "Pee-cans . . . Georgia pee-cans."

"Hmmpf," Nicely had muttered, clearing his palate with the port, and pouring himself another rather quickly, too, tossing that one back uncharacteristically quickly. He poured himself a third, but let that one sit 'twixt his hoary hands, and gave it a long glare before looking at his host.

"Uhm . . . bad news, I fear, Lewrie," Nicely had begun, at last. "A matter's arisen which, ah . . . may preclude your participation in my squadron's mission, d'ye see."

"Some other duty, then, sir?" Lewrie had asked, feeling, in the following order: disappointment to miss a straightforward adventure; some relief that he'd *not* be handy, did Nicely get a wild hair up his nose, and need some derring-do done; who the Devil had requested him for something else, and how much worse might *that* be?

"Not, ah . . . quite," Nicely had struggled on, obviously loath to bear bad news, but . . . "I shall be . . . *we* shall be, sorry to lose your *inestimable* services on the West Indies Station."

"I'm t'go somewhere *else*, sir?" Suspicious, indeed, that.

"Far and fast, I fear," Nicely had gloomed. He wriggled as if the crutch of his breeches had suddenly pinched a testicle. "There's the matter of all those damned Samboes of yours, Lewrie. Your Cuffy sailors. More to the point, where and when you got 'em, d'ye see."

"Ah? Hmm, hey?" Lewrie flummoxed, like to cough up half of a lung suddenly. That was *not* the ugly shoe he'd *expected* to be dropped!

"I *did* note, and wonder, where ye'd found so many free Black volunteers, the weeks I was aboard, whilst you were away, but . . ." his squadron commander had said, doing some fidgetting of his own.

They're going to hang *me!* the irrational part of Lewrie's brain screeched at him. The rational half was too stunned to put forth any opinion. *I'm caught, red-handed! Christ, shit on a . . . !*

" 'Tis the Beauman family, d'ye see," Nicely had carped. "A dozen of their slaves ran off one night. Nothing *too* odd about it, at first glance. One of the risks of slave-holding, with all the tales of the Maroons who've fled into the Cockpit Country, or the Blue Mountains . . . where the Beaumans *thought* they'd run, even was that plantation right on the sea, on the South coast, and rather far from Maroon territory."

"Ah . . . *gerk*!" had been Lewrie's sagacious reply, and his heart banging away like Billy-Oh, about two inches below his tonsils, it felt like. "Bother ye for the port, if you're . . . ?" he asked, trying damned hard not to stammer. "Then, so, sir?" he managed to state.

"Organised as the Maroons are," Nicely had gone on, "it wasn't beyond credence to think that they couldn't arrange an escape for any number of slaves determined enough to join them. And, God knows word can pass secret 'twixt house and field slaves, and runaways, quicker than their masters could manage. No, Lewrie . . . 'twas only after the Beaumans managed to find witnesses who said that a darkened *ship* was in Portland Bight that very night that they began to suspect that the runaways might have had some help, and the ex-slave Maroons are not in *possession* of many boats, none larger than canoes and such, so . . ."

"Perhaps a French, or Spanish, privateer, that . . ." Lewrie tried to say, with a puzzled shrug.

"Then, there was all that folderol 'twixt your friend, Colonel Cashman of that West Indies regiment the Beaumans raised to put down the slave rebellion on Saint-Domingue, and the family," Capt. Nicely had gravelled reluctantly on, "the duel that followed the accusations slung about after that pot-mess of a battle outside Port-au-Prince, just before the withdrawal of all British forces . . . cowardice charges by Cashman, 'gainst the younger Beauman . . . Ledyard Beauman, was it?"

Lewrie could only vaguely nod; he did not trust himself to speak.

"Incompetence charges in reply, then that *duel*!" Nicely sniffed in gentlemanly outrage at what a shambles *that* had turned out to be . . . Ledyard Beauman too scared or drunk to obey the niceties, firing at Cashman's back before "Kit" could turn, stand, and receive; Cashman drilling the foppish bastard in the belly; Ledyard's second, a cousin, Captain Sellers from the disbanded regiment, tossing Ledyard a second pistol and drawing his own; and Lewrie, as *Cashman's* second, shooting *him* dead, too, and . . .

"Your friend sold up and sailed for America, right after?"

"Uhm, aye, he did, sir," Lewrie answered, sensing a reprieve if Kit Cashman was suspected. "Good Lord, Captain Nicely, ye don't think that *Christopher* had a . . . ! Well, I'm damned if . . . !"

"The Beaumans did, at first," Nicely had intoned, so solemnly that Lewrie felt that faint hope shrink like a deflating pig bladder.

"Spite, sir, pure and simple!" Lewrie managed to declaim.

"Spite, perhaps, on Colonel Cashman's part," Nicely countered. "A parting jape on the whole detestable Beauman clan, *and* an expensive one. For, wherever your friend Cashman lit in the United States, the dozen fit and young slaves would prove useful in a new farming venture, or a source or ready funds, if not, but . . ."

Nicely had drawn out that "but," turning it into a descending *glissando* worthy of a dying diva's final *aria*, nailing the first spike into the coffin lid by adding, "Of late, though, Hugh Beauman, head of their clan, has heard-tell that your crew has *quite* a few more Cuffy sailors in it than the usual frigate so long on station in the Caribbean."

"Why, those bastards!" Lewrie spluttered, summoning up every shred he could muster that even *resembled* righteous indignation, and whey-faced innocence. "Cashman slew Ledyard, *I* killed one of Hugh's cousins, so . . . ! Before your time, sir, in my midshipman days during the American Revolution, *Lucy* Beauman and I were, ah . . . friendly. We even considered a union, should I earn a commission, but the Beaumans would have none of it. Almost had t'duel one of 'em *then*! Barred the house, Lucy and I cut off . . . !"

He pointedly *didn't* supply that he'd been rogering a scandalous older "grass-widow" on the side whilst trying to squire *Lucy*, that he had escorted Hugh's married sister, Anne, about town unchaperoned one day, and not *his* fault, that *faux pas* in gentlemanly behaviour.

"So I have learned, Lewrie," Nicely had sternly muttered. "Just as I'm aware of the Beaumans' threats on your life following the duel, which Mister James Peel of the Foreign Office took seriously enough to discover to me, and get you and *Proteus* safely out to sea, and out of their reach. We are all aware of that."

"Ah . . . *we*, sir?" a stalwart Capt. Lewrie had quailed.

"Well, of course, *we*, sir!" Nicely had barked, obviously grown weary with tip-toeing and shilly-shally. "Me . . . Peel, Admiral Sir Hyde Parker, the island governor, Lord Balcarres . . ." he ticked off on his blunt fingers. "Spiteful, vengeful calumnies laid against you by men who've held grudges against you since the '80s may not be deemed *sufficiently* actionable beyond an initial enquiry. But . . ."

The dying diva warbled again.

Didn't know he liked *German operas*, Lewrie fearfully thought at the mere mention of "enquiries." One look aboard by the Beaumans, and he'd meet up with "Captain Swing," and why the *Hell* had he thought the theft of a dozen slaves, no matter *how* perishing-bad he'd needed hands to man his ship, could escape notice forever? A semi-drunken evening with "Kit" Cashman after the defeat and withdrawal from Saint-Domingue, as Cashman was closing his accounts and preparing to emigrate; *"Kit"* sniggering as they schemed a way to punish the Beaumans, and, indeed, it was *meant* to be an expensive, parting jape against them, hitting them where it would hurt them the worst . . . in their pocket books! A way for Lewrie to flesh out his under-strength crew, with

Cashman even offering to urge some of his White ex-soldiers from the disbanded regiment to sign aboard as Marines . . . !

"Such scurrilous charges 'gainst a Commission Sea Officer, and one so *successful*, and *valuable* to the Crown, well!" Capt. Nicely had sniffed again with prim anger. "Baseless charges, of course. . . . Well, *we* feel that the repute of the Royal Navy should *not* be tainted with such, so . . . that is why we thought it best, all round, were you, and *Proteus*, to be sent away on other duties, Lewrie." As he said that, Capt. Nicely had squirmed on his chair like a Hindoo *fakir* trying for a comfortable spot on his bed of nails.

"Ah, hmm," Lewrie had responded with an audible gulp of relief. "So, how far d'ye think I . . . ?"

"There's despatches in need of transport to Halifax," Nicely said with a vague wave of his hand, and a cutty-eyed expression on his face. "Hellishly boresome place, Halifax. Fogs, rocks, and shoals . . . deuced hot summers for that far north, mosquitoes big as wrens, swarms of them as thick as, well . . . fogs. Nothing much there, but for their dockyard and store houses. What the town was settled for, to service ships on the North American Station, and a seasonal haven for line-of-battle ships from our station, as well. Excellent yard facilities, I know, though. And, isn't *Proteus* in need of a bottom cleaning, and a re-coppering?"

"Well, there is that, sir," Lewrie had perked up.

"Of course, with our liners from the Caribbean ready to head up that way, soon, Halifax might be a tad too busy fulfilling *their* needs, so you may end up swinging round the anchor for a considerable bit of time, before they get round to your case."

Oh, don't say case! Lewrie had most illogically thought, ready to titter with relief; *Did I say "case"? Silly old me!*

"So, I should look to closing my shore accounts, d'ye mean, sir?" Lewrie asked, sure then that his departure would be something quicker than "instanter," and he didn't need to add dunnings from tailors and chandlers to his troubles.

"May you achieve all that by dawn tomorrow, it'd be best."

"Dawn! Ah ha," Lewrie had gloomed, with a benumbed nod.

"Frivolous, detestable, spiteful . . ." Capt. Nicely had mumbled, intent on nibbling Georgia "pee-cans," giving them his whole attention, unable to look at Lewrie, or unwilling to do so. And Lewrie wasn't so sure whether Nicely had been griping about the Beaumans, or *him*! He'd also noticed that Nicely hadn't, or couldn't, put Lewrie to a question of whether the Beaumans' suspicions were true. What Nicely didn't know, he could not testify to in a court of law, should it come to it!

"Well, of course *they* are, sir!" Lewrie had spat.

Nicely had squirmed some more, his eyes flicking about as if in search of a basin of water and a towel, like a Roman governor about to remand a felon back to the Court of The Sanhedrin—or so Lewrie's fervid imagination could conjure at that instant.

"Sail under Admiralty Orders," Nicely had grunted, "fly colours of an 'independent ship,' all that."

"Written orders, sir?" Lewrie had had wit enough to press. The last thing he needed was to be charged with stealing his own *frigate*!

"Oh, most assuredly, sir," Capt. Nicely had chirped. Meaning that Vice-Adm. Parker would treat his departure as a trivial matter of a minor refit for a hard-used frigate, which could carry despatches to Halifax at the same time, and could later swear that he'd known not a blessed thing about any legal charges. Nicely's signature would not be on those orders, either; nor would Lord Balcarres's, or Peel's, or anyone else's. "Can't have you just swanning off whenever . . . *damme*!"

Nicely might have said more anent the matter, but was startled by faint brushings of fur against his well-blacked, fashionable boots, as Lewrie's cats, Toulon and Chalky, took that moment to gird up their not very considerable courage to make musky *rencontre* of their former cabin-mate.

Though the cats had made a fuss over Nicely when he'd first gotten aboard to supplant Lewrie, once their master was gone it was another matter, and they'd tormented the man . . . mostly with piss! Stockings, shoes, linens, sheets, and mattress, dressing robe abandoned on the back of a chair, uniforms laid out near to-hand atop his sea-chests, and the contents of the chests, too, if carelessly left open . . . all had gotten Toulon's and Chalky's "liquid blessings"! Teeth and wee claws had marked Nicely's boots, sword-belt, and leather scabbard covering, too, and his bright brass or gilt brassards, buttons, or sword fixtures had gone a gangrenous shade of green by the time Lewrie had come back aboard.

"Why, those . . . !" Nicely had barked, like to lift his boots from assault, draw his knees to his chest, or climb atop his chair and let out a screech like a lady who'd seen a mouse. "Why . . . *there* are the little darlings," he'd pretended to coo, instead, after he'd gotten past the urge to kick them as far as the stern transom settee. Only to be polite to his host!

"Aspinall?" Lewrie had called out. "I assume we've nothing more private to discuss, Captain Nicely, so I might . . . ?"

"Aye, have him in," Nicely had quickly agreed.

"Thought you were keeping an eye on the cats, lad," Lewrie said as his steward returned.

"Oh, I woz, sir. 'Twoz feedin' 'em tasty scraps, but . . ."

"If you'd . . . herd 'em aft, for a bit longer, I'd be grateful," Lewrie had gently bade him.

"O' course, sir. Here, lads! Come, Toulon! Come, Chalky, an' here's more bacon shreds for ye, there's th' good littl'un!" Aspinall coaxed, as they trotted for the day-cabin, tails fully erect. Once by Lewrie's desk, though, the cats *did* take a moment to gloat over their little shoulders, lick their chops, and seem to grin at each other as if highly pleased with themselves!

"I'll see you to the deck, if that is all you, ah . . ." Lewrie offered, dabbing his mouth with a napkin and rising.

"Ah, well, aye," Nicely had replied with a sigh, setting aside his own napkin, and getting to his own feet. "One last thing, sir."

"Aye?"

"Sir Hyde, and Lord Balcarres, both bade me relate to you that they appreciate all you've achieved since coming under their command, Lewrie," Nicely had whispered to him. "They, and I, think you much too valuable an officer to be sacrificed. Though we *all* consider you the *damnedest* fool . . . should the Beaumans' suspicions hold even a *drop* of water. Sir Hyde particularly stressed his approval of your fighting qualities, your, ah . . . *unorthodox* way of achieving whatever you're set to accomplish. We, all of us, wish you to know that, should you have need of patronage in future, you may . . . should the Beaumans insist on laying *false* charges . . . count on our support."

And, were the charges *true,* Lewrie would end swinging in small circles in the wind, at the end of a fresh, new rope, it went without saying!

"I'll miss ye, Lewrie, 'deed I shall," Nicely had said, by way of gruff departure. "Best of luck, young sir," he added, offering his hand for a fierce shake.

"Thank you for that, sir . . . for all you've done for me in the past . . . truly," Lewrie had soberly answered, realising that the thing was still afoot, that formal charges for grand theft could follow him wherever a mail-packet could go, and, unless he walked away from his ship in a foreign port, there could always be a British court near to hand to find him and haul him before its bench.

"I really *do* like you, Lewrie," Nicely had declared, then, as fiercely as privacy allowed. That was as far as he could go, though; that was all he'd allow himself to say on the matter.

"I hope we have the chance to serve together, again, sir," he had replied to that. "Goodbye, sir. May you have a successful cruise down there against the Frogs and Dons, and *continued* success in your career."

"Thankee, Captain Lewrie, thankee," Nicely had gruffly said.

Then it had been time for them to call for their swords, hats, and marks of dignity, then go out onto the main deck; up to the quarterdeck, then the starboard gangway as the side-party had assembled, and the strict ritual for the departure of a senior officer was performed. *Proteus*'s crew, Black *and* White, still mellow from that rum issue, and their own mid-day meal, had doffed their hats and raised a second cheer for good old Capt. Nicely.

And Lewrie had stood by the entry-port, hat raised high over his head in salute to watch Capt. Nicely enter his barge and be rowed away to his bright, new frigate . . . and had suddenly never felt so alone in all his born days.

BOOK I

Dulcis inexpertis cultura potentis amici;
expertus metuit.

Those who have never tried think it pleasant to court a friend in power; one who has tried dreads it.

HORACE, *EPISTLES* I, XVIII, 86-87

CHAPTER THREE

HMS *Proteus* lay peacefully at anchor in the sheltered waters of Spithead, north of the Isle of Wight, just a bit Sou'east of Gilkicker Point, taking her bearings from the Monkton Fort on the point, the buoy marking the No Man's Land Shoals, and a windmill on Portdown Hill. It meant a swim of over two miles to the point, and just over a mile swim to reach the Isle of Wight, and a hard slog 'cross the Ride Sands, when the tide was low, to deter desertion. Desperate as *Proteus*'s crew was for diversion, and the pleasures of the shore, hungry as they were for solid land, reunion with wives, sweethearts, children, and their parents—for free-flowing kegs of beer, tall tankards of grog or unwatered, neat rum, for "ladies of the town," alley prostitutes ready to dole out "knee-tremblers," for sheep or goats, if they were *too* eager!—it was not to be. Lt. Langlie had already posted fully-uniformed and fully-armed Marines along the bulwarks, the beakheads, and taffrails to keep any "inspired" seamen from slipping over the side in the wee hours when no one was looking.

Proteus had come in "all-standing," her best and second bower, and a kedge anchor, ready to loose if a permanent mooring buoy was not available. With a flashy show of seamanship, the well-trained sailors had rounded her up into the wind as soon as the bearings to shore were satisfactory, had swarmed the masts, yards, and running rigging to take in all sails at once, and one side-battery of her guns ready-loaded and thinly manned to fire a slow, metronomic ritual salute to the Port Admiral, the last discharge timed to be fired at the same moment that not a scrap of canvas remained un-fisted, un-furled, or not harbour-gasketed.

Whether such a "scaly-fish" display actually impressed anyone or not, well . . . under the circumstances which might obtain ashore, Lewrie hoped with crossed fingers that coming to anchor "man o' war" fashion *might* mitigate his later reception from his seniors; crossed fingers, as well, that they could actually pull off the stunt!

It helped, of course, that in the sheltered lee of the Isle of Wight, the wind's force had been blunted, and the harbour waters were much calmer. Had the sea and wind been up, he wouldn't have attempted it, no matter how badly he *needed* to make a good impression!

He stood about midway aft 'twixt the helm and the taffrail, in his very best shoregoing uniform, with all his "brightwork" polished as glossy as his boots, and the gilt lace of his coat and hat fit to blind the unwary. He glanced aft to watch one of *Proteus*'s cutters as it was rowed out astern, with the kedge anchor aboard, and a messenger line bound to the stern cable, which was laid out on the quarterdeck ready for feeding. The cutter made slow but steady progress over the harbour chop, which today was heaving barely two feet.

"Beg pardon, sir," Lt. Langlie reported, casually touching the front of his cocked hat, "but the best bower's down firm in nine fathom, same for the second bower, and we've veered off near ninety degrees between 'em. Fourty-five fathom of chain and cable to each, sir."

"You might dis-mount both nine-pounder bow chasers, for later, Mister Langlie," Lewrie decided. "Lash 'em ready to be bound to the cables, should the weather make up. 'Tis winter, after all."

"I shall see to it directly the kedge is bound and set, sir," his First Officer crisply replied. "Your gig is alongside the entry-port, too, sir, and Cox'n Andrews has your boat crew standing by," he informed Lewrie, with a glance down to the large-ish canvas bag sitting on the deck near Lewrie's feet that held the mail and despatches from Halifax. Slung off Lewrie's shoulder was a second, smaller bag; that one held Lewrie's orders, journals, and reports.

"Thankee, Mister Langlie," Lewrie replied with a satisfied nod, though he secretly felt extremely loath to quit the relative safety of his frigate's decks. *They can't take me up, 'long as I have artillery!* he told himself. "And a 'foin marnin' fer it,' as our Irish sailors'd say, hmm?" Lewrie posed with a faint, sarcastic grin.

It was *England* they smelled over yonder; it was England on which they hungrily gazed. It was grey, gloomy, and raining, of course; the sullen sort of fickle showers that could come and go, come and go, for weeks on end, seemingly timed to concur with every *second* chime of the ship's bell, (which was to say at every *hour*) and perversely coinciding with any human need or urge to go outside!

"Any signals from shore, Mister Gamble?" Lewrie asked, turning to face their oldest and most-senior Midshipman, who was getting upwards of twenty, compared to their other 'tween-year "snotties."

"They acknowledged our signal when we made our number to them, sir," Mr. Gamble replied, brisk and efficient as usual, as he'd proved to be since joining months before. " 'Have Despatches' was also acknowledged, but nothing since."

Ooh . . . canny! Lewrie sourly thought, ready to suspect a hearty "good morning" as a veiled threat by then; *Lure mine arse ashore, all unsuspectin', then "slap"! Into irons, and* under *the gaol!*

"Business as usual," Lt. Langlie surmised with a yawn. "And too busy to fret over a single frigate's appearance."

"Well, then . . ." Lewrie announced, heaving a heavy sigh of resignation, seeing as how there was nothing to keep him aboard. "I should be on my way. *Expect* t'be back aboard a few hours hence, but . . . keep the bumboats and doxies away 'til I return, or send you word, Mister Langlie. And when we *do* hoist 'Out of Discipline,' make sure no more rum or spirits get smuggled aboard than we may help, hmm?"

Lewrie glanced forward towards the larboard gangway, where the Bosun and his Mate, Mr. Pendarves and Mr. Towpenny, and the Master At Arms, Mr. Neale, and his Ship's Corporals, Burton and Ragster, already had their heads together. Neale had been *born* burly and gloomy, but a shipboard "liberty" in a British port most-like had his guts in knots, in dread of what riotous excesses *that* could mean belowdecks!

"Side-party, then, Mister Langlie," Lewrie bade, forcing himself to take the first step forrud towards the starboard gangway, the entry-port, the man-ropes and battens alongside the main-chains . . . towards his gig, a dock ashore, then . . . ignominy and court-martial? His feet felt suddenly leaden, as did his innards.

A court-martial, and a quick dismissal from the Navy could turn out to be the *least* he could expect! Lifelong shame, and the life of a haplessly ignorant tenant farmer; a veritable exotic stew of the village drunk, wastrel idler, *and* a black-sheep shame, all in one!

Boot-heels drummed on snowy-scrubbed oak deck planks with an ominous thudding sounding very much like *Doom-Doom-Doom!*

Caroline'll file a Bill of Divorcement, o' course, Lewrie sadly thought as he passed 'twixt the twin rows of the side-party, doffing his hat to all assembled; *she and her brother, Governour, came from old slave-holdin' folk in North Carolina! Why, they'll curse me as a traitor to the nat'ral state o' humankind!*

Of late (with not an inkling of his crime yet revealed to her of course) his wife had actually begun to respond to his letters, again; a *chary* sort of reply, to be sure, after that still-unknown scribbler who had filled her head with tales of his overseas "doings" with a mistress in the Mediterranean, Phoebe Aretino; a tussle or two with the bustily alluring Claudia Mastandrea in Genoa and Leghorn (even if she *had* been a French spy he'd been *ordered* to bed and blab lies to!); about Theoni Kavares Connor, the Ionian Greek widow with the currant-trade fortune who'd removed to London . . . with his bastard son "Alan" in tow! Since he and *Proteus* had departed for the Caribbean back in '97, that vengeful gossip's "dirt" had dried up, but . . . there'd already been enough for Caroline to stew over, and she'd made it quite clear that she was of a mind to shoot him, despised him worse than cold, boiled mutton, and et cetera and et cetera, so there, you faithless bastard!

Caroline's aging mother, Charlotte Chiswick, would most-like go into the wailing vapours, brother-in-law Governour would recall all of his panther-lean and panther-quick reflexes of old, lever his substantial arse from one of his over-strong fireplace chairs, and toddle to a gun cabinet, and her miserly, spiteful uncle Phineas Chiswick . . . his rasping cackles *already* rang in Lewrie's fervid imaginings!

In point of fact, being slung out of the Navy into dreary, civilian misery, with all those vultures flapping round his head like a flock of Harpies, forevermore, just might be a Fate *worse* than Death!

Oh, Death, where is thy sting? Lewrie mournfully chid himself, dredging up a Bible verse (though not exactly sure from *which* Book of the Good Book). Though, as he turned his arse out-board and began his descent of the man-ropes and boarding battens, he made a quick, mental note to re-read the Book of Job . . . carefully!

And, he thought as he took a seat in his smart gig's stern; *if it's a* criminal *trial, there's bound t'be a half-dozen "dominees" near to hand, with Bibles t'loan, just* hot *t'weep o'er my damned soul!*

"Ready, sah," Cox'n Andrews said in a low voice behind him, at the tiller, fetching Lewrie up from his black study to take note that *two* of the six oarsmen waiting to row him ashore were Black, ex-slave sailors: big and strong Jones Nelson as stroke-oar, and the wiry young "George Newcastle" (who'd new-christened himself once free after their King, and a bottle of beer he'd seen but never sampled!) as a larboard oarsman, on the middle thwart!

Take out advertisements, why don't we! Lewrie thought, in a gawpish shudder. "Right, then . . ." he said in a proper sea-captain's low growl of impatience, after re-gathering his courage (which had taken a very sudden tack-about!) "Shove off, lads."

"Up-oars," Andrews called. "Let go dah painter, and shove off, bow man. Out oars, starboard," he ordered as he swung the tiller over hard a'larboard. "Dip oars, starboard . . . two short strokes. Now . . . out oars, larboard, ready, and . . . long-stroke, t'gether."

"Well, I think that should about conclude things, at last, sir," the aging Flag-Lieutenant to the new Port Admiral confessed, finally. "Any other matters wanting?" he cheerfully enquired.

"Topping up supplies expended on-passage from Halifax," Lewrie told him, handing over a fair copy of his frigate's lacks, assembled by her Purser, Mr. Coote, the Bosun, Master Gunner, Sailmaker, Cooper, and others. "Though, I s'pose the Dockyard Commissioner's office would be the best place for it."

"The Commissioner, Captain Sir Charles Saxton, will be relieved to hear of it, Captain Lewrie," the Flag-Lieutenant chuckled. "I note your ship received a bottom-cleaning and re-coppering at Halifax, did ye not, sir?"

"We did, sir," Lewrie agreed amiably. "Amazin' what can be accomplished on a good sand and shingle beach, with such dramatic tides."

"My word, you'll be *more* than welcome, then, Captain Lewrie, I dare say!" the Flag-Lieutenant gushed. "And *Proteus* is, at present, un-attached? Neither the North American nor the West Indies Station will be expecting you back any-time soon?"

"Not that I know of, no," Lewrie carefully admitted, taking time to cross his legs the other way about, guarding his "wedding tackle" as he did so, and striving to sound breezily unworried.

"Well, then! I shall inform Channel Fleet of your availability, sir! As well as London, of course," the other officer gleefully said, all but rubbing his hands. "Our Admiral Nelson has said that there are never enough frigates to go round, and isn't that the truth of it, sir?"

From the beatific look of hero-worship that seized the lieutenant's phyz, Nelson's repute had gone skyward like a sea-mortar's shell after his victory at the Battle of the Nile, so Lewrie thought it politic, and might improve *Proteus*'s future employment, to make a boast or two about his connexions to that worthy.

"Served with him twice, now, sir," he off-handedly tossed about. "Grand Turk Island, in '83, just before the end of the American Revolution, then as part of his squadron off the Italian coasts in '94, and '95. Corsica, too, actually . . .

and saw him in action during the siege of Toulon. Oh!" he cried, fingering the medal for Cape St. Vincent on his chest. "He dragooned me to follow him and repeat signals in '97 at Saint Vincent, as well! *That* was a 'windy' hour or so."

" 'Pon my stars, Captain Lewrie, you did?" the Flag-Lieutenant responded with the expected gawp of astonishment, giving Lewrie a rare chance to preen and forget his impending troubles.

"Prosperin', is he?" Lewrie idly asked.

"Well, aye, sir." The Flag-Lieutenant sobered, looking uneasy, and skittish. "You knew he'd lost his right arm when trying to force a landing at Tenerife, in the Spanish Canaries?"

"Poor fellow, never had a *bit* of luck at land expeditions, did he?" Lewrie said, with the expected clucks of sorrow. "Grand Turk . . ."

"A head wound at the Nile, which I am told still pains him and causes sick headaches," the other officer sadly intoned.

"Why, they'll whittle him down to a nubbin, he keeps that up," was Lewrie's rejoinder to that, which gave the Flag-Lieutenant pause, for a leery second.

"Lately, he's . . . well, there are rumours that he's come under the sway of the King and Queen of Naples, and their corrupt court—"

"Met him, too," Lewrie interrupted. "Runs his own fried fish shop, 'Old Nosey' does. Serves a grand platter. Italians, *well* . . ."

"All sorts of difficulties with the Neapolitans, Captain Lewrie. And, there's scurrilous talk of the Admiral's *dealings* with the Hamiltons . . . the Ambassador's *wife*, most—"

"Lady Emma?" Lewrie butted in, again, sitting up straighter for closer attention to the "dirt" he expected to hear.

The Flag-Lieutenant dared cock a brow at him as if to ask, *You know* them, *too?* before getting cutty-eyed and breaking his gaze. "He is *said* to be led about by the nose, like a prize bull, by that lady, Captain Lewrie. That they've, uhm . . ." he gravelled, actually turning red with embarassment, or remorse for a hero's seeming failings.

Topped her, has he? Lewrie thought, and felt like snorting with derision; Took *him long enough, didn't it? Five years or more, since he met her. The way she went after* me, *Nelson must've been numb from the waist down . . . or held her off at sword-point like a daft saint!*

"I am sure the rumours are indeed scurrilous, and baseless, my good sir," Lewrie pretended to growl in support of Nelson's fame.

"Lady Emma *gambles,* sir," the Flag-Lieutenant bleakly sniffed.

"Uhm, aye, as I recall . . ."

"Gambles to *excess,* sir. And a woman who wagers like a man is utterly *lost,*" the junior officer primly stated, all but wringing his hands that his paragon would even associate with such a woman.

Never been to Bath . . . have ye? Lewrie drolly thought. Seeing in which quarter the wind was blowing, Lewrie decided to trim sails to suit. "She came from low *degree*, don't ye know, sir . . . an *actress* for a time, so I heard. Mistress to Sir William Hamilton's own kin for a bit . . . bought off him as token for gambling debts. Bedded, risen in *foreign* societies, then only properly married *years* later. A dancer *au naturel*, hey? Would've done her scanty-clad 'impressions' for the Hellfire Club, she'd been old enough."

And wouldn't Father have loved that! Lewrie happily considered.

" 'Tis a pity, though, sir, that Lord Nelson cannot be more *discerning* of the company he keeps," the Flag-Lieutenant fretted. "A man so high-minded and intent 'pon defeating the King's enemies might not even be aware of what people in England might construe from, ah . . ."

"Lie down with dogs, at Admiralty Orders, mind," Lewrie said to comfort the older fellow, who most-like would serve out his years as an humble "catch-fart" to shore-bound admirals, never pace a quarterdeck, and could but savour *vicarious* joy from newspapers that cited his hero, "and one cannot help but rising with a flea or two."

And, haven't I just! Lewrie told himself, recalling all those sordid duties *he'd* performed for King and Country in the company of an host of "foreign hounds." Though, some of them *had* been handsomer than others, and delightful temporary company.

"I am certain you are right, Captain Lewrie," the Flag-Lieutenant at last agreed, though nowhere near happy about his hero being slurred. "As I said, I do believe we have concluded our business. May I congratulate you on your return to England, and humbly wish you success in all your future endeavours."

"Whatever those may be," Lewrie said with a smile, rising at the same moment as the other officer. "You've heard nothing of any foreign expeditions that need a stout frigate, or . . . ?"

"Not for me t'say, sir . . . though, with that Frog general, that Bonaparte, just returned to France, there still may be some actions to be taken to clean up the Mediterranean, again. Malta's still in French hands, half of Italy, the Adriatic, and the Ionian Islands . . . my word, Captain Lewrie! You may very well end up serving under our Nelson one *more* time!"

Lewrie was about to blurt out that he'd met that little prick, Napoleone Buenaparte, back at the siege of Toulon, too, but, after a quick second forebore; the Flag-Lieutenant had already looked at him askance for a braggart, once. He didn't wish to leave the impression of a Falstaff—no matter that flag-lieutenants had no say in things, a Port Admiral's ink-spotted clerk most especially, still there was a chance that an off-hand remark might linger.

"I'll call upon Captain Saxton, then, and thank you for all your help, sir," Lewrie amiably said, bowing his way to the door.

A brisk stroll 'cross the sprawling dockyards took him to the Commissioner's offices, where he found half a dozen officers waiting ahead of him, got told that an appointment *could* be made for the next day, but his ship's needs *could* be addressed, had he the requisite ream of chits and documents handy.

"A *total* refit will it be, Captain Lewrie?" a weary clerk asked with a total lack of enthusiasm as Lewrie produced a thick sheaf from his haversack, as the waiting captains smirked among themselves.

"Just done at Halifax . . . stores, mostly," Lewrie replied.

"Thank the Good Lord, then, sir," the clerk brightened. "I *may* work you in tomorrow at . . . shall we say nine, sir?"

"Nine it'll be, thankee," Lewrie quickly agreed. "Fresh mail for *Proteus* . . . stuff not yet handed over to the packet, yet. Might there be any? And, who do I see about it? Lewrie . . . Ell–Eee–Double You . . . Arr . . . Eye . . . Eee. *Proteus* . . ." he said, as the clerk penned scribbles in a ledger-sized book atop his waist-high desk.

"Post storage is down the hall to the right, 'cross the yard to the red-brick building, and there you are, Captain Lewrie."

"Ah! Fine, then. See you tomorrow!"

He left the offices, went down the hall, crossed the yard, was presented by a *row* of red-brick buildings, but found the one that had a "Post-Boy" gridiron flag flying atop it, and entered.

"Not much, sir," a grimy, very old clerk finally told him, with a limp canvas sack in his hands, after a thorough rousting through the dusty shelves and hundreds of similar bags. "Sign here, sir. Then on this line . . . then this 'un," the mail-clerk croupily required, whilst coughing up a lung on the thick fug of coal smoke from a badly drawing fireplace.

Lewrie thought of going back aboard *Proteus* with the sack still bound, of receiving dire news in the privacy and safety of his great-cabins . . . where he could rant, weep, scream at the unfairness of it, toss back several reviving brandies, and plot a solo escape overside in the wee hours, but a most *dreadful* curiosity took him. After years in the Royal Navy, he'd been drilled to paw over the stacks of mail at once to separate the official from the personal, then open and read the official, first; he'd been whipped as a Midshipman for *not* adhering to that nautical custom, so . . .

Near the piers was a lacklustre coffee-house, where Lewrie knew the brew more-resembled dish-water, but an establishment where a chap could sit and sip in relative anonymity . . . were one not a Nelson, of course, whose phyz was on everything from portrait prints to ale mugs, by then. Once there, he could sort out anything horrid addressed to him, and mull over his prospects . . . or a new career as a brothel-master in Calcutta!

"Oh, wait one, sir!" the grimy old clerk called out before he'd laid hold of the office's doorknob. "*Thought* there woz somethin' come in I should'a put in th' sack," the fellow said, shuffling over to the pigeon-hole racks and mumbling to himself. "Come in 'is very mornin', it did, now where'd I, ah! Here ye go, Cap'm Lewrie, o' the *Proteus* frigate! Sign here, sir, ye'd be so kind. An' here . . . an' here."

"Thankee," Lewrie numbly said, taking note of the creaminess of the paper, the heaviness and expense of the bond, as he turned it over and over in his hands, fresh, crisp, new-mailed corners still intact, and not a jot of smut from being transferred from pillar to post . . . except for the clerk's coal-sooted fingers, of course. It was sealed with a large blob of brown wax, which wax topped and cemented two wide bands of black riband together. *Grim-lookin'*, Lewrie shudderingly told himself; *grim as a death-notice!* And, whoever had sent it didn't trust to mere wax to seal the flapped-over paper's corners to keep the contents private, but had bound it north-south, then east-west, to boot! A seal *had* been pressed into the wax, but it was one he thankfully didn't recognise. It wasn't Admiralty, and thank God it wasn't from a Crown Court, not even a barrister or solicitor!

To hell with tepid dish-water! Once outside in the cold airs, he sat *Proteus*'s mail sack at his feet and tremulously pried open the seal and ribands, unfolded the flaps, and . . .

Sir

Upon receipt of this letter, copies of which have been despatched to all major naval seaports where you could be expected to call, you will, AT ONCE, attend me to discuss a matter which may, are you not expeditious, redound to your utter peril and ruin. My address is enclosed, and I shall make my self available to you at any hour you are able to arrive. But, be quick about coming to London!

Z. Twigg

Twigg, Oh Christ! Lewrie quailed with an audible groan; *What'd I ever do t'deserve* his *company, again? Oh, yes . . . that. But . . . !*

Old Zachariah Twigg, that cold-blooded, murderous, dissembling, smug, and arch old cut-throat, that malevolent Foreign Office spy! Had not James Peel said he'd retired, at last; so what good could Twigg do him? "Matter which may redound to your utter peril . . . ," which meant that *some* word of his slave-stealing had gotten to England, but no one "official" had taken notice of it . . . yet! They might not if Twigg still thought it secret, and could do something about it.

Oh, but *Lord*, he'd thought himself shot of Foreign Office plots and errands: with his last time paying for all; Guillaume Choundas in American chains, his every scheme scotched; the former French colony of Saint-Domingue's new masters, the ex-slave armies, isolated, unarmed, and un-reenforced by Paris, and sure to wither and fall into British hands, sooner or later; those French Creole pirates from Spanish Louisiana slaughtered, a *raft* of stolen Spanish silver recovered, and simply a *grand* scheme scouted out for a future invasion of that crown jewel of the Mississippi River, the city of New Orleans, delivered to his superiors at both Admiralty and Foreign Office, *and* getting shot in the process, to boot!

Wasn't that enough? Lewrie appealled to the heavens.

For, did the hideous old Zachariah Twigg still own the "interest" to get him off, Lewrie would owe the skeletal bastard his *soul;* nothing got done without incurring a heavy debt in English Society. And, that meant that Lewrie would *never* be rid of neck-or-nothing schemes!

Worse, yet! Much as he heartily despised that noisome schemer, Twigg, he'd be forced to *grovel,* lick his boots, buss his blind cheeks, fawn, swallow shite and proclaim it plum duff, and pretend to be . . .

Nice to him!

CHAPTER FOUR

Away in the "diligence-coach" at dawn, a day after meeting at the Commissioner's; up Portdown Hill inland, thence to Petersfield, a few miles away from wife and home at Anglesgreen, but there was no time for *rencontre*, just a quick note to Caroline from the posting-house as the horse team was changed. Which note, Lewrie grimly surmised, would be used to light the candles under the chafing dishes to keep her breakfast warm! He didn't know quite why he even bothered.

Onwards to Guildford, once more pretending to nod off, too fretful to accept the usual invitation from sailors travelling with him to "caulk or yarn," passing up the chance, for a rare once, to brag about *Proteus*'s most recent exploits, or share reminiscences about the Caribbean and the West Indies. He "harumphed" himself deep into his cloak, tipped his cocked hat low over his eyes, closed them, and thought about nooses and jeering crowds.

In London, at last, he'd hired a horse at the final post-house, strapped his cylindrical leather *portmanteau* and soft-sided clasp-bag behind the saddle, and set off Northward, following the instructions in Twigg's demanding letter. He found it vaguely reassuring that his route from the post-house took him very near Whitehall, and the seat of Admiralty, Parliament, and the Army's Horse Guards; if Twigg lived on a road that led directly back to town and that august warren of government buildings, might he still have needful influence?

Up Charing Cross, 'til it became the Tottenham Court Road; then onwards 'til Tottenham Court crossed the New Road and became known as the Hampstead

Road, with the dense street traffic and press of houses, stores, and such gradually thinning. Further onwards, and the breweries, metal-working manufacturies, and craft shops predominated, then those began to thin out, replaced by market gardeners' small farms, estates of the middling nature, and roadside establishments, with fields and forests and pastures behind them.

Hampstead, like Islington in the early days, had developed over the years as the seat of weekend "country" get-away cottages, manses, and villas . . . though, Hampstead catered to a much richer, and select, part-time population than Islington's artisan-tradesman clientele. He could espy, here and there, stone or brick gate-pillars announcing the presence of a grand-ish house up a gravelled and tree-lined lane, set well back, and landscaped into well-ordered semblances of "bucolic" or gloomily "romantic," in that fallen-castle, overgrown-bower, mossy-old-but-still-inhabited style that had grown so Gothically popular, of late, and *damn* all moody poets and scribblers responsible for it, and what it cost to be created by gimlet-eyed landscapers!

It was *not*, for a bloody wonder, raining, that mid-day. Lewrie was *not* soaked to the skin, cocooned in a frousty fug of wet wool and chafing canvas. As it was England, though, it *had* rained, recently, thus turning the roadway into a gravel-and-mud pudding, and his snow-white uniform breeches might never be the same, and every approaching dray or waggon, and its mud-slinging wheels, was a "shoal" to be avoided like the very Plague!

His fearful errand was so completely off-putting that Capt. Alan Lewrie, never a stranger to the charms of young, nubile, and fetching farm girls, barely gave them a passing glance, and rarely lifted his hat in salute to a shy smile of approbation, in fact; and must here be noted, if only as a clue to his present state of mind.

Here an "humble" cottage, there an "humble" cottage; a Bide-A-We to the left, a Rook's Nook to the right, or so the signboards said to announce the existence of a destination up those lanes leading off the Hampstead Road. Lark's Nest, a Belle Reve, a rather imposing new two-storey Palladian mansion set back in at least ten acres of woodsy parkland named Villa Pauvre . . . which proved to Lewrie that the rich could *afford* a sense of irony.

At last, Lewrie topped a long, gradual rise, atop which stood a pair of granite, lion-topped pillars flanked by a long-established and nigh-impenetrable hedge to either side. Here, he drew rein and gawped at the house, which lay about two cables off on the right-hand side of the road, up another gradual rise so that the house sat atop the crown of a slightly taller hill that sloped gently down on all four sides . . . and the signboard read "Spyglass Bungalow"!

Very apt, for atop the villa was a squat, blocky tower of stone, open to all four prime compass points, very much like the bell towers seen in a Venetian *campus,* or town square, right down to the wide-arch form of the openings. *Or, a hellish-fancy block-house atop a fortress's gate or corner,* Lewrie decided with a gulp of dread. He gazed about, in search of a further signage that might-well have read "Abandon All Hope, Ye Who Enter Here," but couldn't find it. He gazed fearfully at the house . . . villa . . . bungalow, whatever, and blinked a time or two in confusion.

For the house was light, airy, and its stuccoed exterior painted the palest cream, set off with white stone, its roof made of those sorts of overlapping red-clay tiles more often seen in the Mediterranean, or Spanish possessions. There was a massy, circular flower bed before the house, encircled by a well-gravelled carriage drive, which led under a wide and deep *portico* over the main entrance. Very much like his father's, Sir Hugo St. George Willoughby's, Hindoo-inspired house near Anglesgreen, which stood on the ruins of an ancient Roman watch-tower and villa, that he'd named Dun Roman. Two storeys, and no full basement, but perhaps a hint of a cellar, so the front door and a gallery-porch were sheltered by the over-wide *portico,* only four or five stone risers to the short flight of steps leading from the stoop to the ground. It was altogether such a *pleasant* prospect that Lewrie had to shake his head a time or two, as well as blink a deal more, to realise that this "Spyglass Bungalow" could actually be the residence of a soul-less, calculating, murderous, and callous son of a bitch like Zachariah Twigg!

He clucked his tongue, shook the reins, and heeled his mount to motion, once more, up that welcoming gravelled drive, between the bare-limbed trees that would in summer shade the wide lane with fresh green leaves. There were dozens of abandoned nests in those limbs that told him that a springtime arrival would be greeted by the singing of hundreds of birds. *Nice* birds, who hadn't a clue how dangerous the master of those trees could be, poor things.

Set downhill on all sides round the house (Indian bungalow) was an inner wall of about six feet height, topped with round-cut stone . . . atop which Lewrie could espy the glint of broken glass!

That's more like it, he cynically thought; *Aha!*

Inside the inner wall (fortification?) lay a lawn, unbroken by any trees or shrubs where an interloper might shelter. Lewrie knew a fort's killing-ground when he saw one, and began to hunt for a hidden ditch or moat, a masking *glacis,* a *redan* or *ravenel* or two where the sharpshooters, or the grapeshot-loaded small cannon, might be placed at time of siege. Off to the left of the villa-bungalow was a coach-house of a matching stucco-and-stone, though with an "humble" thatched roof, that led back into the inner enclosure; up against the wall, as if the hayloft above the stalls and tack rooms held loopholes for marksmen! It was only in the immediate vicinity of the house that greenery was allowed. Lewrie took note that a handsome coach stood outside the stable doors, a groom or coachee swabbing the road's mud off it, and a servant tending to a team of four matched roans. Getting even closer, Lewrie could make out a large, enclosed equipage, a lighter convertible-topped coach for good weather and short jaunts, *and* a sporty two-horse chariot inside the building, as well.

Come at a bad time? he asked himself; *Does Twigg have company?*

A guest's coach, its team led out for oats and water, gave him a small shiver of new dread, for said equipage *could* belong to an official from a King's Court, and Twigg's imperious letter the excuse for him to be lured into a trap! He wouldn't put such past him, for Twigg had *always* played people false, whether friend or foe!

"Ha ha, go it, girl! Heels down, that's the way!" came a voice from behind the house, and, down the cobbled stableyard from behind the house came the clatter of hooves, the shrill "Yoicks!" and imitations of a foxhorn's "tara-tara!," as a pair of ponies appeared, both loping (but no faster!) no matter the urgings of their riders . . . a small lad and a girl child, the boy appearing no more than ten, and the girl not yet a gangly teen. They whooped their way out of the stableyard, onto the gravelled drive, under the *portico* to cross Lewrie's "hawse," then headed off 'cross the lawn for another exhilarating circuit of the inner wall, about the house!

Behind them, afoot, came a brace of adults; a rather handsome woman in a dark riding *ensemble,* and a much older, spindlier, man in a drab brown suit of "ditto," white shirt and stock, and brown-topped black riding boots, and waving a crop over his head. Smiling, *beaming* with enjoyment and pleasure.

Twigg? Lewrie gawped to himself, gape-jawed for true; *he* never *smiled, not a day in his mis'rable life!*

But it *was* him, to the life, the spitting image of that coldly calculating "chief spider" behind a myriad of bloody-handed schemes on the King's enemies. And, at that moment, as he shaded his eyes with a hand to his brow—the one holding the *whip,* o' course!—Mr. Zachariah Twigg could be mistaken for the *nicest* sort of genial, and wealthy, country squire who couldn't swat a wasp without regrets.

"Aha!" Zachariah Twigg called out, sounding so welcoming that Lewrie, for an instant, thought himself the victim of a sorry supper and a bilious dream. Or, *wishing* that he was! "Captain Lewrie, you have arrived, ha ha! Alight, and let me look at you, me lad!"

Spur away! Lewrie warned himself; *Spur away, now, and ride like Blazes!* Though he was so taken aback that he meekly let his horse go onwards at a sedate plod to the cobblings of the stableyard, drew rein, and swung down as a groom came up to accept the reins and tend to his rented horse.

"Honoria, pray allow me to name to you one of my young acquaintances from the Far East, and the Mediterranean, Captain Alan Lewrie of the *Proteus* frigate. . . . Captain Lewrie, my daughter, Mistress Honoria Staples. I'd introduce you to my grandchildren, Thomas and Susannah, but I fear they're having too much fun with their new ponies, ha ha! A stout fellow, full of pluck and daring, is Captain Lewrie, my dear, an energetic and clever champion of our fair land, and a perfect terror to Britain's foes, from our first encounter to the present!"

"Your servant, ma'am," Lewrie managed to respond, at last, with a gulp and bob of his head as he doffed his hat to her and gave her a jerky bow, feeling so deliriously put-off that he nearly blushed to be so gawkish and clumsy, like a farm labourer introduced to a princess, all but shuffling muddy shoes and tugging his forelock.

Clever, daring . . . plucky? Lewrie felt like goggling to hear an introduction such as that from Twigg, of all people; *God above . . . me?*

"A comrade of old, of course," Mrs. Staples replied, bowing her head gracefully, and beaming in seeming understanding. "Your servant, Captain Lewrie, and delighted to make your acquaintance. And . . . you have old times to take stock of, I'm bound, Father? The children and I should be going, then . . . may I get them *off* their new ponies," she stated with a merry twinkle, "though you and Johnathon . . . my husband, Captain Lewrie . . . a man as fond of springing surprises on people as Father . . . spent *far* too much on them."

"You'll not dine here, my pet?" Twigg cooed, looking devilish-disappointed that they would not. Damn his blood, but he was almost . . . *wheedling*! Or doing a damn' good sham of it.

"I told cook we'd be back by one, and there's just time for us to get home before everything goes cold," his daughter chuckled, holding up a lace-gloved hand to her children as they completed their lap of the grounds. "Rein in, children, and alight! You've shewn Grandfather your presents, and we must go. I mean it! No, you mayn't ride them back; they're too fractious, yet. It will rest them to be led at the coach's boot, unsaddled."

"Brush and curry, then stable them proper, once you're home, as well, my dears," Zachariah Twigg fondly cautioned. "See to your beasts first. You look after them, and they'll look after you. Remember, you are English, not cruel Dons or Frenchmen."

"Yes, Grandfather," the children chorused, though unhappy about leaving, or dismounting. Quick as a wink, the team of roans was back in harness and the handsome closed coach led out into the drive, ready for departure.

"See you all on Sunday, my dears," Twigg promised as he hoisted the children in, then handed in his daughter, giving her a peck on the cheek like the doting-est "granther" in all Creation. "Church, dinner, then we'll all go for a long ride together, after."

Twigg, in church, hmm . . . Lewrie silently pondered, wondering if even the most enthusiastic missionaries, desperate for congregants, in the worst stews of Wapping or Seven Dials, would dare have him.

"Delighted to meet you, ma'am," Lewrie offered, again.

"And you, sir," she replied, though distracted by keeping both her rambunctious, chatter-box offspring in check. Then, off the coach clattered at a sedate pace, with the ponies trotting in-trail.

"Well, *that* was . . . s'prisin'," Lewrie said with a droll leer, once the coach was out of earshot.

"Think I spent *all* my life lurking in the world's dark corners, 'thout a private life outside of service to King and Country?" Twigg snapped.

"Frankly . . . yes," Lewrie baldly stated, lifting one eyebrow.

"But not a patch on *yours*, Lewrie," Twigg shot back, purring in his old, supercilious fashion, looking down his long nose. "You have spread your 'presence' so widely, and indiscriminately, about the earth, 'tis a wonder you had time for a *public* life, haw haw."

All Lewrie could do was remind himself that he'd come to beg at his superior's table and beggars had to suffer abuse in silence; that, and grind his teeth.

"Well now, you are come, at last," Twigg said, seeming to relent. "Let us go into the house, where we may discover what may save you from a well-deserved hanging."

CHAPTER FIVE

The interior of Zachariah Twigg's "humble" abode was just about as disconcertingly out-of-character to the man he'd known as the stucco outer facade. Once they were past the requisite tiling of the entry hall, done in red-veined Italian marble, the floors of the central passageway were shiny contrasting parquetry, laid out in a complex geometric pattern.

"Teak and holly," Twigg tersely allowed, "the teak brought from India."

"Indeed," Lewrie said, as a servant came for his cloak, hat, and sword. The servant was a Hindoo, a short, wizened little fellow, with a bristling grey-white mustachio that stuck out almost to his ears, as stiff as a ship's anchor-bearing cat-heads, above a thick, round white beard. He wore a tan silk turban above a European's white shirt and neck-stock, a glossy yellow silk waist-coat, and a voluminous pair of native *pyjammy* breeches, his suiting completed by thick white cotton stockings, in deference to the weather perhaps, but with stout leather elephant or bullock hide sandals on his feet.

"*Namasté*, El-Looy *sahib,*" he said, with a faint attempt at a smile.

"Aha!" Lewrie barked back in further surprise. "Ajit Roy, is it you? *Namasté* t'you, too," he said, placing his hands together before his chin and sketching out a brief bow. "Haven't heard myself called that in fifteen years!"

"Yayss," Twigg drawled in his superior, amused manner of old. "There's a thousand *other* things you've been called, since, hmm?"

"Now, damme . . ." Lewrie began to bristle, before recalling what peril he was in, and why he'd come. *Grovel; fawn!* he warned himself.

"The *kutch bohjan kamraa,* Ajit," Twigg ordered. "No need to use the formal dining room . . . 'mongst old companions," he could not help adding with a faintly amused sneer. "*Laanaa hamén* sherry, first, Ajit."

"Je haan, sahib," Twigg's old servant replied, bowing and smiling.

"This way, Lewrie," Twigg commanded, stalking off on his long legs, hands tucked under the tails of his coat, and leaving Lewrie no choice but to follow.

The well-plastered walls were tawny yellow, set off nicely with heavy crown mouldings, wainscottings, and baseboards, false-columned at intervals, with lighter mouldings to frame gilt-framed portraits, and exotic foreign scenes. Clive of India still led his small army versus native *rajahs'* hordes, and grimly-smug relatives peered down with familial asperity. All the floors were teak planking, though strewn with wool or goat-hair carpets, all light, subtle Chinee or colourful Hindi, with not an Axminster or Turkey carpet in sight.

Far East shawls, *saris,* or vivid princes' surcoats did service as wall hangings, next to tapestries painted by native artists of parades, tiger hunts, leopard hunts, or court scenes, with gayly-decorated elephants bearing lords and ladies in *howdahs.* Some walls bore gaudy, silk *mandarins'* coats, stiff-armed with a dowel through the arm-holes, next to the little pillbox hats Lewrie had seen at Canton, with the pheasant tail-feathers and coral buttons on the top that denoted rank and importance.

It would seem that at one time Twigg had been a mighty hunter, himself, for there were boars' heads, leopards' heads, even a bear, its lips still curved back in his final fury. On a jungle-green wood platform there was a *huge* stuffed Bengali tiger—looking a little worse for wear, though, where *someone's* grandchildren had used it as a hobby-horse.

And, there were weapons galore: cirles of wavy-bladed *krees* daggers and knives about a crossed pair of *parangs;* assorted Hindoo edged weapons about a brace of bejewelled *tulwars;* lance-heads, javelins and pike-heads, bill-hooks, and other pole-arm "nasties" that were favoured East of Cape Good Hope.

Behind locked glass cabinets were racks of firearms, from clumsy match-lock muskets and hand-cannon to long, slim, and elegantly-chased and intricately-engraved Indian or Malay *jezzails,* some so bejewelled that they'd fetch thousands; even humble flint-lock Tower muskets, St. Etienne or Charleville French muskets given or sold to native princes' troops had been turned into priceless works of art by Hindoo artisans. There were even *wheel-lock* pieces, musketoons, and pairs of pistols as long as Lewrie's forearms that the Czar of All the Russias might covet.

Armour? Take your pick: fanciful *cuirasses,* back-and-breasts and helmets, gilt or silver chain-mail suits, brass fish-scale armour over thick ox-hide; Tatar, Chinese, Mongol, Bengali, Moghul . . .

"Nippon, there," Twigg commented, pointing to a stand that held a wide-skirted, glossily-lacquered set, seemingly made of bamboo, tied together with bright orange and red wool cords; there was a horned helmet with neck pieces and side flanges so wide and deep that the wearer could shelter from a hard rain under it, with a fierce, wild-eyed, and mustachioed face-mask bound to it. "Them, too," Twigg further stated, indicating a horizontal stand that held a long dagger, a short sword, and a very long sword, all of a piece, bright-corded, and their scabbards so ornately carved they resembled the jade or ivory "boats" with incredibly tiny figures of oarsmen and passengers, all whittled from a single tusk or block of soft stone.

"Nippon?" Lewrie gawped. "You mean Japan?"

"No White man has gone there, and returned to tell the tale, in three hundred years, Lewrie," Twigg proudly said "Though, some of the hereditary warriors, the *samurai,* now and then lose their feudal lord, or . . . blot their copy-books," Twigg added with a taunting leer at his guest, "and become outcasts . . . *ronin,* I recall, is the term . . . some of whom leave their forbidden isles, entire, and take service overseas. Portuguese Macao is a port where bands of them may be hired on. Quite fierce; quite honourable if you *pay* 'em regular. This fellow, here . . . well, let us say he proved a disappointment, and committed ritual suicide to atone. Willed me his armour and swords."

"Did *you* ever manage to land in Nippon?" Lewrie just had to ask.

"Of course not, sir!" Twigg hooted. "I was bold in my younger days, but never *that* rash. Unlike *some* I know, hmmm?"

Swallow it, swallow it! Lewrie chid himself.

Another great room to pace through, this one filled with porcelain, *niello* brass, gilt and silver pieces, the most delicate ceramics, ginger jars, wine jars, tea sets, and eggshell-thin vases, from every ancient dynasty from Bombay to fabled Peking.

"Didn't know you'd always wanted t'open a museum," Lewrie said. As they attained a smaller, plainer dining room that overlooked a back garden, barns, coops and pens, and a block of servants' quarters. It was where the house's owners would break their fast *en famille,* in casual surroundings and casual clothes, before they had to don their public duds and public faces to deal with the rest of their day.

"As the French say, *souvenirs,*" Twigg scoffed, though his eyes did glow with pleasure over his vast collection, worthy of a man who'd come back from India a full *nabob,* with an *emperor's* riches stowed on the orlop. Smugness of owning such grand things, perhaps with happy remembrance of how he'd acquired them. Or, the blood and mayhem required to do so!

"I can see why your grandchildren were loath to leave," Lewrie wryly commented. "My own children'd screech in bloody wonder to play amongst such a pirate's trove."

"Mementos of an arduous life," Twigg scoffed again, perhaps with long-engrained English gentlemanly modesty, "spent mostly in places so dreadful, the baubles were the only attractive things worth a toss. I assume you like goat. Do you not, it doesn't signify, for that's what we're having. Keep a flock to dine on . . . sheep, as well."

"But, no pork, nor beefsteaks, either, I'd s'pose," Lewrie said, with another wry scowl.

"Taboo to Muslims in the first instance, taboo to Hindoos in the second, aye," Twigg replied, his thin lips clasped together in the sort of aspersion that Lewrie had dreaded in their early days. "Old habits die hard. Well, don't just stand there like a coat-rack, sit ye down," Twigg snapped, pointing imperiously at a chair at the foot of the six-place table, whilst he strode with his usual impatience to the chair at the other end, and Lewrie almost grinned to see himself seated "below the salt," no matter there were only the two of them.

The elderly servant, Ajit Roy, bearing a brass tray on which sat two glasses of sherry, shuffled in, obviously waiting 'til they were seated before intruding. Twigg took a tentative taste, looking puckery, as if assaying his own urine for a moment, before nodding assent and acceptance, at which point Ajit Roy came down-table to give Lewrie his small glass.

"*Laanaa shorbaa*, Ajit," Twigg ordered, and not a tick later, an attractive Hindoo woman in English servant's clothing, but with a long, diaphanous shawl draped over her hair and shoulders, entered with bowls of the requested soup on another tray.

"*Dhanyavaad*, Lakshmi," Twigg told her.

"Thankee," Lewrie echoed in English. He'd never learned Hindoo as glibly as his father, Sir Hugo, and had ever sounded *pidgin* barbarian when he did speak it, but it *was* coming back to him, in dribs and drabs. She *was* fetching; did she and Twigg . . . ?

"Ajit Roy's second wife," Twigg said, with a knowing leer after one look at Lewrie's phyz. "The first'un cooks. And no, I *don't*. My tastes these days, well . . . I also own a place in the City, quite near your father's new gentlemen's lodging club, in point of fact. His is at the corner of Wigmore and Duke streets, as you surely recall, while my set of rooms is nearby in Baker Street. We run into each other. . . ."

"Oh, how unfortunate for you," Lewrie sourly commented.

"We speak rather often, act'lly," Twigg said with a mystifying smile. "Sometimes dine, drop in for a drink, or play *écarté* with him at his club, with no need for its lodging facilities."

"And does he give you a discounted membership, sir? Or . . . does he make up for it by fleecing you at cards?" Lewrie cynically asked.

"My dear Lewrie . . . no one has *ever* fleeced me at *écarté* . . . and lived," Zachariah Twigg drawled, with a superior simper. "Your father and I rub along quite well, together, act'lly. We're much of an age, and experienced much the same sort of adventures in exotic climes, so . . . absent the disputes resulting from, ah . . . 'boundary' friction in the expedition against Choundas and the Lanun Rovers . . . his concerns for his *sepoy* regiment, and taking orders from a Foreign Office civilian, we've discovered that we have a great deal in common. Having *you* and your, ah . . . *follies* in common, as well. How is your soup?"

"Simply grand," Lewrie sarcastically muttered, though the soup was as close to a Chinese "hot and sour" as a Hindoo cook could attain, and as tasty as any ever he'd had when moored off Canton in the '80s.

"Amazing, what a *small* world in which we live, Lewrie," Twigg went on, carefully spooning up his own soup, and slurping it into his thin-lipped mouth, then daintily dabbing with his napkin. "Sir Hugo is partnered with Sir Malcolm Shockley in his gentlemen's club enterprise. . . . Sir Malcolm thinks the world of him, and of *you*, more to the point . . . though I've yet to see a valid reason *why*, other than gratitude for getting his wealthy arse out of Venice and the Adriatic before the French took it in '97. *And*, wonder of wonders, Sir Malcolm is wed to Lady Lucy Hungerford, *nee* Lucy Beauman, of the Jamaica Beaumans who wish you hung for stealing their slaves. Well, well, well! Quite the coincidence, what?"

"And Hugh Beauman's already written Lucy and told her all about it?" Lewrie said with a groan, feeling an urge to slide bonelessly or lifelessly under the table, and *stay* there, unfindable, for, oh, say a century or so. "Christ, I'm good as dead!" he moaned, his brow popping out a sweat that was not *entirely* the fault of the spicy soup.

"And . . . here comes the roast!" Twigg enthused as Lakshmi entered, bearing a tray of sliced kid goat, and a heaping bowl of savouried rice, mango *chautney*, and such. "Done to a *perfect turn*, I am bound!" he added, not without a purr and glare that Lewrie took for sheer maliciousness—making him feel even more inclined to slink beneath the table, *un-fed!*

"I take it, an . . ." Lewrie managed to croak, "that Sir Malcolm's mentioned it to Father?"

"B'lieve so, Lewrie, yayss," Twigg responded in a further purr of hellish delight at his predicament, all the time hoisting slices of goat onto his heaping plate of rice and mild, baked red peppers.

Lewrie felt his face flush (*not* from the spicy soup!) picturing Sir Hugo's reaction to his folly, not so much anger or disappointment, really, for they'd never really been *proper* father and son, leaving it quite late—in India in '84 or '85—to *tentatively* reconcile, thence to keep a wary distance ever since, so whatever rage Sir Hugo might display was water off a duck's back. No, what upset Lewrie more was a firm suspicion that he'd chortled his head half-off that Alan had gone and done something so goose-brained, *and* been caught at it, red-handed!

"Damme . . . *Lucy* knows, 'tis a safe wager that all *London* knows, by now!" Lewrie muttered, dabbing his brow with his napery. "The hen-headed, blabbery . . . baggage!" he nigh-stuttered in new dread. " 'Tis a wonder I've not been taken up, already, with . . . !"

"One'd be surprised, Lewrie," Twigg loftily told him. "Do try the kid. There's a *dahee* to go with it, one of those yogurt gravies I recall you liking when in Calcutta. *Tandoori*-roast chicken to follow!"

"Christ!"

"You and Lucy Beauman were, at one time in your mis-spent youth, quite fond of each other, Lewrie," Twigg breezed on, come over all amiable, as he spooned spiced *dahee* on his goat and rice. "She went on to wed a rich'un she met at Bath, her first Season in England . . . dare we speculate on what is called the 'rebound' following her family showing you the door for the utter cad you proved to be, hmm? Lord Hungerford, Knight and Baronet, surely was a great disappointment to her, since he proved to be just about as huge a rake-hell and rantipoling 'splitter of beards' as you . . . though, Lady Lucy seems to have been spared revelations anent your poorer qualities, for some reason. The illogic, and the blindness, that the fairer sex possess towards their un-deserving men, no matter proof incontrovertible served up on a gilt platter, hah!

"She still has, as they say, Lewrie, a 'soft spot' in her heart for you, therefore, and, so far as I am able to ascertain, has yet to utter the first word to anyone, other than her husband, Sir Malcolm, of the matter."

"You *must* be joking!" Lewrie exclaimed, almost leaping from his chair in amazement at such a ridiculous statement. "Lucy is my prime suspect of writing scurrilous, anonymous letters to my wife, about my . . . overseas . . . doings . . ." he trailed off, blurting out more than he'd meant to.

"Ah, those letters!" Twigg said, brightening with cruel amusement. "Why must you suspect her?"

"You *know* of 'em?" Lewrie quailed, though he had to admit that Zachariah

Twigg had spent his entire life as a Foreign Office agent—he just *had* to know a bit about everything!

"Your *father* has, since the mutiny at the Nore, he said, so . . . knowing my old profession, he approached me to delve into things, and discover what I could. 'Smoak out' the culprit. So far without joy. Why do you suspect her?"

"When we met in Venice in '96, *years* later, Lucy, I felt, was . . . still after me," Lewrie told him as he at last accepted a heap of rice, a slice or two of roast kid, and a dribble of the spiced *dahee*. "Even if she was married not six months, still on 'honeymoon' with Sir Malcolm Shockley, she was . . ."

"What a *burden* it is," Twigg amusedly drawled, "to be the romantic masculine paragon of one's age . . . and in *such* demand!"

"All but throwing herself at me, aye!" Lewrie retorted in some heat, and grovelling bedamned. "Her foot damn' near in my lap, even with her husband at-table with us, and when I wouldn't play, she took up with Commander William Fillebrowne, another officer from our squadron. There's another I suspect, the smarmy bastard! Our last words, Lucy caught onto my . . . involvement with a lady I'd rescued from Serbian pirates, and said—"

"Mistress Theoni Kavares Connor, the mother of your bastard," Twigg offhandedly interjected 'twixt a bite of food and a sip. "She of the Zante currant-trade fortune from the Ionian Islands."

"Er . . . yes," Lewrie barely squeaked, having been rein-sawed from a full gallop to a pale-faced, hoof-sliding halt, for a moment. "Well . . . Lucy said something very like 'I should write your wife and tell her what a rogue she wed' . . . *playfully*, but not without a *bite* to it. I told *her* what Sir Malcolm should know 'bout *her* doin's with Commander Fillebrowne, and that's where we left it, but . . ."

"And *was* she, in fact, involved with Fillebrowne?" Twigg asked.

"Well, o' *course* she was!" Lewrie snapped, hitting his stride, "I saw 'em for myself, spoonin' and kissin' on the balcony of a rented set o' rooms, just before we sailed the last time, whoever could notice 'em bedamned . . . only Dago foreigners, I s'pose they thought. An old friend of mine from Harrow, Clotworthy Chute, was with me, too! Chute was doing the Grand Tour of the Continent with Lord Peter Rushton, at the time. And . . . she gambles. Gambles deep," Lewrie added, recalling what that Flag-Lieutenant at Portsmouth said of Lady Emma Hamilton, as if that would be proof enough to sign, seal, and deliver the truth of his account.

Twigg cocked an eye at him as if he thought that Lewrie had lost his mind, and was about halfway towards laughing out loud at such rank priggishness, especially coming from one so "low-minded" as Lewrie.

"Do assay the wine, sir," Twigg instructed after a long ponder. "A Dago wine, how further coincidental. A Tuscan *chianti,* in point of fact, of a very dry nature, that complements the richness of the goat quite nicely. I can understand, on the face of it, why you might susect Lady Lucy, Lewrie, but . . . you say you also suspect that Commander Fillebrowne?"

"Well . . ." Lewrie elaborated, after a tentative bite of kid and rice, and a sip of the *chianti,* which brought back memories of Naples. "When we first met, he was anchored at Elba. Tupping a local vintner's wife, as I recall. Thought I'd take to him, at first, but in the space of a single hour, I came away a bit disgusted. Comes from a very rich family, treats the Navy like a place to kill time 'til his inheritance is come . . . all yachting, cruising, and claret, and his orlop the storehouse for art treasures he was buying up from refugee Royalist French. *Boasted* of it! Fillebrowne's family'd all done their Grand Tours, the war was *his,* and all he cared about was . . . 'collecting'!" Lewrie sneered. "He chaffered me, that very *morning,* with hints he'd taken up with my former mistress. . . ."

Lewrie paused, waiting for Twigg to say, "Phoebe Aretino, better known as 'La Contessa,' Corsican-born, former whore, *shrewd* businesswoman, and collector, trader, and treasures-dealer in her own right," but Twigg kept his mouth shut, or busy with his victuals; and, for the sort of man whose very gaze could turn cockchafers "toes-up dead," his expression was a very bland "do tell" and "say on."

"Threw it in my face, rather," Lewrie growled, shoving rice on his plate with an angry, scraping noise of steel on priceless china. "Nose-high, top-lofty sort, the greedy, callous bastard. Well, Chute saw through him. Clotworthy's a 'Captain Sharp,' makes his livin' by gullin' naive new-comes to London . . . ones who've just inherited some 'tin,' and such. When I told him that Fillebrowne thought himself an *astute* collector of fine art, Chute cobbled up a brace o' bronze Roman statues o' some sort, *I* never saw 'em. Amazin' what a week's soaking in salt water'll do t'make 'em look authentic, and Fillebrowne bought 'em, straightaway. *Pantin'* for 'em!

"I suspect Fillebrowne figured out he'd been finessed, sooner or later, learned that Chute and I were old friends . . . acquaintances, really . . . perhaps he and . . . my former mistress," he said, avoiding Phoebe's name, as if to deprive Twigg of un-necessary information . . . just in case, "had an angry parting? Sharp an eye as *she* had, when it came t'treasures, if *she* tipped him that they were frauds, he'd've gone off like a bomb on her. On me! And, he'd have seen, or heard, just enough needful t'pen scurrilous letters to Caroline, in revenge."

"One *could* see his reason for *pique*, yayss," Twigg mused, those long fingers of his steepled thoughtfully under his chin, not *exactly* mocking, at that instant. "Though, you *do* have that effect on people. But, was Commander Fillebrowne still possessed of active commission, I do not see how he could stay . . . current anent your, ah . . . pastime."

"There's been *nothing* . . . current," Lewrie querulously replied. "Not since I sailed for the Caribbean. Well, the last bits . . . about Mistress Connor lodging with me at Sheerness for a week before we departed . . ." he admitted with a squirm. "*And*, afore that, about the two-dozen doxies my solicitor was t'pay, for services rendered. . . ."

"Two-*dozen* prostitutes?" Twigg barked, as if in breathless awe, going so far as to lay one hand on his heart. "What stamina! Damme, Lewrie, but I am *impressed*!"

"For helpin' me kill belowdecks mutineers, so I had enough true men t'take back my ship and escape the Nore Mutiny!" Lewrie retorted. " 'Wos innit f'me? Wos innit f'me?' " he snipped, impersonating lower-class dialect main-well, after twenty years of exposure to it. "They wouldn't've tried it on, else! Christ, my report to Admiralty got 'em letters of *appreciation*, ev'ry last one of 'em! And, I didn't lay one single finger on *any* of 'em, but *someone* twisted it into a scandal!"

Idly, and illogically, the face and form of the then-tempting young Sally Blue *did* cross his mind. Black hair, blue eyes, promising poonts, and a waist 'bout as slim as a sapling pine . . . !

"And *was* Commander Fillebrowne's ship at the Nore at this time?" Twigg pressed, looking grimly intent. "And, do you believe Lady Lucy was aware of your doings, as well?"

"No, don't think so," Lewrie had to confess, going as slack as a sail in the Atlantic Doldrums. "So, damme if I know who."

"No other suspects, then?" Twigg asked, one dubious brow raised.

"Well, in my madder moments, I sometimes fancy it was you!"

Both of Twigg's brows leaped upwards at that statement. He sat back so quickly in his chair that Lewrie could hear the joinings squeak in protest. Then, to make Lewrie feel even worse (was such a thing possible at that instant), Twigg quite uncharacteristically threw back his head, opened his mouth, and began to guffaw right out loud!

In an evil way, it went without saying.

CHAPTER SIX

Lewrie had to bite the lining of his mouth to keep a tranquil face on, as Mr. Twigg exhausted his highly-amused outburst; he eased off from red-faced brays to napkin-covered "titters," thence at last to a top-lofty and nose-high sardonically-superior air of very *faint* humour—lordly chuckles of the arrogant kind, which more suited Mr. Twigg's usual nature.

"Oh, Lewrie . . ." Twigg finally drawled, after a restorative sip of wine. "Believe me, sir, did I wish you destroyed, professionally or personally, such a nefarious ploy would never be required. All I'd have to do is sit back and watch you do in yourself! Besides . . . what reason would I have to attempt such . . . hmm? Merely because your ways of prosecuting the King's enemies now and then row me beyond all temperance?"

"Well . . ."

"Which they do . . . now and then," Twigg intoned, with a vicious twinkle in his eyes, as if he enjoyed turning this particular victim on his roasting spit. "Despite the mute insubordination you've shewn me whenever we've been thrown together . . . your truculent reluctance to sully your hands with underhanded duties that force you to get out of bed earlier than is your wont . . . or, out of some *doxy's* bed, more to the point . . . I have always been *more* than amply-gratified with the results you achieved, and have expressed my satisfaction with you, and your methods of fulfilling my aims, to your, and my, superiors following our ev'ry assignment.

"*Secret* reports, of course," Twigg added, with a casual wave of his free hand, the sort of gesture that put Lewrie in mind of someone tossing tidbits overboard to the sharks. "Bless my soul, must I have *gushed*? Does your long-held enmity arise from a lack of vocal praise? Was I remiss in not patting you on the back . . . or the top of the head? Would a box of *sweets* make up for it?" Twigg posed facetiously.

"Damn my eyes . . . !" Lewrie began to say.

"No matter what you've thought over the years, Lewrie, I admire your good qualities," Twigg stated as he reached for his knife and his fork once more. "On the other hand, your good qualities have at times been rather *damned* hard to *find*, but . . ."

A mouthful of food, a cock of the head as he savoured it, then a palate-cleansing nibble of bread and a sip of wine followed Twigg's admission.

"I will confess that my sense of duty, and urgency in the fulfillment of that duty, might have given you the impression that you're little more than an occasionally borrowed gun-dog of doubtful lineage," Twigg said on, dabbing at his mouth with his napkin. "I have gathered that I sometimes *do* act more brusquely with others than they might've preferred, but . . . to use a military simile, it little matters to me do the officers' mess dine me in as a 'jolly good fellow,' just so long as they perform as required to attain success 'gainst our foes."

No! Really? Lewrie thought tongue-in-cheek; *Such an out-going and amiable fellow like yourself? Perish the thought!*

"Believe me when I tell you, Lewrie," Mr. Twigg continued, now stern-faced and cold, "that people who've displeased me in the past I *have* ruined, for the good of the country, and, when naval or military force was involved, for the good of their respective services, in the long view. Had I really felt call to ruin *you*, whyever had I not had you cashiered *years* ago, hey?"

"Well . . ." Lewrie was forced to realise.

"Your personal life . . . such as it is . . ." Twigg scoffed on, with a leery roll of his eyes, "has no bearing on your public life, or your service to the Navy. Unless you were a drunkard, a rapist, or a brute so heedless and flagrant as to become a public spectacle, and a newspaper sensation. Thankfully, you're rather a *mild* sort of sinner. You know how to keep your 'itches' scratched with little notice. *Sub rosa*, as it were. As an English gentleman should, or he ceases *being* a gentleman, and then you'd deserve ev'ry bit of your come-uppance."

Lewrie could have little to say to that. He squirmed a little more on his chair, and blushed like a Cully chastened by a *very* stern old vicar, ready to swear he'd never do whatever it was, again.

"Put me in mind of the Scot poet Robert Burns, you do, Lewrie," Twigg said with a thin-lipped smile and a simper. "Know of him, hey?"

"Aye," Lewrie allowed himself to admit.

"Burns said of himself that he was, ah . . . 'a professional fornicator with a genius for paternity,' " Twigg quoted with a chuckle.

"Ah-*hmm,*" Lewrie said, clearing his throat with a fist against his mouth.

"Despite that, Burns wrote simply marvellous songs and poems," Twigg allowed, thawing a little. "Despite your shortcomings, you are an invaluable asset to the Navy, and the Crown, Lewrie, and I'll not let you be 'scragged' over this smarmy jape of yours 'gainst the Beauman family. Not 'til this war is done, and we've wrung the last drop of usefulness from you. You're as much a weapon as any broadside of guns ever you, or anyone else, fired."

"Thank you, sir," Lewrie felt called to reply, with a shiver of relief that someone, no matter how horrid, was on his side. Under the circumstances, perhaps horrid, devious, and brutal aid was just what was needed!

"Besides . . ." Twigg simpered again. "Watching you twist about in the wind is devilish-amusing . . . now and then. Eat up, man! Your food's going cold, and 'tis too tasty to go to waste. More wine? See to him, Ajit Roy *jee. Bharnaa opar!* Fill him up!"

Suddenly in a much better mood, Lewrie accepted more piping-hot rice, more yogurt gravy, more slices of meat, and began to eat, about to rave over the exotic, long-missed, flavours, 'til . . .

"How to achieve that aim, though . . . aye, there's the rub," Mr. Twigg mused over new-steepled fingers, with his fierce hatchet face in a daunting scowl. "Stealing those slaves and making sailors out of 'em rather *exceeded* your usual harum-scarum antics. Left 'em in the shade, as it were."

"You mentioned that Sir Malcolm Shockley might be of some help, sir?" Lewrie dared to suggest, with curry sauce tingling his lips.

"Aye, Shockley. He *likes* you, and he isn't your run-of-the-mill backbencher in the Commons, either. No Vicar of Bray, is he, nor is he the Great Mute, either. Allied with Sir Samuel Whitbread, and those younger 'progressives' who associate with him. Shockley's not a typical 'Country-Put,' like most of our rural, squirearchy, 'John Bull' Members are . . . damn 'em for the unsophisticate twits they are. There's *wit* behind *his* eyes!"

"Fox, perhaps, sir?" Lewrie chimed in, hopefully.

"The Great Commoner?" Twigg sneered. "Following the Spithead and the Nore naval mutinies, the Prime Minister, Pitt the Younger, and the Tories crushed the man. I fear that the formerly-esteemed Charles James Fox is as powerless as a parish pensioner . . . and has about as many friends. That will be a real problem for you, for most of those who revile the institution of slavery are the same ones who spoke out so openly in praise of the French Revolution in the late '80s . . men like Jeremy Bentham, Doctor Joseph Priestley, Wedgwood, the pottery fellow, Boulton and Watt, the steam-engine men, and the light-headed scribblers such as Blake and Coleridge . . . even Robert Burns, come to think of it. All the so-called Progressives, what? They run with the same pack. Still, that was ten years ago, and memories fade. No one got round to hanging *them* for uttering such rot, even if the French made them honorary citizens for their vocal public support."

"But, that was before the Frogs lopped off King Louis's head," Lewrie sourly observed.

"Well, that changed everything . . . but for the *true* hen-headed, of course." Twigg smirked most evilly. "No, knowing those worthies as I do, the vehemence with which they revile slavery will naturally make them raise up a *too* public hue and cry, a veritable *crusade,* with you the heart of their righteous blather. Make a martyr of you. . . ."

"And don't most martyrs end up *dyin'*, Mister Twigg?"

"Well, of course they do, Lewrie! Can't have martyrs without a good bonfire, and shrieks of agony!" Twigg chortled. "What we need is the subtile backgate approach, else the pro-slavery colonial and shipping interests in Parliament *demand* your cashiering, and hanging . . . to spite the do-gooders, if for no better reason. No, we must go to cleverer men, who can see the longer view. Wilberforce, perhaps. Aye, Wilberforce would be your man!"

God save me! Lewrie thought, shrinking at the mention of that name. William Wilberforce and his coven of familiars had been a bane on English Society for years, marching on age-old morals (or the lack of them!) like a vengeful army of pitchfork-armed Puritans through the "Progressive" wing of the Church of England, evinced by the so-called Clapham Sect; on another front via the House of Commons since so many Members were of like minds; and through Philanthropy in the public arena, a third front led by rich and influential *women* like Mrs. Hannah More and Elizabeth Fry . . . by Jeremy Bentham, himself, with his Vice Society and his damnable concept of Utilitarianism. If things didn't meet his strict and narrow key-holes of the most benefit for the most people, then damn it to Hell and do away with it . . . whatever it was. Lt. Langlie had gotten a copy of Bentham's *Panopticon,* his view of an ideal England, and had been aghast, as had Lewrie, that it called for total surveillance of everyone's waking actions by a "morality police" as an infernal machine to "grind rogues honest"!

Over the years, maypoles and dancing about them had been banned, village football and Sunday cricket had all but disappeared; good old Church Ales were completely gone. Fairs, bear-baiting, dog- and cock-fighting, throwing at cocks, greased-goose pulls, beating the bounds (and springtime beating of boys to keep them honest!), pig-racing, and all sorts of light-hearted amusements had been done away with, which had reputedly led Mrs. Hannah More to declare that sooner or later, all that would be left would be the new-fangled Sunday schools, and that the people of England "would have nothing else to look at but ourselves"!

Why, by now, the reformers might've even done away with fox-hunting and steeplechasing! Damn 'em. Newly-rich *arrivistes*, Non-Conforming Anglicans, Dissenters, and Methodists barred from Public Office, Service, or Honours; jumped-up tradesmen become wealthy, grand landowners; even that ex-slaver John Newton (who'd written Mr. Winwood's poem and hymn and had been Saved) . . . oh, but it was a devious conspiracy of do-gooding that opposed almost all that Lewrie thought he *fought* to preserve! Why, give them a few more years, and topping goose-girls, milk-maids, and serving wenches would be right out, too!

"Such flam," Lewrie muttered. "Bentham, Fry, those sort. That writer, Macauley, and Wilberforce and the Evangelical Society, they're all of a piece, Mister Twigg. Are you *sure* we need their . . . ?"

"Sarah Trimmer, don't forget," Twigg added. "She who thinks our old fairy tales too indecent for today's children. 'Dick Whittington's Cat' leads the poor to aspire above their proper stations, for instance. 'Cinderella,' which my granddaughter adores, by the way, is too harsh on step-mothers and step-sisters. To Trimmer's lights, we need tales more *uplifting*, instructional, and *useful*. Gad, though, just try reading some of her alternatives. *Horrid*, simpering, blathering *pap*!

"It's the war, I suppose," Twigg continued, after a moment of gloom. "You were in England during the naval mutinies, which, for a time, looked to become a nationwide Levellers' rebellion that might've overthrown Crown, Parliament, and the Established Church, to boot! In dread of the French revolutionary Terror being replicated *here*, perhaps the Mob *needs* taming, and our upstarts quashed.

"Thankfully, however," Twigg said with a sardonically amused leer, "our earnest reformers wish to do their chiefest work among our semi-savage *poor*, not the well-to-do. So far, that is. More wine?"

"Uhm, aye . . . but!" Lewrie replied, impatient with the niceties. "Let *that* lot get their hooks in me, and I'm done for, Mister Twigg!"

"You are surely 'done for' do they *not*, Lewrie," Twigg sombrely pointed out. "Where else could you find aid?"

"Well . . ." Lewrie said after a deep breath, shrugging without a single clue. "Damn my eyes."

"Exactly," Twigg said with a sage simper. "How was the ride up from London?"

"Just bloody lovely!" Lewrie snapped. "Bucolic, and . . ."

"I meant the state of the *roads*, and the *weather*, Lewrie!" Mr. Twigg snapped back in exasperation. " 'Less there's a thunderstorm and washed-out roads, there's daylight enough to get us down to London and lodgings . . . where I may write to those I believe most-able to give you aid. No time like the present, what? If pouring rain, we'll take my coach, if not, my chariot. Much faster. Your hired 'prad' I'll stable here and have my groom send down, later. Leading an indifferent horse at the cart's tail will only slow us down. Eat up, and we're off."

"Do you really think we'll be able to . . . ?" Lewrie asked in awe of Twigg's alacrity, and in great relief that, dubious as he was, there was *one* ally willing to save him from a "hemp neck-stock."

"Hope springs eternal . . . all that," Twigg responded, roughly shovelling in a last bite or two, taking a last sip or two of wine.

Damme, but this is going to irk, but . . . ! Lewrie thought; under the circumstances, there was nothing else for it.

"Then I thank you most humbly and gratefully, sir," Lewrie was forced to say. "However things fall out, I will be forever in your debt."

"Yayss . . . you *will* be," Twigg drawled with a superior expression on his phyz, and his eyes alight in contemplation of future schemes.

A chariot . . . Jesus!

Oh, it had seemed perky enough, at first. Just a rapid jaunt, what? The sporting blades of the aristocracy and the squirearchy were simply *daft* for speed, and bandied about the names of famous coachmen who made their "diligence-" or "balloon" coaches fly on the highways of the realm. Some of them would offer substantial sums to take the reins from an indifferent (and bribable) coachee for a single leg of a coach trip. They knew the names of the famous whip-hands, and bragged about a mere handshake from a hero coachee as one would boast about a meeting with a champion jockey or boxer, forever comparing records of how quick Old So-And-So shaved five whole minutes from a run 'twixt The Olde Blue Rabbit tavern and the Red Spotted Pig posting-house, or some such rapid run of umpteen-ish miles, and the odd casualty bedamned.

If an urchin or two, one of the cheap fares who rode on the top or clung to the footmen's seats atop the boot, were bounced off and got turned into imitation cow-pies in the road, then so be it. If the slow and unwary hiker got trampled, well . . . it only made for a better tale at journey's end!

Chariots were even better, for well-to-do young bloods could be, *had* to be, the drivers, and, but for a hallooing chum or two in the wee open compartment with them, any accident wouldn't claim any innocents, who just might know a lawyer and sue for damages! Chariots were "all the go" and "all the crack," meant to be whipped into breathtaking speed, and there was nothing grander!

Lewrie had, rather inconveniently, forgotten all that.

And dour old Zachariah Twigg, so precise and Oxonian a fellow of the older generation, surely his chariot and matched team of horses was merely a retired fellow's affectation . . . wasn't it?

Unfortunately, no. Once aboard, Twigg had revealed a new facet to his character. There was a mischievious glint to his eyes, an evil little chuckle under his breath, and a sly smile on his lips as he took the reins in one hand, a long whip in the other, and turned into a Biblical Jehu.

They were off in a flash, headed downhill for his estate's gate quicker than a startled lark, making a fair rate of knots even before they passed the gate in the inner wall surrounding Spyglass Bungalow, moist dirt and gravel flying in twin rooster-tails from the madly-spinning wheels. At the highway, Twigg didn't slow *that* much, either; they shot out into the road, other traffic bedamned, "heeled" over on one wheel, and slewing about like a wagging cat's tail!

"Brisk . . . ah ha!" Twigg exulted as they thundered along, *really* beginning to gain speed.

"Duh-duh-duh-duh-duh!" Lewrie replied, unable to form words, if he cared a whit for his teeth and tongue, as the chariot drummed, banged, and juddered. His *portmanteau* bag and valise at his feet, between his legs, were bouncing so high that he had to press his knees together if he cared a whit for his "nutmegs," as well.

Down the long, slow rise they tore, the chariot's axle starting to *keen* about as loud as Lewrie wished *he* could. He would have been wide-eyed and gape-mouthed in utter terror, if doing so would not end with a mouthful of muddy road, or the loss of an eye from gravel flung up from the team's rear hooves.

"On, boys! On!" Twigg cried, cracking his whip over the horse team's heads. "*Marvellous*, ah ha!" Followed by a madman's cackle.

"You're a bloody shite-brained . . . !" Lewrie tried accusing, but the chariot took a jounce or two, wheels *above* the ground, and it only came out as another series of "duh-duh-duh-duhs!" Twigg was swaddled up in an old, shabby overcoat, an ancient (wind-cutting) tricorne hat jammed low on his brows, with a muffler about his neck and halfway up to his nose; he was getting spattered, but it might not matter. Alan, though . . . his heavy grogram boat cloak was no use at all, for it flew behind him like a loose-footed lugsail, the gilt chain riding high on his Adam's apple and damned-near strangling him. What was happening to his pristine white waist-coat, shirt, neck-stock, and his very best uniform coat he didn't want to even contemplate.

Lewrie looked ahead of them (with one slitted eye, it here must be told) just in time to screech, "Watch out for that . . . Oh, Christ!" as Twigg swerved their chariot over almost to the verge of the highway to miss an offending hay-waggon drawn by a yoke of plodding oxen, that flashed past in a twinkling, so quickly that all Lewrie could sense of their near-collision was an ox-bellow, a startled cow-fart, and a waggoner's thin cry of "Yew *bloody* damn' . . . !"

And, by the time they'd slewed back into their proper lane, the light pony trap coming the other way had had time to move right over, and they missed that'un by *yards*!

"Aah . . . ha ha ha!" Twigg exulted, his long whip cracking, and Lewrie shut his eyes and tried to summon up a prayer.

Twigg, damn him!, drove as if the Devil was at his heels (which in Twigg's case, Lewrie thought, was an apt description!) chortling and whooping delight like Billy-O; like an ancient Celt warrior, mead-drunk and painted in blue woad, out to smash through a Roman legion, just one more good charge for good, sweet ancient Queen Boadicea; like Pharaoh raced in pursuit of that damned Moses, upon discovering that the wily bastard had decamped for the Promised Land *without* finishing his mud-brick quota, and had absconded with a dozen of his favourite concubines to boot! All Pharaoh could expect from Dissenter religionists!

All Lewrie could do was hang on for dear life to the front and the side frame and light screening wood, and try hard not to get thrown clean out of the infernal machine, have his "wedding tackle" knackered by his luggage, or lose his only change of clothing, entire! A time or two, on the flat stretches (without competing traffic, though Lewrie wasn't going to peek to determine that), it was even hard to breathe at their mad pace. Facing forward, it felt like he was aboard the quickest frigate ever built, going "full and by" into the apparent wind in a half-gale. Of course, the muck flung up from the team made breathing difficult enough.

Finally . . . after what seemed an interminable term in Hell, the drumming of horses' hooves slowed from a Marine drummer's "Long Roll" to summon a crew to Quarters to rather sedate, and distinctive clops.

He, at last, dared take a peek 'twixt the fingers of one hand, the one he used to rake mud-slime from his eyes, and was amazed to see that they were on the Tottenham Court Road, just about to the crossing where it became Charing Cross.

"We're here," Twigg commented with a grunt of satisfaction, and a peek at his pocket watch, as if he'd just beaten his old record for a "jaunt" to town. Indeed, they were; Lewrie's addled senses re-awoke to the sights, sounds, and smells of bustling London. Twigg had removed his ancient tricorne (now much the worse for wear) and had replaced it with a natty new-styled hat; his grimy muffler now lay at his feet, as did his old overcoat, revealing the "country squire" suitings he'd had on during dinner. He looked clean as a new penny-whistle . . . damn him!

With a twitch of his reins, Twigg swung them onto Oxford Street, headed west. "I will drop you at your father's gentlemen's hotel and club, Lewrie," he told him. "You are sure to get lodging there . . . and at a significant discount, I'd wager, hah? Right round the corner to mine own house in Baker Street. Convenient, that, for our purposes."

"Should I dine with you tonight, then, sir?" Lewrie asked, flexing his hands, now that there was no need to cling to the chariot with a death-grip.

"Not a bit of it!" Twigg barked, back to his old, imperious self. "There's too much for me to do, tonight, to put your salvation on good, quick footing. *Eminent* people with whom to dine, and consult over victuals, hmm? Speed's the thing, before any news from Jamaica makes you a *pariah*, subject to arrest, hah!"

"What a pity," Lewrie said, tongue-in-cheek, now that he could trust using it without the end of it getting snipped off on a deep rut and a bounce. Which statement made Twigg glare down his nose at him.

"It would be best for you if you kept close to your lodgings, Lewrie," Twigg instructed. "No gadding about. No drunken sailor's antics, for a time. And I'll thank you to keep your breeches buttoned up snug, as long as we're here, sir. Let us not give your anonymous tormentor any *more* grist for his, or her, mill. And, the influential men and women whom we wish to espouse your cause are a *prim* lot. Even the slightest whiff of new scandal or dalliance, and you'll lose what hope they could offer you, *n'est-ce pas*?"

"Lor', wot a caution ye are, yer honour, damme if ye ain't, har har!" Lewrie returned in a mock lower-deck accent, fed up with Twigg's top-lofty scorn. "Nary e'en *one* saucy wench, nor drap o' gin, neither, yer honour, sir? Why, wot's th' world comin' t', I axs ye? Tsk tsk."

"And yet you *must* make a fool of yourself," Twigg said, sighing in exasperation, his eyes and lips slit; one *might* have also heard him almost growl in frustration.

"Sorry, sir. My nature, I 'spose," Lewrie said, sobering.

"Well, keep a taut rein on your . . . nature," Twigg snapped back. "I'd keep you caged in a basement or garret, if I could, but I suppose at *some* point, your potential patrons will *have* to see you, and speak to you . . . more's the pity. Whilst in your lodgings, I suggest that you polish the tale you told me of how your crime occurred, and make it *damned* short. I'll send round a list of queries your sponsors are, to my mind, most likely to make to you, and include suggestions as to how best to explain yourself.

"And, when they see you, Lewrie . . . should they, that is to say," Twigg added, his acidic aspersion dripping, "I adjure you to display a proper *gravitas* suitable to your station, and circumstances. One might even practice *righteousness* in a mirror . . . though I doubt you're that familiar with it. Play-act a 'tarpaulin sailor,' perhaps, all blunt, and tarry-handed. Rehearse responses of wide-eyed honesty to the most probable questions they might put to you . . . a list of which I'll send round . . . damned short responses, it goes without saying. Do you give your . . . saucy nature free play even for a moment, such as your last, witless fillip, and I assure you that you're truly lost."

A short turn north in James Street, a tack westerly to Wigmore Street, and they were at last arrived at the corner of Duke Street, and Twigg drew them to the kerbings before a splendid converted mansion that now boasted a discreet blass plate by the entry that announced the place as the Madeira Club, Lewrie's father's "gentlemen's hotel."

"Hellish-fond of their ports," Twigg said with a sniff. "Sup in. Do *not* stray to your usual low haunts," he brusquely ordered as Lewrie *most*-thankfully alit on solid, un-moving, ground. The doors opened and a liveried porter came down the steps to help carry his traps. "I will be in touch with you, anon. And for God's sake, Lewrie! Have yourself a good, long bathe, sponge your uniform, or purchase a new'un. You are as filthy as a Thames-side mud-lark!"

With that to cackle over, Twigg whipped up and away, leaving Capt. Alan Lewrie muttering under his breath, and slowly dribbling road-slime on the sidewalk.

CHAPTER SEVEN

Righteousness came rather easy to hand at the Madeira Club, for most of its lodgers and guests were of the very same sort of "made men" whom Twigg had disparaged over dinner at his Hampstead bungalow, newly rich or at least moderately well-to-do off steam engines, the mills and manufacturies that had sprung up due to the war's demands, expanding overseas trade *despite* said war, and clerks and functionaries returned from India or other colonies as "chicken *nabobs*," worth £50,000 at the very least, even some "*nabobs*" and "gora-*nabobs*" with *nouveau riche* fortunes of £100,000 or more, even some few who could nearly be called by the new-fangled term "millionaire." Even with his Spanish silver, Lewrie was a piker compared to most of them. After he let drop that he was a friend of Sir Malcolm Shockley, Baronet, one of the club's founders and major investors, though, once he declared that his father was Sir Hugo St. George Willoughby, the other founder, he was welcome enough there. Serving officers, in the main, holders of King's Commission, were not expected to be anything *but* middling-poor, so he was forgiven! And if he wasn't *exactly* a paid-up official member, he surely would be, soon.

God, but they were an earnest lot, though! Early to bed, early to rise, no loud noises after ten in the evening, their wagers on card games in the so-called Long Room never ventured much above a shilling or two, and every meal was preceded with a prayer. Alan Lewrie had to give his father credit, though, when it came to the victuals, and most especially to the contents of the wine cellar. If one had no valet or manservant to assist, a gentleman could trust the staff to fill a role temporarily, and with all the quiet, unobtrusive competence of the best private mansion's staff.

The maidservants, of course, were homely, old trullibubs.

The chariot ride did require Lewrie to purchase a complete new uniform at his old Fleet Street tailor's; whilst there, he also got a rather drab and sober civilian suit, imagining that if the city's bailiffs were on the lookout for a Capt. Lewrie, RN, they might not look twice at a natty fellow in *mufti*, as the East India Company officers put it. And, if he *appeared* to be sober, grave, and righteous before his potential patrons in unremarkable (but well-cut) clothes, it might go a long way towards furthering his cause. Lewrie didn't imagine that prim Clapham Sect and Evangelical Society sorts would care very much for "flash" on their own backs . . . or on their penitents, either. With his fellow lodgers' attires to go by, Lewrie thought he'd made a wise move.

"That's the question, d'ye see, Captain Lewrie," one member told him as they sat side-by-side in matching leather chairs before a cheery fire one night in the Common Rooms. After a hearty supper, and two bottles of smuggled French cabernet sloshed down, Mr. Giles, who'd made his fortune in the leather-goods trade, had turned nigh-gloomily voluble in his maunderings, to which Lewrie, in his new "sober" guise, was forced to listen, nod, and make the appropriate "ah hums" and "I sees."

"What t'do with sudden wealth, sir," Mr. Giles said with a sigh, as if £250,000 was an intolerably sinful burden. "To spend and get and waste it on mere pleasures and fripperies, as most do, when presented with a windfall, an un-looked-for inheritance? Why did God intend for *me* to prosper, and not others? Thankee for the port, sir . . . aahh! If one ponders it a bit, one sees that wealth hidden under the proverbial bushel basket, greedily squirreled away, benefits no one. The Lord may mean for us to make ourselves *comfortable*, but not *showy*, then use His rewards for our hard work and diligence to the benefit of *others*, d'ye see. To be useful, of avail to improve *others'* lots. . . ."

Mr. Giles was a Methodist, *and* a Utilitarian.

"Treat the sick," Lewrie surmised, "feed the poor, all that."

"New hospitals, yes sir," Mr. Giles replied. "Work-houses, and parish poor-houses to relieve the unfortunate, the orphans, the widows. *Good works* among 'em, too. Not outright *charity*, though. Schools for the lower classes, so that they learn *honest* trades, thrift, sobriety, and obedience to the laws of the realm—"

"Chastity . . ." Lewrie stuck in, feigning an agreeable air.

"Oh my, yes, Captain Lewrie!" Giles heartily agreed. "As well as cleanliness in their persons and habitations, *and* the way they live their lives. Now, Mister Putney, yonder . . ." Giles said, indicating a sallow stick of a fellow who looked as if an entire host of tropical diseases had had fun playing with him, "was the Collector of, uhm . . . some Indian city or province . . . Sweaty-Pore, or some such like that. Came home with an hundred thousand pounds, and what's the very first thing he did with it?"

Found a better physician, was Lewrie's best guess.

"Donated two thousand to tract societies, to spread word of new morality throughout London *and* Portsmouth, ha!" Giles boasted, clapping a palm on the wide arm of his leather chair—which act resulted in a waiter fetching them both a fresh bottle of the house's trademark Madeira, which wasn't exactly what Mr. Giles had in mind, but was welcome nonetheless.

"And the poor academies and Sunday schools, I trust, teach them to actually *read* those tracts?" Lewrie asked, smiling congenially, but bored about to tears and wide yawns. "All improving, and . . . useful."

"Exactly, sir, exactly," Giles chummily agreed. "Now, our Major Baird is also a 'graduate' of our Indian possessions," he said, indicating another well-tanned man in his thirties in a "ditto" suit of such starkly unrelieved black that Lewrie had taken him for a "dominee." "I heard he only came off, of late, with thirty thousand, mostly in looted pagan baubles, tsk tsk." Lewrie wasn't sure whether Mr. Giles was sad that Maj. Baird hadn't piled up loot by the keg, or had had a bad run of luck at plundering the poorer *rajahs*. "Invalided out of East India Company's army, sad t'say for him, poor fellow, but before he departed, I'm told he donated enough to hire a C. of E. chaplain to minister to the needs of the native soldiers in his regiment. He and his Colonel held Sunday Church Parade, rain or shine, and succeeded in converting a fair number of heathens to the Lord, before coming Home. In the market for a wife is Major Baird, at present, and I'm certain that the Good Lord will reward his efforts a thousand-fold, by steering his steps to a most suitable and companionable match, of a like mind."

Giles leaned closer to whisper, "Baird's dead-set against *novels*, don't ye know, any wastrel reading matter that does not uplift or serve the greatest good. Thinking of forming a society of his own, I believe, to which I do believe I may donate an hundred guineas, ha!"

"A creditable endeavour, sir," Lewrie said, fighting a stricken expression from showing; in his rooms he had four new novels he'd found in the Strand, all of a lubricious or lascivious nature. Lewrie thought of hiding them away, before one of the ugly chambermaids found them and denounced him to Maj. Baird, fearing that the Evangelical Society might just drag him about the city in chains, for an example of how "rogues were ground honest"! At the Madeira Club, *reading* about sex was about as close to the genuine article as one could get! In strict privacy.

"One may *try* to be a good, Christian Englishman," Giles stated, all but wringing his hands, "one may attend Divine Services, hold deep and abiding faith, and *strive* to shun the lures of the world, Captain Lewrie, but, without Good Works, one is not a complete Christian, and is but a *drone* in Society. One must strive to *be* and *do,* not just to *seem,* hey what?"

"Now, where have I heard that before?" Lewrie asked, his tongue firmly in his cheek by then. "Did Doctor Priestley say it, or . . . ?"

"Bless me, but I can't recall," the wine-fuddled Mr. Giles said with a vague shake of his goodly head. "So, what is it that *you* do to make your mark on a sinful world, Captain Lewrie? Where do *your* interests lie when it comes to improving and uplifting?"

"I exterminate godless Frogs and heathen Dons, thus making our world safe for moral Englishmen, sir," Lewrie declared, pretending as if it was his true calling, though ready to snicker aloud.

"Ha ha! Capital, capital, ha ha!" Giles exclaimed, bellowing his delight and slapping the chair arm, again. "A glass with ye, sir, a brimming bumper!"

"Well . . . if you insist, Mister Giles," Lewrie replied, fraudulently trying to demur. "Though 'wine's a mocker,' and I've not much of a head for deep drinking. Not my nature, d'ye see, and . . . I really did intend to read at least another chapter of the Good Book tonight, before retiring . . . clear-headed, but . . . hang it. A glass it is!"

Soon after that convivial "slosh," he made his excuses, further pretending to yawn in a prodigious, jaw-locking manner, and made his goodnights to one and all.

Once out of the Common Rooms, though, he headed for the bar for a pint flask of decanted (also smuggled) French brandy, which he hid in his breast pocket. He almost made it to the stairs, but for the noble Maj. Baird, who managed to impede his progress long enough to hold a whispered conversation, enquiring just where an "inquisitive" fellow could "covertly witness and gather damning evidence upon" the immoral doings of the city, the cock & hen clubs, the dissolute dens of iniquity where wagers were laid, and where "women of the town" plied their trade . . . "to document in eye-opening tracts," of course.

"Ask the barman for a copy of the *New Atlantis,*" Lewrie winked back, "that guide's your boy to *all* the dissolute. Slip him sixpence. Failing that, just wander down Charing Cross, this very night."

He left the upright Maj. Baird to sort Sin out for himself.

⚓

"Well, you *look* presentable," Mr. Twigg said as Lewrie entered his hired coach, thank God a closed one, and not another damn' chariot, this time. "You're well-practiced in your responses?"

"As well as may be," Lewrie told him in a fretful tone as he sat across from him on the cold and damp-feeling leather bench facing Twigg. Twigg had decreed that Lewrie's new uniform would be best, complete with his sword and both the Cape St. Vincent and Camperdown medals hung low on Lewrie's mid-chest from their coloured ribbons.

"Sir Malcolm Shockley and some others have put in good words for you," Twigg informed him, sounding almost breezily unconcerned. "Your old school chum, Peter Rushton in Lords, sent a letter, as well. With *his* reputation for vice, God knows what use it'll be . . . though I must declare it was well-written. Clerk gave it a polishing, I expect."

Lewrie gave that a short, jerking nod of agreement; at Harrow (in the *short* time in attendance before his expulsion) trying to read a sniggery, surreptitious note from Peter Rushton had been all but indecypherable, like getting a scouting report on the defences of Biblical Canaan from one of Moses's spies, and *hastily* scribbled in Aramaic at that! "Meet us behind the coach-house and share a bottle of brandy" in Peter's idea of a "copper-plate" hand could have very well meant "We've hid five dead mouse and they're randy," which of course had earned them both a caning, even if the instructor or proctor couldn't make heads or tails of it, either.

"We're to speak to William Wilberforce, himself, Lewrie," Twigg informed him. "You followed my directives? Had a last bathe, a good night's sleep . . . alone . . . and you're not 'headed' by spirits?"

"Sober as a hangman," Lewrie answered.

"How apt," Twigg said with a sniff. "Here's the line you're to take . . . 'twas your old compatriot, Colonel Cashman, late of the King's Service in a West Indies regiment, and local planter—"

"And un-findable for corroboration in the United States," Lewrie stuck in.

"—whose utter revulsion over the institution of slavery, even was he a participant and slave-owner for a time," Twigg drilled onwards, "that led you to despise slavery, yourself. Very John Newton–ish, you see. It will strike a chord with Wilberforce and what possible *entourage* of the like-minded who might be present, for it slightly coincides with Newton's own experience of being a slaver, then shipwrecked, and enslaved by the very people he sought to capture and sell. That poem of his, describing his enlightenment and salvation . . ."

" 'Amazing Grace,' aye," Lewrie said with a grunt and a new nod.

"You actually know of it," Twigg nigh-gasped with surprise that Lewrie, of all people, had been exposed to it. "Well, damme. Wonders never cease! No matter . . . when asked, you will clew to this point as if your life depended on it . . . which it does, by the by," Twigg said, with another sniff of faint amusement, "that it was *Cashman* who thought it all up."

"Damme, sir!" Lewrie said, recoiling. "Even if it's half-true, he's a good friend, and it's not . . . quite honourable to shift the—"

"He *did* think it up, you said so, yourself!" Twigg archly objected. "As a cruel jape on the Beaumans. In my version, however, the former Colonel Cashman, disgusted with slavery and his own part in it, manumitted all his own chattel, then, grieved by the unremitting, and inhuman, beastly cruelty with which the Beaumans kept their slaves, he schemed to free as many of them as he could . . . encouraging them to go into the mountains and join the free Maroons, the young men and boys to 'steal themselves' and join your crew as free men."

"But . . ." Lewrie tried to say, loath to put the onus on "Kit" Cashman, no matter that he was far out of reach of British justice.

"They . . . stole . . . *themselves*, Lewrie!" Twigg insisted. "*You* did *not* steal them, d'ye understand the significance of that? It's a lawyerly niggle, but, under current statutes, you only aided and abetted, but did not instigate, or *commit*, hah! And, you did it in a fine *cause*. Think of yourself as the noble hero from a free land, *England!*, where slavery has already been banished. Suddenly exposed in the Caribbean Sugar Isles to the utter barbarity of slavery's realities. And it sore-grieved you. Consider also your experiences on Saint-Domingue, where you witnessed the, ah . . . desperate courage of self-freed Blacks trading their lives by the thousands, so their children could be free. I still have friends at Admiralty . . . I've read your reports of intercepting those sailboats full of ex-slave soldiers, who almost blew you out of the water with suicidal gallantry . . . the survivor who slit the throat of one of your sailors as his last act of defiance, and you were touched . . . to your very soul," Twigg spun out, and Lewrie could see it was all a cynical sham that Twigg was creating, merely an interpretation of what really happened. Ordinary Seaman Inman's throat had been slit out of savage hatred of *any* White man, not gallantry, but . . . it was much of a piece with what a barrister would argue at his trial, and if such an interpretation of evidence and happenstance took place at an informal *hearing*, not a formal trial (which would *preclude* a trial for a hanging offence should it succeed in gaining him sponsors, protectors), well . . . so be it. And he hoped Christopher Cashman would forgive him, should he ever even hear of it.

"I'll do most of the exposition, Lewrie," Twigg ordered, leaning back against his facing coach bench. "You just sit there and be stoic, stern, and honourable. Refuse wine, but accept tea or coffee. The sun isn't 'below the yardarm' . . . all that. Try not to fidget or squirm on your chair. Sound resolute. Boast only when describing what fine tars your dozen Black hands are. You *might* allude to any religious instruction they've gotten since signing articles. It'd go down well, hmm?"

Like a boxer getting last-moment cautions on his opponent, there was not time enough for Mr. Twigg to impart all of his last suggestions. Before Lewrie knew it, their coach pulled to a stop before an imposing row house's stoop (where, exactly, a preoccupied and benumbed Lewrie in later years couldn't say, and couldn't find with both hands and a whole battalion of flaming link-boys) and their coachman's son, serving as a footman, was folding down the metal steps and opening the door.

Lewrie stepped out onto a fresh-swept sidewalk, looked up at the gloomy, coal-sooted sky, and drew what felt like his last free breath, his left hand fretting on the hilt of his hanger, and his right hanging limp by his side, loath to take a single more step forward, or climb up the steps to the row house's door.

For London, with all its stinks, the air he drew in was rather fresh; it wasn't raining, for a bloody wonder, and as he looked up, as he would to read the set of the sails and the wind's direction, Lewrie could actually make out shape and form in the clouds, even espy several patches of open, wispy blue, here and there. Then, as if the wicks of theatrical lanthorns had been turned up, the sun peeked out briefly, to stab bright shafts down on the city through those wispy cloud-gaps, and brightened the street they stood in.

"Marvellous," Mr. Twigg smirked as he shot his cuffs and tugged down his fashionable waist-coat. "Why, Lewrie, I do declare the sacrificial birds' entrails are found flawless, the auguries are auspicious, and the old gods smile upon us, haw!"

"Bugger the old gods," was Lewrie's muttered reply to that. "If we must, we must. Let's get it done."

CHAPTER EIGHT

The row house fairly shouted Respectability, though in a muted, subtle way; "shouting" would have been thought too "common" or enthusiastic by its owners, perhaps. The terrace of row houses was a relatively new development outside; once one was in the entry hall, however, it was obvious that materials from older, razed houses had been re-used, for the entry's panelling looked to be authentic Jacobean Fold woodworking, the immense and intricately carved marble staircases had the sheen from many hands and feet over a very long time, too well-crafted to be sent to the scrapyard. The tables and such were of a heavier, past-century style, too, and the framed paintings and mirrors were gilt-framed in a Baroque style. Bright new red, blue, and buff Axminster or Winton carpets covered the usual black-and-white chequered tile floors, and ran up the staircase to cover slick, worn spots on the treads. *The house of a serious collector?* Lewrie wondered, taking in the statues in the recesses, the noble Greco-Roman busts on plinths; the house of a rich merchant or banker, or someone titled?

A balding old major-domo in sombre black livery took their hats, cloaks, and Lewrie's sword, then ushered them abovestairs without more than a begrudging word or two. Once up, he opened a glossy wooden set of double doors and bowed them into a parlour-cum-library done in much the same You-Will-Be-Impressed decor, but for the massive walls of bookcases from floor to ceiling on two sides; more new-ish, bright Turkey carpets on glossy wood floors, a world globe on a stand in one corner about a yard across, a heavy and ornate old desk before the windows and surprisingly bright and cheery (though heavy) draperies; a desk stout enough for Cromwell and an entire squad of fully-armoured Roundheads to have fought upon, if they'd felt like it. There were several wing chairs and settees, done in brighter chintzes, on which sat some *very* Respectable and Seriously Earnest men and women, who stared at the newcomers like a flock of vultures waiting for "supper" to go "toes-up" and die.

"Sir," Mr. Twigg intoned with suitable gravity, and a head bow.

"Ah ha," a slim older man seated behind the desk replied, as he rose to his feet. His coat was a sombre black, too, though enlivened with satin facings and lapels, a fawn or buff-coloured waist-coat, and new-fangled ankle-length trousers instead of formal breeches, slim-cut, and light grey. "Ladies and gentlemen, may I name to you Mister Zachariah Twigg, late of the Foreign Office, and his protégé, Captain Alan Lewrie . . ."

Hell if I'm his *protégé!* Lewrie irritatedly thought.

". . . man of the hour, and sponsor of human freedom," he heard the fellow conclude.

"Hurrah! Oh, *hurrah*!" a young lady cried, leaping to her feet and clapping her hands, all enthusiastic Methodist-like, which sentiment was seconded an instant later by all the others present, who stood and began to *applaud* him, making Lewrie gawp, redden in confusion, and almost start out of his boots. Then, to his further amazement, damned if they didn't begin to sing "For He's a Jolly Good Fellow" (not at all well or coordinatedly, mind), but, they *sounded* genuine in their approval. Lewrie decided that lowering his head and coming over all modest was called for, and considered scuffing his boot toes might not go amiss, either. *What the bloody Hell?* he thought, though.

"Though there are troubling aspects, indeed, to your feat, sir," the fellow behind the desk said as the song (mercifully) ended and he came to where Lewrie stood, "it is an exploit which I, and many others, wish to become commonplace, in future. Allow me to shake you by your hand, Captain Lewrie." Which he did, so energetically that his long, wavy hair nigh-bobbed as he took Lewrie's paw in his and gave it a two-handed pumping. "William Wilberforce, sir . . . and it is a pleasure to make your acquaintance."

"Erm . . . well, thankee, sir," Lewrie managed to say. Wilberforce wasn't *half* the glum ogre he'd imagined; and, for a Reverend, he dressed in the latest fashion, with the help of an excellent tailor, too!

"Some of your admirers, Captain Lewrie, and the leading lights in the movement to eliminate the scurrilous institution of slavery in every British possession, not merely in the British *Isles,* which we've already accomplished, thank the Good Lord . . . Reverend Mister Clarkson . . . Mistress Hannah More . . ."

The faces and names went by in a mind-muddling rush, too many at once for Lewrie, though Mistress Hannah More was another surprise to him . . . she might look him up and down like taking measure of a rogue, with her lips as pursed as Twigg's, but she was, in the main, a rather handsome woman, not half the infamous and forbidding "Kill-Joy" he'd imagined, either. Though granite and ice *did* come to mind as he made a graceful "leg" to her, getting a coolly-imperious curtsy back.

". . . host, Mister Robert Trencher," Wilberforce said, passing Lewrie on to a stout but handsome man in his late fourties, another of those who espoused the latest London fashions, in brighter suiting than one might expect from a run-of-the-mill "New Puritan."

"Your servant, sir," Lewrie said, taking the offered hand.

"Nay, Captain Lewrie, 'tis I who hold that I am *your* servant," Mr. Trencher heartily replied. "'Twas a risky business, but commendable, *most* commendable! And I shall be pleased to do everything in my power to see that you should not suffer for it. Ah . . . allow me to name to you, sir, my wife and daughter. Captain Lewrie, Mistress Portia Trencher. My dear, Captain Alan Lewrie."

Time to make another "leg" as Mrs. Trencher, a fetching older woman in shimmery grey satin, curtsied her greetings in proper fashion, and state that he was her servant, as well.

". . . Captain Alan Lewrie, my daughter, Theodora. My dear . . ."

The young lady, no more than nineteen or twenty, Lewrie guessed, had no patience for staid, languid "airs." She bobbed him a very brief curtsy, but also reached out to take both his hands in hers, fingertips gripping fingertips, and her grip trembling but strong.

"Your servant, Miss Trencher," Lewrie dutifully tried to say, noting that this Theodora was the very same lady who had leaped to her feet, cheered, and clapped him.

"I echo my father, Captain Lewrie," she nigh-breathlessly gushed, "for in gratitude for the bold step you took to free so many who cried out for rescue from abominable cruelty, it is I who are yours . . . your *servant,* I meant to say! Delighted to be!" she exclaimed, a higher blush rising to her face over her hapless *innuendo,* in what was obviously a rehearsed speech of welcome.

Careful, old son! Lewrie chid himself, feeling lusty stirrings in his groin; *Let go of her,* now. *Hands t'yourself . . .*

He took a half-step back and lowered his hands to break free of her fervent grip, taking note of her parents' stern cringes over her enthusiasm; her parents taking note of his own "chaste" reticence and surprise at her departure from the normal graces, he also hoped! One more bow of his head, which let Lewrie take a better peek at her.

God Almighty! he thought. For young Mistress Theodora Trencher was the very personification of elfin beauty! She stood not a whisker above five feet, two inches, in her soft-soled "at-home" slippers, very slim and wee. Her hair was a dark brown that was almost raven, curled with irons, and banged over a well-shaped, thoughtful-looking brow; a firm jawline and sweetly tapering chin, but with very full mouth, and lips he was sure would be eminently soft and kissable . . . ! She did not wear the artifice of cosmetics, and had no need of them, for her complexion was the epitome of English "cream," and her eyes, huge at that moment in enthusiasm, were the most intriguing, and rare, violet!

"I really did very little, Mistress Trencher, though I am grateful for your good opinion," he responded, with a dash of gruff, "sea-dog" modesty, as Twigg had rehearsed him. He managed to tear his eyes away from gawping at her impressive bosom; the newest women's fashions evidently allowed even the Respectable to sport low necklines, and her "poonts" or "cat-heads" could not be faulted! Turning to her parents, he added, "Part of it, I must confess, was need, d'ye see. The Fever Isles are hard on European sailors, and we'd had a bad bout of Yellow Jack aboard. . . ."

Even with his back to him, Lewrie could feel Twigg cringe and slit his mouth, for him to blurt out that his actions were anything less than humanitarian and selfless!

"Indeed, sir? I was informed . . ." Rev. Wilberforce said with a wary sniff.

"Had we not, though, sir," Lewrie quickly extemporised to save himself, "there'd have been no vacancies for the escaped slaves. The Admiralty frowns on captains who recruit, or accept, volunteers above the establishment deemed proper for a frigate of *Proteus*'s Rate, even to the number of cabin-servants and ship's boys allowed, unless they are paid from a captain's purse. They're jealous of every pence spent on rations, kits, clothing, shoes, and what not.

" 'Tis said, sir," Lewrie concluded, striving to recall what a pious expression looked like, "that the Lord moves in mysterious ways, His wonders to perform. The slaves' prayers, and mine, coincided nigh miraculously."

"Amen!" Theodora seconded.

"Just as Admiralty has broken captains who cheat the Exchequer by overstating the number of their crews, despite losses to desertion and death," Mr. Twigg informed all present with a knowing and casually world-wise air (even if he was glaring daggers at Lewrie), "who pocket the lost hands' pay, and connive with the Purser, who will sell off the un-issued rations and slop goods, Reverend, ladies and gentlemen, just as often as they would one who over-recruits."

"Well . . . shall we be seated and have tea?" Mr. Trencher suggested, waving his guests to the settees and chairs about the parlour. Twigg practically snagged Lewrie by the elbow and led him to a settee too short for more than two, looking as if he'd love to hiss cautions, but couldn't. As they sorted themselves out, waiting for the ladies to sit first, Lewrie took happy note that he'd have a grand angle on the fetching young Miss Theodora, who dipped her head most gracefully, exposing what a fine and swan-like neck she had above her lace shawl.

"Or, might Captain Lewrie and Mister Twigg prefer refreshments more stimulating than tea?" Mrs. Hannah More enquired with a wary cock of her head.

Playin' fast an' loose with the Trenchers' hospitality, ain't we? Sly witch! Lewrie spitefully thought, though answering her with another of his "special modest" grins, a shrug and shake of his head.

"As we say in the Navy, ma'am, the sun is still high over the yardarm, for me," he replied. "Tea would be delightful."

The next hour passed much as Twigg had warned him; they asked careful questions as to his motives, how his "theft" had occurred, and what sort of fellow was his fellow-conspirator, ex-Col. Christopher Cashman. Was he a spiritual man, and just when had *his* revulsion of slavery arisen? In his new enterprises in the United States, was he a slave-owner there, or . . . ? And, more to the point, when and where had the (so far) noble Capt. Lewrie developed his own detestation?

So he told them of his first experiences in the Caribbean, back during the American Revolution; of the fugitive Yankee slaves who had run to British-held towns and garrisons, seeking the freedom promised should they aid the Tory cause.

"I was at Yorktown during the siege," Lewrie related, addressing Mrs. Hannah More, his most-insistent and most-dubious inquisitor, "in charge of a weak two-gun battery of landed guns . . . only a Midshipman, then. For labourers and help loading the guns, we had several runaway slaves. We were all on short-commons, we ate the same rations, slept in the *redan* together, kept watch and drilled together, with the same chance of being killed in battle, did the French and the Rebels attack.

"Well . . . they stood a worse chance, 'cause they faced lashings, a return to their chains, being lynched or shot, if we lost . . . which we did, and, I fear, some of them *did* suffer such fates, for very few of them escaped before the Lord Cornwallis's surrender, and it *shamed* me, ma'am . . . the way they looked at *me,* the veriest boy Midshipman, as their saviour, and I could do nothing, in the end," he told them.

Damned if they didn't, and damned if I didn't, Lewrie took pause to recall; *And every bloody word of it the Gospel Truth!*

"And you were made prisoner, Captain Lewrie?" Mr. Trencher asked.

"No, sir. Two boatloads of light infantry, North Carolina Loyalist troops, I and my few hands, were blown downriver while trying to ferry the army across York River. Got stranded on the mud shoals down Guinea Neck, the morning of the surrender. We sheltered at a tobacco plantation, a *slave* plantation, 'til we could re-work our barges so we could sneak out to sea and escape. The orders were to abandon all but British, or White, troops, d'ye see . . . the horrid conditions that the plantation slaves had to stand, their near nakedness . . . pardon . . ."

"Fought their way out, 'gainst a company of Virginia Militia and a company of French troops from Lauzun's Legion," Mr. Twigg added with a sage nod of his head, to boot. Lewrie snapped his gaze to Twigg; he didn't know that anyone but the participants knew the details of that long-ago horror. "Nigh a week on the Atlantic, before being picked up by one of our warships. Might have sailed all the way to New York if he had had to. A most resourceful and determined man is our Captain Lewrie . . . even as a mere boy of a Midshipman," Twigg ended, bestowing on Lewrie a most-admiring grin, one which Lewrie was sure was costing his soul a pinch or two. But, it was a welcome diversion, one that went down well with all present.

"Then . . . in '86, I was in the Bahamas," Lewrie continued, "in command of a ketch-rigged gun-vessel, *Alacrity*. A Lieutenant, finally. There was a James Finney, there . . . known as 'Calico Jack,' like that pirate, Jack Rackham. A war hero, a successful privateer, and a merchant of great fortune . . . made by *continuing* privateering against every trading ship, under any flag, even British. He was *very* big in slaves. Practically *owned* the Vendue House at Nassau, and always had what they call 'Black Ivory' . . . 'cause he was pirating slave ships on their way to the Americas, murdering the crews, and selling the Africans off, as well as the re-painted, re-named, re-papered ships. With official connivance, sad t'say. We raided his secret cache of goods, his lair, on Walker's Cay, finally, and found the bones of nigh an hundred pirated slaves too old or sick to auction off . . . some still bound in coffles by their chains, after they were murdered. Some not," he grimly said. "Evidently, 'Calico Jack' and his cut-throats thought it a waste to let perfectly good chains and manacles be buried."

"Broke up the pirate cartel," Twigg stuck in, again, with even more (faint) praise, "and pursued Finney right into Charleston harbour in South Carolina, recovered what the brute had looted from the most-prominent island bank, and captured the last of his minions for trial, and righteous hangings, at New Providence. Put a *very* permanent end to 'Calico Jack,' as well, didn't ye, Lewrie?"

What doesn't *he know about my doings?* Lewrie gawped to himself, half-turning on the settee to see Twigg's eyes all steel-glinted.

"Well, 'twas personal by then, Mister Twigg," Lewrie admitted. "After Finney'd tried to seduce or assault my wife while I was at sea."

"And," Twigg drawled, looking back at the others with a smile on his phyz that was almost beatific, "made the man pay for his brute importunity by his own hand." *That* made 'em gasp and shiver!

"By personal experience with Captain Lewrie, I may also relate to you that his own Coxswain, any captain's most trusted aide, is also a runaway Jamaican house slave by name of Matthew Andrews," Mr. Twigg further informed them, once they got over their vicarious thrill. "He has been with him for years, and most-like had a great influence upon Captain Lewrie's views on the despicable institution of slavery."

"My *word*, sir," that Mr. Clarkson exclaimed, "I am certain we were unaware of the depth of your feelings upon this head."

"A *house* slave, ladies and gentlemen," Lewrie said for himself, "better fed, clothed, and sheltered than field hands, one might even say *pampered*, to some extent, yet . . . Andrews risked three hundred or more lashes, or the noose, to flee it, and be a whole, free man."

Hang on a bit, Lewrie suddenly thought; he might as well have, for his brow and face were already furrowed with *some* sort of intensity. *Do I really despise slavery as much's I'm protesting? Well, mine arse on a band-box, but I really think I do!*

"Don't rightly know what his name was before," Lewrie admitted, suddenly of a much cleaner soul, relieved that he was not *completely* playing a role to save his neck, "lest his old owners spot him and try to haul him back, I s'pose. Won't even tell *me*, just in case, but . . ."

"And your man Andrews, your newly rescued Negroes," Wilberforce enquired, "has any attempt been made to see to their souls, Captain?"

"Uhm . . . the night they came aboard, sir," Lewrie said, with a feeling that his soul-washing had been very temporary, for he was now back to tip-toeing 'cross a *fakir*'s bed of nails. "I hope that no one thinks this a presumption, but . . . 'tis customary for new hands to doff their civilian clothes, go under the wash-deck pump, and get bathed, be rid of fleas and such, before being issued slop-clothing. Well . . . our Sailing Master, Mister Winwood, a *most* devout

Christian, thought it much like *baptism,* d'ye see. At his suggestion, each chose a new name for ship's books, as if they *had* been baptised, or christened."

They ate that fact up like plum duff, with many a pleased, prim simper or shared smile, and softly whispered "Amens."

"*Proteus* doesn't carry a chaplain, sorry t'say," Lewrie added. "Only line-of-battle ships, admirals' flagships, generally do, with the charge to minister to a squadron's, or a fleet's, spiritual needs, and are paid either by Admiralty for their services, or are supported by a devout senior officer, and, as I'm sure you're aware, the pay isn't all that grand . . . the same rate as an Ordinary Seaman, with so many groats per hand in the crew atop that. Hardly ever *see* a chaplain on a ship below the Third Rate. Mister Winwood, therefor, is my chiefest aid at Sunday Divisions. We hold a *form* of Divine Services . . . Morning rites with a Collect or two, as specified, a suitable Epistle, perhaps even a brief Homily, and, of course, rather a lot of hymns. No Sacraments, of course! Though," Lewrie just had to add, feeling free enough for a bit of waggishness, "right after the final hymn, we *do* issue the rum-ration at Seven Bells of the Forenoon. But, totally secular and Navy, you understand."

"But, are your Negroes cabin-servants, waiters, and such, or do you employ them as sailors, Captain Lewrie?" Mr. Trencher asked him.

"Sailors, Mister Trencher," Lewrie firmly stated. "Most, rated Landsman, like volunteers or pressed men un-used to the sailors' trade. In gun crews, waisters at pulley-hauley, aye, the older ones. One is a dev . . . an outstanding cook, I must admit, but that was his plantation trade. Our five youngest, though, do go aloft, are rated Ordinary Seamen . . . spry topmen, sure t'be rated Able Seamen in a few years . . . oh, and one young fellow's a crack shot with a musket or Pennsylvania rifle. And, they're all drilled in musketry, cutlasses, pikes—"

"They have fought, under arms?" Mrs. Hannah More intruded, with a slit-lipped squeamish look at the image of *armed* Negroes, not merely *freed* Negroes. Was that too *much* equality for her, too soon?

"But, of *course,* ma'am!" Lewrie replied, surprised by her fret. "They *must,* if they're to serve in the Royal Navy. They have, indeed, and hellish-well, too!" he boasted, though wishing he could un-say the "hellish" part. "Like any English tar must, to serve his King, and to uphold the honour and liberty of his ship . . . to aid their shipmates in time of peril, whether storm or battle, ma'am.

"Shipmates . . ." Lewrie prosed on, only thinking himself *half* of a fraud, "paid the same, garbed the same, fed and doctored the same as each other, swing elbow-to-elbow in their hammocks belowdecks . . . you may see such for yourself aboard any ship in the Navy, for Free Black volunteers are everywhere. In the Pool of London this very morning in any merchantman you'd care to board . . ."

"Oh, we've seen them!" Mistress Theodora exclaimed, one hand on her mother's arm. "Those poor souls dismissed their ships between one voyage and the next . . . those horrid captains who turn them ashore to save money 'til they're needed, again. They live as hand-to-mouth as the poorest unemployed Irish. What did that brute call them, Father, that disparaging . . . ?"

"Ah, erm . . . 'Saint Giles Blackbirds,' dear," Mr. Trencher managed to say, waving a hand to excuse getting even close to commonness, or Billingsgate slang. "Where they gather, mostly . . . Saint Giles."

"Indeed, they evince such *heart-warming* gratitude whenever some of us circulate among them with clothing," Mrs. More piously said, in a righteous taking, "or provide a hot-soup kitchen for sustenance once their few pence are lost to vice, to *drink*, to . . . the sort of debased women who . . . well," she said with a grim roll of her eyes. "They're, dare I say, *avid* to receive our improving tracts and penny Testaments. It is quite *encouraging* to witness the *thirst* they have for the Good News of the Gospels. Why, I could even conjure that in every glad eye, one may actually see the spark of uplifting enlightenment blossom! In point of fact, when we lead them at hymns, their simple, joyous expressions put the lie to the contention that Negroes are forever bound into darkness and savagery. I fancy them budding *saints* in their patience, their eagerness to *please*, and improve themselves . . . with God's help, of course . . . and ours," Mrs. More primly, and firmly, concluded.

"And, do you sense the same patience, gratitude, and, dare we say, budding saintliness in your own Negro sailors, Captain Lewrie?" Mrs. Trencher asked.

"They do sing better than most of my crew, ma'am," Lewrie said. "Though . . . I fear that that French scribbler, Rousseau, had it wrong, when it came to the nobility of the simple savage. Whether still back in Africa, or dragged unwilling to Civilisation, *by* Civilisation, men, women and children are pretty-much the same, at bottom, the wide world over."

Why, you damned heretical cynic! Lewrie could imagine he could hear them all say; they certainly pruned up and sat back, at that.

"Some will drink too much, and try to smuggle rum aboard during a shore liberty, or when anchored in harbour," he explained. "Some are clever, some are dull . . . the same as us. The younger ones will cock a snook and be playful imps, if they can get away with it, the same as my Midshipmen or powder monkeys. Some serve chearly, some will always be bitter they've traded one form of slavery for another, just like any Navy or merchant sailor aboard any ship, in peace or war, even if they are paid regular, and get some prize-money to hand.

All get homesick and lonely, now and again . . . miss loved ones, wish to *have* loved ones, someday, somewhere.

"I'm sorry, but I've never met anyone even *close* to saintly in the Navy, and very few might earn such an appellation ashore, either, ladies and gentlemen," Lewrie told them in measured tones. "Negroes or Swedes, or British, it doesn't signify. They aren't saintly, nor are they child-like; they fit no playwright's cast of sympathetic characters, for each one's different, an individual. Aboard my frigate, they're . . . Proteuses. All of a piece, but each one a unique piece of the whole. When this war ends, and they're turned loose on their own devices, who *knows* what they'll make of themselves, but, for the meantime, they're . . . my crew."

"And quite right, too!" Miss Theodora piped up, ready to clap her hands, again. "Full equality!"

"Even if enforced," the Rev. Wilberforce commented, musing on all that Lewrie had said. "Well, I think . . . and I believe I am safe in saying for all of us, Captain Lewrie, that what you have related to us this morning has been enlightening . . . as to your motives, and what sort of man you are." He arose, leading the others to their feet.

It sounded very much like the interview was over and he had not won enough of them over. Well, there *was* the girl, but . . .

"There is the grave matter that what you did *officially* might be termed theft of chattel property," Wilberforce went on, "and property is the heart of Common Law, but . . . could it be intimated that you intend to offer the Jamaica Beaumans perhaps a modest recompence to assuage their rancour . . ."

"The Jamaica Beaumans hold too hot a grudge against Lewrie for even a princely sum to soothe them, sir," Mr. Twigg countered. "That would be for a court to determine, and, as I said when I first placed the matter to you, a court is the absolute last resort for Lewrie's cause, the very first for the Beaumans."

"Because you duelled," Mrs. More sniffed with disgust.

"Because I *seconded* Colonel Cashman, ma'am, and they cheated," Lewrie corrected her. "It was that, or allow my best friend get shot in the back. I'd not have *that* stain on my honour."

He could see another vicarious thrill cross their features at the image of Lewrie as a duelling man, a "killing gentleman," even if they did profess to abhor the deadly practice. At least it was done among the "better sorts," not the scurrilous poor and the riff-raff! And, if one intended to be Respectable in this new England these Reformers wished to make, honour went *with* Respectability.

"Whether you intend to aid Captain Lewrie," Mr. Twigg told them as they began to drift towards the double doors, "or not, his presence in Great Britain will be a hindrance to both his cause . . . and yours, sirs, madames. I have spoken to people I know at Admiralty, whichever way things fall out, d'ye see. HMS *Proteus* will soon be departing for foreign waters . . ."

Thank bloody Christ, and it's about time, too! Lewrie thought.

". . . support in the Commons, assisting Sir Malcolm Shockley and his allies," Twigg suggested, "depicting the Beaumans as the *epitome* of cruelty, greed, and . . . crude rusticity. Sordid 'Country-Puts' of a brutal and spiteful nature, hmm? Speaking of saints, here's Lewrie and his magnificent list of achievements as a naval hero. Details of which I and my associates may supply you, as we also drop a few hints here and there . . . in the public press, if absolutely necessary," Mr. Twigg said, with an obvious dislike for newspapers.

Here now, just a tick, you said we'd not *become a public spectacle!* Lewrie cringed, wishing he could openly disagree to the idea of being . . . *celebrated.* And right vehemently, too!

"Else, sirs, *else,* ladies," Twigg ominously told their assembly, with a stern forefinger raised, "'tis the Beaumans who will prosper in this affair, and the cause of emancipation in the Empire will suffer a grievous backwards step. *Hang* property, I say! For this touches more on Morality, and ultimate Justice . . . not Man's niggling laws. Well, then . . . we thank you for receiving us so kindly and attentively, and, no matter your final decision, are both most grateful that you allowed us our say."

"D'ye think we did my . . . 'cause' a damned bit o' good, Twigg?" Lewrie fretfully asked, once they'd been hatted, sworded, caned, and cloaked, ready to re-board their hired carriage, outside. "Damme, we didn't even *touch* on my involvement with the Saint-Domingue uprisings, respect for Toussaint L'Ouverture's slave rebellion, like we planned to, and . . ."

"Oh, I think we did, Lewrie," Twigg rather distractedly replied as he clambered into the coach and took seat upon the rear bench, hands crooked over the top of his cane, fingers flexing as his acute mind also churned odds and probabilities, going over what had been presented, as well as what had *not* been said, for lack of time or the right opening. Lewrie settled in across from him and felt like gnawing on one of his thumbnails as the coach lurched into motion, for Twigg was quite ignoring his presence.

Finally, Twigg's fingers did a last little dance on the handle of his cane, and a sly smile spread across his harsh, ruthless face.

"What?" Lewrie simply had to ask; that smile was just *too* odd.

"Bless me, Lewrie, but 'til now I never knew just how *convincing* you can be.

Damme, but I am impressed by your seeming sincerity!" Mr. Twigg said with a simper.

"Wasn't a *total* sham, Mister Twigg!" Lewrie groused. "Mine arse on a band-box, but I *do* despise slavery. No person with the slightest bit of feeling could do else. The idea of court-martial and cashiering, a criminal trial and hanging, might've made me *urgent* and . . . glibber. . . ."

"I don't think that's actually a word, sir," Twigg snickered.

"Damn dictionaries!" Lewrie griped. "With my name and neck on the line, maybe I *did* do a stellar stage performance to convince those people to aid me, but 'twas *not* a conversion by indictment, like your common criminal! Slavery makes me queasy, aye, but 'tis not a thing I thought to do anything *active* about, 'til . . . it just *is,* and . . ."

"What is the saying?" Twigg amusedly said. "That the threat of hanging concentrates the mind most wondrously, hmm? Well, of *course* most people in England despise slavery, Lewrie, whether they have ever been exposed to its evils, or not. They think, most patriotically, in Arne's song, 'Rule, Britannia' . . . 'Britons, never, never, *neh-ver* shall be slaves.' Now, how that squares with suspicion, xenophobia, and the Mobocracy's general hostility towards 'Samboes,' Cuffies, Hindoos, and Lascars if they turn up in this country, well . . . that's rather hard to say. Englishmen like the *idea* of emancipation . . . just so long as they don't have to rub elbows with the *results,* ha ha! Free as many as you like . . . just keep them out of *England,* what?"

"So . . ." Lewrie warily said, wondering just where Mr. Twigg was going with his prosing. "You're saying, then . . . ?"

"That once this matter becomes public, almost everyone in the British Isles . . . minus those actively engaged in the slave trade and colonial trade, it goes without saying . . . will *adore* you for what you did, Lewrie. Do the Beaumans dare sail here to press their charges in court . . . as they simply must, if you are allowed to be faced by your accusers, as the law requires . . . I fully expect them to be greeted at the docks by *hordes* of the Outraged Righteous . . . with the further addition of the idle, drunken, and easily excited Mob, of course."

"There'll *be* a trial, you're saying," Lewrie responded, with a groan and a sigh. "I'd hoped . . ."

"I fear there must be, sooner or later," Mr. Twigg said with a shrug, his eyes alight, making Lewrie feel as if he felt that it was no skin off *his* back if Lewrie got pilloried and dunged, or carted off to Tyburn. "But, only after such a public spectacle as to poison any jury empanelled, from Land's End to John o' Groats. Public sentiment will uphold you, and *spit* upon the Beaumans, and slavery. I do imagine that, 'twixt Wilberforce and his strident associates, and what covert efforts I and *my* associates may contribute, public sentiments may be played like a flute. But for one potentially harmful distraction . . ."

"Which is?" Lewrie asked, one eyebrow up in wariness.

"You," Twigg replied, tilting back his head to gaze down that long nose of his, looking as if he was having difficulty stifling his chortle of glee. "You're a much easier man to extol at long-distance, Lewrie, with none of your warts and peccadiloes on public display! It is foreign waters for you, me lad. At sea, where I believe you once told me . . . or Peel . . . either of us, it don't signify, that you did not get in a *tenth* the trouble you did ashore. 'Out of sight, out of mind,' whilst your allies at home strive mightily to put a gloss upon your valiant repute, hmm? Very far away, for an *extended* period of time, where, one may hope, you garner even more-glorious laurels with some laudable achievement 'gainst England's foes. That'd go down nice, did you—"

"You said you'd already spoken to people at Admiralty?" Lewrie said. "So I s'pose that's in-hand, too?"

"I fear you've no time to dilly-dally, Lewrie," Twigg assured him, still simpering in a most haughty manner. "No *recontre* with the little wife, no visiting your children. Not even time to drop in on Sir Hugo for a *brief* meal . . ."

"No loss, there," Lewrie sarcastically said; it wasn't so much the *active* dislike of his sly sire that had dominated his early years—people who "press-ganged" one into the Navy in the middle of a war and stole one's inheritance had a *way* of fostering distrust!—but, more a eeriness that, no matter Sir Hugo St. George Willoughby's new repute, fortune, and "rehabilitation" in Society, one should keep one hand on one's coin-purse at all times, and reject any proposed investments!

"Twigg, you're smiling like you already know where I'm going," Lewrie sullenly accused.

"Perhaps," Twigg slowly and cagily drawled back. "I will allow that it will *not* be back to the Caribbean. And . . . *weeks* from summons to court," he mystifyingly added. "Good God, sir . . . you should now be doing handsprings or Saint Catherine's wheels. Are you not grateful?"

"I *am*, but it's the *way* you . . . !"

"Were I you, I'd gather my traps from the Madeira Club at once, and book a seat on the 'dilly' to Portsmouth, instanter," Twigg went on quite blithely. "Make haste to return aboard your frigate, before your new orders beat you there, and the Port Admiral takes notice that you've been absent rather a bit too long for one still holding active commission and command. Well, perhaps I might run you down, myself, in my chariot. *Much* faster than a diligence-coach . . ."

"Ah, no . . . thank you!"

"Or, does Sir Hugo wish to have a brief bit of time with you," Twigg drolly continued, "he could drive you to Portsmouth in *his*. He purchased a chariot and team, recently, d'ye know. We *race,* when we have the time to weekend at my country house. They're all the crack, haw haw!"

"I'd rather *walk,*" Lewrie bleakly replied, with a shudder.

BOOK II

"I, bone, quo virtus tua te vocat, i pede fausto, grandia laturus meritorum praemia! Quid stas?"

"Go, sir, whither your valour calls you. Go, good luck to you!–to win big rewards for your merits. Why [do you] stand there [still]?

HORACE, *EPISTLES* II, II, 37-38

CHAPTER NINE

"Anyone looking for me, Mister Langlie?" Lewrie asked, once all the honours had been rendered to welcome him back aboard. He tried to make it sound like a casual enquiry, not a furtive fret.

"We've heard nothing from shore of any note, sir," Lt. Langlie crisply reported as Lewrie's shoregoing traps were borne below by his steward, Aspinall. "Beg pardon, sir, but . . . in your absence, I felt that a few days 'Out of Discipline' mightn't go amiss, and allowed the hands 'board-ship liberty. Once the water butts had been scrubbed and scoured, and the hoys fetched us fresh."

"Good thinking," Lewrie commented, his mind elsewhere, kneeling on the quarterdeck to stroke his affection-starved cats, which had come scampering to the starboard gangway at the very first tweetles of the bosun's calls. "No one knifed, poxed, or run?"

"Poxed, I could not say, sir," Langlie replied with a chuckle. "A few fist-fights and drunken rows over the doxies, of course, but no runners. Erm . . . I also sent ashore to the yards for spare spars and Bosun's stores, replenished our salt-meat and biscuit, and indented for live animals, so . . . *Proteus* is stocked with the full six months' worth of supplies, Captain," he reported, with a touch of pride.

"Very good, Mister Langlie," Lewrie congratulated, looking up at him, then rising to his feet, now that Toulon and Chalky had had their immediate fill of "wubbies." "I apologise that London required me to be away longer than I expected. In my absence, you've done well . . . as you always do. Of course, I expected no less, after our years of being thrown together," he tossed off with a grin.

That's enough praise, Lewrie thought; *don't* trowel *it on! Else, it'll go to his head.*

"Once I've gone below and changed into working rig, bring me the indentures and all to sign," Lewrie said. "Any more mail come aboard?"

"Some, sir. Yours is on your desk," Langlie told him, as they began to stroll towards the ladder to the gun-deck. "When in the City, sir, did you discover where our future orders might take us. sir?"

"Nothing definite, no," Lewrie cryptically informed him. "Damn, lads! Give me space in which to walk, will you?" he said to his cats, which thought it their "duty" to *closely* escort him down the ladderway, weaving back and forth from one riser to the next. "Pray God they do not come immediately. No time for shopping, and my personal stores are in need of re-stocking, too. Quite unlike the wardroom's . . . hmm?"

"We're all quite . . . happy, sir," Langlie rejoined, laughing. "I vow the Purser's actually done us proud . . . for a change."

Lewrie quickly changed into dark blue slop-trousers, a worn old waist-coat, and his plainest, and heaviest, uniform coat, for the great-cabins were chilly, and the two cast-iron stoves did little to heat the space. Evidently, Aspinall hadn't slept in his quarters temporarily, or lavished Lewrie's limited supply of coal on himself whilst he was away—good, honest lad!

Bills, which Lewrie read over, then addressed to his solicitor in London, Mr. Matthew Mountjoy; official documents opened first, of course, but they were nothing demanding—most were fleet-wide announcements of changes in admirals', captains', and lieutenants' lists, some new soundings taken of far-flung coasts or harbours, of more interest to Mr. Winwood, the Sailing Master, than to Lewrie, right off.

Hardly any personal correspondence, though, Lewrie broodingly noted as he sat slumped at his desk in the day-cabin. A mocking note from his father, Sir Hugo, was the most recent, japing him on staying at his Madeira Club; something brief from Lord Peter Rushton, wishing him joy of his return to England—nigh indecypherable, of course, in his own hand. Peter *might've* included cheerful words of how he would do what he could in his cause in the House of Lords, since Lewrie *did* manage to make out a reference to having spoken with Mr. Twigg, but it was hard going without a magnifying glass and a Sanskrit or Arabic dictionary.

Slam! went the Marine sentry's musket butt on the deck without the great-cabins' main-deck doors. "First Off'cah, SAH!" he bellowed, all full of piss, vinegar, and temporary officialdom.

"Enter," Lewrie called out. Lt. Langlie ducked under the deck beams and door frame to come in, bearing a thick-ish bundle of paperwork, just as Aspinall bustled in a second or so behind him with his coffee-pot.

Two cups, and half an hour, later, and there was another twitter of calls from the gangway, the thud of a boat coming alongside, below the entry-port, in the midst of their reading and scribbling. Not one minute later, and Mr. D'arcy Gamble, their smartest and eldest Midshipman, was announced by the sentry, and entered the cabins.

"Captain, sir," Gamble reported with his hat under his arm. "A messenger from shore is come aboard with orders," he said, eyes bright with excitement for new adventures and new horizons.

"Have him in, then, Mister Gamble," Lewrie instructed.

"Aye aye, sir!"

A smartly-dressed and languidly-elegant older Midshipman entered next, all but yawning in boredom with his work-a-day duty, all but sniffing in disdain at such casually, comfortably garbed officers, so unlike himself.

"Captain Lewrie, sir?" he asked, as if he had to be convinced before he would turn over his precious documents to just any "hobble-de-hoy."

"Last time I looked, that would be me," Lewrie said from behind his desk, still seated, taking an instant dislike for the fellow, even if he *did* see a bit of himself, back when he'd been stuck ashore in the service of the Port Captain of English Harbour, Antigua. In younger days, when he'd appalled himself by actually wishing for another shipboard assignment despite his early loathing for a naval career, he had been just that supercilious, himself, to disguise his delight to be *on* a warship, even temporarily. "Orders, have you?"

"I do, sir," the young man replied, reaching into a tarred and waterproofed canvas haversack slung from one shoulder, and producing a ribbon-and-wax-sealed letter. "Just come from Admiralty, sir," Mr. Midshipman "Top-Lofty" formally intoned, as if uttering the magic word "Admiralty" made him a grander fellow.

Didn't beat 'em aboard by much, *did I?* Lewrie mused to himself as he stretched out a hand to accept them; *Twigg must be working like a Trojan t'get me out of harm's reach.*

"We done, Mister Langlie?" Lewrie asked his First Officer, who sat across from him, legs crossed, in one of Lewrie's leather-covered collapsing chairs, looking eager as a hound when the gun-cabinet was opened.

"Done to a turn, sir," Langlie replied, gathering up the last of his "bumf" into a neat pile; one copy for the ship, one copy for the yards.

"Then perhaps Mister . . . whatever your name is . . ."

"Catlett, sir. Midshipman Cat . . ."

". . . would be so good as to bear all these back ashore for us, hey, Mister Langlie? Kill two birds with one stone, seeing as how he is on his *way*, hmm?" Lewrie dismissively suggested, quite enjoying his brief bit of spite. "Anything *else*, Mister Catlett?"

"Uhm, nossir," the crestfallen Midshipman replied.

"Well, there you are, then!" Lewrie said with a bright grin as he indicated that Langlie should hand Catlett the paperwork. "Do stay dry as you can, on the row ashore! Wouldn't want 'em smudged!"

"Very good, sir," Catlett intoned, sketched a brief bow, then departed, escorted by an equally disappointed Mr. Gamble, who had been hoping for at least a hint as to their new duties, and destination.

"A 'no-sailor' tailor's dummy," Lt. Langlie softly commented in dismissal of their visitor. "*He'll* never see the outer channel marks. I'll go, sir, and allow you . . ." he offered, starting to rise.

"Stay, Mister Langlie," Lewrie objected, waving him back down. "This concerns you as much as it does me," he said, breaking the seal and unfolding the large sheet of paper. He laid it on the desk-top, smoothed the crisp folds flat, and hunched over it under the slightly swaying lanthorn for the best light.

Uhmum, Lewrie thought; *"required and directed," and all that . . . "making the best of your way," uhmum, "with all despatch,"* he read to himself, frowning over the urgency implied by those stock Admiralty phrases. *What in Blazes has Twigg talked 'em into?* he wondered.

"Oh, buggery," Lewrie uttered at last. "Mine arse on a band-box! He's *not* gone barking mad, yet? Holy shit on a . . ." he griped.

"Sir?" Lt. Langlie hesitantly asked, his brow furrowed.

"Convoy duty, Mister Langlie," Lewrie told him, looking up and sitting back into his chair. "We're to make all haste up-Channel for the Goodwin Sands, meet up with a 'Trade' of East Indiamen, and escort 'em at least as far as the Cape of Good Hope. Saint Helena, Recife in Portuguese Brazil, to Cape Town."

"Africa, sir!" Lt. Langlie enthused. "I've never been there."

"Haven't missed much, then," Lewrie told him.

Africa! Bloody Africa? Lewrie furiously thought; *Is this some sort of galling jape on my predicament? Want me t'turn my Black tars* loose, *there? Recruit even* more, *do they, damn their eyes? And damn Twigg, too. It* must've *been him who suggested it, the sly . . . !*

"Uhm, far be it from me to presume further, sir, but . . . *who* is not yet daft, did you say?" Langlie curiously asked.

"Captain Sir Tobias Treghues," Lewrie bleakly said, "Knight and Baronet. One of my old captains in the American war, when I was still a Midshipman aboard HMS *Desperate*. Prim as a dowager, 'til a Frenchie swotted him in the head with the hard end of a rammer, and turned mad as a March Hare . . . on his off days . . . so, God knows what he's like now. Depending on the temperature, the latitude or longitude, what he's eat for breakfast . . ."

"Grim, d'ye expect, then, Captain, sir?" Langlie asked.

"Far be it from me to slur senior officers, Mister Langlie . . ." Lewrie gravelled, though recalling that yes, yes he always *had,* "but, are his wits flown him for a week or two, he can turn into a *spherical* bastard . . . a bastard no matter *which* way ye look at him. Next week, you're in his good books, and couldn't do wrong if you rammed him, on purpose! The Navy must be hellish needful, if *he* still holds active commission. I'd have thought Captain Treghues had been dismissed, or 'yellow squadroned,' years ago, when he inherited his title and all."

Lewrie took note of Lt. Langlie's "bland" expression; was that worthy trying to keep a straight face, or was he wondering whether his own captain was consistently "up to snuff"?

"Why, next you know, Mister Langlie, Admiralty might even be so desperate they'd offer *me* command!" Lewrie japed. "The damned fools."

His First Officer responded as junior officers should: grinning and issuing a silent chuckle over a senior's self-deprecating wit.

"Where stands the wind, then?" Lewrie snapped.

"An hour ago, 'twas a 'dead muzzler' from the South, sir, but I did feel a pinch of veer to it," Langlie answered. "By dawn, it could be more Sou'easterly."

"Damme, by dawn, there might be enough Easting for Treghues and his 'trade' to set sail," Lewrie gloomily speculated, conjuring up a sea-chart in the mind's eye. "We *could* make an offing, but it'd take days to beat up-Channel t'meet 'em. Off western Kent, at the very best if they can manage the narrow channel from out behind the Goodwin Sands. Lots of short-tacking close ashore for us, *bags* of sea-room for them, and I just *know* he won't keep his anchors, waiting for us to show up! Damn. Just damn my eyes!

"Best pass the word to take in kedge anchors, Mister Langlie," Lewrie ordered. "We'll swing to our bowers 'til it looks as if we may fall down to Saint Helen's Patch, safely, then . . ."

"Aye aye, sir, directly," Langlie replied, getting to his feet, and tucking his discarded hat under his left arm.

"Pass word for Mister Winwood, as well, sir," Lewrie said as he strode to the chart-space up forward against the main-deck bulkheads. He stopped short, though, looking into Aspinall's tiny day-pantry and wondering just how much he had in the way of personal stores, and estimating how short-commons he'd be by the time they reached St. Helena Island, much less Cape Town! "And I'd admire did you pass the word for Mister Coote, to boot. I run out of wine, Mister Langlie, and I might turn as mean as Treghues can, hah?" he added, feigning surliness. "Tea and water, and I'll *not* be responsible for my actions. Aarr!" Lewrie concluded, in one of his patented "piratical" snarls.

"At once, sir!" Langlie answered, and departing the great-cabins right speedily, as if that snarled "Aarr!" was *not* meant in jest.

No time to go ashore for leisurely shopping for himself, Lewrie decided; jams and jellies, mustards, vinegars, cases and barricoes of spirits, personal livestock, fresh eggs . . . food for the cats! . . . it would all be "catch-as-catch-can," all done by the Purser in a slapdash, last-minute rush, with no allowance for suiting his tastes; even whisky might be hard to come by in English shops, much less good wines!

Books, to fill the many boresome hours and days to come, Lewrie bemoaned. Well, there were the few he'd managed to obtain in London. *The Innocent Adultress*, *Venus in the Cloister*, *Cuckholdom Triumphant*, and a compendium of testimonies from infamous adultery trials. Lewrie pawed over the volumes in the fiddle-racks above the chart table; hmm, he *did* have the newest *Whoremonger's Guide to London*, his sturdy *Moll Flanders*, a translated *Les Liaisons Dangereuses* that he'd acquired in the Bahamas in the '80s, his *Fanny Hill*, his *Shamela*, and a selection of other amusing Fielding or Smollett novels. . . .

By God, what are these? he asked himself as he dug his newest novels from his still-packed valise, and came across his own copy of the latest *New Atlantis*, the very same guide he'd recommended to that seemingly upright Maj. Baird at the Madeira Club (and which wouldn't do him a bit of good at sea, would it?), and out spilled a loose pile of *tracts*! Penny one-sheets, folded-over four-sheets, even pamphlets and chapbooks . . . all, by their bold titles, declaring them to be of the most cautionary, uplifting, and "improving" sort of Evangelical Society flim-flam.

"Who the Blazes put these in here?" he muttered aloud, immediately suspecting Twigg, or one of his unofficial minions, who had slipped them in at Twigg's behest. Just one more jibing, mocking jape, on top of everything else, and secreted so their presence wouldn't ram it all home up his fundament 'til he was far out to sea!

Lewrie considered what to do with 'em; there was always a need for shredded paper in the cats' litter box; there was also need for a supply of scrap paper for his own quarter-gallery toilet, and he just might be able to save a crown or two from what the Purser was to buy ashore for him, or . . .

Leave 'em out in plain sight, does Treghues come aboard, Lewrie thought. *Push 'em off on him, if he hasn't seen the latest issues, hah?*

CHAPTER TEN

By dawn of the next morning, the winds had, indeed, come more out of the Sou'east, allowing HMS *Proteus* to up-anchor and short-tack down to St. Helen's Patch, nearer the main channel round the Isle of Wight. By mid-day, just about Four Bells of the Watch, the winds actually were coming off the distant North Sea and the Danish/German coast, and *Proteus* up-anchored once again, this time for good, and thrashed out an offing into the Channel.

As the last headland of the Isle of Wight slipped astern, Lewrie could admit to himself that it felt good to be back at sea . . . even if the weather conditions were pretty-much a pluperfect bastard! Thrice-reefed courses, tops'ls and t'gallants, with the royal spars and masts struck down, and HMS *Proteus* was *still* laid over twenty or twenty-five degrees, practically sailing on her lee shoulder, and green seas were shipping over the forecastle, jib-boom, and bowsprit with every plunge, sluicing down the main deck, wave-breaking round the companionway hatches, and gurgling out the lee scuppers like the town drains. The so-called "Chops of the Channel" behaved more like a series of granite terraces that the frigate clambered over, then skidded down, with many thumps and thuds, among the high-pitched whining of the Easterly wind tearing through the miles of rigging aloft, and standing upright on her quarterdeck took the skill of an acrobatic rider, with legs spread and each foot placed on the bare back of one of a pair of fractious, galloping horses . . . and headed for a series of log jumps.

To make matters even dicier, every bloody merchantman or naval vessel that had been stranded in every harbour east of Portsmouth had used the wind shift to make *their* offings, too, and scud downwind for the Atlantic. Trades, convoys, squadrons, whole *fleets,* or individual ships ordered somewhere round the world could be muzzled in port for weeks before the winds shifted, allowing them out, and it seemed as if half the Royal Navy and *all* the Merchant Service, from coasting smacks to Indiamen, had set sail that morning.

All bearing Westward, in gaggles and streams, a positive flood of hard, unyielding, impatient shipping, their captains and masters in such a hurry they'd not give opposing traffic a single inch more than absolutely necessary to avoid collision as *Proteus* short-tacked against the flood, seemingly the only ship headed East that vile morning.

To make matters a *tad* worse, *Proteus* had to tack rather a lot; if Treghues and his trade had already sailed, they would not venture too far Sutherly, else they'd end up wrecked on the rocks and shoals of the Channel Islands or the French coast, or run the risk of privateers operating out of Normandy or Breton harbours, so Lewrie could not let himself stray too much to the South. No, he must remain in the Northern half of the Channel, slicing 'cross the hawses of hundreds of those "running," "both sheets aft" merchantmen on the larboard tack, and the starboard gun-ports almost in the water for a time, then come about in a flurry and thrash Nor'east 'til the Kentish coast was almost in sight from the deck, making civilian captains and watch-standing officers and mates curse him on starboard tack, too!

To make things just a *wee* bit worse on top of all that, squalls and patches of nigh-blinding rain came swooping down-Channel, now and again, driven by the "fortuitous" wind shift so beneficial to Commerce—squalls which perfectly blotted out both *Proteus* and whatever high speed, Couldn't-Get-Out-Of-Their-Own-Way traffic bearing down on them.

And, as the final fillip of Fate, there were the damned tides in the Channel, which perversely seemed yoked to the winds like a pair of surly oxen. The tides had turned an hour or so before, right after HMS *Proteus* had cleared Selsey Bill, and going like a racehorse. But, for the next few hours, until the tides turned, all of their efforts to go East, no matter how close their frigate lay to the eye of the wind as she bashed "full and by," no matter how manfully *Proteus* struggled up to windward, *damned* if there wasn't Selsey Bill off their bows at the end of every starboard tack inshore in search of Treghues's convoy!

"*Sane* people go West in weather like this," Lewrie muttered to himself, "and the *wise* stay in port 'til it moderates."

"Gained a bit, though, sir," Mr. Winwood, the Sailing Master, assured him after a long, gloomy peek at that "magnetic" headland with a heavy brass telescope to his eye. "Might've made three miles to the good, this last tack. Speaking of, though, sir . . ."

"Aye, thankee," Lewrie grumbled, turning to Lt. Catterall, the officer standing the Forenoon Watch. "Time to tack, I believe, sir!"

"Aye aye, sir!" Catterall bellowed back with great glee, turning to his helmsmen and lifting his brass speaking trumpet to roar, "Stations for Stays! Tail on, and prepare to come about to larboard tack!"

As he waited for sailors to ready themselves, Catterall clapped his raw hands together before him like a performing seal, all swaddled up in tarred canvas foul-weather clothing, then turned to address both Lewrie and Mr. Winwood. "Going like a thoroughbred at Derby, she is, sir! Damme, what *fun*!"

"God save us," Lewrie whispered to Mr. Winwood, "but he's ready for Bedlam. Certifiable!" He plastered a broad, agreeable grin on his phyz, though, and shouted, "Carry on!" to his manic Second Officer.

All hands, and all officers, too, up from naps in the gun-room, just to be on the safe side. Judging his moment very carefully, Lt. Catterall rose up on the balls of his feet, taking a deep suck of wind into his lungs, and turning just a tad blue as he held it for a long second or two, judging the scend of the sea, the pressure on the sails from the gusting winds, the wave-sets smashing against the starboard bows, and what they might be like halfway through the evolution . . . and, what gaps in that shoal of merchant traffic he thought he could thread *Proteus* through once she got a way back on, sailing nearly 140 degrees off her present course, and lay slow and loggish before the winds snatched her like a paper boat on a duck pond, and sent her tearing off once more.

"Ready, ready . . . ease down the helm!" Catterall screeched, at last, loud enough for his trumpet-aided voice to carry all the way to the forecastle. Then, "Helm alee!" after a last peek, a last breath.

Proteus swung up closer to the wind, fore-and-aft headsails now "Flowing," and, in such a brisk wind, the fore bowline kept fast, and the fore sheet "checked" or "braced to" in pilot boat fashion, as they would when short-tacking in a narrow channel. "*Rise*, tacks and sheets!"

Tacking in such weather really *wasn't* recommended; steady winds and fairly smooth seas were best, but . . . wearing the frigate about off the wind could end with them scudded a mile or more West of where they had started, by the time they had described a full circle and pointed her bows Sou'-Soueast . . . and Selsey Bill even further out of reach on their larboard bows!

There was a heart-stopping moment when a series of combers met *Proteus*'s bows with wet and hearty smacks, threatening to slam her to a full stop and put her "in-irons," unable to fall off to either beam, but the knacky Mr. Midshipman

Gamble, on the forecastle, feeling what shift of wind that the men on the quarterdeck could not, ordered that the inner jib and foretopmast stays'l be flatted to larboard for a bit, which put just enough wind-pressure on her to force her over enough to cross over. Then, right-smoothly, the starboard sheets, the new lee sheets, he ordered belayed snug, and hauled in in concert with loosening the new, larboard, windward sheets, and hernias and tumbles among the foc's'le hands bedamned.

"Whew!" Lewrie, Winwood, and Lts. Langlie and Catterall all uttered, once *Proteus* recovered from her dramatic heel over to the starboard side, and she began to make way once more. "Whew!" again a moment later, as a heavily-laden cargo ship actually altered course to miss them, and passed down their larboard beam with at least a quarter-cable between them. With her captain and first mate shaking their fists and cursing a blue streak, of course.

"Selsey Bill . . . again," Lewrie muttered late that afternoon, as the headland loomed into sight once more. This time, after the turn of the tide, it was *astern* of them, for a wonder, could almost be said to be on their larboard quarter as *Proteus* angled in towards the coast on starboard tack, and readied herself to come about and hare off to mid-Channel. The winds, which had acted much like a gust-front preceding a storm, had moderated nicely, and the seas had flattened a bit, though they still broke green and white around her. When Lt. Adair, the Third Officer, directed the latest tack, the manoeuvre went off as smoothly as anyone could ask for, and the nearest other vessel that could cause a collision was at least three cables off.

"The wind *seems* to be backing, sir," the Sailing Master opined, with a wary lift of his nose and a deep sniff at the apparent winds. "More out of the Nor'east by East, now . . . well, perhaps a point *shy* of Nor'east by East, but *trending* that direction . . . it very well may be."

"Making our best course up on the wind East by Sou'east, aye," Lewrie decided, consulting that mental compass rose that he had been forced to memorise in his midshipman days, so he could "box" it whenever a senior asked . . . usually with a rope starter in his hand if he got it wrong, and a Bosun's Mate waiting to wield it, and breathing hard in expectation of the joy that came with serving Mr. Midshipman Lewrie "sauce" for his ignorance.

"About that, aye, sir . . . a point more Easterly, does the wind continue backing," Mr. Winwood ponderously, cautiously agreed.

"A long board, this time, I think," Lewrie further decided with a chart replacing the compass in his head. "With wind and tide since the turn early this morning, Captain Treghues's trade would most-like have headed Sou'west, at first, once clear of Dover. Hug our coasts for safety from the Frog *chasse-maries* through the Straits, then take a slant South of West with the wind right up their skirts. Avoiding Dungeness, Beachy Head . . . I don't expect we'd see them *too* close in-shore."

"Unless they haven't sailed at all, Captain," Mr. Winwood said with a heavy frown. "Did the East India Company wish to add one more ship or two to the trade, still lading in London, and now unable to get under way 'gainst a 'dead muzzler' up the Thames or Medway, sir?"

"The only joy we can take o' that, Mister Winwood, is in knowing there'll be fewer damn-fool merchant captains out t'ram us amidships," Lewrie scoffed with a dry chuckle. "That, and the chance to flesh out our cabin stores from the bumboats in The Downs. Even if those buggers would steal the coins from their dead mothers' eyes."

"There is that, sir," Winwood agreed with a faint simper that, on him, was a sign of high amusement.

"Two hours more on larboard tack, I should think," Lewrie opined. "Tide's with us, the sea's flatter. We should fly over the ground like a Cambridge coach, thirty miles or more. Next tack . . . the middle of the First Dog, most-likely, then a short board at . . . Due North. With any luck at all, we'll fetch some coastal mark *other* than Selsey-bloody-Bill! Bognor Regis, perhaps? I'll be below 'til then, sir."

"Very good, Captain, sir."

Once in his quarters, Lewrie paused to warm his hands over the single coal stove he trusted to be lit, under way, and that one lashed down tautly, and secured in a deep "fiddle-box" filled with damp sand. Even with the sky-lights in the coach-top overhead closed, all the gun-ports lashed shut, and the sash-windows above the transom settee right aft closed, it was still grindingly, damply cool in his great-cabins.

Toulon and Chalky were curled up together in a snoring bundle on the starboard-side collapsible settee in the day-cabin, faces buried in each other's fur, and had even managed to burrow a bit under the light quilt that Aspinall usually spread over the settee's removable pad, to save the upholstery from a quarter-pound of hair . . . left daily.

After two and a half years and a bit in commission, HMS *Proteus* was getting a little "ripe," despite the continual efforts expended to dispel the odours of a working vessel; they smoked her with smouldering bunches of tobacco, scoured with vinegar monthly, swept down the lower decks daily, and both swabbed and holystoned weekly, but . . . one could not put upwards of 150 men and boys aboard in such a confined space as the gun-deck and officers' quarters, keep six months of perishables on the orlop and in the holds, without the reek of over-ripe cheeses, the faint carrion-in-brine smell of salt-beef and salt-pork kegs, the salt-fish right aft on the orlop, or the stinks of the livestock up forward in the manger below the forecastle from filtering into every nook and cranny, from seeming to soak into the very fibre of the ship, and her bulwarks, beams, and frame. Add to that her "ship's people," who went without bathing for a week at a time, unless caught in a heavy rain on deck, who must fart, and belch, and sneak a pee in the holds or cable tiers when caught short when the beakheads were too far to walk. Not to mention the muddy fish-reek of the cables themselves.

At sea, Lewrie got to the point where he hardly noticed it, but a few days ashore, even in such a rancid place as London with all her garbage middens and hordes of people, and the change was noticeable in the extreme. He wrinkled his nose in disgust.

There was no steaming pot of coffee or tea, so Lewrie remained wrapped snug in his boat cloak and sat down at his desk, under a swaying coin-silver oil lamp that was putting out its own contribution to the ambient effluvia, and looked over the last bits of mail that had come aboard just before they departed from St. Helen's Patch.

His ward, Sophie de Maubeuge, once French royalty but now penniless and orphaned, had written him a chatty letter, describing how his father Sir Hugo had furthered her introductions in London Society, with the promise of sending him a new oval pocket portrait that "Granpère" had commissioned. Once she had moved away from Anglesgreen—she and his wife Caroline had had a major falling-out, with Caroline even suspecting Sophie and her "faithless, adulterous pig of a husband" with being lovers, if not fellow conspirators to conceal his overseas amours, for a time—Sir Hugo had taken her in, and, to everyone's surprise, had developed quite an avuncular affection for Sophie and her welfare, and her future as an *emigré*. Now, he positively doted on the girl as she blossomed into a ravishingly-attractive young lady, expressing that he felt beyond "grandfatherly," perhaps had even attained "paternal" sentiments! Lewrie *still* suspected the old rantipoler's intentions.

There was a letter from his wife, too, in answer to his brief note hastily scribbled at the Guildford posting-house. Caroline was appreciative of what the so-far small share of his Caribbean silver paid out to him had bought to improve their house and middling tenant farm. Lord, it was dry and stand-offish, though, all sums of profits from the farm, and lists of outlays made, with a pointed direction for him to write his children at their new public school, at the least, if such a chore wasn't beyond his ability, before he sailed. And, what was this, she had asked, about rumours of some criminal deed he'd done on Jamaica? What *new* shame had he brought on his family name; not that it was all that good to begin with . . . damn him. Had he *no* consideration for his children's futures, for his long-suffering wife's repute?

There was an encouraging letter from the Trencher family, wife, father, and daughter, which expressed their wishes for his safety and continued success. They didn't have that much new to say about *defending* his "good name," but assured him that their continual prayers were with him. Their daughter Theodora had offered to send him a package of goods for the betterment of his crew: pocket-bibles, New Testaments, and chapbooks of the newest, most inspiring hymns . . . along with reams of tracts fresh from the printers, of course.

Lewrie looked up from re-reading that letter, speculating most idly (of course) on what sort of figure Theodora Trencher might boast, feeling even a tad risable at the fantasy . . .'til he saw the framed portrait of his wife Caroline that hung on the bulkhead facing him in the dining-coach. Odd . . . he'd never noticed the leeriness the artist had captured in her expression, before!

Coughing into his fist, he lowered his gaze to the desk, again, lifting the letter that the Rev. Wilberforce had sent him, wherein he offered much the same sort of spiritual comfort for HMS *Proteus*'s tars, both Black and White. Wilberforce had even proposed placing an eager young chaplain aboard her, his pay and his keep to be supplied by the Evangelical Society! Could the young man he had in mind be able to go aboard before *Proteus* sailed . . . could Lewrie "vet" him once he arrived at Portsmouth . . . and, was *he* not suitable to Captain Lewrie's complete satisfaction, perhaps there might be time enough for Wilberforce and his associates to select another?

Well, he'd done as Caroline had bid him; he'd written to both of his sons, Hugh and Sewallis, had even penned a loving letter to his little daughter Charlotte . . . all done into the wee hours of the final night in the inner harbour at Portsmouth, long past the Master At Arms' official "Lights Out" at nine of the evening. Though, what good *that* letter would do Lewrie rather doubted, since Charlotte was still with her mother, home-tutored, not schooled, and exposed to all the grumbles of his wife and in-laws, who'd never thought him quite "up to chalk."

There'd been that letter from his father, who had mentioned one Sunday after Services, in the churchyard, when the vicar of ivied old St. George's had preached a homily on Sinners, and little Charlotte had so taken it (and other things she'd heard) to heart that she had *loudly* told one and all present in the churchyard that "*my* father is a Sinner . . . *and* a filthy beast!" His father'd found it delightfully droll at the time, even if Lewrie hadn't, and God knows what poisons had been poured into her ears, since!

Children, well . . . there had only been a few years on half-pay ashore to get to *know* them, then the war with France had erupted back in '93, and he was back in Navy harness, and there hadn't been a whole month with them since then. Sewallis, Hugh, and Charlotte had become more the *concept* of children, just as he had felt himself merely the *shadow* of a father, and every reunion had presented him with sprouted *strangers*, and little Charlotte the most unknowable of all. To whom he wrote platitudes . . . *well-meaning* platitudes, but no matter how he reminded himself that he, indeed, *loved* them, he still felt so oddly disassociated.

There came the heavy thud of the Marine sentry's musket on the deck outside, and the cry of "Mister Midshipman Grace, SAH!"

"Enter!" Lewrie called out, sitting up straighter, and shoving his letters into the desk drawer.

"Captain, sir . . . Mister Langlie's duty, and he wishes to shake out to second reefs in courses and tops'ls. He said to tell you that the winds are moderating, sir," the lad said. Grace, the son of Nore fishermen, who had come aboard a ship's boy in company with his father and grandfather, who had risen to "Gentleman Volunteer" Midshipman once *Proteus* had been won back from the mutineers. He was upwards of sixteen, now, and shaping well to become an extremely reliable and tarry lad. His grandfather, whom they'd dubbed Elder Grace, was gone, lost to the Yellow Jack, and his father, Middle Grace, was now rated an Able Seaman, and bore the shipboard rate of Captain of the Afterguard, the petty officer in charge of the mizen-mast.

"Very well, Mister Grace," Lewrie said in agreement. "Give to Mister Langlie my respects, and permission. I'll come up, directly."

"Aye aye, sir."

Lewrie had himself a paternal sigh, then got to his feet, gathered up his hat and mittens, and went on deck, pausing to give Toulon and Chalky a chin and ear rub or two.

At least on deck, the nippy wind was much fresher than what he breathed in his great-cabins, and the Channel was calming, too. Where agitated green rollers and white-spumed crests had been, there were now darker green or steel-grey waves, though the "chops" still made *Proteus* ride like a brick mason's dray on a cobbled street. Her heel had altered to a mere fifteen degrees from vertical, according to the clinometer by the compass binnacle and chart cabinet, as well.

"We're making a better way, sir," Lt. Langlie reported, with a sketchy salute tossed up to the brim of his cocked hat. "The coast is completely under the horizon, and Mister Winwood thinks we are nearly twenty miles to the good, East'rd, and about the same to seaward."

"Came up early, did you?" Lewrie asked.

"A bit fuggy, below, sir," Langlie allowed with a wry grin. "I was in need of fresh air, and . . ."

Eight bells chimed slowly, in pairs, from the foc'sle belfry as a ship's boy turned the watch glass: four in the afternoon, and an end to the Day Watch, and the beginning of the First Dog.

"Carry on, Mister Langlie," Lewrie bade, and his First Officer went through the ritual of relieving Lt. Adair and his watchstanders. The men of the larboard division shuffled up to take the place of the hands in the starboard division, the men going off watch lingering to savour fresh air, themselves.

"Very well, sir, I have the watch," Langlie intoned, saluting Adair with a doff of his hat. "All hands!" he bellowed not a moment later. "Mister Pendarves, Mister Towpenny, mast captains! Trice up and lay aloft to make sail to the second reefs!"

Lewrie paced up to the larboard, windward, quarterdeck bulwarks to watch things done, as spry topmen and older yard captains climbed the ratlines in the weather shrouds; out to the mast-tops' edges and for a time upside down on the futtock shrouds before some scampered up higher to the tops'l yards, whilst others scooted out the course yards, carefully balanced on the foot-ropes with their chests pressed to the canvas-bound main and foremast course yards.

Lewrie thought to remind Langlie to overhaul the spiral set of the yards once more sail had been made, but forebore; that would just be "gilding the lily," an unwanted intrusion on a competent officer's performance. Good and trustworthy lieutenants could almost make his job irrelevant, at times, which suited Lewrie's well-hidden lazy nature right down to his toes.

"Sails, ho!" the mainmast lookout cried, pointing up to larboard. "Deck, there! Ships in comp'ny . . . nine, ten, or more! Three points off th' larboard bows, an' hull-up!" he sang out as the clutch of ships appeared from the misty rains.

"Glass, please," Lewrie called over his shoulder, and thought of going aloft as high as the futtock shrouds, but decided not to; it was already too crowded aloft, and he'd just be in the topmen's way. Midshipman Larkin fetched him a day-glass, and he had himself a good and long look at them.

"Deck, there!" the lookout far aloft wailed. "Eight Indiamen, a frigate, two sloops o' war, and a Third Rate in the van!"

"Our 'John Company' trade, sir?" Lt. Langlie took time from his duties to enquire, with excitement in his voice.

"Unless they're running more than one a month, aye, sir," Lewrie told him. "And, on the leading seventy-four, I do b'lieve I can make out a flag with yellow-red-yellow stripes . . . East India convoy in the code book they gave us. Mister Larkin! 'East India' flag to the foremast, the Union flag to the mainmast halliards, where they can see it, and know we're not a Frenchman. And hoist our number to the peak of the mizen signal halliards."

He counted off the massive East Indiamen, admiring their glossy and rich hulls and fresh canvas, so big and impressive that they could be mistaken for 74-gunned ships of the Third Rate, though the 74-gunner leading that "elephants' parade" was the genuine article, and could be discerned as such after close inspection, for her own sails were worn, mildewed, and parchment tan by comparison, and her hull did not glisten as the others did; too much wear, salt water, and not enough linseed oil or tar and paint, and that not refurbished lately. By comparison, his frigate, relatively fresh from the Halifax yard, gleamed like a bright, new-minted penny.

A flurry of flag signals from the lead 74 created an answering blizzard of bunting from the frigate on the forward Southern quarter of the convoy, was repeated by the trailing sloop of war to seaward of the trade's stern quarter, and answered by the other Third Rate that brought up the rear, which, after a long moment, made a new hoist that the lead frigate repeated as she wore a bit off her "soldier's wind" and started to come down nearer *Proteus*.

"Can't read 'em, sor . . . sir, sorry," Midshipman Larkin said as he stood atop the bulwarks by the mizen shrouds, a telescope to his own eye. "They're streamin' right at us, but I *think* she's askin' just who we are, I do! 'Tis in the private signals for this month . . . I think."

"Must believe we're a French fraud," Lewrie agreed. "Mine arse on a band-box, we've our Number aloft, already. Can you read his?"

"Er, aye, sor . . . sir," Larkin, the Bog-Irish by-blow, replied, drifting back into brogue as he always did when flustered. "She's ah, HMS *Stag* . . . Fifth Rate, thirty-eight-gunner, Captain John Philpott," Larkin stammered, fumbling through his bundle of lists and almost losing both his telescope overside and his grip on the shrouds.

"Last *Stag* would know, we're still in the Caribbean, sir," Lt. Langlie commented by Lewrie's side. "A good ruse for a French raider."

"Aye, Mister Langlie," Lewrie said. "Mister Larkin, hoist that we are ordered to join the escort. Perhaps the latest signals book'll convince them. 'Tis only three weeks old, after all."

"Aye aye, sir."

A long minute or two passed as Larkin and his "bunting tossers" made their hoist, which was acknowledged by *Stag;* then, they had more minutes to wait 'til *Stag* made a reply, for she had to pass the message back to the repeating sloop of war, which passed it to the trailing 74-gunner, which was obviously the flagship. More time was taken for the flagship to hoist a new order, which had to come down the chain to the sloop, to the frigate, to *Proteus*.

And, all during that time, the convoy was plodding along under reduced plain sail, bound roughly West, Sou'west, while *Proteus* still was on larboard tack, heading about Sou'east by East and drawing apart slowly.

"Wear her about to West, Sou'west, Mister Langlie," Lewrie told his First Officer. "Nothing more convincing than showing leery people your arse. Like a dog rollin' over on his back."

"Aye, sir. All hands! Stations to wear, ready . . . !"

"What did they ask that time, Mister Larkin?" Lewrie asked.

"Order, sir. 'Come Under My Lee,' the flag said t'do," Larkin puzzled out at last. "HMS *Grafton*, seventy-four. Captain Sir Tobias . . . Trey . . . Gwees? Triggers?"

"Truh-*Gewz*," Lewrie corrected him. "An old captain of mine, me lad. Damme, they didn't do him too proud, did they? *Grafton* was commissioned in 1771. Why she hasn't been hulked . . . or rotted apart . . ."

"Ready to wear, sir," Langlie reported.

"Very well, Mister Langlie. Once about, reduce sail so we may fall astern of *Grafton* yonder, then come up under her lee. With winds full astern, I *s'pose* he means come alongside her inshore beam. Might be, either'd do," Lewrie said with a shrug. "Mister Larkin, alert yon suspicious frigate that we're wearing about. Try *not* to make it look like an order to Captain Wilkinson, hmm?"

"Aye aye, sor," Larkin sheepishly replied.

"Wear about, then, Mister Langlie."

"Aye aye, sir."

Perhaps half an hour later, HMS *Proteus* had fallen far enough towards the tail-end of the trade to make a bit more sail so she could angle in towards HMS *Grafton*. When she was close enough, it was an easy matter to duck under her high, old-fashioned stern and make a brief dash before the sails were reduced once more, so that she ended up off the 74-gun ship's starboard quarter, about half a cable inshore of her.

Lewrie left the details to Langlie, busy with his telescope by the larboard bulwarks to study the people gathered on *Grafton*'s quarterdeck. Officers, sailors of the afterguard, some gloomy-looking corn stalk of a fellow in drab, dark clothing, and . . . a woman? An officer, perhaps *Grafton*'s First Lieutenant, lifted a brass speaking-trumpet to his mouth to shout across. The swash of the sea between the two ships, the wind, and the normal creaks and groans of *Proteus*'s hull made what he shouted quite un-intelligible.

"Croror? Is'll pot?" Lewrie mimicked, cupping a hand behind an ear and shrugging at that worthy. "What the Devil does he mean by that, I ask you? Must be a Welsh insult," he japed to his own officers.

"Come . . . up . . . to . . . *pistol* . . . *shot*!" Grafton's senior officer cried, again, all but screeching this time, and waving an arm to direct them to sidle up alongside *Grafton*, almost hull-to-hull.

"Ease a spoke or two o' lee helm, Mister Langlie," Lewrie said, tossing back his boat cloak so the single gold epaulet of his rank on his right shoulder could be seen, as *Proteus* tentatively angled a bit to larboard, closing the distance between the ships to about twenty or so yards. "Ah, *there's* the bugger," he muttered under his breath.

Capt. Sir Tobias Treghues, Baronet, had thrown back the wings of his own cloak, to display his pair of epaulets, with his chin high, as if he'd smelled something rank. Treghues had always been lean and tall, and so he still was, though his aristocratic face was thinner in the cheeks than Lewrie recalled, and there *was* a hint of the beginning of a gotch-gut 'tween groin and chest that strained his pristine white waist-coat, the sign of good living, Lewrie surmised, once Treghues had inherited his father's estates and title . . . though Lewrie also could recall that Treghues was the *first* son from a poor holding, forced to sea to earn the better part of his living.

Lewrie lifted his cocked hat to doff it in salute, and after a moment, Treghues lifted his in response, revealing that his formerly dark brown locks had receded above his temples, and were now streaked like a badger's pelt with grey.

"*Captain* Alan Lewrie, is it?" Treghues shouted across, after he had replaced his hat on his head. "Will wonders never cease!"

"To the life, sir!" Lewrie shouted back, wondering what sort of answer one could really make to that opening sally. He would have said that it was good to see Treghues, again, but didn't have a clue whether the man was in the proper half of his wits to accept it.

"You are *late*, sir!" Treghues primly said.

"Only got our orders yesterday, sir, and had to wait on the wind in Saint Helen's Patch!" Lewrie replied, his own hands cupped to make a trumpet. "I *thought*

I'd catch you up, at sea, once the wind arose from the East." *I'm* tryin' *t'be jolly*, he told himself.

"You should deal with your signals midshipmen, Captain Lewrie!" Treghues instructed. "They are . . . slack in their duties!"

"Dead downwind of you, sir, all signals were edge-on to us!" he explained, "The leading seventy-four did not repeat them!"

"Just like the old days!" Treghues seemed to scoff at that. "As I recall, you *always* had glib and ready answers!"

And bugger you, too, ye prim turd! Lewrie silently fumed.

"Take station out yonder, sir!" Treghues cried, pointing off to the Southwest corner of the convoy. "Tell Captain Hazelhurst, of the *Chloe* sloop, that he is to re-position himself ahead and to larboard of *Horatius*!"

"Just asking, sir, but my orders did not list all the ships in the escort!" Lewrie yelled over to him. "May I assume *Horatius* is the van sevety-four?"

"Aye, she is!" Treghues shouted, sounding both impatient and petulant together. "You will learn them soon enough! Make all haste to your proper station, Captain Lewrie! It is growing *dark*, sir!"

"Aye aye, sir!" Lewrie replied, doffing his hat once more, in sign of departure; and, hopefully, that his "joyful" *rencontre* with a shipmate of old was mercifully at an end.

"Clew up, Mister Langlie . . . Spanish Reefs, to slow us. Helmsmen, helm hard up and slew a knot or two off us," Lewrie snapped.

Proteus swung wide away, acting as if she'd been stung by the flagship. Course sails were briefly gathered up in their centres to spill wind, until she'd fallen far-enough astern of *Grafton* to avoid a collision when she swung Sou'-Sou'easterly, putting the wind on her larboard quarter to fall down towards the distant sloop of war, clews freed, and her course sails now drawing taut and full.

"Me pardons, sor," Midshipman Larkin meekly muttered, wringing his hands over his supposed faults. "But I really couldn't read 'em."

"No one could," Lewrie gently told him. "Not your fault."

"Uhm, not a *horrid* beginning, was it, Captain?" Langlie queried in a soft voice at his captain's elbow. "After what you said of . . ."

"But not a good'un, either, Mister Langlie," Lewrie resignedly replied, turning to look astern at the flagship in the gathering dusk. "I fear this'll be a hellish-long voyage. And feel *twice* as long."

CHAPTER ELEVEN

"Signal from the flag, sir . . . our number!" Midshipman Gamble sang out, with a heavy brass day-glass to one eye.

"*Damn* it!" Capt. Alan Lewrie spat, and thumped a fist on the cap-rail of the larboard quarterdeck bulwark for good measure, bleakly muttering under his breath, "What the bloody *flamin'* Hell does he want *this* time?" Before turning to face Midshipman Gamble he took a moment to re-collect the proper nautical stoicism, heaving a deep sigh.

"Aye, Mister Gamble?" Lewrie enquired, with what a disinterested observer might mistake for bland and idle curiosity. His play-acting was wasted on Midshipman Gamble, for that young worthy had clapped the telescope back to one eye, and had screwed the other shut, intent upon the distant HMS *Grafton*'s hoists. Lewrie was, therefore, allowed to scowl, taking note that the First Lieutenant, Mr. Langlie, and Bosun Pendarves, with whom he was discussing the renewal of chafing gear to save the currently-strung running rigging, both lifted their eyes in sympathy, and pointedly looked away.

"Take Station . . . Alee, no . . . Ahead," Mr. Gamble interpreted, after a quick peek at the sheaf of unique signals that Capt. Treghues had composed whilst they were hammering their way Sutherly across the dangerous Bay of Biscay, just in case the French raiders had managed to snag a copy of that month's code book. To simply obtain their copy of the convoy's code had required them to go close-aboard *Grafton* and put a boat down to fetch them; into *Proteus*'s captain's hand, only, in the middle of a roaring Westerly winter gale!

Once soaked to the skin and nigh-drowned, Lewrie had clambered up *Grafton*'s side to the entry-port whilst the line-of-battle ship had ponderously rolled, pitched, heaved, and even seemed to "wiggle," only to be greeted by the First Lieutenant who had given him the signals, wrapped in oil-skin, then sent right back into his swooping boat, with nary a sign of Treghues to be seen! Lewrie didn't imagine that Capt. Treghues had *meant* for him to perish . . . but, the sight of his demise *might* have fetched their senior officer up from below to do a little "what a pity" horn-pipe!

". . . five miles leeward of convoy, sir," Mr. Gamble concluded.

"Crack on sail, Mister Langlie, all to the royals," Lewrie said.

"Very good, sir," Langlie replied. "More chafing gear, Mister Pendarves, once we're settled down. For now, I'd admire did you pipe 'All Hands.' "

"And here we go, again," Lewrie muttered, turning to stomp aft and peer 'cross the quarterdeck at *Grafton,* now up on their starboard bows, and about five miles distant. Could he really shoot fire from his eyes like an ancient Greek god, the flagship would explode before he blinked, all his problems immolated in a towering ball of flames.

It had been like this for weeks, going on for the better part of two months since the rendezvous in mid-Channel. Did the shallows or rocky shoals of the Breton coast need scouting for fear of lurking Frog warships or privateers, one could count on *Proteus* to do it; were any of the towering East Indiamen dawdling astern or straying too far away, the safest wager would be that *Grafton* would hoist their number as the ship to dash off and play "whipper-in." Did one of their merchantmen lose spars or sails in the generally horrid weather in the Bay of Biscay or off the equally-belligerent Spanish coasts, it was usually HMS *Proteus,* and Lewrie, given the task of giving her both close escort and succour, to the point that Lewrie's carefully hoarded supply of bosun's stores, sail canvas, light upper mast, and yardarm replacements had been sorely depleted . . . and would any of the other warships among the escort force whip round a share-out? Hell no, of course.

In point of fact, the only signal that *Grafton* had not hoisted was "Captain Repair On Board," and an invitation to supper, as was made to every other warship captain, and even to some of the "better-behaved" Indiamen.

The third time I blink, she blows to smithereens, Lewrie fantasised, and feeling a bit of disappointment when *Grafton* did not, after a last shutting and snapping-open of his eyes.

Their trade was now well South of the Tropic of Cancer, steering mostly Sou'-Sou'west with the weakening Nor'east Trades fine on their larboard quarters, to churn out enough Southing in mid-Atlantic so the Westward-flowing

Equatorial Current did not slosh them too far over to the New World and onto the shoulder of South America, where they could end embayed against the coasts, and hit bows-on by the Sou'east Trades. It was theoretically possible to shave the Cape Verde Islands without being forced too far West, then do a long and labourious tacking course direct to St. Helena, if the weather allowed, though that would require fighting the Equatorial Current *and* the Trades all the way.

Anything t'make this hellish voyage shorter, pray Jesus! Lewrie fervently prayed, and quite often, at that.

The easier way, so their Sailing Master, Mr. Winwood, insisted, would be to let the current and winds waft them West'rd, as far South as the bleak and lonely St. Paul's Rocks, then haul their wind to fall down upon Cape St. Roque for a landfall, and coast South to Recife, in neutral Portuguese Brazil. But, somehow Lewrie just knew by then that Capt. Sir Tobias Treghues, Bart., would demand that they do things his way . . . the hard way. He was charged with convoying the Indiamen to St. Helena, and by God, that's where he'd escort them.

Besides, heading over to Recife would require that their trade would have to run down the coast of Brazil, then down the hostile shore of the Spanish possessions, 'til they could strike the strong Easterly winds round the 40th Latitude, "The Roaring Fourties," using them to be gusted over to the Southern tip of Africa, and exposed along their way to the odd Spanish or far-roaming French warships or privateers.

At least the weather's warmer, Lewrie could console himself.

Though it was mid-December, and the Atlantic was still a lively place, and the skies were rarely completely clear enough for reliable sun or star sights, the seas *were* a cheerier blue, and the rising and setting of the sun each day was dramatically and colourfully tropical. Equally dramatic were the height of the waves and the spacing between their sets that they encountered, which made both deep-laden Indiamen and sleek men o' war wallow, soar, and snuffle atop them.

One blessing to that moderation in the weather was that Lewrie no longer had need of his coal stove for heat during the days, but for the rare night when the wind had a nip to it after sundown, and most times, one of Caroline's quilts, and the cats, made his swaying bed-cot snug and cozy.

God, but the thought of even an extra week, an extra day, more in Treghues's company was enough to curdle his piss, and even the sudden turn of speed that *Proteus* was now displaying could not cheer him, even were they ordered to take station a blessed five sea-miles ahead and apart. And, Lewrie dourly speculated, once at St. Helena, they'd take aboard wood and water, then turn the bulk of the escort force on a course for England, leaving but one ship of the line and perhaps no more than two lighter ships to see them all the way to Cape Town; and there was the strong possibility (a hellish-gloomy one!) that Treghues would choose his frigate to be his goat. Had not Twigg as much as said that he was on his way—all the way!—to Africa? And, had that perversely mischievious man sent a letter to Treghues of Lewrie's need to be far away from England, perhaps had intimated the *why* of it, and had chortled over the thought of a primly-outraged Treghues deciding to make Lewrie's life under his authority a living Hell? He wouldn't put such dastardy beyond Mr. Zachariah Twigg . . . damn him!

"And . . . belay ev'ry inch of that!" Lt. Langlie bellowed, satisfied with the set and angle of the sails, at last, bringing Lewrie back to a *somewhat* pleasing reality. HMS *Proteus* now had a "bone in her teeth," her cutwater, forefoot, and bows smashing a mustachio of white foam below her bowsprit and jib-boom, the seas creaming either side of her hull, and spreading a wide, white highway in her wake. In comparison to the plodding merchantmen and other escorts bound closely to them, *Proteus* seemed the only vessel under way, with the slow ships looking as if they merely tossed and wallowed in place. The convoy's best speed—the speed of the slowest to which all the others conformed—was no better than five or six knots, while *Proteus* was in her element with the Trades on her best point of sail from nigh-astern. A quick cast of the log showed her already making nine knots, easily able to better that at the next cast, and attain ten or better. East India Company captains were even more conservative than most civilian merchant masters; they had priceless cargoes to safeguard, and paying passengers (some of them rich, titled, and well-connected, and Members of The Board, to boot!) who demanded coddling, so "dash" simply wasn't in their Sailing Directions. They plodded mostly under "plain sail" in daylight, and dramatically reduced canvas after sundown, and drove him to testily impatient, leg-jiggling fits.

Savour it, savour it, Lewrie chid himself, determined to take as much fleeting joy of their temporary freedom as possible.

"Will ye take a cup o' tea, sir?" Aspinall enquired, making his rounds aft from the galley with his ever-present steaming pot.

"Tea'd be capital, Aspinall, just capital!" Lewrie replied with relish, allowing his body to loose the Treghues-inspired tension of his back, neck, and jaws. Once he'd gotten a battered tin cup of tea in his hands, he turned aft to look astern, going so far as to slouch like the veriest lubber against the bulwarks. The freshness of the stern winds kissed his cheeks; and, there was the gladsome sight of HMS *Grafton* as she slowly dropped astern, going hull-down in *Proteus*'s wake.

"Mister Langlie?" Lewrie announced in a quizzical tone, and with his head cocked to one side.

"Love a cup, sir," the First Lieutenant replied, mistaking that quizzical tone as an invitation, and grinning cheerfully wolfish.

"Oh, that, too, but . . ." Lewrie added, "once we're the requisite five sea-miles alee of *Horatius* yonder, instead of reducing sail again, I think we should weave a zig-zag course under full sail. We could cover a wider swath of ocean that way."

"Of course, sir," Langlie said, holding a cup for Aspinall as he poured it brim-ful. "Ah, thankee kindly!"

"And, before Bosun Pendarves overhauls the chafing gear, let us also see to the dead-eyes. On this tack, we may re-tension the shrouds on the lee side, first, then wear and tighten the starboard shrouds as they become the lee stays."

"Very good, sir," Langlie said with his hot cup just below his lips, and blowing to cool his first sip.

"We've not had a chance to exercise at the artillery of late, either," Lewrie further decided. "Once we're all ataunt-to, I'd like the rest of the Forenoon be spent at live-firing the windward guns of both broadside batteries, depending on which tack we stand. A little more work to run them out up a sloping deck, but good practice for our people, don't you think, sir?"

"I do indeed, Captain," Langlie dutifully responded, as if he'd *ever* demur with a hearty "Hell, no, what a daft idea, sir!," no matter *what* a captain might dream up. "Good physical exercise, too, sir," he added.

"Who knows, Mister Langlie, the crew might even enjoy the extra exertion!" Lewrie said with a chuckle. "Full sail, hearty breezes . . . and no more bloody . . . *plodding!* . . . might perk them right up. By God, it does me! All of a sudden, I feel as gingery as a feagued horse!"

"Bow to stern, by numbers . . . fire!" Mr. Carling, the Master Gunner, bellowed over the roar of wind and water, and the starboard gun-captains jerked their lanyards, tripping the flintlock igniters of the starboard battery's 12-pounders one at a time. As soon as a gun fired, the first and second loaders dashed 'cross the deck to the guns waiting down the larboard side. The gun-captains and hands on the tackles stayed at their stations at the starboard guns long enough to overhaul any potential tangles in the recoil and run-out lines; the smoking vents were checked by leather-guarded thumbs as the rammer men swabbed out with sopping wet sheep's wool sponges; once the tubes were safe to handle, tackle-men, who normally didn't handle loading, got a bit of cross-training inserting cloth powder bags and ramming them home to the rears of the tubes, at choosing the best round-shot from the racks about each main deck hatchway or the thick rope shot garlands between each piece. They then ran their guns up to the port sills once fresh shot had been inserted down the muzzles and tamped down atop the powder bags, stoppering the blocks so they would not roll back free, then abandoned the starboard pieces to join the men who had been readying the larboard battery.

"Wear, Mister Langlie," Lewrie ordered.

While the gun crews panted and gasped, the brace, sheet, and sail tenders went to their stations once more, and *Proteus* was worked 'cross the stern winds, again, the fourth time in a half-hour. And, as those Trade Winds swung round onto the larboard quarter, and the deck began to heel in the opposite direction, Mr. Carling was there to cry for the ready-loaded larboard battery to prime and cock and stand ready.

"Signal, sir!" Midshipman Gamble called from the taffrails. "A 'Repeat' from *Horatius* . . . our number. 'Suspend Action,' and 'Conserve Powder And Shot,' sir!"

"Damn that man!" Lewrie griped under his breath, hands gripped white-knuckled on the forward quarterdeck railings overlooking the gun-deck and waist. "Aw, Dad!" he said louder, for all to hear. "You just *never* let me have a *bit* o' fun!" Loud enough for his gunners and sail tenders to hear, which drew a hearty laugh at his good imitation of an adolescent's peevish whine. "Very well, Mister Langlie. Secure guns, seal the ports, and insert tompions. Drill's done. Have Mister Coote fetch a fresh scuttle-butt up from below so the hands can slake their thirsts. We'll stay on this point of sail for a while, too, once you've gotten everything flaked or flemished down. Mister Gamble?"

"Sir!"

"Signal to *Grafton* . . ." Lewrie began, then paused.

Buss my blind cheeks, ye spiteful bastard, Lewrie considered; *Go shit in yer cocked hat an' call it a brown tie-wig?*

"Signal 'Acknowledged,' Mister Gamble," Lewrie directed with a weary, and much-put-upon, sigh. *No way t'put* that *in code,* he thought.

Six Bells chimed at the forecastle belfry, and ships' boys turned the hour and half-hour watch glasses; eleven in the morning, almost the end of the Forenoon, and a half-hour from when any Forenoon drills would end, anyway, and the rum-issue ceremony would be held.

"Mister Carling?" Lewrie shouted down to the Master Gunner. "I will join you once the guns are secured to your satisfaction, and see what needs doing, in your estimation."

"Aye aye, Captain!" Carling shouted back, and Lewrie was sure that the Master Warrant Gunner would have his people filling that half-hour 'til "Up Spirits" was piped with greasing, sponging, and prissy fussing about tackles and blocks. With Lewrie by his side during the inspection, Carling would most likely find a way to wheedle more goods from Bosun Pendarves's stores, as well, and the much-put-upon Bosun still had that worn-out chafing gear to rig this morning; perhaps that task would fill the better part of the afternoon, if nothing else came up . . . or Capt. Treghues spotted it and chaffered Lewrie for its lack. Of a sudden, Lewrie was determined that it would be done before *Grafton* ordered them back within "close-telescoping" distance!

The bosun's calls twittered in unison as "Clear Decks, And Up Spirits" was piped. The red-rum keg with the King's seal painted on it in gilt came up from below, and the hands queued up for their sailors' anodyne, loafing and nattering each other in "matey" camaraderie about sips or gulpers owed, debts already paid, or had they been forgotten. A pair of Lt. Devereux's fully-uniformed Marines, complete with muskets, escorted the keg forrud, behind the young boy drummer beating a jaunty roll to announce its coming. Now that duties were done for a time, and all the hands expected for the following half-hour was their call below to their mid-day meal, it was a welcome bit of idle leisure.

Lewrie paced along the windward quarterdeck bulwarks, from the larboard ladderway to the main deck, to the taffrails and signal flag lockers right aft, his undress coat and hat discarded in his own sort of casual leisure, readying himself for participation in the measure of the sun at Noon Sights, when all his commission officers, and the Sailing Master, and his students, the midshipmen, would ply sextants together, and, at the first chime of Eight Bells ending the Forenoon, record their sums on slates or foolscap paper, then perform the "mysteries" of navigation.

Proteus was still under all sail, cracking along quite nicely, most pleasingly. This far South, the day even began to feel a touch more tropically warm, moderated by the winds, and Lewrie untied his neck-stock and opened his shirt collars. He leaned on his hands atop the taffrails for a bit of lonely peace from the demands of his ship, and his senior officer's pique, right by the larboard stern lanthorn, slowly shaking his head at the far-off convoy.

The lead 74, HMS *Horatius*, still plodded along at the convoy's head, with only her sails, at times a sliver of her upperworks, visible when pent atop a rising swell. Astern of her lay the four short columns of Indiamen, two-by-two in line-ahead, with only their beige courses, tops'ls, and t'gallants in sight. The entire gaggle was now about five miles off, as ordered, but an equal five miles off *Proteus*'s larboard quarter, and slowly falling to full astern.

Lewrie didn't relish the idea of interrupting the rum issue, but in the few minutes between the issue's end and the pipe for Dinner, they would have to come about one more time, he decided, before they sailed too far astray of the convoy's mean course. Once settled on a long starboard tack once more, they could then eat in peace.

"Deck, there!" the mainmast lookout shrilled of a sudden. "Sail, *ho*! *One* sail, *one* point off th' *larboard* bows!" he sing-songed.

Damn the rum, and victuals, too! Lewrie turned about, looking outward, as if he could spot their mysterious interloper from the deck. "How . . . bound?" he cried back, hands cupped round his mouth. "How . . . far . . . away?"

"Tops'ls an' t'gallants, sir, 'tis all I see! Hull-down, she is, an' . . . bound West!" the lookout decided, after discerning which were the leaches of the stranger's upper sails, and how they were cupped to gather wind.

That'd make her about eight or nine miles off, Lewrie decided to himself, nodding in agreement with the lookout as he pictured a "plot" in his head. They were sailing Sou'-Sou'east, with the Trades fine on the quarter, which put the stranger due South of them. Bound West, did the lookout say? They were close enough to the Cape Verde Islands for it to be a ship bound for Brazil from there, scudded along by wind and current. It could be an innocent merchantman, even a British-flagged ship, or . . . it could be a French or Spanish warship or privateer outbound from taking on wood and water, and seeking prey.

"Mister Gamble?" Lewrie shouted, stomping his way forward. "A signal to *Grafton* for *Horatius* to repeat . . . 'Strange Sail, Due South. Will Investigate.' Mister Langlie? Soon as dammit, put the ship about three points alee to South by West. There's just enough time for our people to eat, but *whoever* it is down yonder, we will beat to Quarters when we've fetched her hull-up!"

CHAPTER TWELVE

"Just what in the name of God is *that*?" Lt. Langlie asked once they had gotten within hull-up distance of the strange vessel that they had spent most of the afternoon pursuing Westward. The closer they got to her, the odder she'd looked.

First had come the sight of her royals and t'gallants above the sea's sharp-edged horizon; some were pale, jade *green*, others were such a pale red they seemed *pink*.

"Faded, perhaps, sir," Lt. Catterall had speculated with a leery expression, as if he'd just been presented a bowl of dog-spew at a two-penny ordinary. "Might've been dark green and red, once?"

"Well, we know about *fading* . . ." Lt. Adair had commented with a snorty chuckle, obviously referring to his captain's unfortunate choice of light cotton uniform coats he'd had made by a Kingston, Jamaica, tailor, which had bled for months before fading to a very pale and washed-out blue, even where white fabric or gilt lace had been intended.

"*Arr,* Mister Adair" had been Lewrie's comment to that sally.

Next had come full sight of her tops'ls and courses, one of them—her main course—was vertically striped like pillow ticking in a red, white, and blue, all now reduced to pink, parchment, and off-white, whilst her fore course was a more conventional mildewed and sunburned light tan, but bore some large design painted on it.

"Spanish warship?" the Sailing Master had wondered. "They hoist crucifixes to their cross-trees before battle, sir, and paint crosses on their fighting sails."

"Must martyr more than a few sailors, too," Lewrie had replied, "when someone shoots the big wood crosses free t'drop on their decks."

Last had come the sight of her hull, and the very *size* of her, as long as a First Rate fleet flagship, as towering from waterline to midships cap-rails as the loftiest Indiaman . . . but from the normally black-tarred gunn'ls upwards painted a vivid blue, all picked out with bright yellow paint on rails, round her entry-port, beakhead rails, and twin stern galleries and quarter-galleries, and decorated along her upperworks with what looked to be yellow-painted *rosettes*!

"Gun-ports, sir," Lt. Langlie had suggested. "Old, *Elizabethan* style gun-ports, with fancy woodwork framing them. Might even mount a side battery of dragon-mouthed cannon, like the Chinese. What in the *world*?"

"Garish," Catterall dismissed.

"Tawdry," Mr. Winwood sneered.

"Whore transport?" Lewrie whispered, his face creasing broadly into a grin. Which had required him to explain the jape played on the younger officers of the gun-room when he was aboard HMS *Cockerel* in the Med in '93. Though, for a moment, the very strange ship had put him in mind of those "floating emporiums" moored on the South bank of the Mississippi opposite the wharves of New Orleans, the aging hulks that served as nearly duty-free stores for Spanish, British, and American merchants; all of them had been just as gaudily painted, and so plastered with an assortment of signboards or sales' broadsheets that it had been hard to make out what colour they actually were, underneath.

"Sir!" Midshipman Grace called from the mizen shrouds, where he had climbed with a telescope. "They've *boarding* nets strung from every yardarm! Nets strung to catch falling blocks and such from aloft, too!"

"Close enough," Lewrie snapped, as that *outré* seagoing joke was within a single mile, his amusement fading. "Mister Langlie, I'd admire did you beat the ship to Quarters!"

"Aye aye, sir!"

"Mister Larkin, you're signals midshipman of the watch?"

"Aye, sor . . . sir," their little Bog-Irish imp soberly replied.

"Hoist colours," Lewrie ordered, "and stand by with our Number, and private signal. Does that gaudy fraud try to bluff us, she'll not have *this* month's proper reply."

As the crew went about stripping the ship for action, lumbering furniture, sea-chests, and flimsy objects deep below, hanging their own anti-boarding nets and "protectors" aloft across the gangways and the gun positions against falling wreckage, *Proteus* changed her course to reduce the angle at which she closed the odd "duck" of a ship, baring her larboard broadside to her, and starting to steal a little of the Nor'east Trade from her sails by placing her in the frigate's "wind shadow." The course change also gave *Proteus*'s gunners time to ready their pieces, light the last-ditch slow-match igniters, and open their gun-ports. As the strange ship loomed up within a half a mile of them, gun-captains raised their free arms to indicate that they were prepared in all respects to fire into her the moment the command was given.

"Colours and private signal, Mister Larkin," Lewrie snapped, as he fiddled with his sword and brace of double-barreled pistols freshly fetched from his great-cabins by his Cox'n, Andrews. The Royal Navy ensign broke high aft of her spanker sail, with a match on her foremast halliards; a string of five code flags soared up the mizen halliards as bundles, which opened like blossoms at a single twitch on the light binding line. *Now we'll see just who ye are, ye . . . sonofabitch!* Alan Lewrie thought in amazement for . . .

At the *very* last moment, a British merchantman's Red Ensign shot up her after running stay, and a blue house flag soared to the top of the strange ship's mainmast, trimmed in bright yellow at every border, and bearing yellow masks of Tragedy and Comedy!

"Think I can make out her name, sir," Lt. Catterall commented, busy with his telescope. "There, on her quarter board . . . *Festival*."

"Mine arse on a . . ." Lewrie gravelled, as dozens of people suddenly appeared along the *Festival*'s bulwarks and rails, waving, shouting, and . . . cheering? Some of them, most skimpily dressed in the tightest garments, scrambled up those "boarding nets" and scampered high aloft . . . to begin swinging back and forth above their "protector" nets. Lewrie lifted his own telescope to behold a white-painted, and loosely-garbed, Fool, who plucked his large red pom-pom "buttons" down the front of his smock, and hit himself in the head with what appeared to be a pig bladder!

"God A'mighty, 'tis a circus!" Ordinary Seaman Liam Desmond, on the larboard gangways, cried. "Look, Pat!" he called to his thicker-witted compatriot, Ordinary Seaman Furfy. "A seagoin' *circus*, arrah!"

"Sonofa . . . a whole afternoon chasin' bleedin', tom-noddy . . . twits!" Lewrie fumed, slamming the tubes of his glass shut. "Play a jape on *me*, will ye, ye . . . *clowns*!"

Wonder if anybody'd fuss much if I just sank 'em, anyway! Lewrie wondered; *There's bound t'be* mimes *yonder. Mimes, clowns, fools, and "Captain Sharps." Might be doin' the world a favour!*

"Gawd, they's *wimmen* thar!" a sailor in the afterguard gawped.

"Deck, there!" the mainmast lookout shouted. "Nekkid wimmen!"

"Still!" Lewrie howled to shut down the bedlam. It wasn't his way to run a totally silent warship, as some captains might, where no talking or unnecessary sound beyond the bosuns' pipes calls passed an order, but . . . might this be a sly ruse to get him within gun range, all unsuspecting and almost completely "disarmed," then . . . ?

"Silence on deck, silence all!" Lt. Langlie sternly shouted.

Lewrie jerked the tubes of his telescope open to full extension again, so angrily he could hear the brass grinding against the stops, and lifted it to his eye. There were even *more* clowns, all prancing about in a dance that looked inspired by St. Vitus, giving each other the odd bash with their pig bladders, turning St. Catherine's Wheels . . . the nearly-nude people aloft . . . no. They wore costumes sewn so snugly that they at first had *appeared* nude, but he could now see that they wore tights and similar upper garments, with equally-snug wraps about their groins as skimpy as a Hindoo's underdrawers. And, they were swooping to and fro on swings hung from the masts, leaping from one to the other as agilely as so many squirrels. Two or three twirled *horizontally* from taut ropes being swung by people on deck, and even a few were playing at sliding down the braces of the sails, riding perilously from the royal yard and the stiff windward edge of the sail to the t'gallant, to the tops'l, then down the edge of the course!

"Wonder if they'll charge admission, heh heh," Lt. Catterall quipped to the helmsmen.

"I said *still*!" Lewrie snapped. "Mister Larkin. Do they have this month's private merchant code?"

"Uh, nossir." Larkin sobered from being lost in amusement.

"Then make a hoist," Lewrie ordered. "Fetch-to at once. Do not use the trade's private signals . . . use the common book."

"Aye, sor."

And *damned* if a brace of clowns didn't leap atop the quarterdeck bulwarks, make exaggerated gestures of cupping their ears, then waving large handkerchiefs and shouting, "Yoo-Hoo!," even blowing kisses!

"Trumpet!" Lewrie barked, taking the one that Lt. Langlie meekly offered. He turned back to the rails, lifted the speaking-trumpet to his lips, took a deep breath, and *bawled* across the narrowing range between both ships, "Fetch-to, or I will blow you out of the water!"

He heard a faint "Yoo-Hoo!" returned, as one of the clowns got his hands on a speaking trumpet, too, though at least some of the men on the *Festival*'s quarterdeck realised that Lewrie was serious, and tried to claw the fellow back down, and retrieve the brass instrument.

"Mister Langlie!" Lewrie snarled. "Larboard chase-gun! Put a round-shot under that bastard's bows. *Close* under!"

BANG! The 9-pounder chase-gun on the larboard forecastle went off terrier-sharp, and in the blink of an eye a "feather" of disturbed spray leaped into being right beneath *Festival*'s jib-boom, collapsing in a salty mist over her own beakhead rails.

At least the clowns stopped crying, "Yoo-Hoo!"

"God's *sake*!" a man Lewrie took to be the ship's master cried in alarm from her quarterdeck. "We're *British*! Hold yer fire for the love o' *God*, sir!" He lowered his "recovered" speaking-trumpet, and took off his old-style tricorne hat, mopping his forehead on his free sleeve. "Merchantman *Festival*, three days outta the Cape Verdes, and bound for Recife!" he continued, with a fresher breath.

"Fetch-to, *Festival*!" Lewrie yelled back. "I will inspect your papers!" To his officers, he ordered in a softer voice, "Lower away a cutter, and muster a boarding party."

Lewrie completed his climb up the battens and man-ropes to the *Festival*'s starboard entry-port, once both ships had fetched-to, cocked up into the Trades at a relative halt. Sailors, acrobats, and women in scanty casual clothing stood about her decks awaiting him, as did her master and mates. A man in a battered old tricorne doffed his hat, and Lewrie began to doff his in return, but . . .

Three white-garbed clowns ran up to "toe the line" along a plank seam; one widely *salaamed* in Arabic fashion, a second banged his head on the deck in a Chinee *kow-tow*, whilst the third parodied bosuns' calls on a nose flute.

"*Don't* make me shoot you!" Lewrie harshly warned the flutist as he gathered a fistful of pom-pommed smock in one hand, and tapped the butt of one of his sashed pistols with the other.

"Gerroutofit!" the ship's master angrily shouted. "Jesus!" he added half under his breath as he came from his quarterdeck to shoo them away. "I'm that sorry for that, sir. That sorry, too, to be such a bother, but we had no idea you were Royal Navy, and ran from you. I am Amos Weed, master of the *Festival*, and you'd be bein' . . . ?"

"Captain Alan Lewrie, sir, of the *Proteus* frigate," Lewrie said, his humours still unsettled by the jeering amusement the circus people expressed as they congratulated the clowns on their jape.

Smells like the cats' sand box, Lewrie told himself as he got a good first whiff of the air aboard the merchantman.

"Our owner, Captain Lewrie," Capt. Weed said, waving at a portly fellow tromping up the starboard ladderway from the waist. "Mister Dan Wigmore, of Wigmore's Travelling Extravangaza."

"'Ow do, sir, 'ow do!" Mr. Wigmore cried as if Lewrie was a long lost brother as he joined them. He was garbed in a bilious green wool tweed coat and *loudly*-embroidered tan waist-coat, a pair of taupe-grey corduroy breeches, and top-boots. He bobbed from the waist jerkily as he doffed a very fashionable, narrow-brimmed "thimble" hat. "An' werry glad we are t'see ye, Cap'm! Daniel Wigmore . . . but I 'spects ye know o' our Extravaganza a'ready. Th' finest, most h'amazin' portable show h'ever ye did see!" Wigmore declared in a pronounced Cockney accent. "Circus! Bareback riders . . . h'acrobats an' h'animal h'acts. Dramas s'tragic they'll make ye blub, comedies s'funny ye'll split yer sides laughin'! Jugglers, fortune tellin', death-defyin' h'aerialists, an' feats o' magic done by mystic *gurus* o' th' fabled Far h'East, a li'l bit o' h'ev'rythin' under th' sun, *and* a men-*ag*-erie gathered from th' four corners o' th' *world*, aha!"

"Lewrie, Royal Navy," he said in stiff reply. "We have—"

"An' 'aven't ye come in Puddin' Time, Cap'm Lewrie!" Mr. Wigmore energetically prattled on. "Wot a wonder, h'arrivin' h'at th' werry instant in our 'our o' need!"

"Need, sir?" Lewrie asked with a snort. "What need?" Damned if he'd give up spare spars and canvas to *this* . . . circus!

"Why, pertection, Cap'm Lewrie, pertection!" Wigmore exclaimed. "We're h'all h'alone out 'ere, an' th' wide ocean full o' two-legged sharks o' th' French an' Spanish persuasion, like. Now ye're 'ere, we kin sail t'Recife in comp'ny wif a stout British frigate, so . . ."

"You've seen enemy warships, Captain Weed?" Lewrie demanded of the soberer merchant master, *trying* to ignore Wigmore's patter.

Trying, too, to ignore the semi-exposed charms of the women the *Festival* carried: flaming-hennaed redheads, lithe little blondes, and an assortment of brunette or auburn wenches, who were slowly drifting over to starboard to listen to the conversation . . . or flirt with the file of Marines and the sailors from his boat crew. One of 'em . . .

"Seen *sev'ral* odd sail, sir," Capt. Weed told him, "and we ran from a few that gave me the odd itch. *Festival*'s not a swift sailer, laden as we are, but a sure ol' girl. Can't rightly say they *were* warships, but none pursued us too long. And, we've nought but eight old pieces, and them but puny, converted Army six-pounders, as like as not t'burst, and none o' my hands what ye'd call proper gunners . . ."

"Mmhmm," Lewrie said with a sage nod, more than half-distracted.

"Frets me critters somethin' 'orrid, sir!" Wigmore bemoaned at his elbow. "Oh, 'tis 'ard, shippin' 'orses an' such, an' them a pitch away from broken legs, an' h'after *years* o' trainin' that'd be wasted. 'Cept on wot Cap'm Weed calls a 'reach,' th' h'upset . . . damme! There they go, again. An' h'after we just got 'em settled, too."

Evidently, lying fetched-to didn't suit his "menagerie," either, for Lewrie heard a sudden cacophony of grunts, roars, bleating goats, burbling *somethings*, fierce moos or hee-haws, yelps, bugles, and enough dog barks for a whole hunting pack. One set off the others, then some parrot squawks and shrill peacock cries arose, too.

"Might ye be good h'enough t' h'excuse me, Cap'm Lewrie. I've beasts t'settle, damn 'em," Wigmore griped, then scampered down to the main deck and down a midships hatchway, bawling for his keepers.

"Tell me ye're bound for Recife, sir," Capt. Weed nigh-implored.

"We're, ah . . ." Lewrie temporised, loath to tell Weed too much. "Perhaps, sir. Bound South, at any rate. But, let me ask you, sir . . . what took you to the Cape Verdes, and from where did you sail, before you fetched 'em?"

"As to yer second question first, sir," Weed explained, "we'd just done a whole year o' shows all up and down the coast of the United States of America, ev'ry seaport city from Maine to Savannah, down in Georgia. Right successful, too, and huge crowds ev'rywhere we lit. The Yankee Doodles are starved for entertainment, I expect. We did a show or two in the Bahamas, then planned to head South, ourselves, for Cape Town and the Far East. *Could've* fetched Recife, but Wigmore was leery of how the dramas'd go over in Brazil, with so few folk speakin' English, there, for none of *our* folk speak Portuguese, e'en the fortune tellers, *and*, bein' a Catholic country, they might not've taken kindly to our costumes, neither. A bit . . . scant, for some tastes, ah . . ."

Lewrie could see the sense in that worry, as he let himself be distracted by the women clad in muslin or sheer cambric underskirts and chemises, exchanging recited lines from slim booklets he took for the scripts of a new dramatic work. One of 'em that particularly caught his eye was an exotic, foreign-looking girl with raven-dark and long curling hair, high-cheeked features, and a complexion that put him in mind of Spain or the New World. *Bright* amber-brown eyes, or were they hazel, but very attractive, and firm young breasts straining against her loose chemise, damned *impressive* and *full* "poonts" . . . !

"As to yer first question," Capt. Weed continued, dragging him back to reality, "we hit the Equatorial Current, and the passage turned longish . . . so much so we were runnin' low on water for the critters, Cap'm Lewrie."

"There's been drought in the Cape Verdes, the last fourty years, Captain

Weed," Lewrie scoffed, his un-formed suspicions of such an odd ship revived, and took a moment to glance over his shoulder to see if his Marines or sailors had found anything piratical in their searches.

"Aye, and so there is, sir," Capt. Weed sadly agreed. "I *told* Mister Wigmore it'd be iffy, but . . . The few folk still livin' on those isles were damn' tight with what they had, too. Sold us barely enough t'fetch Recife, after all, then shooed us outta port, nigh at cannon-point. Wouldn't even let us land the beasts for exercise, nor any of our people, either! Got a low opinion o' circus and theatre people in the Cape Verdes! I *hope* we can make it all the way to Recife, and we just *may*, do we not meet slack winds, or have to run from any more of those strange sail. We'd *much* appreciate escort, Cap'm Lewrie, do ye be bound that way," he almost pleadingly stated.

"We, ah . . ." Lewrie hedged once more, then finally had to spill it. "That would be up to my senior officer, sir, and the East India Company's civilian 'Commodore.' We're part of a rather large escort to a 'John Company' trade. Should the winds suit, those gentlemen may even plan for us to beat our way direct to Saint Helena."

"A 'John Comp'ny' convoy, up to windward of us?" Capt. Weed gladly exclaimed, rubbing his hands together in such an avaricious way that he put Lewrie in mind of a new-day Blackbeard, who had just heard news of tops'ls in the offing. "Though I never heard a good word said o' Saint Helena water, either, nor decent anchorage, that'd be better than swanning about these seas, alone. Aye, 'John Comp'ny' masters'd not discomfit their paying passengers with *too* long a passage, 'thout putting in for fresh stores. *High* on fresh, Cap'm Lewrie . . . manger beasts and wines, flour so they can bake fresh, daily, aha! I'd lay ye any odds ye wish, ye'll fetch Recife *long* before ye see the hills of Saint Helena! Why, by sundown, we'd know one way or t'other!" he happily went on, rubbing his hands together again.

"You know the rules of convoying, sir?" Lewrie had to ask him. "The Acts and Admiralty regulations, that you'd have to post a bond with the Commodore, before. . . ."

"And follow ev'ry rule, aye, Cap'm Lewrie, aye!" Weed replied. "An' Daniel Wigmore's rolling in 'chink,' so the bond'd be no bother. A very profitable bus'ness, is entertainment! 'Tis another reason to wish to join yer convoy, sir . . . there's lashings o' profits hidden in Dan's cabins, most of it in silver coin, so . . ."

Lewrie's interest drifted off, again, as a pack of nigh-naked people swarmed down from aloft where they'd been swinging or leaping about. And, there was that raven-haired girl, again, too, and this time, she was done with reciting her lines, and was leaning against the larboard bulwarks on the opposite gangway, her arms crossed under her breasts, her legs-parted stance through the sheerness of her underskirtings hinting at slim hips, a taut belly, and *long*, fine limbs. A narrow slit of bare flesh was bared 'twixt the waistband of skirt and chemise bottom. Freed of rehearsing, she was frankly and openly *staring* at him, with the slightest hint of a promising smile upon her lips. She began to grin as he stared back at her just as boldly, and her eyes widened, she drew in an expectant, *impressive* breath, before clapping a hand to her mouth, as if she found him as attractive as he found her, felt as "risible" as Lewrie did. Then her grin widened to gape-mouthed, and she *pointed* at him, saying something aside to those other wenches near her (rather *gauche*, that, but who knew *what* foreign girls thought proper, Lewrie wondered), and he half-raised a hand to wave at her, 'til . . .

Something butted the back of his booted calves, something hairy encompassed his lower legs, something as reeky as his cats' sand box after a month's neglect, and he looked back and down.

"*Jesus* fuckin' . . . !" Lewrie screeched, of half a mind to break into a panicky gallop to the taffrails, or leap for *Festival*'s lower yardarms.

"Whuff!" the thankfully leather-muzzled bear said as he tried (thankfully) unsuccessfully to lick and chew on Lewrie's ankles!

". . . Christ!" Lewrie yelped.

"Oh, pay Fredo no mind, Cap'm Lewrie," Capt. Weed told him as he let out a guffaw, "but don't do nothing sudden-like, either. Old Fredo's just curious 'bout a new-come. His teeth are dulled, and his claws've been clipped short. Gentle as a baa-lamb . . . mostly. One of our dancing bears, he is, and ain't he a beauty? Does a whole series o' tricks . . . when we feed him regular. He'll give up and lose interest, in a bit."

"*That'd* be nice!" Lewrie shudderingly said as the bear's great bulk, gentle or no, made him stagger as the beast began to scratch his hairy hide on the back of his thighs.

"Jose! Come do something with Fredo, will ye, *por favor*? He's an Andalusian bear, him and his brother, quite rare where they come from, they are. Raised 'em from cubs, Wigmore did," Weed told him.

"Uh huh?" Lewrie whinged, fearful of taking a deep breath.

"Fredo, *amigo*!" his keeper, Jose, cajoled, coming to take hold of the bear's thick collar. "Chu beeg seelly, leggo de chennleman."

Instead, the bear rose up on his hind feet, laid a heavy paw on Lewrie's right shoulder and epaulet hard enough to make him *sag*, and started to sniff his coat and head all over. Fredo gave him another chummy "Whuff!" and a soft but rasping bawl, then slapped his cocked hat off. At least *that* got him off and *down*!

The bear gave it a lick or two, then skittered it along the gangway like an amusing new toy . . . a football, perhaps. Jose swept it up from him, eliciting another disappointed bawl, and handed it back to Lewrie, towing better than five hundred pounds of furry appetite by the collar like he would a wolfhound.

"He mean no harm, *senor,*" Jose said in a friendly manner, even going so far as to tap the bear on his long snout. "Fredo and Paulo, dey are poosycats. Say jello to de chennlemun, Fredo, say jello!" he urged, and the bear stood up, again, raised a foreleg, and "waved" his paw at Lewrie, uttering another "friendly" squalling bawl that *might* be taken for a pacific greeting . . . did one ignore the paw, the size of a soup bowl!

"Geef heem a scratch on de head, *senor,*" Jose coaxed. "He like de head pat, an' den he be chur vriend. Say jello to my widdle vriend, *senor Capitano.*"

"Uh . . ." Lewrie began to demur, rather shakily it here must be noted, but, so many of *Festival*'s people were watching by then, that spectacular and highly-amused raven-haired wench included, that Lewrie couldn't refuse, so . . . he (tentatively) reached out one hand to stroke the bear's broad head, to dare skritch his fingers in Fredo's coarse, thick fur, knowing that his hand would reek afterward, as if he petted a wild goat or badger, and wouldn't Chalky and Toulon be pleased when he went back aboard, to snuffle, savour, and go gape-mouthed in wonder over such exotic new stinks!

Fredo seemed pleased, giving out a raspy "Whuff " or two.

"So, mightn't ye put in the good word with yer Admiral an' them, Cap'm Lewrie?" Weed asked as Jose mercifully led Fredo away, finally. " 'Bout us joinin' your convoy for a spell?"

"Uh . . ." Lewrie dazedly reiterated, seeing another keeper come up on the main deck, just done leading a burbling, spitting baby camel into the sunshine, and *damned* if he'd pet that! "Perhaps it's be best did we retire to your cabins, Captain Weed, so I may study your manifests, registries, and such."

CHAPTER THIRTEEN

"Absolutely not!" Capt. Sir Tobias Treghues snapped. "A band of seagoing . . . *Gypsies*! Might even be pirates in a gaudier garb."

"Well, *Festival*'s papers are all in order, sir," Lewrie pointed out, with as much deferential patience as he could. "And, while there very well may *be* some Gypsies among the circus folk . . . fortune tellers and such . . . I don't b'lieve we've any pots need mending, nor are there any babies aboard our ships to steal, so . . ."

"Oh, well put, young sir!" Capt. George Clowes hooted, lifting a handkerchief to his mouth as he had himself a good guffaw. Clowes was the senior civilian master of the East India Company "trade," and therefore the temporary "Commodore," who would see them all the way to Calcutta or Bombay, perhaps onwards to Canton in China, too. "We indeed are bound for Recife, Captain Lewrie, and I see no valid reason why the circus ship should not be given our protection, seeing as how we're all going the same way. Really, Sir Tobias . . ." he "tsk-tsked."

"They could have been lurking off the Cape Verdes, just waiting for a fat convoy to come along, sir," Capt. Treghues continued to demur. "If not pirates themselves, perhaps they serve as the eyes and ears for enemy privateers, perhaps a small French raiding squadron. Their claim of water shortage might allow them alongside one of Captain Clowes's vessels to be succoured, and . . ."

"They look slit-eyed dangerous to you, Captain Lewrie?" Clowes asked, giving Treghues a long up-and-down look as if his patience was long, but not limitless.

"I'd not turn my back on their dancing bears, sir," Lewrie told him. "But, my boarding party and I searched the entire ship, looking for anything odd . . . well, *piratical* odd, not outrageous odd . . . and we found nothing amiss. They've but eight light six-pounders, and those are British Army cast-offs. There are only thirty-odd in her crew, and perhaps an hundred circus and theatrical folk, all told. The *Festival*'s master, Captain Weed, possesses but a dozen muskets and fowling pieces, and a dozen rather dubious Sea Pattern pistols, all under lock and key in his great-cabins. Of course, there are boarding pikes and cutlasses in their one arms locker, also locked up securely. Oh, I fancy those sailors of theirs have personal knives, there's a knife-thrower with a small chest full, and a sword-swallower with a small arsenal, and among the 'artists' one'd find pocket pistols and daggers and such. Hat-pins among the women, but . . ."

"And she's a slow sailer, this Captain Weed admitted?" the East India Company captain enquired. He was a trim and spare fellow in his late fourties, rather distinguished looking, and, with the salary of a "John Company" master, dressed extremely well, with a vague attempt at a uniform look that emulated Royal Navy fashion, 'less all the gold lace folderol, and with silver buttons instead of gilt or brass.

"Aye, and there's another reason she should be shunned," Treghues snapped, fidgeting in his leather-covered chair behind his desk in HMS *Grafton*'s great-cabins under her old-fashioned poop. "She'll slow our progress. We'll take *weeks* more to . . ."

"And my Indiamen *won't*, Sir Tobias?" Capt. Clowes tittered, as he shared an amused look with Lewrie. "You've already made sufficient remonstrances for more sail, and quicker progress, sir, and complained of our customary reduction of sail after sundown. 'Bare steerage-way' you called it, I seem to recall? It's the Company's *way*, sir, for the comfort of our paying passengers." Clowes stated more soberly, laying down the law, in a manner of speaking.

A way of speaking that a Royal Navy captain, a putative "Commodore" in his own right with a triangular red pendant to prove it . . . even if it did bear the white ball of an officer not *officially* listed in that rank, yet . . . found both egregious and insufferable, it would appear, from Lewrie's observation this evening, and from his previous service under Treghues.

God knows he *was always smug and insufferable!* Lewrie thought.

Treghues was the son of a poor but titled family, and had been raised with all the deference given to members of the peerage; he had entered the Navy despite being the eldest, for there was little to inherit but the empty title, with "The

Honourable" following his younger rank, and preceding his Christian name. Even so, people *would* tug at their forelocks and doff and scrape to nobility, and . . . unless he had proved himself *monumentally* unsuited . . . would continue to be courted in a midshipmen's mess, the officers' gun-room, or as a captain second but to God. He never *had* been the sort who took disagreement with his notions easily, had ever been sublimely cock-sure of himself, and was primly "strong in the Lord." Lewrie was certain that Capt. Clowes and his casual nature, and his quick, amusing wit, was a constant trial to Treghues. Treghues was the sort who expected pot-holes to be filled before he crossed them, stairs to flatten themselves, and Clowes, and Lewrie himself, were deep, sloppy road ruts and trip-snares!

"If it makes you any easier in your mind, Sir Tobias, perhaps . . . since *Festival* will be as slow as my Indiamen," Clowes suggested, "you could keep her under your guns at the rear of the trade. Where it most certainly appears she will end up."

Were a long-suffering Christian permitted to snarl, slam fists on the desk, perhaps even aspire to rising and kicking cabin furniture, Capt. Treghues looked more than ready to turn from a Job to a Samson in the pagan temple! Crash-bang, and down come the pillars to bury smarmy "John Company" captains under the rubble!

Lewrie could not help himself; he felt a fit of "smarmy" coming on, and let it take wing.

"Besides, Sir Tobias," he said with a sober, straight face, "to allow *Festival* to make the best of her way alone would undermine Orders In Council . . . or was it an Act of Parliament? Can't quite recall its origin, but . . . Thirty-three George the Third, Cee-Sixty-six of Seventeen Ninety-eight. All British merchant vessels . . . and the *Festival* demonstrably *is* . . . must attach themselves to convoys under Royal Navy escort which either go *to* their destination, or as close to it as may be, sir. For a merchant master to do otherwise, he would be subject to a fine of one thousand pounds."

Sir Tobias Treghues did two things simultaneously; he scowled at Lewrie as if he'd turned into a steaming, gore-dripping Beelzebub liable to ruin an armchair, *and* seemed to perk up at the mention of a substantial fine to levy.

"Of course, *Festival,* on her initial voyage to America, *was* in a Halifax convoy," Lewrie explained, hiding his delight at what he had read up on once back aboard *Proteus*. "Sailing alone from one Yankee Doodle port to the next, down to Savannah, Georgia, this last year entire, she was not *strictly* on the high seas, and therefore not liable to the Compulsory Convoy Act, *and* departed Nassau alone for the very good reason that no South-bound convoy originates from the

Bahamas. Captain Weed assures me that it was his intent all along to join any convoy he met which could see him to Recife, Saint Helena, or Cape Town," Lewrie laid out, ticking items off on his fingers. "And, so he has," he concluded, then folded his hands back in his lap, behind his cocked hat.

Pecuniary interest quite flew Treghues's head, and utter disgust for the beslimed Imp of Satan seated before him rose to the fore. His mouth flapped open, then snapped shut with an audible click of teeth.

"I never expected *you* to become a sea-lawyer, Lewrie," Treghues sarcastically drawled, fidgeting a deal more in his chair, and uttering a faint, subdued sound that seemed very much like one of Lewrie's own "patented" "Arrs," perhaps with a slight improvement of Treghues's own devising resembling a parrot's "Rwark!" that he stifled rather well by raising a fist to his lips, as if caught in mid-cough.

"Captain Weed and Mister Wigmore have put up the bond for their passage, sir," Lewrie further explained, reaching into an inner pocket of his coat and withdrawing a letter. "I laid out to them the penalty of failing to obey escort instructions, lagging behind, or departing a convoy without proper leave, sir, and the fines liable for disobeying. As well as the one hundred pounds penalty for not making all efforts to avoid boarding by a foe, or failing to alert the rest of the convoy to such incident, by night or day. Now, as of this hour, *Festival* doesn't possess our private signals book which you devised, nor have they posted the pertinent articles of Thirty-three George the Third, Cee–Sixty-six on a board on their quarterdeck, but . . . perhaps did you send an officer aboard her in the morning with those, one who could ascertain how much they have done to be in compliance with Thirty-three George, and the Compulsory Convoy Act . . . perhaps go yourself, Sir Tobias? To satisfy your worries, for yourself? And, they're circus and theatre folk, sir, so you're bound to be amused."

"Grr-umph!" Treghues thundered into his fist, louder and more acidic than before, fidgeting forward in his chair as if he wished that he could leap across it, take Lewrie by the lapels, and shake him back to subordinate sobriety. That, or slap him senseless!

"Would that suit you, Sir Tobias?" Capt. Clowes innocently asked, though he had a slight trouble with his own throat, it seemed, for he had need for a fist at his lips, too.

"If!" Capt. Treghues barked. "If, ah . . ." he repeated in calmer takings after a moment, "the law *requires* us, requires *them*, rather . . . and, given Commodore Cowles's assent to this *des . . . !* this particular, ah . . . vessel's joining the convoy, then, well . . . hmm," he flummoxed, trailing off whilst trying to

put the best face on abject surrender, or humiliating defeat. "I s'pose we must allow it, though . . ."

"And will they keep *strictly* to themselves, sirs?" came a harsh voice from aft, from Treghues's sleeping space, which was screened off by some rather nice glossy deal partitions and "homey" chintz drapes. "Or, will such low and *amoral* people be allowed to contaminate us *all*?"

It was a female voice, which made Lewrie start and swivel about in his chair (made easier by the slug-trail of satanic slime he'd left in it, perhaps?) to seek the identity of the speaker.

Thought *I saw a woman on the quarterdeck, the first day*, Lewrie told himself; *Damme, did Treghues marry, at last? And does he carry her aboard?*

Long, long ago, when the old HMS *Desperate* had helped evacuate the last British garrison and American Loyalists from Wilmington, North Carolina, Treghues had been rather taken by Caroline Chiswick, had even very clumsily and embarassingly sniffed about her; even more embarassingly trolled about Lewrie to see if the girl might prove willing for him to sling a tentative "woo" at her. Damned near grovelling, he had been, blushing as if it nigh-killed his prim soul to discover what he could of the girl from such a *low* source!

And, did he ever hear that she married me *in '86, I wonder?*

The heavy draperies were pulled back, and the lady in question appeared, with her knitting still in her hands, and both bone needles clutched in a white-knuckled grip like all-conquering Brittania ready to heave spears or cross swords with the foe.

Yoicks, what a bloody horror! Lewrie silently gawped, keeping a level expression on his phyz as he rose from his chair at her entrance. Lady Treghues was the *severe* sort! *Wouldn't care t'run into* her *in a dark alley!* was his thought as he clasped his hat to his breast, and made a "leg" to her, as did Capt. Cowles, which nicety she ignored in her pique. Hair which might have once been lustrous and fetching was now a drab mousey-brown, and drawn back from her face; her face, of a particularly-pale complexion, bore not a trace of fashionable cosmetic artifice. A firm square jaw, lips so thinly pursed that she could be mistaken for one of Zachariah Twigg's kinfolk; harshly high, *knotty* cheekbones, and the only feature that might draw favourable comment was her light, jade-green eyes, which were now spitting glittering Arctic icicles like a shower of cross-bow bolts. Despite the lingering warmth of an evening near the 20th Latitude, in a stuffy, closed great-cabin, Lady Treghues was simply *swaddled* in a Puritan-dark heavy gown, covered from scrawny throat to her wrists, *and* draped in a wool shawl of her own making, to boot! Oh, she was a long and lanky gawk!

"Milady," Capt. Cowles soothingly intoned, bent over in a bow worthy of St. James's Palace.

"*Good* Captain Cowles," Lady Treghues cooed back to him, could a vulture *actually* coo, of course! "And *you* must be Captain Alan Lewrie, sir!"

"Milady," Lewrie rejoined, dipping her an additional bow.

"My husband has told me *all* about *you,* Captain Lewrie," came a much cooler address. Had she a fan instead of knitting needles, she'd have been whacking it back and forth to fight her "virtuous vapours" like a loose and flagging jib! All that was missing was a scandalised "Hmmph!" and a stamped foot.

"It was my pleasure to serve aboard his ship, milady," Lewrie replied, rising upright instead of "grovelling" like a Russian serf.

"Hmmph!"

There it is! Lewrie told himself, now sure that an exasperated stamp would soon come.

"I rather doubt there'll be much visiting 'tween ships, dear," Treghues grumpily said, put out that his wife had intruded upon men's business . . . but seemingly at a loss as to how to prevent it. Perhaps the grey hair in his thinning auburn thatch had come from his wife and her "for his own good" interventions?

"Once the weather calmed, there *has* been, Treghues," she objected, "supper invitations, and I don't know what all. Surely, do *circus* people, *actresses,* and base, low-born itinerants get a whiff of money to be made off the better sorts we convoy with their sleights of hand, mountebank antics, and . . . *pick-pocketing,* they'll swarm every ship in a twinkling. Like a Biblical plague of locusts!" she fumed, shifting her knitting needles from Low Guard to Present-Arms.

Lewrie never could make sense of how "loving couples" addressed each other. Commoners' wives might refer to "The Mister," or cry out their husband's surname to get his attention . . . perhaps even in the "melting moments" before orgasm! "Oh, Smith, oh, Mister, yes, yes!"?

Calls him Treghues, not Tobias, does she? Lewrie took quiet note; *And it's* our *convoy,* our *crewmen,* too? *My "husband" or "the captain" says . . . God spare us!* he thought with a shiver.

Capt. Treghues looked as if he'd like to tell her to mind her own business, put a sock in it, or simply bugger off, but . . . years in harness with her, years of bleakness, might have *already* daunted what meek remonstrances he'd made . . . and the wiles she'd used on the poor bastard to make sure he knew just which of them wore the breeches! A quick perusal of the great-cabin's bulkheads and partitions revealed an assortment of "art," but nothing personal, no children, no portrait of Lady Treghues in her younger days. *Talk of bleak!* Lewrie thought.

"Of course, I will issue a directive that there will be none of that, dearest," Treghues announced, stiffening his back and lifting his chin, as if to make his surrender to her will seem all noble. "And, it goes without saying that any chicanery or pilferage on the part of the mountebanks will be severely punished, as such crimes would in fact be were they committed on any street in England."

Good luck with that, Lewrie amusedly thought; *bored as the passengers and officers aboard the Indiamen already are, t'will be* them *to swarm* Festival. *For a peek at the menagerie, o' course. So educational. As improving as Sunday school, ha!*

"Hmmph!," in a *somewhat* satisfied sniff, was Lady Treghues's conditional comment on that.

"Well, perhaps I should return to *Proteus,* sir, now that that's out of the way," Lewrie offered. Speaking of offering, no one had yet offered him a glass of *anything,* and he rather doubted they'd trot out the good china and sit him down to supper, in their current snit.

"Yayss," Capt. Treghues drawled, turning his forbidding gaze in Lewrie's direction once more. "Perhaps you should, Lewrie."

"Very well, sir."

"Tomorrow night, though, sir," Capt. Cowles said as he gathered up his own things preparatory to departing himself. "Let us say about the end of the First Dog, I would admire did you dine aboard my ship, *Canterbury.*"

"I should be absolutely delighted, Captain Cowles, thankee very kindly," Lewrie answered, most pleasantly surprised that *someone* would dine him in, at last. "Should I fetch a brace o' bottles along?"

"No bother, Captain Lewrie," Cowles most agreeably replied. "We bear a perfectly ample and varied wine cellar aboard, surplus to the passengers' personal stores. I dare say a fresh-butchered roast would go down nicely . . . with fresh butter and piping-hot rolls baked not a quarter-hour before, hey? Can't beat the victuals of an Indiaman!"

"Before I begin to slaver, sir, let me say that you do me *too* proud," Lewrie happily told him. "Well, it appears we're both off. Good evening, Sir Tobias, Lady Treghues."

"Last Sunday, Captain Lewrie . . ." Lady Treghues said, instead. And Capt. Treghues stiffened in wariness for which bee had got in her bonnet, this time. "We ordered Divine Services, and your frigate was fairly close under our lee. Though, I do *not* recall *Proteus* holding a *proper* service. You lack a chaplain, sir?"

"Now, dearest . . ." Treghues began, with much "ahemming."

"We do not, Lady Treghues," Lewrie told her. "Few ships under the Third Rate ever do. We hold what lay portions of the liturgy as are allowed, without the presumption of a real chaplain's offices. It would be a touch . . . sacrilegious to do otherwise, milady."

"Treghues, this coming Sunday, we simply *must* see that Reverend Proctor is rowed over to them, must we not?" Lady Treghues triumphantly announced.

"Of course, dearest," he just had to agree.

"Reverend William Wilberforce offered, milady," Lewrie couldn't help say in parting. "Sadly, we had to depart Portsmouth before a man of his selection could come down from London and come aboard."

"The Reverend . . . *Wilberforce*?" Lady Treghues goggled. And it wasn't pretty.

"*Proteus* had just come from the Caribbean, milady," Lewrie said with his tongue firmly in one cheek. "He and I, and Mistress Hannah More and some others, had a long discussion about chattel slavery that I witnessed overseas. The Abolitionist Society, d'ye see. It was very kind of him to offer a chaplain, but . . . Admiralty would brook no delay . . . even for the Lord." he concluded, giving "pious" a good shot.

"I . . . see!" Lady Treghues intoned, much subdued, and sharing a fretful look with "the captain" of hers.

"Your offer for your Reverend . . . Proctor, did ye say? . . . to conduct a proper service aboard is, may I say, equally kind, milady," Lewrie told her with a reverent bow in *congé*, and a thankful smile that only Treghues, a long-time Navy officer, might recognise as one of Lewrie's "shit-eating" grins. "I quite look forward to it. 'Til then, I s'pose . . . *adieu*, all!"

And what they make of that, the Lord only knows! Lewrie told himself as he stood by the starboard entry-port waiting for a cutter.

"The Abolitionist Society!" Capt. Cowles snickered at his side in the companionable darkness, looking out on the riding lights of the convoy that glittered on a slow-heaving dark ocean. "My *God*, Lewrie, but you're a *proper* caution, hee hee!"

BOOK III

"Fornix tibi et uncta popina
incutiunt urbis desiderum, video, et quod
angulus iste feret piper et tus ocius uva,
nec vicina subest vinum praebere taberna
quae possit tibi, nec meretrix tibicina, cuius
ad strepitum salias terrae gravis."

"'Tis the brothel, I see, and greasy cookshop
that stir in you a longing for the city, and
the fact that that poky spot will grow pepper
and spice, as soon as grapes, and that there is
no tavern hard by that can supply you with wine
and flute-playing courtesans to whose strains
you can dance and thump the ground."

HORACE, *EPISTLES* I, XIV, 21-26

CHAPTER FOURTEEN

Lanndd . . . Hhoo!" the lookout on the mainmast cross-trees high aloft shrilled. And this time it wasn't false. Dark cloud-heads that loomed over the horizon could *appear* solid, and they had been mistaken several times for the tall mountains of St. Helena . . . just as thunder heads earlier in the voyage had been mistaken for the lonely St. Paul's Rocks, for Cape Roque. One particularly-solid and seemingly-unmoving storm ahead of the trade's course on-passage for Recife had resembled an island so much that *Grafton* had despatched HMS *Chloe* to "smoak" it out, sending her dashing ahead of the convoy, as if Capt. Sir Tobias Treghues might gain undying fame by discovering one of the "long lost" isles described in early Spanish sea-charts, sometimes reported by seafarers ever since . . . just as "High-Brazil" and its archipelagos were once cartographers' rumours, yet never found where others had reported them. She'd returned hours later, empty-handed.

These hills and mountains were real, though, at long last. They solidified as the convoy butted its slow way towards them against both Trades and current; other clouds scudded *behind* them as they got near, and even at ten miles rough details of rocks and bluffs and greenery (such as it was) could be discerned on barren, windswept St. Helena.

"Almost done," Lewrie whispered to himself with mounting, yet wary, enthusiasm, as he studied the isle from a perch on the foremast fighting top. "Almost *there*!"

Soon to be free of Sir Tobias and Lady Treghues? Pray Jesus! A break in their long, *very* long passage, and the bulk of the escorting warships would turn about for home. And, was God just, *Proteus* would be one of them.

One more circus performance, then . . . ! Lewrie thought as he put his brass telescope to his eye. It *was* land, by God; it had to be St. Helena, and not another of those portable mysteries, for this was even in the correct latitude and longitude, for a wonder.

Though he still despised clowns and mimes worse than he ever did cold, boiled mutton, Capt. Alan Lewrie had come to rather like circuses and such. Or, rather, *certain* circus folk.

Recife had been a friendly port, a wondrous place to break their passage, go ashore, and stretch their legs. Well, for "John Company" sailors and paying passengers, for Navy officers or working-parties under the ships' pursers to fetch supplies . . . but not for Jack tars.

Treghues had ordered his squadron anchored farther out, so that even the strongest swimmers might be daunted from hopes of desertion, with armed and fully-kitted Marines posted at entry-ports, sterns, and bows, round the clock. Once re-victualled, and glutted with firewood and fresh water, Treghues *had* allowed the "Easy" pendants hoisted, the warships put "Out of Discipline" for two whole days and nights; *aboard-ship* liberty, not *shore* liberty, so the local bumboats could swarm out with their wares—shoddy slop-clothing, cheap shoes, exotic parrots and monkeys for sale, fruits and ades, smuggled spirits . . . and whores.

What had then ensued had not been a pretty sight, and Treghues and his wife and chaplain had taken shore lodgings to spare their finer sensibilities the sights and sounds of the wild ruts that had followed.

Any sailor with the "blunt" could hire a doxy for a tumble, for an hour or so; those who could afford more could declare to the watch officers that his chosen wench was his "wife," with whom he'd share his food (and whatever extra he could buy from the bumboatmen) and his rum issue with her, plus a fee to her and her "agent" for her loaned charms.

The Surgeon, Mr. Hodson, and his Mate, the exiled former French physician, Mr. Maurice Durant, made what attempt they could to determine the women free of venereal, or other communicable, diseases. The Bosun and his mates, the Master-At-Arms, and his Ship's Corporals searched incoming goods, and the whores' underskirtings, for contraband liquour, but *that* was a losing proposition, and small bottles of local rum or arrack always got past them.

Watches would still be stood in harbour, and the cry to rouse a division, a watch, usually was no longer "Wakey wakey, lash up an' stow" but "Show a leg, show a leg." Hairy-legged men got chivvied out of a hammock; smooth and (mostly) hairless female legs were allowed to sleep in! Everyone got as drunk as they could afford, danced as exuberantly and sang as loud as they could holler, and coupled in hammocks, or on the deck between the guns, whenever they felt the itch, with a blanket hung from the deck-head for only the slightest modicum of privacy. It sometimes required the Master-At-Arms, the Bosun, *and* those Marines who *weren't* whoring or talking-in-tongues-drunk to break up fights over a woman, a parrot, puppy, or kitten, a dram of rum or a suspect run of the cards, dice, or backgammon.

Lewrie slept aboard, but wisely took his gig ashore right after breakfast, and didn't return 'til after Lights Out round nine o'clock. What he hadn't seen he wouldn't have to punish, and would usually hold a rather lenient Captain's Mast, unless relatively innocent sins turned into crimes against the Articles of War.

The Portuguese were neutral in the war against France, and the people of Recife were friendly towards most visiting seamen. Without wartime taxes, and with the higher value of the Pound Sterling, he had gone on a frenetic shopping spree. Fresh low-tide sand by the barrel for the cats' "necessary"; jerked meats and sausages for their feeding; hard-skinned citrus fruits by the bushel, cocoanuts for their novelty; both local and imported wines to restore his wine-cabinet and his lazarette stores; fresh ink and paper, new batches of candles and oils to fill his lanthorns; a new shirt or two; Christmas presents to ship to Caroline and his children, Sewallis, Hugh, and Charlotte, for he'd not had enough time to do so in London or Portsmouth, and here it was not only *past* Christmas, but almost two months into both the new year of 1800 and a new century as well!

Lewrie had bought a personal store of Jesuits' Bark, *cinchona*, just in case of Malaria breaking out after a shore call, along with a box of citronella candles in tiny wooden tubs, that Mr. Durant found useful to defeat the sickening tropical miasmas that had engendered an outbreak of Yellow Jack aboard *Proteus* when first in the Caribbean in '97. And, when they were anchored near shore, the candles seemed to shoo away the pesky mosquitoes, too, allowing one to sleep at night without diving completely under the bed-covers.

New linen or cotton bedding, too, a spanking-new and more comfortable cotton-stuffed mattress for his hanging bed-cot, since the old one had begun to reek, from both his own sweat and the odd claim laid upon it by Chalky or

Toulon, most especially when Capt. Nicely had supplanted him for a time last year.

And, *laundry*! And hot baths!

At sea, laundry was done in a wood bucket with seawater or part-fresh, part saline, in which the lye soap the Purser, Mr. Coote, sold could barely raise a lather. The freshwater ration was a gallon a day per man, officer or ship's boy, and most of that was used to boil the salt-meat rations or rare duffs or puddings in net bags in steep-tubs in the galley. To rinse, other net bags were used to tow the washing astern in the ship's wake, so clothing smutted and stiff with tar and "slush" stains from the skimmed fat from the galley used on all of the rope rigging to keep it supple, reeking of human sweat and fleshy oils and grease, came back aboard but a *tad* cleaner, and simply stiff with salt crystals, once they'd been dried. After a while, everyone, from the aristocrat to the powder monkeys, erupted in painful, suppurating salt-water boils. Lewrie included.

Laundry done in boiling-hot *fresh* water, though, *oceans* of it, then rinsed and re-rinsed in colder fresh water, churned and paddled, wrung and beaten, then sun-dried on a line of clean rope, could hold the boils at bay for weeks, months, if one carefully rationed changes of underclothes and sheets, and didn't go *too* potty on fastidiousness!

The officers and midshipmen had decided to go shares on fresh livestock, too, and had asked if their captain might wish to join in. They'd hunted up a nanny-goat with two kids, which could be milked for addition to coffee or tea, so sweet that even hot cocoa didn't require too much sugar stirred in. And, a good kid goat was tender eating as well! They bought chickens and new coops, so they could have eggs at least three days a week, along with a lusty rooster to quicken chicks so the flock would prosper, if the noisy little bastard did his duty. A fat duck or two, some pigs, including a pregnant sow sure to birth some roast sucklings sooner or later, and a bullock for consumption in harbour, and one for later fresh beef.

Even a permanent guard had to be put on the manger under the break of the forecastle, to help the ship's boy who tended livestock—genially known as the "Duck Fucker"—keep the Marine's pet, the champion rat-killing mongoose, from stealing chicken eggs. By now, she was *very* well-fed on dead rats (which upset the midshipmen's mess no end for taking *that* source of meat), sleek, and well-groomed, and wore a red leather collar, and the semi-official rank of Corporal, listed in their muster book as Marine M. Cocky.

Then, after a sublime first night ashore's supper of local seafoods, fresh salad, soup, and mango pudding, washed down with a moderate lashing of wine, Lewrie had decided to toddle over to the plaza to take in the show at the Wigmore's circus.

Capt. Weed of the *Festival* was right; the language problem was insurmountable, so the planned dramas and comedies, and the songs they usually sang in English, had been dropped, but there was still a lot to see, and the performers of Wigmore's Travelling Extravaganza were Jacks and Jills of all trades, able to play any role called for on stage, or flesh out acts in the arena, both aloft and alow.

Lewrie paid his admission, and got a seat several rows back on a shaky set of locally run-up tiers of benches set about an open area at one end of Recife's typically large colonial plaza. Before him, there were two foot-high rings formed by garishly painted wooden boxes, the outer ring about ten feet closer to the audience, the inner ring about sixty feet across. Temporary masts and spars and shear-legs inside the inner ring stood with the aid of rope rigging. Colourful flags flapped in the slight evening breeze, and long strings of cast-off signal flags or small, cheap burgees were hung everywhere a rope could be stretched. Torches or large lanthorns illuminated the inner ring, and the air was heavy with expectation of something out of the ordinary, and the local crowd, half of them children, stirred, squirmed, and chattered. Lewrie made sure that his watch and fob, and his wash-leather coin-purse, were safe in the front pockets of his breeches, for though he wasn't exactly in the "cheap seats," some of the better-dressed Brazilians nearest to him still bore a shifty, pick-pocket's look. At least he was back far enough to be spared the attentions of the damned clowns and mimes!

All in all, it was rather enjoyable. There were fire-eaters or sword-swallowers, bareback riders who performed acrobatics while their mounts cantered or loped about the inner ring, strongmen billed as Hindoo *jettis* who drove nails with their fists into wood, or broke stacks of bricks. Human pyramids of acrobats, jugglers who threw knives back and forth, people who went aloft above the "boarding net" to twirl on taut vertical ropes, or leap from one swing to another. There was a rope-walking act, followed by dancing and trick-performing bears, Fredo and Paulo of his recent acquaintance.

In the slim outer ring, there were parades of animals, though Lewrie *did* think that the zebras more-resembled the four burros he had seen aboard *Festival*, docked-tailed and mane-shorn, and tarted up with soot and chalk stripes. There were performing dogs, a rooster who did a dance (even if his iron dance floor *had* been heated beyond endurance, Capt. Weed had told him). There was a horse who could add, subtract, or multiply, a camel race (with the baby camel chasing them, ridden by a monkey in a red vest and turban), followed by an eye-patched scrawny man with a whip who worked a pair of mangy old lions, and went so far as to put his head in one's mouth, which set the locals into paroxyms of fear; followed by trained parrots which could play fetch from children in the crowd, if shown a matching item first.

And, the clowns and mimes, of course, as *entre actes*, whacking each other with pig bladders or whatever fell to hand, who also worked a troop of monkeys for all they were worth, and that right-lewdly, too. Though that seemed to go down better with the mostly Catholic audience than Lewrie might have expected.

Earlier on, Jose had made a second appearance as a knife-thrower, with both the brassy wee redhead "actress" and the little blonde as his assistants, or targets on a huge revolving wheel; he could even do it blindfolded—or so it appeared, at least.

And, there was "Eudoxia," the raven-haired wench who had caught Lewrie's eye the first day aboard *Festival*. She'd assisted with a dog act, been one of the bareback riders, all in garish, revealing costume, but, her final showing put all those in the shade. Out she came in a scanty outfit to do a solo turn. She wore a spiky, glittering tiara of what looked to be old sword tips and too-big-to-be-real paste gems, all that atop both her own hair and a black wig of tight-curled tresses so long they reached her arse, and looked like old ropes. Eudoxia had on a sheer upper garment, a hip-length, one-shouldered Greek *chlamys*, sheer enough to show off her silver *lamé* corset (that did wonders for lifting her breasts, and Alan Lewrie's libido!), skin-tight breeches, and knee-high suede boots, with a large, recurved Asian horn bow and a sheaf of arrows.

". . . *cruelly* h'exiled. Princess Eudoxia, ladies an' gentlemen!" Daniel Wigmore cried by way of introduction, pausing to let a locally-hired gentleman translate for him. Wigmore had more gilt lace, silver chain mail, and brass buttons on his bright red coat than a dozen generals were authorised. ". . . h'escaped from th' myster'yus steppes o' th' Roosias! . . . wif th' blood o' h'ancient Parthians, Scythians, an' Cossacks in 'er 'ist'ry! Daughter o' th' fabled h'Amazon female warriors wot shot their arrers from th' walls o' Troy, h'itself, fightin' fer ol' King Priam in th' h'*Iliad*! I gives ye that h'archer *par excellence* . . . that most beautiful an' *deadly*, 'oo revenged 'erself on them 'oo slew 'er own true love wif 'er silent *steel* . . . *h'Eudoxia*!"

It started slow, but built right craftily, Lewrie thought. She began with regular straw-stuffed canvas targets, but then progressed to playing cards, candle flames to snuff, large rings flung aloft, which she snapped a beribboned arrow through. Locally-gathered, expendable, pigeons released from wicker cages didn't stand a chance as they fled towards the far end of the plaza, even right overhead of the audience! The wee blond "actress" turned up with a canteloupe on her head, and that got skewered, too. Then a grapefruit, then an orange, finally an apple, *a la* William Tell!

For the *pièce de résistance*, a gaudily caparisoned white horse trotted out into the inner ring, and Eudoxia gave a great shriek, and ran after him, springing and rolling astride, and proceeded to perform her art on targets from horseback, too: seated upright, kneeling atop her mount, *standing*, even scissor-legged along her horse's side, and shooting from below his belly, from under his neck! "Eudoxia" finally drew rein after squarely hitting the ace of spades on a playing card at the full *gallop*, then reined back her horse so hard that he skidded to a halt on the plaza's stones, to rear and prance, pawing the air with his fore hooves to a tumultuous applause, as the small band did a triumphant fanfare, and, over the roar of the crowd, uttered a howl of victory that the Portuguese *might* mistake for an Amazon or Cossack phrase, but which to Lewrie sounded suspiciously like "*Sic semper tyrannis!*," before she wheeled away behind the gaudy sailcloth draperies that screened the performers and beasts from view.

As her horse dropped to all-fours, though, she swept the upper tip of her bow across the audience, stiff-armed, and ended aiming at Lewrie! A *salaam*-ish bow from the waist from the back of her horse, then a very wide grin, and she blew kisses to everyone, with a final one again directed at him, and a vixenish, impish smile, to boot!

Well, then! he thought; *Well, well, well, hmm! Wink's as good as the nod! Though . . .*

As he'd suspected, there *had* been visiting back and forth from one plodding ship to another, on days when the winds and seas weren't up, and *Festival* had indeed drawn more than her fair share of callers. *Proteus* had spent half her time close under *Grafton*'s lee, close under the slow *Festival*, too, though unable to partake of an hour of two of diverting amusement, probably so Treghues could keep a damn' wary eye on the both of them! By telescope, Lewrie had noticed that civilians off the Indiamen had gone aboard much tenser than they departed. All callers had been warmly greeted, and the female members of the troupe had always been the first to welcome them, and the last to see them off.

Perhaps she really was *a whore-transport!* Lewrie had sniggered; *Pays for new costumes . . . atones for poor salaries, and damme if those camels and "zebras" o' theirs don't need a* lot *o' fodder!*

Now, as he paid only half his attention to the magic act which followed the girl's performance, the rational half of his mind warned him that Eudoxia, or whatever her name was in real life . . . Mabel, or Peg most-like, from Liverpool? . . . might be a *well*-used strumpet, but . . . that *other* moiety of his higher faculties kept nudging him with an elbow to remind him that he was the owner of a round two-dozen sheep-gut cundums of Mother Green's very best construction, purveyed in old Half Moon Street, and English, by God, the finest in the world, and in the end, if she *was* for temporary hire, then her socket-fee, no matter how steep, would be more than worth it with a body so slim, her legs so long, lean, and shapely, "cat-heads" so bountiful, and so athletic and strong a ride that he very likely might only half-survive it! No commitments, no embarrassing entanglements, no . . . !

His *sane* moiety pointed out that, surely, "Eudoxia" might have a lover or protector among the circus or theatrical troupe, already, someone jealous, hulking . . . someone like Jose, perhaps, who'd proved his skill with knives, who had wild beasts to sic on him, someone who might pester him to death with *clowns,* if nothing deadly fell to hand.

No matter, he felt . . . "Invited."

And, damme, I am *curious!* he told himself; *What harm in that?*

So, now without a certain amount of trepidation, lest he'd misunderstood the wench's broad gestures, he alit from the stands once it appeared that the night's entertainment was winding down, and casually *ambled,* as innocently as he might, over towards the circus's screened-off area, even going so far as to stick his hands into the pockets of his breeches, most un-officer-like, and attempt to whistle a gay air to disarm the squinty looks he was getting from the thickly-muscular "Hindoo strongmen," and some equally strong and daunting sailors off *Festival,* who did double duty as roustabouts and guards over Wigmore's property. He could reassure himself that he still *owned* a watch, and a full purse, if nothing else!

Before he got quite to his destination, though, the curtained-off backstage area *erupted* performers and beasts, out to take a final parade and their last bows from an adoring audience, and he ended up standing there looking foolish. A minute later, he felt even more of a Cully as smarmy, slick-looking local young gentlemen and pretenders came stroking their mustachios and leering, with flowers in hand, on much the same mission as his!

Oh, bugger this! Lewrie scowlingly thought, feeling hot under the collar, and even more embarrassed to be lumped in with such sprogs. He turned away and shaped his stroll out towards the empty end of the vast plaza, towards the fountains, statuary, and such, when . . .

"Cap'm Lewrie!" Daniel Wigmore gaily called out, as the torches and lanthorns were doused, and the tinny little band strangled their last notes and fell silent. "Why, bless me soul, Cap'm sir, but 'ow'd ye h'enjoy me show?" Wigmore came bustling up through the departing crowd, beaming and bobbing at one and all to take bows of his own from them for a successful performance.

"Why . . . I thought it was simply capital, Mister Wigmore, sir, and I dearly wish my sailors could come ashore to witness it!" Lewrie cried back, stopped in his tracks and removing his hands from his pockets to doff his cocked hat. "Enjoyed it immensely, especially . . ."

" 'Owever not, then, sir?" Wigmore wondered aloud as he came up and not only doffed his own huge, Austrian-style fore-and-aft bicorne, adrip with gilt lace and egret plumes sufficient to stuff a large and fluffy pillowcase, but stuck out his hand for a hearty shake. "Fetch 'em ashore t' next night's performance, why don't ye?"

"Ah, that'd be up to our Captain Treghues, Mister Wigmore, and he'll not allow shore liberty, not in Recife, at least," Lewrie said. "Perhaps at Saint Helena, which is more a garrison than a civilian, and desert-ible, liberty port. My lads'd relish that, aye, sir."

"Aye, that'd bulk th' gate, 'sides th' few poor sodgers stuck h'out there wif nary a di-wersion," Wigmore happily agreed, the sound of silver coins dropping into his receipts sack in his mind's fantasy. "Why, there must be 'undreds o' th' buggers, ah ah!" he purred, with his hands rubbing greedily together. "Promise me, Cap'm Lewrie, ye'll do all ye may t'git yer sailors, all *yer* sailors, an' them off t'other warships, ashore so'z we can h'amaze 'em, an' I'll give yer officers an' ye free h'admittance, h'often'z ye'd like!"

"That'd be grand, too, Mister Wigmore," Lewrie told him, "and, at Saint Helena, you'd be staging your plays, as well, so, did Captain Treghues allow, we might even be able to attend several nights . . . one night the circus, the next a comedy, the next a drama, or opera, or, in this case, what they call an *operetta*. I was quite taken with how your performers filled so many roles. Surely, what they may do on a stage would be even more interesting, revealing such a well of talent, so to speak. Does, erm . . . Eudoxia, for instance, or whatever her real name is . . . play dramatic roles, as well?"

I sound like a "Country-Put" sniffin' round a Pimp! Lewrie chid himself, feeling a burn rise up from his collar once more; *like a young buck tryin' t'sneak backstage at Drury Lane!*

"Why, h'Eudoxia *h'is* 'er real name, sir," Wigmore declared with a wry squint of understanding at him, "th' 'princess' part's a bit of a stretch, but she *did* come from somewheres 'round th' Greek or Turkish 'Ellespont . . . s'truth! 'Er King's h'English h'ain't all that good t' play *h'important* talkin' parts, but she goes down well when it come to *supportin'* roles, h'at comedies an' such . . . chorus singin', and, wot we calls in th' trade the *h'ingenue*. Like *'er* show, par-tic'lar, Cap'm Lewrie?" he asked with a knowing nod and smile.

"Most impressive, indeed," Lewrie confessed, reddening more.

"Why, ye should *tell* 'er 'ow much ye were h'impressed!" Wigmore exclaimed, all but taking Lewrie by the elbow to steer him towards the tentage. "Come backstage wif me, an' we'll do that this werry minute!"

"I'd be, ah . . . delighted!" Lewrie agreed, much took quickly to make it sound casual, so he amended, "if that would be no imposition on your performers' privacy, o' course, ah . . ."

Wigmore looked at him *most* disbelievingly, damn' near *goggled* in point of fact, as he led him past the hopeful, leering local *senhores* and into the backstage area. And, knowing the goal of Lewrie's wish to "congratulate" his performers, took his own sweet time getting round to the object of Lewrie's quest. Lewrie was, perforce, made acquaintance with the horses; the parrots, who made use of his shoulders and arms for roosting branches; the terriers of the dog act, who found the permanent scent of cats on him equally delightful; a joyful *rencontre* with Fredo, and his brother Paulo (once the dog pack had been forcibly removed), both of whom seemed devilish-glad to see him, again; and both mother and baby camel, which involved rather a great deal of slobbers.

Hello to Jose, hello to almost everyone; a handshake with that eye-patched skeleton who made the lions perform, though without having to ruffle any lion fur, for those beasts were already back in a stout iron cage, gnawing on what little was left of their earlier supper.

Finally . . .

"An' surely ye remembers our darin' h'archer, Cap'm Lewrie," Wigmore said with a sly simper. "H'Eudoxia, darlin' . . . ye recollect Cap'm Lewrie o' th' *Proteus* frigate, wot stopped us?"

"*Da*, I do . . . yes," Eudoxia purred, cocking a brow at him as if to ask what took him so long. The scanty outfit and wig were now gone and she sported a thin silk dressing robe belted at the waist, looking as if she'd had a quick sponge-off right after the final parade. Her own hair had been brushed back into a single long mane, and the garish makeup she'd worn in the ring had been removed, as well. No cosmetics of a more conventional nature had replaced it, either; even so, Eudoxia appeared nigh-flawless, fresh-scrubbed, with her natural colour still high from her satisfaction with her performance, and her excitement at being in the public eye for a bit.

There was no curtsy or bow; she stuck out her hand man-fashion to shake with him, catching him in mid-"leg," forcing Lewrie to shift his hat from his right hand to his left to respond in kind, and finding her grip surprisingly strong, her slim fingers tautly lean.

"Your servant, Mistress Eudoxia," Lewrie said by rote.

"You are havink parrot shit on your shoulder, Kapitan Lewrie," she said, instead, reaching for a damp towel to sponge his coat, with an impish grin on her face; which kindness and care for his appearance required her to step overly close to his left side. With her in flat slippers, Eudoxia's chin was just below the point of his shoulder; shod in shoes with fashionably, and sensibly, low heels, she might stand within two or three inches of his own height of five feet nine. Looking larboard at her work, her face *seemed* solemn, but her eyes glittered and crinkled with well-hidden glee.

"Very kind of you, Mistress Eudoxia," Lewrie told her. "Normally sponging off my coat would involve cat fur."

"You havink pet cats?"

"Two of 'em . . . Chalky and Toulon," Lewrie said. "Grand company for sailors, cats. For a captain."

"A lonely think," Eudoxia agreed, stepping back at last. "I am seeink Kapitan Veed liffing alone in . . . great-cabins, *da*? *Weed*, I am to say, not Veed. New to the *Engliski*, but learnink quickly, do you think, Kapitan Lewrie?"

"Doin' main-well, Mistress Eudoxia . . . extremely well," Lewrie amended, since "main-well" was an idiom she hadn't yet met, it seemed. "Mister Wigmore says you came from beyond the Hellespont? Turkish, or Greek, or . . . ?"

Her face hardened of an instant, her almond-shaped, almost Oriental eyes slitted in fury, and her nostrils flared; Eudoxia all but stamped a foot! "Turkman, *nyet*! Greek, *nyet*!" she fumed. "Ve beink *Ukraine* people . . . *Cossack*, not Mongol, not Tartar! What fool Wigmore know, hah. *Not* Muslim, but Russian Orthodox, *yob tvoyemat!** Come from Volga! East of Volga!"

"The, ah . . . river, aye," Lewrie said, shrivelling up and shying from her sudden fury.

"Mans who say Cossack be bastard Tartars or Turkman is damn *lie* they tell!" Eudoxia snapped; this time she did *stamp* her foot, dainty though it was. "We Christian, see?" She opened the throat of her robe to display a silver cross with an odd diagonal extra bar, showing him the proud top-swell of her breasts, an expanse of flawless skin, and a promising depth of cleavage, too . . . though Lewrie didn't think that was her intent at the moment.

Why, I'll wager she's that yummy, right down to her toes! Lewrie told himself; *Creamy* . . . damn' *creamy!*

*"Fuck your mother."

"I apologise for any misunderstanding, Mistress Eudoxia. Maybe I did not hear him right, and I was not aware of your . . . heritage," he said, red-faced. "Forgive my ignorance of your part of the world, but I've never been near the Volga, in the Black Sea."

"Um, I beink sorry, too, Kapitan Lewrie," Eudoxia meekly replied, looking down and all but biting her lower lip for a moment. "For saying the bad think . . . *yob tvoyemat. Pajalsta* . . . please, forgive? It mean to . . . do something bad vit' your own mother." She half-whispered that, blushing and lowering her gaze again, though finding it a *tad* funny.

"Would that be with, or without, bells on?" Lewrie asked with a grin. "An English expression, to . . . go do something to *yourself*, ye see . . . with bells on? Of course, you're forgiven, and thankee for a new phrase to add to my vocabulary. Should I ever sail to the Russias . . . d'ye think I might find it useful?"

"Get you killed," Eudoxia all but giggled, looking up at him, directly, and with all her impishness back. "Is *very* bad. My poppa hear me say, he beat me."

"Then don't tell him you did," Lewrie leaned closer to suggest, snickering and laying a finger alongside his nose for a sage tap. His experience with foreigners was fairly broad, though he could not claim a working knowledge of any tongue but his own, and he was thankful that flirting with the girl wouldn't require a hired interpreter or a glossary of useful phrases. Her accent, thick as it was, was nowhere near as incomprehensible as that Hungarian officer in the Austrian Navy, Lt. Kolodzcy, he'd been saddled with in the Adriatic back in '96, sailing along "the Balgan goast" in search of "Zerbian pirades," and, "bud ov gourse, ve must fint ourselfs some wirgins"! All delivered with his double heel-click of precise *punctilio*!

"So . . . are *all* Cossacks from the Volga as skilled in archery as you, Mistress Eudoxia?" Lewrie enquired. "I came to congratulate you on your skill, and accuracy. I've heard that Cossacks are superb horsemen, o' course, but my word, I must say that you are possessed of a fine seat, as well."

They hit another language snag, for Eudoxia furrowed her brows at that compliment, and all but groped her slim bottom, peeking over her shoulder to survey her arse.

"On your *horse*!" Lewrie chuckled in explanation before she took off on another angry outburst. "Excellent riders in England are said to have a 'fine seat' . . . in the *saddle*, or, in your case, bareback. How did you learn all that?"

Her hands flew to her mouth for a second as she saw the comedy in misunderstanding his idiom. As her hands came down, she didn't just giggle girlishly, she laughed right out loud. "Oh, *that* seat! *Da*, all Cossack learn ridink from babies. Poppa is teachink me from a *little* girl. Have brother, but *he* go serve vit' Czar in cavalry. We beink circus people all my life, I only child left, so he teach me like he teach brother. Poppa do act vit' bow, do shootink vit' guns, too, but act vit' gun is . . . ex-pen-sive, *ponyemayu*? Unnerstand? Powder, shot, . . . and, be uhm . . . need *rifle* guns . . ." She frowned, searching for a word, and looking to him to supply it, right-fetchingly coquettish.

"To be accurate, aye," Lewrie supplied.

"*Da*, the ac-cer-rut," Eudoxia smilingly agreed, waving him to a pair of rickety cane chairs so they could sit facing each other, with a respectable yard between them. "Gun act, be very slow. To re-load? Or must have *many* rifle guns, cost too much, make not so much money."

"So, you can shoot as keen with a gun as with your bow?"

"Oh, *da*!" Eudoxia exclaimed, feckless, not boasting, but merely stating a manifest fact of life. She gloomed up, though, mercurially quickly, and laid her hands on her knees. "Poppa, one night . . . pan or flint go 'piff!' by his *good* eye. Cannot do *no* shootink act, anymore. I beink twelve, I think, when it happen?"

"And you had to take over, to earn the family income," Lewrie surmised, feeling genuine concern, though he did trowel it on thicker, for her benefit. "How terrible for you, Mistress Eudoxia."

"*Nyet*, not take over, I too little," she corrected him. "Work dog and monkey act, ride bareback horse. Poppa is tendink horses and beasts, but is very little we make, for long time. And, Momma . . ."

Eudoxia squirmed fretfully on her chair, dropping her gaze, and looking both pensive and a tad angry, too. "She very good singer, and actress, but must help Poppa, too? He lose place, act is over, so . . . I am fourteen, she run away vit' damned French clown! Is *also* singer, actor, oh, opera *grand*, he thinkink! Very handsome, *da*, think circus and clownink is too low. Boast he be *bolshoi* opera czar in Vienna or Paris," she sneered, "and Momma run 'way to be opera czarina, too!"

"*Damn* the French!" Lewrie commented with long-accustomed heat. "Never can trust a one of 'em, I say. The arrogant bastards."

Clowns! he derided to himself; *French clowns, worst of all!*

"Finally join Wigmore show in Lisbon," Eudoxia related, heaving a heavy sigh. "Begin bow and horse act when I am beink sixteen, after Poppa teach me all he know. Old lion tamer sick and old, Poppa is good vit' beasts, so he learn new act, but very hard on him. Poppa is proud. But . . ." she said with a fresh smile and hopeful expression, "now we makink the *good* money, ev'rything is *karasho*! Engliski, 'bloody fine'!"

"Good for you!" Lewrie said, patting the back of her hand that rested atop her nearest knee. "So, you've been doing your act how many years, now? No wonder that you're so skilled, having honed your craft, your . . . *art*, so long."

"*Art?* Pooh!" Eudoxia spat, figuratively *and* literally, with a brief scowl. "Is reason Momma run 'way. In letter she leave us, she say must follow her *destiny,* her *art,* hah! As for my act, I doink it six years, now. Now, twenty-two."

"You seem to have coped rather well, for all your heartbreaks, mistress," Lewrie responded, "and I'm sorry if my mention of 'art' is a reminder of past sorrows, but . . ."

"Hurt no more, Kapitan Lewrie," she assured him, smiling back, and twining lean, strong fingers in his, with her impishness returning. "So, you are kapitan of *bolshoi* . . . big Engliski frigate, an Engliski gentleman. Must sail the whole world over, so many new places, like we do in circus. Is excitink? Meet many excitink new peoples . . . ?"

"Sometimes it *seems* just like a circus," Lewrie laughed. "But, let's speak of you, instead. I heard you'd done an entire year along the American coast. How did you like that, wild Indians and such?"

"Oh, is *grand,* America!" Eudoxia enthused. "Big as all Russia, vit' peoples so rich and clean, not serfs. *Not* like Russia! Where I get my boots, wild Indian . . . moccasins, at Savannah . . . !"

"Ahem!" came a voice near Lewrie's left ear, making him freeze in dread; would he have to pet *another* new (mostly harmless) creature?

"*Here* is Poppa!" Eudoxia exclaimed, leaping to her feet, letting go of Lewrie's hand. "Is our lion tamer!"

"Errp!" Lewrie gawped as he shot to his own feet.

The man with the eye patch stood near them, one hand on a dagger in his waist sash, the right holding his whip, uncoiled to the ground. The look on his harsh face could curdle sperm, piss, or strong brandy!

"*B'lieve* we were introduced a few minutes ago, sir, but I didn't exactly catch your name?" Lewrie smoothly offered, sticking out a hand in hopes the fellow would take it, thus *partially* disarming him.

"Kapitan Lewrie, of the *Engliski* Royal Navy, here is my poppa, Arslan Artimovich Durschenko," Eudoxia contributed with all the guilelessness of the righteously innocent, going all giddy-giggly. "Poppa, Kapitan . . . ?"

"Alan."

"Kapitan *Alan* Lewrie, *spasiba* . . . thank you, I meanink to say," Eudoxia repeated, all but bouncing on her (chaste) toes. "Is proper manners to say Christian name and patronymic, Kapitan, to speak to my poppa."

"Mister Arslan . . . Artimovich, yer servant, sir," Lewrie said.

"Ummm," Durschenko responded, not even looking down at Lewrie's offered hand, and making that "ummm" rise from deep in his chest, like a bear awakened, grumpy and deadly, from his winter nap. The fellow's jaws flexed and worked from side to side as he ground his teeth, *very* much, Lewrie thought, like a slavering mastiff eager for his dinner.

"You must be very proud of your daughter, sir," Lewrie quickly extemporised, striving for another of his "shit-eatin' grins" and his nigh-perfected smarm. "In her skill, her poise, and talent, that is. I came to offer my congratulations to her, and ev'ryone *else,* d'ye see, for a most enjoyable show, which I hope my sailors will be able to see, once we reach Saint Helena . . . ah ha."

This ain't workin', Lewrie nervously considered.

"Hah!" Durschenko Senior barked, not buying that for a minute. His live eye glared bullets, but he did shift his whip to his other hand, and un-handed that dagger!, to at last take Lewrie's hand as if all was forgiven. Giving it a vise-like squeeze, so hard that Lewrie felt his eyes were almost ready to water.

"Heh heh heh," Durschenko muttered with a feral, toothy grin.

Lewrie gave back as good as he got, though, clamping down with all the strength he had. *Never try that on with a sailor, Arse-lick Artimovich,* he thought; *nor a swordsman, either, ye old fart!*

They stood there, arms beginning to quiver, fingers going numb and white, shuffling closer to each other like two wrestlers looking for an opening to a sudden throw.

"Oh, *stoy*!" Eudoxia snapped in exasperation, at last, seizing them by the wrists to pull them apart. "Stop that, both of you! The Kapitan is nice man! He mean no harm!"

Don't lay wagers on it! Lewrie thought, wishing he could shake feeling back into his hand without anyone seeing him do it.

"Low bastard . . . fine gentleman, no difference," Eudoxia cried, "no matters. I never meetink *nobody* that Poppa do not . . . oh, tell me what is word?" she flustered, looking to him for aid.

Murder? Lewrie wryly supposed. "Distrust?" he said, instead.

"*Da,* distrust, *spasiba,* Kapitan Lewrie," Eudoxia hotly agreed, her eyes glinting as cold as the snowy steppes that had birthed her. She turned to face her father and launched into a rapid, gutturally-garbling bit of foreign "argey-bargey." Durschenko Senior glowered, scowled, gawped, and stamped a booted foot, by turns, leaning back and almost tittering at one point during her harsh tirade, growling and barking like the aforesaid mastiff in the same lingo whenever he could get a word in, which wasn't often.

Other circus people, including those smarmy clowns and mimes, were drawn to their little domestic "tiff," and Lewrie wondered if he could crawl away, unnoticed, for every now and then, Arslan Artimovich would snap his head about to glower and snarl at Lewrie, and everyone in Wigmore's Travelling Extravanganza surely had seen him and Eudoxia "at loggerheads" before. Perhaps, Lewrie dourly fantasised, they had also seen Durschenko lash an interloper away from his precious girl, and were waiting with rising expectations of a good show, perhaps even laying wagers on the outcome?

Their business, now, not mine, Lewrie told himself, giving up all hopes of sporting with the girl, no matter how entrancing. *I had a good, hot, freshwater bathe, a fine meal, and the circus* was *nice, really. Just toddle off? Stand here and look foolish?*

For a second, Lewrie wished he had thought to fetch his penny-whistle ashore with him . . . or knew how to juggle.

The best he could do was manage a *semi*-dignified departure, if that, he sadly supposed. There was no point in risking being fed to Durschenko's lions at the worst, or being whipped bloody, at the best. Flirtatious and coquettish as Eudoxia was, as *welcoming* of his attenions, there didn't seem to be a rosy future in it.

Their palaver ended, finally, with a sideways cutting gesture on her father's part, which got his hand off the dagger and a "*nyet*!"

"Well, I'll take my leave . . ." Lewrie said, doffing his hat.

"Eudoxia . . . goot girl, *ponyemayu*?" Durschenko rumbled deep in his chest. "*Keep* goot, me. *Dosvidanya, bolshoi* Kapitan. Goot *bye*!"

"Understand completely, sir," Lewrie replied, sketching a bow to him. "Ev'nin', Arslan Artimovich. Good ev'nin', Mistress Eudoxia. Hellish-good show," he added, making a finer "leg" to her.

"We see you again at Saint Helena, Kapitan Alan Lewrie," she responded in kind, making a more graceful curtsy than he had suspected she knew how to perform. Dressing robes weren't made for such, though.

"Nyet," from her father.

"Da!" she hotly retorted.

Time t'scamper, Lewrie thought, feeling the need to employ his hat for a fan, at the charms that curtsy had briefly revealed.

He left them, still yammering away at each other, slinking red-faced and feeling like the veriest perfect fool, as he threaded his way through the circus folk.

He could not help looking back, though, when he attained the draperies, to see the father leading Eudoxia away by her elbow, and she turned her head to watch him leave . . . for one last sight of him? She gave Lewrie a large-ish shrug as if to say, "Well, what can we do?" yet . . . a second later, began to grin, her mercurial, minx-like impishness returning. She pursed her lips for a distant kiss!

Well, Lewrie thought, lustily stunned past dread; or close to it, anyway; *Well well, well well, hmmm!*

CHAPTER FIFTEEN

"To where might they *run,* Sir Tobias?" Capt. Graves of *Horatius* asked with a weary note to his gravelly voice after listening to Capt. Treghues expound on why he had decided not to allow shore liberty for their hands, now that they were snugly anchored in James's Valley harbour, at the East India company *entrepôt* of St. Helena.

"Why, aboard an East Indiaman for the better *pay,* sir," Treghues rejoined in his best "tutor's" voice, as if speaking to a student with all the tired patience required to get through a dull scholar's skull. "Most especially, aboard a *homebound* Indiaman, so they may jump ship in England, and desert their bounden duty to the Navy!"

"All of which, sir, anchor here in James's Valley harbour, for the very good reason that the only other possible anchorage where any ship of worth or deep draught may come-to is Rupert's Valley, which is totally uninhabited . . . for the very good reason that there is not a drop of fresh water to be had, there, sir," Capt. Graves belaboured. "In *this* anchorage, Sir Tobias, any seaman who takes 'leg bail' could easily be restored to duty by the very simple task of enquiring of, and going aboard to search, any Indiaman before it sails."

Capt. Graves (no kin to the influential Royal Navy Graveses) exhibited reasonably great patience, himself, and, for a tarry-handed and *direct* sort of old salt phrased his rebuttal slowly, borrowing a formal choice of words usually alien to his nature, Lewrie was pretty sure . . . but a volcanic simmering was just below the surface.

"Then we could flog them blind, as an example to the others," Capt. Philpott of HMS *Stag* added, almost tongue-in-cheek.

"The island is thinly settled, Captain Graves," Treghues said, with a thin-lipped aspersion. "All they'd have to do is scamper into the hills, live off the land for a few weeks to wait us out, *then* come down and sign aboard an Indiaman."

"The island's thinly settled, sir," Capt. Graves quickly said, "for *another* very good reason. Compared to Saint Helena, the Scottish Highlands are as lush as Tahiti! Can't *farm* hills this steep, except for this valley, so there's nought to steal and eat. Every resident of this bleak rock's a member of the militia, and bored to *tears*, most-like. Raise the hue and cry, and they'd run 'em down in a Dog Watch! And enjoy the adventure, to boot, sir!"

"Then 'John Company,' or the garrison of the forts, gives them their floggings, and holds them in gaol 'til the next warship arrives, sir," Capt. Philpott stuck in, again. "Pity."

Treghues snapped his head about to glare his displeasure at such a waggish comment, but found Philpott's phyz composed in a wide-eyed, benign expression which expression made Lewrie hide a grin with his fist to his mouth, and stifle a snort of amusement. Treghues swivelled about to bestow upon him an even sterner glare.

"You said something cogent, Captain Lewrie?" Treghues snapped. "Is there a notion you wished to contribute, sir?"

"Erm . . . only that I am quite in agreement with Captain Graves, and Captain Philpott, Sir Tobias," Lewrie declared. "Though I've not called here before, it seems evident that there's nothing upon which a deserter might victual, outside this little one-street village, and no place where any such might even find shelter. No trees to cut down to make a crude lean-to, to get out of the incessant winds. There are no beaches from which to fish. With only four hundred or so soldiers in the garrison, not over a thousand residents all-told, unemployed tars would stick out like sore thumbs, and be taken up right-promptly."

"A sailor *intent* to run would take *any* risk, Captain Lewrie," Treghues countered with an impatient wave of his hand. "The fools."

"Though, may I point out, Sir Tobias," Capt. Philpott eagerly added to Lewrie's remarks, finding a willing ally, "that sailors who were not allowed ashore in England before our departure, kept aboard at Recife, kept aboard here at Saint Helena, possibly denied liberty ashore at Cape Town, too, might be *more* eager to desert than sailors given a *slight* bit of free time, of leisure ashore . . . of trust, sir."

"Oh, rot, sir!" Treghues sneered, all but rolling his eyes in scorn. "Your average English tar is a drunken, ignorant, and irksome lout who'd sink into sloth, crime, and alcoholic stupors given the opportunity, Captain Philpott. Without continual watchfulness, without unending discipline to rein in their baser desires, they'd run riot in a twinkling! Oh, I'll grant you, there are *some* honest volunteers who look to improve themselves, some men pressed under dubious legalities who come aboard imbued with sobriety and industriousness as a result of their former civilian employments, but . . ." Treghues waved away as if the situation was hopeless, and would always be so.

HMS *Grafton*, so they had all learned on their long voyage, was a "taut" ship. Lewrie didn't remember Treghues being quite so strict during the American Revolution, perhaps because old HMS *Desperate* had been a much smaller ship, with a smaller, more familiar crew. He *had* always stated that "a taut ship was a happy ship," though how Capt. Treghues translated that to his present crew was reputed to be harsher. Then again, Treghues had been younger and full of promise, and hadn't spent so many years idling ashore on half-pay, either. Nor had he wed such a dour termagant of such a bleakly forbidding nature.

"But two whole days 'Out of Discipline' since departing England, Sir Tobias," Capt. Graves cautiously pressed. "'Gainst currents, and winds to here as long a voyage as it took to fetch Recife, with perhaps better than a month more 'til we break passage at Cape Town, assuming we even do . . . liberty here at Saint Helena is the *least* we may do for them. Do they face the prospect of an unbroken voyage all the way to Bombay, to Canton in *China*, well . . . compared to those ports, liberty granted here is safest of all, sir!"

That's why there were two ships of the line in the escort; once past Cape Town and Madagascar in the Indian Ocean, some of their trade would head for Bombay, some would bend their course for the Strait of Malacca, and China, with a two-decker 74 for escort. Treghues would choose which duty HMS *Horatius* might perform, which half he'd escort onwards in *Grafton*.

"Jack Ass Point, and the foreign factors' compound at Canton, sir," Lewrie said, "I *have* been there. No risk of desertion, there, since the Chinese lop the heads off 'red-haired foreign devils' when they get into *their* part of the city—"

"I was not aware you took *merchant* service, Lewrie," Treghues interrupted, sounding as if involvement with "trade," or its nautical assistance in a civilian capacity, was rather sordid.

"Wasn't merchant service, sir," Lewrie responded with a smile. "Some secret work for the Foreign Office aboard a false trader, armed and crewed by the Navy. Bombay, too, sir. Well, my experience was in Calcutta, up the Hooghly, but . . . there's nowhere for English tars to run among the Hindoos, either. Not for long, if they don't speak a word of the language, sir. Ports in India might not be walled off from the local population like Canton is, but they might as well be, for all the good they'd do potential deserters. And, as I recall it, every ship that put in was allowed shore liberty . . . liberal liberty, sir. If our hands'll be allowed liberty at Bombay and Canton, what's the harm in allowing liberty here, where they have *no* hope of jumping ship, sir?"

"For the very good reason, sir, that they will run *amok,* as the barbarians of the Malay Peninsula say!" Treghues snapped, now rapidly losing his patient, all-knowing-father air.

"On *what,* may I ask, Sir Tobias?" Capt. Graves gravelled, near the end of his seeming serenity, too. "The *very* few public houses of James's Valley? Upon the veritable regiment of bawds, now a-tip-toe on the strand, awaiting their arrival with open arms?"

"Sir!" Capt. Treghues barked, slamming a palm on his desk for punctuation. "You exceed proper bounds, Captain Graves! Aye, there's very few public houses or taverns hereabouts, and *should* we allow our people ashore, they'd be *swamped* by so many sailors all at once!"

"Exactly what the publicans and tavern keepers look forward to, I'd expect, sir," Capt. Philpott blandly suggested. "How'd they make their livings, else? The garrison and the locals can't be much of a livelihood, sir."

"And, there's Wigmore's Travelling Extravaganza, too," Lewrie quickly seconded. "They've a decent band, and do musicals, comedies, and dramas, in addition to their circus performances, sir. All quite innocent, no more harmful than letting discharged sailors free in Covent Garden or Drury Lane, sir. It'd go hard for our people, to know that they're performing for the garrison, but *they're* not allowed to go ashore and attend, sir. Might make 'em . . . surly."

"You're entirely right, Sir Tobias," Capt. Graves was quick to exclaim, scooting forward to the edge of his chair in his eagerness to make his point, "a taut hand and consistent discipline's the very thing to make an efficient ship, but it *can* become too much of a good thing, d'ye see, do you not give them a bit of slack, now and then. If my hands must sit aboard, close enough to see soldiers, civilians, and 'John Company' sailors going ashore to take in the shows, it *will* make them surly, as our good Captain Lewrie suggests, sir."

"Even more eager *t'be* aboard an Indiaman, perhaps, sir?" Capt. Philpott tacked on, sounding breezy, and trying hard not to smirk at his impious suggestion. "Never can tell."

Lewrie wasn't sure which comment made Treghues bristle up, go puce-faced, and bluster more . . . Graves's hint that strictness might prompt rebelliousness, Philpott's heretical idea, or Graves calling Lewrie "good"!

"Aye, that *circus*," Treghues seethed. "Whacking good time you had ashore, did you, Captain Lewrie? At that circus, hmm?"

Damme, what does he know, and how did he learn it? Lewrie had to take pause to ask himself, crossing his legs the other way round to guard his "wedding tackle."

"An amusing, and innocent, distraction, Sir Tobias," he replied. "Half the audiences at Recife were children and their parents, and the local authorities seemed satisfied that nothing prurient or bawdy had insulted their rather austere sense of morality, sir."

"I enjoyed it, too, sir," Capt. Graves chimed in, as did Capt. Philpott a second later: "Aye, it was innocent and amusing. And, I suspect, Sir Tobias, that were our sailors seated in their audiences, that'd be hours they'd *not* be spending in taverns or brothels. Half a day's liberty, watch and watch, say . . . Noon to Midnight. A fresh dinner, time enough for at least a *mild* drunk, then a bought supper and a ticket to a show, and . . . by the time the final curtain comes down, 'tis time to return aboard their ships, hmm?"

"Depends on local sunset, full dark," Lewrie speculated, "when they light their illuminations, I s'pose. Perhaps from Seven Bells o' the Forenoon 'til Seven Bells of the Evening Watch'd work better. The usual arrangement of two 'hostages' still aboard for each libertyman, their own run ashore dependent on t'other's behaviour, and return?"

"Wouldn't have to expend rations, do they debark before the rum issue, or call to messes," Capt. Philpott slyly said. He and Graves had turned their attention upon each other to thrash out arrangements, as if the decision had been made in their favour, and Captain Treghues was no longer present. "And wouldn't our 'Pussers' love *that*, hey?"

"Masters-At-Arms, Ships' Corporals, and Provost guards from the garrison to keep a wary eye on 'em, perhaps?" Lewrie further suggested.

"Aye, that'd work out well, Captain Lewrie," Graves exclaimed, turning to include Treghues, at last. "Garrison troops told-off as the Provosts might attend the shows in an official capacity, but . . "

"Could watch 'em, in essence, for free!" Lewrie hooted.

"An easy arrangement to make with the garrison commander, I'd think, Sir Tobias," Philpott chortled, turning to face Treghues with a puppy-eyed, eager child's expression, waiting upon Treghues's say-so, as they all did, with a "please, Father, may we *please*?" expectancy.

Treghues stared them down, as stonily as the Egyptian Sphinx, lips down-curled, as pruned up as if he'd bitten into a sour citron. His fingers drummed on the desktop, nails chittering as if he wished to hone them for a clawing in the near future. He heaved a great sigh and leaned back in his chair to stare at the overhead and the painted and lacquered deck beams. Perhaps he was consulting the Almighty as to the best course of action, praying a silent apology to Him for being a weakling, imploring the Lord to keep his sinful sailors from *too* much exuberance ashore, or . . . calling down *all* the Pharaoh's plagues upon his contemporary Moseses, who pleaded to "set their people free."

"A third of each ship's complement, sailors and Marines, each day, sirs," he glumly, sullenly, announced, at last. "Two-thirds will bide aboard, dependent upon the libertymen's behaviour, and if those miscreants depart one jot or *tittle* from decorous comportment, then I will cancel *all* further liberties, hear me, sirs?"

"Very good, sir!" they almost managed to say in chorus.

"I will consult the tables to determine full dark, hereabouts," he further decreed, "does the circus require full dark for their performances . . . as *good* Captain Lewrie is *so* certain that they require," Treghues could not help loftily sneering.

"Makes for a better experience, sir . . . like a darkened hall in Drury Lane draws the audience into the lit stage," Lewrie explained to him, off-handedly. "Or, so I am told," he added, withering under that steely gaze.

"Do *not* interrupt, sir," Treghues gravelled. "As I was saying, perhaps an adjustment from *Six* Bells of the Forenoon to Six Bells of the Evening Watch . . . Eleven to Eleven, would suit, depending on what the tables say. I will send you word by dusk. In the meantime, you will see to wood and water for your ships. Liberty is . . . allowed."

From behind the deal partitions and privacy curtains leading to his sleeping space and quarter-galleries came a faint, outraged "Hmmph!" from Lady Treghues, and, for a moment, Lewrie wasn't sure if he didn't feel sorry for the poor fellow. It was one thing to be talked out of a firm decision (no matter how rigidly daft) by officers junior to him, but it was quite a rather *grim* other to have to beard that harridan in her "den," probably after making assurances to her that he would *not* allow sailors of his squadron access to Sin!

They rose and made their parting salutes, and Treghues rather languidly, perhaps even a tad weakly, waved them on their way. They had not quite attained the starboard gangway and entry-port, not even attained their own gigs or cutters, before *Grafton*'s crew began muttering and buzzing, all atwitter with the glad news that they'd be going ashore, even before it could be announced officially. Such was usual aboard ships, though . . . what was whispered aft in gun-room or great-cabins had a way of spreading "before the masts" by a nautical grapevine older than mythical Jason's good ship *Argo*. By the time Lewrie, as the least-senior officer, had settled himself on a stern thwart in his gig, with Cox'n Andrews ready to order "Out Oars" (and didn't *he* have a huge grin on his face, too!) *Grafton*'s people were beginning to cheer!

We're going to the circus! Lewrie could not help thinking like a beamish tyke; *We're going to the circus, again, hurrah!*

CHAPTER SIXTEEN

The circus, yes; Lewrie saw every performance—perhaps hoping for an aerialist to fall and kill a clown, or for Arslan Durschenko's lion to mistake his head for a chew toy at that climactic high point of his act—definitely to savour Eudoxia's archery and horsewomanship. Pigeons to skewer were a bit thin on the ground on St. Helena, but the seagulls used in their stead were equally delightful.

Lewrie doubted there were more than a corporal's guard standing watch on the ramparts of the cliffside forts guarding Rupert's or James's Valley, or manning the massive 32-pounder guns in the Mundens Fort that dominated the main harbour, for the audiences at every show were filled by red-coated soldiers. Even here on a bleak and remote outpost isle, Mr. Wigmore looked to be in the way of making a "grand killing," what with the garrison and the locals so eager for *anything* novel in their isolation, with the addition of the thousands of East India Company or Royal Navy sailors in port—not just the sailors from their convoy, but an additional eight Indiamen which had broken their passage after departing Cape Town, and had been waiting for the arrival of warships to escort them to England, along with the hundreds of passengers and "John Company" officials there gathered.

Wigmore made the most of it, with the circus scheduled for the late mornings, and taking just long enough to whet appetites and very dry throats by the time performances ended (which pleased the taverns and inns to no end) and the comedies or dramas staged just after the sun went down.

There wasn't all that much timber available on St. Helena, so this time there were no tiers of shaky seats. Everyone had to sit on the ground or rocks, catch-as-catch-can, up the beginnings of a slope of a hill that framed the little one-street "company" village, much like the sketches that amateur artists brought back from their Grand Tours of the Continent, and the edifying sights of tumble-down ruins of ancient Roman amphitheatres in the capitals of southern Europe.

It wasn't grand theatre, either, not when the lead performers were still smarting from their circus acts of a few hours before, and were mostly as amateurish as a cast of public school boys putting on a springtime "lark" just after their final examinations. When at "meaningful dramas," they tended to over-emote most portentously, turning Shakespearean classics into shouted declamations, and Lewrie could not recall any performances he'd seen of *Othello, The Merchant of Venice*, or *The Tempest* done quite so energetically, as if the entire cast was made up of very frenetic fleas. Or inmates of Bedlam.

They were much better at comedies and musicals. They did *The Beggars' Opera*, of course, since everyone English, high-born or low-, knew the tunes by heart, knew the japes word-for-word, and could sway and sing along in nostalgia, or shout, heckle, cheer, or laugh a bit too early, throwing the performers off their paces so thoroughly that that show had turned into a mugging contest.

Two Gentlemen of Verona got completely plagiarised, becoming a farce titled *A Day At The Forum*, with many foot chases and slamming doors, slave girls in skimpy gauze costumes, and lusty, but foolish, Roman lads who didn't know they were related.

Then, there was *The Sultan's Hareem*, loosely borrowed from the many horrid novels (some running to eight volumes!) written about some plucky English girl kidnapped by Corsairs and sold off to an Ottoman Turk, fending off the old lecher's advances quite cleverly, if quite implausibly, 'til rescued by the Royal Navy. That'un featured skimpy costumes, too, perhaps the same ones worn earlier by the Roman slave girls. Both farces were heavy on popular songs incorporated wherever they even slightly fitted into the plots, *The Sultan's Hareem* ending with "Rule, Brittania!"

And didn't Eudoxia look grand in barely-concealing gauze!

Since no clowns could throw buckets of confetti or water on him at the temporary theatre, nor any mimes drag him out for their victim or laughing-stock, Lewrie sat down front at the dramas and comedies, with the other captains, officers, and East India Company officialdom, and their wives, mistresses, or doxies.

Where he could get a good view of her charms.

Eudoxia, indeed, didn't get many lines in the dramas, but more than held her own in the comedies. She was a slinky-sultry Egyptian slave girl in one, a star belly-dancer in the other (doing much the same routine in both, actually), and would never be said to possess a fine singing voice, but . . . who cared? Lewrie certainly didn't, for her natural, nigh-exotic beauty, her graceful, long-limbed carriage as she made her paces across the extemporised stage, and her innate impishness when delivering comic dialogue, combined with the sombrely serious way she went at her nearly-salacious solo dances, transfixed him into gape-jawed, and highly appreciative, awe.

And, just as she singled him out with her bow at the end of any circus act, when the *dramatis personae* took their final bows, lined up just before the footlights, her eyes always found his, her triumphant smile grew brightest, and her last blown kisses and lowerings of her head were to him . . . *despite* her father, who always seemed to be just at the edge of the stage curtains, or in the shadows of the circus's screening drapes, also looking fixedly at Lewrie, and that furiously, too, with his teeth grinding themselves to pea-gravel and dust!

That was as close as he actually got to her, in point of fact, as close as any hopeful gentleman or lusty tar got to her, either, for just as soon as Eudoxia exited the ring or the stage, Poppa Durschenko was there by her side, now sporting *two* daggers in his waist sash, and bestowing upon one and all cautionary glares so black and menacing that they might have killed birds on the wing, before taking her by the arm or elbow and hustling her behind the safety of the tents or drapes.

Until their last night in port.

Wigmore had staged *A Day At The Forum*, again, the bawdiest and funniest of his offerings, that seemed to go down so best with sailors and soldiers. Most captains and officers had already seen it, as had the local lights, "squirearch-ish" passengers, and officials, but the audience was still fairly large, most of it garbed in Army red, or in Navy blue, and Lewrie had gotten himself a place in the very front on a low stool he'd fetched off the ship.

No matter that the crowd that night were repeat attendees, the farce went down even better than before. Knowing that this was their last performance before packing themselves and their scrims, costumes, and props aboard *Festival* for a long, boring voyage, the actors played up even broader and bawdier, altering dialogue and the ends of jokes to suit their less sophisticated, but more loudly-appreciative, crowd. The music was louder and livelier, even the songs leered or eye-rolled more comically, the pace of the foot chases and door slams even more frenzied, and drawn out 'til people in the audience were nearly *retching* or *choking*, they had laughed so hard, could not even titter a jot more, yet found something new over which to howl.

Lewrie's own eyes were squinted, tear-filled, his sides ached, the corners of his mouth nearly hurt, and he had guffawed so forcibly that when he could draw a full breath, his lungs felt as abused as if he'd smoked the foulest Spanish *cigaro* in all Creation.

At last, both noble families were reconciled, the villains were confounded, the long-lost brothers reunited, and the little blonde who played the first *ingenue* slave girl, and Eudoxia, who played the sultry Egyptian dancing girl slave, were freed and espoused. The entire cast gathered to sing the last song, linked arm-in-arm, then took the final bows. Arslan Artimovich Durschenko slunk out to the edge of the thin curtain on one side of the stage, ready to help haul it shut, glaring at everyone, and . . .

Eudoxia did her last, deep curtsy, head inclined as grandly as a countess, clad only in a peachy *lamé* chemise, a *very* sheer goldish sheet of gauze gathered to resemble a Roman *stola,* ankle bangles, and white-leather sandals. As before, after she had made acknowledging bows to left-right-and-centre of the audience, blown kisses to the four winds, and waved to those who shouted loudest from far in back, higher up the slope, her almond eyes and widest smile was for Lewrie, making him sit up straighter and squirm in lust, no matter the danger lurking in the wings.

Then . . . Eudoxia stepped to the edge of the stage as the rest dropped their linked hands to depart, bounded lithely over the footlights from the low wood stage, onto the stretch of ground separating the stage from the audience, and, with her most playful laugh, landed in Lewrie's lap, arms about his neck, and one lean, slim leg extended towards the starry sky!

"Merciful God!" Lewrie gawped, beaming fit to bust, with an arm about her waist. "Well, hallo there!"

"*Zdrasvutyeh, Engliski* sailor boy," Eudoxia said with a laugh. "You comink here off-e-ten?" One hand came up to stroke Lewrie's cheek to steer his head, then planted a broadly-drawn, loud, and wet kiss on his lips, to his, and the crowd's, amazement and delight.

"Woo-hoo!" Sailors cheered, jeered, and whistled, while her kiss turned from playful to fierce. "That's our 'Ram-Cat' for ye!" a sailor off *Proteus* loudly hooted, one who knew the sobriquet by which his captain was known in the Royal Navy and the reason for it, which had nought to do with Lewrie's choice of pets.

"Your papa is going to *kill* me!" Lewrie carped, stunned, pleased, but very worried, as she gracefully rose to her feet and drew him erect with her, draping her slim body against his, her arms about his neck and fingers toying with the short, tied queue atop his coat collar. "Might even take his whip to *you,* girl! We'd best . . . !"

"Then it be good you run away, *da?*" she teased back, whispering, her lips half an inch from his, and Lewrie could not stop himself from running his hands up and down her back, giving her a firmer squeeze so he could lift Eudoxia's toes off the ground, marvelling at how sinewy, how firm, her body was, compared to most women's, yet how silky-smooth.

"Running away . . . now," he told her. Yet, didn't. Now eye-to-eye with him, she grinned, and bestowed on him another, more serious, enflaming kiss before leaning her head back and crying, "Hah! Now is good time we *both* runnink!" He let her go, thinking it a *most* sensible suggestion, and she fled with a playful hop and a skip for the right-hand side of the stage platform, farthest from her papa, though she did stop, spin about, and cry, "Was much fun! *Dosvidanya,* Kapitan Alan Lewrie."

He stood staring after her like a Greek hero who'd caught too good a direct look at the Hydra, and been turned to stone. He felt a need to gulp, and did so, a time or two. He also felt a need to grope at his crutch to ease the sudden tightness of his breeches, for surely no human could *have* a cock-stand the size and hardness of a belaying-pin, but forebore, given the audience about him . . . and the fear that her father was still watching. He shook himself back to reality, bent down to pick up his hat and stool, and saw the now-drawn stage drapes nigh-churning with a struggle behind them.

*"Tot tarakan!"** he heard, recognising Arslan Artimovich's raspy shrieks. "Let go, *yob tvoyemat*! *Chort!*† *Doh*!‡ *Tot sikkim siyn*!"** Or, whatever *that* meant. In punctuation, a long arm emerged through the curtains' partings, a hand at the end clutching a dagger, with several other hands struggling to disarm him, and Lewrie determined that, aye, it *would* be a good time to bolt . . . in a dignified manner, o' course, though with *some* purposeful haste. *"Tot gryazni sabaka!"*++

As he headed for the piers and his waiting gig, taking *longish* strides, he tried to recall what it was the London papers always said of a new play in Drury Lane, or Covent Garden. Right, that was it!

A most enjoyable time was had by all!

*"That cockroach!"
†"Shit [or] Damn!"
‡"God!"
**"That son of a bitch!"
++"That dirty dog!"

CHAPTER SEVENTEEN

"First Off'cer . . . SAH!" the Marine sentry without the door into the great-cabins cried, thudding the brass-bound butt of his musket on the deck.

"Enter," Lewrie bade, interrupting his breakfast in the dining-coach and rising to his feet, almost wincing with dread anticipation of what report Lt. Langlie might make; he had already gotten a letter from HMS *Grafton,* even before his sailors had finished washing and stoning *Proteus*'s decks.

Lt. Anthony Langlie stepped through the door into Lewrie's forward cabins, 'twixt the dining-coach to larboard and the chart-space to starboard, cocked hat under one arm, and a rolled-up set of papers in his free hand. Toulon and Chalky, who had been breakfasting on the fresh bacon bought ashore, raised their tails and tricky-trotted over from their dishes to greet him, as was their usual wont, for Langlie was always good for a kind word and a skritch. They were disappointed, though, for Langlie paced right past them, for a rare once, to attend to the grim matter at hand.

"Coffee, Mister Langlie?" Lewrie offered, dabbing at his mouth with a fresh napkin. "Buttered toast and jam, too, perhaps?"

"Ehm . . . the coffee'd be welcome, sir, thankee," Langlie said, a frown upon his usually-placid and (some said) handsome features.

"Sit ye down, then, sir. Aspinall? Coffee for the First Officer, and a refill for me," Lewrie directed. Aspinall fetched a fresh cup and saucer, his battered black pot, and did the honours, before, at his captain's firm nod, retreating back into his tiny pantry abaft the chart-space. "Well then, Mister Langlie . . . just how large a pack of sinners are we?" Lewrie finally asked.

"Ehm . . ." Langlie commented with a sigh, unrolling his reports. "A total of twenty-two hands on report, sir. I comfort myself with the fact that *Proteus* isn't the greatest offender, but . . ."

"To paraphrase those Americans with whom we cooperated in the Caribbean, Mister Langlie," Lewrie stuck in with a scowl, " 'when the captain ain't comforted, ain't *nobody* comforted,' hmm? I've already had a note from Captain Treghues on the matter. Tell it me."

"Aye, sir. Ahh . . ." Langlie sadly replied. After one sip from his sugared and goat-milked cup of coffee, he referred to his papers. "First off, I suppose, there was the 'zebra' race, though that Mister Wigmore's made no formal complaint about the ah . . . borrowing of his beasts, or the condition in which they were returned. It *did* draw an undue amount of attention, though, sir, so . . ."

"Could've been worse, Mister Langlie," Lewrie opined. "Might have been camels, not . . ."

"The camels put them right off, sir," Langlie told him. "All that biting, bawling, and spitting green goo. In point of fact, one could hold Wigmore partially at fault for allowing our Black hands to mount them at all."

Some of their "liberated" Jamaican Blacks, Landsmen or Ordinary Seamen, had been allowed to view the circus's menagerie in their pens down by the piers where they'd been kept after the last circus performance, prior to re-loading aboard *Festival*. God knows why, but they had also been allowed to *mount* the so-called zebras, and, on a drunk lark, had decided to race them bareback all the way uphill through the town to the last tavern at the head of the valley, the loser to pay for all.

They had been highly displeased to find that the "zebras" were only tarted-up donkeys, whose "cosmetics" stained their cleanest shoregoing uniforms. Equally displeasing was their discovery that, having been born Black African, they had no more innate "zebramanship" skills than your run-of-the-mill drunken tar. The race had been a shambling, short-tacking disaster, and, once at the distant tavern, they had taken a peevish load of ale aboard themselves, and gotten the *donkeys* drunk, into the bargain! The garrison's Provost Guard had fetched them Hood, Howe, Bass, Whitbread, and Groome . . . and the donkeys . . . home, giving the men Hell for "cocking a snook" at them and giving the Provosts false, and highly improbable, names!

"And what's this about stolen azaleas, roses, and a . . . *tree*?" Lewrie asked, referring to Treghues's note by his plate.

"Well, that was mostly our Irish hands' doing, sir," Langlie informed him with a grunt of obvious distress. "Furfy, Desmond, some of the other lads. Once I got *them* back from the Provosts, and a *bit* sobered up, their explanation was that they'd heard sailors off those homebound Indiamen talking about how profitable is the importation of exotic foreign . . . shrubs, and they thought that it might be a two-way trade. Make a bit on the side, sir? . . . There was, also, some talk about emulating 'Breadfruit' Bligh . . . the *saplings,* not the mutinous part. And . . . they wished to do a bit of . . . gardening, sir. Spruce *Proteus* up?"

"Were they of a mind t'plant 'em in the water tubs between the damned *guns,* Mister Langlie?" Lewrie gawped. "Or, would just any-old where suit?"

"Ehm . . . I gather they'd have gone either side of both entry-ports, the quarterdeck and foc's'le ladderways, and . . . your door, sir. Decorative door-stoop flowers," Langlie lamely confessed.

"But, the island governor's *wife's* roses and azaleas, Mister Langlie!" Lewrie exclaimed, referring again to Treghues's damned note. "The bloody *tree* from right outside the governor's courtyard!"

"Ahern was especially covetous of the roses, sir," Lt. Langlie morosely commented. He'd been up all night, from the first alert he'd gotten from the garrison's Officer of the Guard, and was, by now, much the worse for wear. "His old grannie was a herbalist healer, or so he says, and highly recommended rose *hips* for those feeling poorly. The, ah . . . argument over which ship got the roses and such never really *did* get to an outright *brawl,* though *hundreds* of sailors were involved, not just our Proteuses, sir! Men off *Grafton, Horatius,* and Navy tars off the *homebound* escort ships were actually the greatest offenders . . . or so I heard from the other First Lieutenants, once we were all summoned to the Mundens Fort at dawn, sir. Once there, we compared notes, held a little 'guild meeting,' as it were. . . ."

"The *tree,* Mister Langlie?" Lewrie pressed.

"The tree, aye, sir," Langlie said with a put-upon sigh. "Furfy clapped eyes on it, and *swore* it was the very sort of tree that stood just outside his childhood croft back in Ireland, sir, and . . ."

"And was it?" Lewrie asked, most dubiously.

"I rather doubt it, sir," Langlie replied with a brief grin on his phyz. "It was a twenty-foot Chinese magnolia. Furfy said, though, that it'd look grand forrud of the roundhouse. Give shelter and shade for hands at the beakhead rails, and the 'seats of ease'? It *required* hundreds of sailors to up-root it, and bear it back to the piers, sir, where they discovered that it wouldn't go in even the largest cutter without swamping it, so they *did* return it, and *tried* to re-plant it . . . sort of, sir. That's when the garrison mustered a company of infantry."

"Mine arse on a band-box!" Lewrie attempted to growl, picturing it in his mind's eye. The only scene he could conjure up was a horde of tars dancing and weaving ribbons 'round a mobile May Pole. He used his napkin to conceal his snicker.

"Well, was it returned, and *mostly* re-planted, it wasn't rightly stealing, was it, Mister Langlie?" he hopefully asked. Under English Common Law, the theft of anything worth more than a guinea would earn the perpetrator—in this case, perpetrators!—a hanging. There were urchins in London who'd met "Captain Swing" or been transported for life for the theft of a loaf of bread or silk pocket handkerchief!

The governor-general and his wife might *be that wroth*, he told himself; *Sir Tobias-bloody-Treghues, for certain, if they're not!*

"I gathered Saint Helena's governor has seen a deal worse, sir," Langlie told him, "though he may be a long time forgetting this one. I was informed he'd only press for monetary damages, though that may be subject to change. The shrubs suffered no permanent harm, though that magnolia tree may be ruined. 'Tis a shallow-rooted thing, and, there wasn't a single blossom or leaf left on it when it was returned. The spoils of war, *victory* laurels, I suppose the Mob thought, sir. There is also mention of a Chinese lap dog missing, a pug something or other, very dear to the governor's *wife*. All ships are to be searched for it."

"*Not* aboard *Proteus*, thank God," Lewrie sighed, for a search had already been made. "Now, what about this low brawl?" he asked as both his cats, eager for attention from two such affable people, chose a lap or the table top; Chalky to Langlie's lap, where he rolled over onto his back and wriggled for "pets" or "play," all four feet pawing air, and trilling shut-mouthed for amusement. Toulon sniffed about the edge of Lewrie's breakfast plate, first, then flopped on his side, just out of easy reach, with his thick tail thumping the table, and his own paws "rabbited" against his chest, issuing louder, more insistent "Mmrrs!"

"Now, that wasn't *our* lads' doing, sir!" Langlie objected in an insulted manner. "Hands off *Adamant* objected to sailors off *any* ship drinking in 'their' private tavern. One of the homebound two-deckers she is, sir . . . the greatest offenders, as I earlier said. The tavern in question is the one nearest the piers, and too convenient to be the sole property of one ship, so . . . the last hours of liberty, our lads popped in for a last pint . . . or two . . . the Adamants took exception to not only *our* lads, but any Navy sailors they didn't recognise, and *especially* to our Black hands, and fell on our people.

"Well, sir . . . the rest of our tars weren't having any of *that*, neither were our *Marines*, sir!" Lt. Langlie further explained. "Just before it got completely out of hand, Mister Neale, the Master-At-Arms, and his party turned up, mustered petty officers off every ship, and broke it up. The publican's damage claims are rather piddling . . ."

"Nineteen pounds, ten shillings, five pence," Lewrie muttered, "Grossly inflated or not, 'tis not exactly 'piddling,' as you see it, Mister Langlie! Not being in a position to negotiate, it'll be up to me to make quick restitution, before we sail on tomorrow's tide, does the wind suit. That'll be above and beyond the sum for damages asked for the damned tree and shrubbery, and a deep bite out of *my* purse and ready funds! In recompense for which, I'll expect the gunroom and the cockpit, and every Man Jack cited in your reports, to whip out 'chink'! Just imagine what *your* share o' that'll be, Mister Langlie, before you call it 'piddling.' "

"Aye, sir. Sorry," Langlie muttered, hang-dog and meek.

"For all those reasons, Mister Langlie, Captain Treghues is now utterly convinced of our entire squadron's irredeemable depravity, in general, and *Proteus* filled with Satan's Spawn, in the specific! We have, to quote that worthy, directly," Lewrie sarcastically said, referring to the note, " 'smutted the good name of the Royal Navy, cast a stain upon the repute of every ship involved, and by your libidinous and drunken conduct besmirched mine own escutcheon with Admiralty' . . . to wit, Mister Langlie, we've shat on his copy-book, and will now have to pay the piper."

"How so, sir?" Langlie was forced to enquire, frowning more.

"The *usual* practice is to escort 'John Company' trades beyond Saint Helena or Cape Town with a pair of seventy-fours, perhaps with a seventy-four and a single frigate, depending on how strong the French squadrons out of Réunion and Mauritius, are reputed to be," Lewrie said with what might uncharitably be deemed a groan. "Now, though, Captain Treghues is of a mind that only a long, depriving sea voyage, a total ban on even *shipboard* liberty, and *lashings* of discipline will restore the ships of this squadron to the paths of the righteous. And, there was no pun intended."

Of course, he left out the juicy part wherein Treghues had taken him personally to task for associating with a nigh-naked circus person and actress . . . a Lilith, a Jezebel, a corrupting Delilah! What was he, a Captain of Less than Three Years' Seniority even so, a Commission Sea Officer of their King, *and* supposedly a married man, *and* the father of three *innocent babes*, doing in company with such a jade, and cavorting so *publicly* before common seamen, to boot, to the detriment of sailors' morals, the dignity of officers, and respect for English gentlemen, and *et cetera* and *et cetera*?

"So, Captain Treghues may deem it seemly for us to sail further than we expected, sir?" Langlie asked, twigging to the meat of the affair at once. "Damme, sir! We knew we stood a good chance of going as far as the Cape of Good Hope, but . . ."

"Now, it appears we're down for Bombay, or all the way to Canton in China, aye," Lewrie sourly mused, idly fluffing his fingers through Toulon's belly fur.

"But, sir . . . such a long voyage, with no additional break in our passage, and without even shipboard liberty, much less shore liberty, is the very thing that dispirited the crews of the homebound warships," Lt. Langlie protested. "They'd not have run riot here, had they been given a chance to carouse at Cape Town."

"I'll grant you the point, Mister Langlie," Lewrie said with a sigh as he shifted in his chair. "Now, assuming Captain Treghues allows us even a *whiff* of land at the Cape, and it's all wooding and watering, and no liberty at all, at least Mister Coote, the Purser, and officers will be let ashore. Do we, indeed, sail 'cross the Indian Ocean, we'd best hunt the settlements over for some handy phrase books in Chinese and Hindoo. That, or kidnap likely Lascar or Asian translators."

"Ehm . . . don't you own some Hindoo, sir?" Langlie asked. "And, I believe I heard that you had been to Canton, 'tween the wars?"

"My Hindoo is barely good enough to order drinks and supper," Lewrie sourly admitted. "And as far as Chinee goes, I doubt I knew a half-dozen people who had a handle on it. Was 'Ding-Dong-Dell' a real Chinese phrase, it'd mean twelve diff'rent things, depending on which syllable, or syllables, got sung higher than the rest. We may be in need of a translator, a social guide. And, damned if the Navy's going to re-pay us for his hire."

"Well, we're still a few hands short, sir," Langlie suggested, almost tongue-in-cheek. "Perhaps we could hire them on as Landsmen, to perform two tasks. In that case, the Navy *would* pay us for them, much like our, ehmm . . ." The First Officer bit off the rest, blushing.

Like our Black sailors, hah? Lewrie thought, silently completing Langlie's slip of the tongue for him; *And wouldn't that make this ship an "all-nations," as varied as a dram shop? Kidnap a few, and the rest come easier.*

"Well, we'll see, once we attain the Cape," Lewrie said, "which will depend on Captain Treghues's mood at that moment. Before we sail tomorrow, though, Mister Langlie . . . you'd best alert the Purser, Bosun, and your fellow officers, warrants, and midshipmen that we may be in for a lean spell. Any needs or comforts they presently lack they had best make good, here."

"Aye aye, sir."

"I will hold Captain's Mast, tomorrow's Forenoon, once we're at sea," Lewrie further announced. "My respects to Mister Pendarves, the Bosun, and he's to make up a round dozen cat-o'-nine-tails and the red baize bags for 'em."

"Aye, sir," Langlie numbly agreed, though with one brow cocked in surprise at such an order, for Lewrie had never, in his association with him, been much of a flogging Tartar, nor *Proteus* been known as a "whippin' ship."

"Captain Treghues, our putative 'Commodore,' has ordered me to administer punishment for our malefactors," Lewrie said. "*Condign* punishment for all involved, he wrote."

"Can he do that, sir?" Langlie uneasily asked. "Just *order* . . . ?"

"Not strictly, under the Articles of War, no, Mister Langlie," Lewrie replied with a chuckle, and a wink. "The drunkness happened on *shore*, as did the brawling and such, on *liberty*, and not aboard ship, where they *would* fall under the strictures of line-of-duty discipline. What individual captains may make of civil infractions, not Admiralty infractions, is up to them, and any interference from outside the hull . . . even from a senior officer commanding . . . would be looked upon as a violation of captains' traditional, and jealously protected, prerogatives.

"Make up the 'cats,' anyway," Lewrie further said, looking all "sly-boots" at his perpetually put-upon First Officer. "The sight of 'em will put the fear o' God in our people. Let 'em stew on what they *might* receive, what I might *do*, a day or two, and they just may have a fresh think on what grand larks they *think* they had, this time. Which might make 'em think twice, the next time I let 'em off the leash."

"Oh, I see, sir, you . . . oww! you little . . . !" Langlie exclaimed, first in mirth, then in pain, looking down in his lap at Chalky.

The cat had delighted in having his belly and chest rubbed and gently tickled, but evidently had desired more energetic amusements, and had nipped unwary fingers to initiate a wee romp. Chalky stuck up his head over the edge of the table, ears half-flat, and a mischievious cast to his eyes as he scrambled to his feet, tail whicking impishly.

"Chalky . . ." Lewrie chid him in a gently-scolding tone, gaining his attention. "We do *not* bite Commission Officers. No, we don't . . . not even Midshipmen. No matter how distracted and vulnerable they be, hmm? Bleeding overly much, Mister Langlie?"

"Skin not even broken, sir," Langlie chuckled.

"Give me your list of incorrigibles, then, Mister Langlie. Was there anything else you wished to discuss? Anything *pleasant* to tell me, to lighten my gloom?"

"Well, we're still *afloat*, sir." Langlie said with a wider grin. "That about covers it."

"On your way, then, Mister Langlie," Lewrie bade him, watching as he finished his coffee and rose from the table, depositing Chalky on it, who immediately bounded to hurl himself on Toulon, who might be more up for play. Louder, with a meaningful glance upwards at the open skylight windows in his coach-top, where sailors of the afterguard and the quarterdeck Harbour Watch could always be trusted to eavesdrop for a clue to future developments, Lewrie concluded his remarks to Langlie with "And don't forget to tell the Bosun to make up those damn' *whips*!"

CHAPTER EIGHTEEN

Long though the voyage had been so far, it was roughly two thousand miles, as the square-rigger tacks, from St. Helena to the Cape of Good Hope, and the first day on-passage had only logged 110. The trade steered somewhere between Sou'west by South, did the Trade Winds allow, and Sou'west, if they did not. Three-masted, square-rigged ships could only get within six points up to the wind, even when sailing "full and by," close-hauled.

The middle of the second day, however, brought dark cloud-heads that swathed the horizon from the East-Nor'east all the way down to the Sou'east, and with them, a backing, rising, and much brisker breeze, a "soldier's wind" that gave the convoy and its escorts a welcome "lift."

To sail Sou'west in search of the perpetual Easterlies for their ride to the Cape would have added more nautical miles to their passage, and would force them down into the vast, swirling heart of the Southern Atlantic, where the great currents that circled counter-clockwise-about between South America and Africa became weak, confused, or nonexistent, where the counter-clockwise winds that could sweep a vessel South along Portuguese Brazil and the Southernmost Spanish colonies, or batter them on the nose in their guise of the Sou'east Trades, faded away, becoming an area larger than North America where ships could chase zephyrs weeks on end . . . the Doldrums. The usual course from St. Helena to the Cape was one large Zee-shaped detour.

As the winds came most unexpectedly Easterly, though, with rains and high seas for accompaniment notwithstanding, those "soldier's winds" were looked upon as a blessing, a raree that perhaps would never be encountered again in an entire life at sea, and one to take advantage of!

The trade turned their bows Due South, cutting off the Sou'west "Zee" almost before it began; they reefed down, or completely took in, their royals and t'gallants, but left their tops'ls, courses, stays'ls, spankers, and jibs full-bellied with wind to *sprint* Southward, even the most hide-bound, passenger-coddling Indiamen masters, and reeled off an average of seven or eight knots for nearly two whole days, and a fair portion of a third, before the skies cleared, the seas moderated, and the wind shifted back into the Sou'east. So rare was it that even after full dark, they pressed on, rocking, scending, and heaving over a white-spumed ocean under full sail, for not a cap-full of that precious wind could be let go to waste; even *Festival,* that cranky old jade, got a way on and looked almost lively as she bowled along at the rear of the convoy, with as much of her gaudy-but-faded, parti-coloured, and patched canvas bellied out taut and straining!

It pleased everyone, even Capt. Sir Tobias Treghues, Bart., for brisk winds and high seas precluded any more of that scandalous traffick 'tween ships, most especially to *Festival,* which he had referred to as "that demned hoor-ship!" It ended the bare-steerageway crawl of the nights, which was always pleasing to one who deemed himself a seasoned salt and "tarpaulin man." And, Lewrie happily considered, the weather had reduced the necessity for Treghues to speak face-to-face with those fractious, nigh-rebellious captains of the other ships in his squadron to virtually nil! Which Lewrie also deemed a blessing of another kind from *his* point of view, and he was mortal-certain that Capts. Graves and Philpott felt much the same!

For, "condign" punishment for those who had misbehaved had been interpreted more leniently than Treghues might have wished, or exacted aboard HMS *Grafton*'s malefactors.

For the most part, Lewrie had awarded more subtly grievous punishments: five days' biscuit and water for rations, denied their hearty morning burgoo, sugar and butter, their duffs, cheeses, pease puddings, or "portable soups," with the eight-man messes temporarily shifted, so that all twenty-two offenders ate together and could not beg or borrow even a morsel from their usual messmates who might not have run *amok*.

What had drawn the most groans, though, had been his decree that for an equal five days, none of the those twenty-two sailors would have leave to smoke or chew tobacco, or purchase or borrow from the Purser or their shipmates, *and,* horror of horrors!, for five days those men would get no *rum* issue, either! No "sippers" or "gulpers" presently due for past favours, and none to be snuck off innocent mates for a present or future duty or favour pledged during their time in Hell!

Those "cats" he'd had Mr. Pendarves make up had mostly been put away in the Bosun's locker, and only three had actually been "let out of the bag" to use on Landsman Humphries, and Ordinary Seamen Grainger and Sugden, who had been witnessed striking petty officers, Masters-At-Arms, or Ship's Corporals from other ships at the tavern brawl, as the roving shore parties broke the melee up, or for being so drunk they had tried to fight their own petty officers as they were brought aboard. A dozen lashes apiece, bound to the upright hatch-gratings, the minimum, since those were their first offences. Enough, Lewrie hoped, to drive the message home so they would not be disputatious with their seniors the next time, but not enough to make it seem vindictive, and ruin the men's morale or loyalty to what had been, 'til then, a fairly "happy ship." Who they fought ashore on their next rare dry-land liberty he could really care less!

Under *Grafton*'s lee to shout across a verbal report, Lewrie had taken sly advantage of Treghues's lust for strictness, by declaring his intent to *work* the Devil out of his hands, as well, with which, at that moment, Capt. Treghues could form no dissenting opinion. *That* resulted in holding the gun-drills that Treghues had earlier peevishly curtailed.

The light 6-pounder chase-guns fore and aft, the carronades, and the long 12-pounder great-guns were manned, run-in and loaded, run-out to the port sills, levered about to aim, elevated by use of the quoins below the breeches, then "fired" in dry drills, first, then actually lit off for real later, once the "rust" had been scaled off his hands, for with so much fairly peaceful passage-making of late, and more time spent in various harbours, there'd been little reason or opportunity to keep his gunners from turning slack. He and his officers began at the very basics, as if introducing new-comes to their duties, stressing safety, caution with their dangerous charges, and attention to duties.

Lewrie, who had fallen in lifelong lust for artillery as a most angry-to-be-there Midshipman in his early days, the winter of 1780 on his first ship, finding in the power of the guns the one, perhaps the *only* joy a displaced dandy (as good as "press-ganged" by his own father for his own damned lust for soon-to-be-inherited funds!) relished in an ordeal that had seemed at the time as miserable a drudgery as a long prison sentence! He had, therefore, high standards, higher even than those of the experienced officers who had taught him Navy gunnery.

Lewrie was disturbingly surprised by just how "rusty" his men had gotten, but promised himself that by the time they reached the Cape he would have them back up to "scratch," even re-acquainting them with the rarely used light swivel-guns and 2-pounder brass boat-guns to be mounted in the bows of the gig, cutter, and launch.

"Oh, they'll come up to par soon enough," Lt. Adair, their Scot Third Officer, cheerfully opined, swiping a hand through goat-curly and dark brown hair as he raised his hat to air out his scalp in the rain and the warmly-moist, green-smelling winds that blew from the far-off shores of Africa.

"Par, d'ye say?" Lt. Catterall, the Second Officer, scoffed. "Whatever the Devil's that, some Gaelic word? Par-*broiled* makes some sense. *Par*-tici-*pate*, par-*ty*? But half a real word, Mister Adair?"

"It is a *golf* term, Mister Catterall," Adair impishly replied.

"And what the Devil's *golf*?" Catterall hooted in his bearishly burly way. "Once more ye've lost me, sir."

" 'Tis a game we play at home, Mister Catterall, and great fun, actually," Lt. Adair explained. "A game which requires great patience and skill . . . well, perhaps it might be lost on *Englishmen,* sir," he said with a twinkle. Then Adair proceeded to describe "golf" to him—tediously and minutely.

"Mean t'say," Lt. Catterall querulously asked, *minutes* later, "you take yer 'mashie' with a 'whuppy shaft' and whack a 'sma' leather-bound rock . . . that never did harm to anybody . . . 'cross yer 'braes,' rain, fog, cold, or snow no matter . . . 'til it lands in a rabbit hole, then do it all over again? Why, I never heard the like! Is there a prize in it? Does the *rabbit* keep the rock, or do ye haul the rabbit out of its hole, take it home, and jug it for yer reward? Sounds daft t'me, but, I s'pose 'tis amusing to *Scots* . . . who have so *few* amusements."

"Par means 'average' for getting there, Mister Catterall," Lt. Adair said, biting off an exasperated sigh, as he usually had to do in dealing with "Sassenach" heathen Englismen in general, or the sardonic Lt. Catterall in particular. "The number of whacks necessary."

"Then less than yer 'par' is doing *worse*?" Catterall chuckled.

"*Better,* Mister Catterall," Adair insisted, with a slight edge to his voice; he *knew* Catterall's cynical humours, *knew* he was being twitted, but never could help himself. "The fewest strokes win a . . ."

"Well, that's arsey-varsey, then," Catterall snickered. "*Over* average is worse, *under* average is best, and someone actually keeps a score of it!"

"Then 'par' will never do, gentlemen," Lewrie commented, after listening with amusement to their typical bantering from his post by the windward bulwarks. "I'll not be satisfied with *average* gunnery, not after our experiences in the Caribbean. I'll settle for two shots per gun, every three minutes, but I'd rather we get off *three* in that time. In the early minutes of engagement, at any rate, when the hands are not fatigued . . . and well-aimed 'twixt wind and water. Remember what that American captain from Georgia said. . . ."

" 'The captain ain't happy, ain't *nobody* happy,' sir!" Lt. Adair piped up with a laugh. To which, in *lieu* of a hearty "Amen!" or "Here, here!" for a second, Catterall added one of Lewrie's patented, piratical "Arrs!," which he'd become quite good at imitating.

"I fear I must stand more aloof to you, gentlemen," Lewrie said as he tucked his hands into the small of his back and peered back up to weather. "No more dining *some* of you in," he pointedly commented over his shoulder. "*Some* seem to have come to know me, and my ways, simply *too* well, alas. And Mister Catterall and the Surgeon were to dine with me this very night . . . on fresh beef, too, what a pity."

He swivelled about to face them, quite enjoying the smirk upon Adair's phyz, and Catterall's strangled expression. With a droll grin, and an energetic clap of his hands, he announced:

"Once gun-drill, the rum issue, and noon mess is done, sirs," he said, "I think we should strike topmasts, then re-rig them, should the winds abate. Just to see how quickly the evolution can be performed, 'rusty' as we seem t'be, hmm? *Then* . . . with the wind abeam, and sailing mostly on an even keel, I will also have the hands work off excess energy by going aloft, waisters, idlers, and all, along with the topmen. Larboard division 'gainst starboard division."

"Aye, sir."

"Up and over, from the windward foremast shrouds to the fighting top, then down to the lee gangway, up the lee main shrouds and down to the larboard gangway, then up and over the mizen-mast. Encouraged, and *led* by their officers, o' course. Mister Langlie and I shall observe, and time it." Lewrie continued with a smirk of his own, "Much like the Irish whore instructed . . . 'up, down . . . up, down . . . up, down, repeat if necessary'! Winning division gets extra grog on completion of their Dog Watch."

The fortuitous winds abated, at last, shifting back to Sou'east, forcing the trade to steer wider to the Sou'west, but they *had* logged nearly six hundred nautical miles, mostly at Due South, more than a quarter of the total passage, placing the convoy and its escorts more Easterly to Africa, and even sailing six points off the wind they would only skirt the edge of the Doldrums, not get becalmed in it.

For a much shorter time, the Trades and the Equatorial Current that flowed the same direction in concert with each other would impede them, then . . . though the Sou'east Trade might still rule, an *Eastward*-flowing current that girded the southern rim of the Doldrums, parent to the one they now fought, would kiss them on their starboard, lee, bows to counter the leeway lost to the winds. A few slogging degrees more of latitude, and the winds would shift to out of the West, in concert with *that* current, and they'd all be be there!

And, so it was, one mid-afternoon in March, that HMS *Stag*, far ahead of the convoy, hoisted a string of signal flags in the private code that Capt. Treghues had invented that read:

"Land—Four Points—Larboard Bow."

"Table Mountain, that'd be, most-like, sir," the Sailing Master, Mr. Winwood, carefully opined. "Visible from seaward on a clear day as far as fifteen leagues . . . or, so my book of pilotage tells us."

Almost over! Lewrie quietly exulted; *This part, at least*.

"We'll not enter harbour tonight, sir, beg pardon," Winwood said. "I'd expect we'll stand off-and-on 'til morning, so we may be able to spot the rocks and such. A poor set of anchorages, even so, sir, this Table Bay or Simon's Bay. Bad holding ground, the both of them, both subject to sudden and contrary afternoon clear-weather gales, it says."

"Cape Town, or Simon's Town," Lewrie said with a shrug of resignation. "With any luck, we'll not be in either, very long, sir. In point of fact, 'twill require a great *deal* of luck should we come to anchor, at all!"

"The, ah . . . results of our sailors' deeds at Saint Helena, I should think, Captain?" Winwood, ever the sombre Christian, whispered.

"Exactly so, Mister Winwood," Lewrie agreed. "There's odds we might just sail right on by, do Captain Treghues and Captain Cowles, as Commodore of the Indiamen, concur."

"Might be just as well, sir," Winwood commented, though with a slightly disappointed sigh. "I've never really been ashore, here."

"The 'tavern of the seas,' Mister Winwood," Lewrie told him with a chuckle. "An infamous sink of sin, no matter the stiffness of the Protestant Dutch."

"Even so, though, sir . . ." Winwood said most wistfully.

"I wonder if they have corn-whisky?" Lewrie wondered aloud.

CHAPTER NINETEEN

It was a rather abstemious little gathering for supper in the great-cabins: the Sailing Master, Mr. Winwood, who never drank much at all, seated to his right; Lt. Devereux, in charge of *Proteus*'s Marine detachment, to his left, and (for a sea-soldier) never known as one who over-indulged in tipple; and his three midshipmen, Mr. Gamble the older, Mr. Grace, and wee Mr. Larkin, at the table's foot, as the Vice. All of whom were so daunted by Mr. Winwood, who was the midshipmen's tutor in matters navigational and mathematical, and by dread of making a fool of themselves by taking too much "aboard." Mr. Winwood's grave, mournful scowl when his sense of primness was offended could make the "middies" scurry like cockroaches. Lt. Blase Devereux was a languidly elegant sort, whose gentlemanly mannerisms they wished to emulate, anyway, and the captain was, well . . . the captain, not a man to disappoint, if they wished to stay in his "good books."

Once Capt. Treghues had signalled that the trade would, indeed, stand "off-and-on" the coast 'til dawn, they had sailed legs North and South abeam the wind, with the Indiamen back to their usual custom of reducing sail to bare steerageway, which had let the avid fishermen in the crew dip a line, ending in the catch of a middling-sized tunny, which had been shared between the gun-room and the captain's table.

They had had reconstituted "portable soup," a sea-pie made from shredded salt-beef and salt-pork, diced potatoes fried with bacon, and the tunny for the last course, great slabs of it, dredged in flour and crumbled biscuit, spices, and lemon, then fried in oil. There had been a decent claret with the sea-pie, and an experimental white wine bought off a homebound Indiaman. One of the first things the Dutch settlers at the Cape had planted was vineyards, though with mixed results, so far. The white had gone well with the fish, though not as smooth or sweet as a German hock, but *miles* better than the Navy-issued "Miss Taylor," the thin, vinegary, and acidy wine that could double for paint thinner, and Lewrie was intrigued enough to think of buying more, once at anchor.

There had also been the promise of an apple stack-cake to come, a dessert that his wife Caroline had brought from her native Cape Fear in North Carolina, shrivelled and wrinkly older Kentish apples that had not gone over, or been wormed, pulped and boiled with dollops of molasses and sugar, then spread thick between several layers of pancakes. Once the tablecloth would be removed, there would have been a tray of "bought" sweet biscuits, nuts, and port. Midshipman Larkin to propose the King's Toast, Mr. Winwood to make one to the Navy, and, as it was a Saturday evening, it would have fallen to Lewrie to propose a traditional Navy toast, "To Our Wives And Sweethearts, May They Never Meet!," which Lewrie found excrutiatingly apt.

But, just as Aspinall was lifting the cloth cover from the cake, the Marine sentry slammed his musket butt on the deck outside, with a strident, rather urgent, cry of "Second Off 'cah . . . SAH!"

"Enter, Mister Catterall," Lewrie bade, cocking a brow over Lt. Catterall's exquisite timing, imagining that the Second Lieutenant, who had the appetite of all three midshipmen together, had thought to wangle himself a hefty slice of cake, or at least a free cup of coffee.

"Signal rockets from the convoy, sir!" Lt. Catterall announced, though, his usually saturnine demeanour much agitated. "Fusees and an alert gun from *Horatius*, as well!"

"Pipe 'All Hands,' Mister Catterall, and Beat to Quarters, at once," Lewrie snapped, rising and tossing his napkin into his plate. "Sorry 'bout the cake, gentlemen, but it appears there may be Frogs in the offing. Your posts . . . shoo, scat, younkers!"

As they quickly rose and tumbled out without ceremony, Lewrie went aft for his baldric and hanger-sword, looking about for Aspinall and his Cox'n, Andrews.

"Andrews, do you fetch up my pair of pistols, soon as you can. Aspinall . . . save the cake, if that's possible. Then, see yourself and the cats to the orlop, with the Carpenter's crew."

In a twinkling, sailors would rush to man the 12-pounders mounted right-aft in Lewrie's cabins, knock down the deal partitions, and bundle fragile furniture, sure to be turned into deadly flying splinters in battle, below. One last snatch off a rack in the chart-space for his cocked hat, and he was off himself, out onto the main deck and up the windward ladderway to the quarterdeck, amid the mad, but well-drilled, bustle of sailors clearing their ship for action. Off-watch men rushed up with the long sausages of their hammocks and bedding, perhaps not rolled as tightly as they would each morning to pass through the ring-measure, to stow them in the iron stanchions and nettings, to turn them into a feeble defence against grapeshot, splinters, and musket fire.

"Where away?" Lewrie demanded, grabbing a spare night-glass by the binnacle cabinet. The Marine drummer was beating the long roll, bosuns' calls were peeping, hundreds of feet, shod or bare, thundered on oak decks, and *Proteus* nigh-shuddered to the sounds of loose items, sea-chests and stools being rushed to the orlop or holds, mess-tables being hoisted to the overheads on the gun-deck, of gun-tools removed from their overhead racks.

"Starboard side of the convoy, sir," Lt. Langlie breathlessly reported in the dark. He and the other officers and warrants had come in a rush from their own suppers. "Lieutenant Catterall reported that he'd seen a rocket and fusee from *Stag,* then heard the night signal gun 'board *Horatius,* before he summoned you. Ah, there's another!"

One Indiaman, then a second astern of her at the forward end of the starboard-most of two columns, both were now burning blue warning fusees high aloft, and launching amber rockets from their swivel-guns.

Lewrie lifted the night-glass to his right eye, straining ahead and to starboard. The convoy was at present bound South, about twenty miles off the shore, a dark coast lit only by a single, feeble bonfire atop either the Lion's Rump or Green Point, near the entrance to Table Bay, high enough above the sea to still be somewhat visible. They had nearly sailed that sea-mark below the horizon, and within the hour had need to come about and plod North, but for this.

Lewrie picked out ships by their large taffrail lanthorns: HMS *Horatius* far ahead, and now sporting a blue fusee at her main-top, and four Indiamen astern of her, the "threatened" pair that sailed on the starboard flank also lit up with the bright, blue pinpoint lights on their mastheads. They were turning away to larboard, pairs of stern lanthorns pinching together, and the vaguest hints of canvas growing like spectral spooks in the faint starlight, and what was thrown by a mere sliver of moon. Farther out lay Captain Philpott's HMS *Stag,* a black smear of hull, a pair of taffrail lights, and her upper sails visible by the burning fusee at her mainmast tip.

Damn this bloody thing! Lewrie furiously thought, cursing the night telescope, for its series of lenses was one short to allow more light into the tube, making everything appear backwards, and upside down. With the glass, *Stag* was headed North; without, she was headed South . . . foreshortening as she turned up into the West wind to face . . . something. HMS *Horatius* was also turning Sou'-Sou'west, as close as she could lie to those winds unless she tacked and came about.

"Can't make out a bloody thing," Lewrie griped aloud, lowering the telescope and rubbing his offending eye. "There's *something* up to the West of them, but damned if I can spot it. Any word from *Grafton*?"

"None, sir," Langlie was forced to say. "Same flares as us."

"Well, of course," Lewrie said with a frustrated sigh. Captain Treghues possessed the customary Navy signals book, as well as the one of his own devising, but *both* of them were based on the precondition of daylight! Nighttime signals could alert the merchantmen and warships to threat, but could not convey any tactical orders as to which action they might take, together. It was up to each captain's judgement as to how he might respond from his own, scattered, position at one of the convoy's four corners. Here, on the larboard, and landward, flank of the dark ships, it was up to Lewrie alone how best to act.

"Now, the near-hand column's hauling their wind, sir," Langlie pointed out. With his naked eyes, Lewrie took note of the two nearest Indiamen's lights; their hulls were beginning to occlude the starboard lanthorns, the blue masthead fusees swinging almost atop their glowing larboard taffrail lights.

"We're going t'get trampled, are we not careful," Lewrie griped. "Shake out the reefs in courses and tops'ls, Mister Langlie, and get a way on, so we pass ahead of those tubs."

"Aye aye, sir! Topmen! Topmen aloft, trice up and lay out!"

"Great-guns manned, loaded, and ready, sir!" Lt. Catterall said from the foot of the quarterdeck ladder. "The ship is in all respects prepared for action."

The gun-deck forward and below Lewrie's post amidships by those freshly hammock-stiffened quarterdeck nettings was dimly lit for night action. A well-spaced row of battle lanthorns marched down each beam, thickly-glassed and made of heavy metal, so gun crews could have just enough illumination to see to their duties, robust enough to resist a spill of the candle flames inside them, and create a fatal fire or an explosion of a serge powder cartridge after it had been removed from its wood or leather carrying sleeve. Beside them, tiny red "fireflies" glowed between the glossy, black-painted artillery; smouldering ends of slow-match coils wrapped round the tops of the swab-water tubs by each piece, the last-resort means of igniting the priming quills full of the finest mealed gunpowder, should the flint in more modern flintlock strikers break or fail. Far up forward, there were another pair of small lights by the forecastle belfry, normally used by the sleepy ship's boys, whose duty it was to keep track of the half-hour and hour glasses, turn them, and ring the bells of the watch.

"Charge *both* batteries, Mister Catterall," Lewrie ordered. "We don't wish to be taken by surprise. Open the ports and run the guns into battery, both sides . . . just in case."

"Aye aye, sir!"

A quick look astern satisfied him that the convoy was turning alee, all of them, earlier than scheduled. A quarter-hour longer, and they would have been alerted by *Grafton* to "Ready About," and, at the proper night signal—a fusee at the end of each foremast royal yard—would have hauled their wind and worn off the wind, as much as one might be expected from civilian shipmasters. Now, they were wearing individually, the most threatened bearing down on the larboard ships, startling them to haul off and fall alee like stampeding sheep, order lost, and if this turned out to be nothing, they'd be half the following day rounding them back up!

"Both the near-hand merchantmen *seem* to be bearing astern of us, sir," Lt. Langlie announced, with the faintest bit of relief apparent in his voice. "Should we be going about as well, Captain?"

"I've a mind to let 'em fall far enough astern, *then* tack, and see what aid we may give *Stag* and *Horatius,*" Lewrie decided, looking forward and to starboard, again, noting where Capt. Graves's lumbering two-decker had gotten to in the meantime. "A moment, Mister Langlie."

The threat *seemed* to be from seaward, but . . . on such an ebony night, nothing could be taken for granted. The French squadrons that haunted the Cape passage and the Indian Ocean were rumoured to be at least two large 36-gun or 38-gun frigates, operating separately, but paired with one, possibly two, *corvettes* apiece, three-masted, full-rigged, equivalent to Sloops of War in the Royal Navy, armed with a battery ranging from 14 to 20 guns, *and* sometimes sailing in concert with well-armed, over-manned privateers, as well. Such a pack could prowl like wolves—sea wolves!

And, like wolves, Lewrie realised with his "wary bone" wakening, could attack from all quarters, not just the one, dashing in to nip or intimidate, 'til their quarry was encircled and doomed.

"Mister Winwood?" Lewrie called over his shoulder.

"Aye, sir. Here," the Sailing Master reported, coming to join him from his usual post before the binnacle cabinet and double helm.

"We've a goodly way on? Sufficient for a quick, clean wear?"

"So I would adjudge it, sir, aye," Winwood ponderously answered.

"And, no reefs, rocks, or shoals to loo'rd?"

"Not for at least sixteen or seventeen miles, no, sir," Winwood was forced to avow, after a wince and a tooth-sucking noise, obviously much more comfortable with such a statement after a *long* perusal over his charts, a set of fresh star sights, taking the height of the moon by back-staff, and auguring the entrails of the odd passing gull.

"Very well, sir, we'll come about," Lewrie announced. "Mister Catterall? Check tackle, and be ready for a wear. Mister Langlie, I wish hands to stations, ready to come about to larboard, then steer a course Nor'easterly."

"Aye aye, sir! Bosun! Pipe 'Stations For Wearing Ship'!"

Lewrie paced to the leeward bulwarks to study the ocean where they meant to go as the fresh bustle broke out round his ears. With the heavy night-glass to his eye once more, he saw grey-black sea and a few white-flecked rollers, that now and again caught the faint glim of the waning moon, a complete pall of utter blackness that showed the veriest upper tier of far-off African cliffs, thin on the horizon. A complete sweep from Due South to Due North showed nothing else.

"Up mains'l and spanker, clear away the after bowlines! Brace in the afteryards! Up helm!" Langlie was bawling through his speaking-trumpet, and *Proteus* began to swing, to heel over as she slowed, bowsprit and jib-boom sweeping alee across the black face of the night.

The winds dead aft, now. "Clear away head bowlines, lay the headyards square! Shift over the head sheets!" Lewrie walked over to the starboard side with his telescope, looking into the stern quarter, and abeam as *Proteus* continued to swing, the wind now striking her on her larboard quarters. "Man the main tack and sheet! Clear away rigging! Spanker outhaul! Clear away the brails!"

There seemed to be nothing dangerous to landward. Lewrie eased his straining eye by lowering the night-glass for a second, as sudden gunfire rolled down on them from windward!

He spun about to catch the ruddy after-flash from gun muzzles, the briefly-lit spurts of whitish-grey smoke from some ship's pieces, and the pyrotechnic, spiralling yellowish embers from cartridge cloth. Distant as that gunfire was, his ears could discern the deep boomings of 24-pounders of *Horatius*'s lower-deck artillery, the crisper barks of what he took to be HMS *Stag*'s 12-pounders, and some light, terrier-like "yaps" from even lighter guns!

"Missing all the fun!" he heard Midshipman Grace whisper in the relative silence, once those distant guns fell silent.

"Brace up headyards, overhaul weather lifts . . . haul aboard!" Lt. Langlie bellowed, as the ship came rapidly back to nearly abeam of the winds.

"Mister Catterall," Lewrie called down in the tumult. "Man the starboard battery. Excess hands to chock trucks and snug the run-out tackles, *then* re-join their mates!"

"Aye aye, sir!"

"Steady out bowlines, haul taut the weather trusses, braces, and lifts!" Lt. Langlie concluded, at last. "Clear away on deck, there!"

They were about, bearing off the night wind to the Nor'east, and, by the sound of the hull, making a goodly way, again, well clear of the ships of their convoy, now fleeing North in no particular order, with, as Lewrie could espy, the sluggard *Festival* and HMS *Grafton* now ahead of them all.

"Thankee, Mister Langlie, well done," Lewrie took time to say as he took one last, long sweep of the sea to the East and Sou'east, but was drawn back to larboard by a new storm of gunfire, sounding as if *Horatius* had spotted something and had loosed an entire two-deck broadside at it.

"Deck, there!" a lookout atop the mizen shouted down. "Black ship astern the starboard quarter, close in!"

"Up helm, Mister Langlie! Stand by, the starboard battery, and be ready to engage, short range!" Lewrie cried, whirling about, again. "Get her bows down and—!"

But, it was too late. Somehow, a ship had sneaked up on them, all her lights extinguished, perhaps with her sails sooted, or so old that dark tan, weathered canvas would not reflect enought light to see her by! Even as the wheel was put hard-over, more gunfire split the night! Until the very moment that her guns lit off, no one on deck could have spotted her, not the night lookouts normally posted at the bulwarks, not the watch officers, not even Lewrie, for all his urgent peering. He froze, caught, like his frigate, with his breeches down, and there was nothing else to do but stand and take it!

BAM—BAM—BAM! Eight guns hammered out a slow, metronomic broadside as the hostile ship crossed *Proteus*'s stern, serving her a vicious rake, by the size of the muzzle blasts at a range of about two cables! Round-shot screamed or moaned, the howling rising in tone as they lashed towards them. Then came the crashing noises, the sound of timbers being smashed with the parrot "Rawrk!" of rivened wood, the shattering of glass sash-windows a few feet below the taffrails as the round-shot pierced through Lewrie's great-cabins to bowl, richochet, and carom past where the temporary partitions that normally shielded his privacy had stood, down the gun-deck among sailors standing by their pieces, shattering truck-carriages, glancing off pristine white-sanded decks, thudding into the mizen-mast trunk, sparking off gun tubes with deep, bell-like Bongs!, and raising a cloud of splintered wood flying like terrified pigeons into flesh!

Eight guns . . . corvette! Lewrie's panicky brain told him as he stood stiff-legged, almost unable to move, to think of much more; *She shot her bolt! Minute and a half t're-load. Good as our Navy?*

There was a great pall of spent powder smoke astern, the hint of masts and sails above it, and the fore end of a warship emerging from behind it, sailing what looked to be Nor'westerly.

"*Belay* the last helm order!" Lewrie shouted, forcing himself to motion, seething with sudden rage for being caught so flat-footed, so *stupidly*, and with shame for letting it happen, to *him*, to *his* ship! "Put yer helm *down*, steer Due North!"

Might open us to another rake, but, do we get a bit *off from her . . . !* he thought. Open the range, duck into the gloom, and hope the French *corvette*—for what else could it be?—lost sight of them for a moment. The wind was from the West, and the *corvette* was close-hauled, steering no better than Nor'-Nor'west, six points off of the wind, and obviously trying to get after the convoy and take at least one prize. With a relatively clean bottom and "all plain sail" aloft, she might attain nine or ten knots, slightly better than what *Proteus* was making, Lewrie's senses told him. They could not hope to surge up abeam of her to swat the *corvette* with their heavier broadside, but . . . what was sauce for the goose was sauce for the gander!

"Mister Langlie, you still with us?" Lewrie called out.

"Aye, sir. Still here," came a reassuringly firm reply.

"Good. I *want* that saucy bastard! Free the last of the night reefs from the t'gallants, let fall and sheet home the royals, and let the main course stay full, fire hazard bedamned," Lewrie schemed aloud. "That Frenchman's after an Indiaman, hard on the wind, most-like, and should be about . . . there," he said, pointing out into the darkness off the larboard quarters. "Perhaps three or four cables off. With luck, we may be able to out-reach her and *tack* 'cross her bows, then serve her a bow-rake!"

Taunt me, *will ye?* Lewrie thought, in fury to be fired upon by a lighter warship, one that usually would shy away from action with a frigate . . . if the Frenchman had *not* mistaken *Proteus* for a Sloop of War or gun-brig, then his feat of tweaking the "Bloodies'" noses with such daring could get him dined-out for years.

"With a knot or two more in-hand . . ." Lewrie began to say, but a fresh series of explosions split the night; another eight bursts of hot, white powder smoke, bright amber juts from muzzles, and showers of embers! "*There* she is!"

The *corvette* was, as he'd speculated, about three cables astern and farther up to windward than before. At that range, in the gloom, the Frenchman's new broadside was more of a threat than a killing blow. Reverting to the usual French Navy practice, these balls were fired at full elevation, on the up-roll, meant to dis-mast and cripple *Proteus,* not hull her, forcing her to fall away Eastward and astern to let the *corvette* get on with her depredations without further interference.

Lewrie involuntarily flinched into his coat as the round iron shot bowled overhead, ahead, and astern in a hopeful spread, but all of them clean misses, this time. And, by firing that broadside, "M'sieur Frog" had given away his best weapon . . . his location and the direction of his course. He was still close-hauled, bound Nor'-Nor'west.

"Signal rockets, Mister Langlie," Lewrie snapped. "Let *Grafton* and the others know there's a wolf 'mongst the sheep, and carry on."

"Aye aye, sir."

Swivel-guns on the midships larboard gangway bulwarks were made ready by the few brace-tenders and waisters not part of the gun crews below on the main deck. Four yellow-white rockets flung themselves to the skies with sulfurous whooshes, slanting out over the dark sea that lay to the West, creating brief golden sparkles and fire-glades on the waters . . . faintly illuminating their foe, as well. Most-hearteningly revealing a frigate off to the West, as well, one which flew the Red Ensign of the Royal Navy, which looked to be sailing Due North or one point alee, a little ahead of *Proteus* and in a prime position to haul her wind and fall down to counter the French *corvette,* too!

"Mister Catterall!" Lewrie shouted down to the deck below him. "Chock and check, starboard, and be ready to engage the Frog *corvette* off our larboard quarters when we wheel up to windward!"

In the last lingering glimmer of the signal rockets, Lewrie had time for a look into the waist, and was appalled. The 12-pounder gun nearest to the larboard ladderway sat on a shattered truck-carriage at a crippled angle, and there were two bodies beside it, in the awkward sprawls of the dead that could be mistaken for piles of old clothes! Four more corpses had been laid out round the trunk of the main mast, the broad pools of spilt blood glittering evilly in the light of the battle lanthorns. Even as he watched, Mr. Hodson's loblolly boys were bearing a gasping wounded man to the main hatchway ladders on a mess-table for a stretcher, a sailor so quilled with finger-thick splinters he more-resembled a hedgehog! A bit farther forward, another gun had not only been dis-mounted, but had been struck so hard with a cannon ball that a large divot had been taken from its thick breech!

Thirteen guns left? No, Lewrie fumed to himself; *Ten, more-like, for God knows what happened to the ones in my cabins, aft!*

"All sail set, sir, ready to go about," Lt. Langlie reported.

"Begin, Mister Langlie," Lewrie ordered, tight-lipped. "Mister Catterall, we're bearing up! Fire as you bear!"

"Stations for stays! Quartermasters, put your helm down!"

Proteus was now sailing at nearly ten knots, her bottom was as clean and swift as could be expected, so recently after a re-coppering, and her turn up towards the wind was quick. Leaving that to Langlie, Lewrie went to the larboard, soon-to-be engaged, side, gripping at the cap-rails and peering wide-eyed into the night, and, *yes!*, there she was, four cables off, but making a goodly way, her location revealed by the creaming white swash of her wake and bow-wave! Lt. Catterall's gunners groaned, grunted, and cursed as they levered their loaded guns about to point so far aft in the gun-ports, lifting, bodily shifting the rears of both gun and carriage to the right, heaving on the run-out tackle and breeching tackle so, when fired, those monsters didn't slew about and crush their tenders, or snap free. At this angle, the guns' right-hand second re-enforcing rings were *out* the ports, the trunnions, upon recoil, might barely clear the bulwarks. The gun-captains urged them on with shouts and fists, blows un-noticed by the sweating tars, for all of them, just as much as Lewrie, craved at least *one* broadside for revenge . . . for pay-back! And, to prove to the world, and to themselves, that they could give as good as they got.

"Ready . . . !" Lt. Catterall was bellowing, stepping well clear of his charges, the crews gathering well away from the possible result of recoil, too, each gun-captain standing with one fist in the air, with the triggering lanyards to the cocked flintlock strikers taut in the other. "Well, damme!" Catterall barked, frustrated.

As *Proteus* came up on the wind, as waisters and tenders braced her sails and yards up sharper, she began to wallow as if sailing with the wind nearly right-aft on a long-scending following sea. Lewrie looked to the helm, of a mind to curse the four helmsmen on the double wheel for the worst sort of lubbers, to see them heaving away, making the spokes blur . . . first to helm down, then to helm up!

"Steady her, dammit!" Lewrie bawled. "Thus!" he snapped, using his right hand to indicate the best course. By the light of the blue fusee at the main-mast top, he could see the commissioning pendant, so why couldn't *they*, for God's sake? "Steady on!"

She *did* steady up, though with a manic effort on her helm; she came to a constant course, at last. "As you bear . . . fire!" came the eager and relieved shriek from Lt. Catterall, and the 12-pounders began to bellow! Lewrie turned back to watch the *corvette,* picking her up by her frothing wake along her waterline, again, as the first round-shot was fired. There! A tall feather of water leaping up under her bows, a second about amidships of her length, a "short," but close enough to graze up and hit her 'twixt wind and water! Her forecourse twitched as a ball punched right through it; there came a faint "Rrawk!" from a direct hit into her scantlings or timbers; he saw her foremast shiver from top to trunk, vibrating like a harpsichordist's tuning-fork as a ball struck it! *Another* feather of spray from a ball that just barely cleared her starboard quarter, *another* close-aboard her after thirds, and caromed off her at a shallow angle, ripping side planking to bits!

Proteus began to wallow, again, bowsprit and jib-boom swinging and hunting left and right in wide and lazy yawings, with the convoy's stern lanthorns, now faint and far-off glows, to track by.

"Dammit to Holy Hell, what . . . ?" Lewrie roared, about ready to strangle someone.

"No helm, sir!" Quartermaster Austen shouted back. "No helm!"

"Christ shit on a biscuit," Lewrie muttered. "*See* to it, Mister Langlie!" he shouted back, though fearing the worst. That stern-rake surely had blown away steering tackle, smashed into the tiller-flat or the rudder, itself! Could relieving tackle be rigged and re-roved . . . else, *Proteus* would go from warship to drifting hulk in a twinkling. A helpless hulk, at the mercy of a pitiless Frenchman's guns!

The last gun in the larboard battery erupted, even though a hit was out of the question as *Proteus* fell off the wind. Only nine had fired, by Lewrie's count . . . even worse than he'd feared. On this wind and without steering, *Proteus* could do nothing but slump shoreward, her stern and weakened gun battery open to the foe.

Lewrie turned back to peer after the French *corvette*. Her wake still gave her position away, but she seemed farther away, not quite as long as she'd been before, perhaps, that creaming froth too short for a ship within four cables, he speculated. There came a bellowing up to windward, a series of gun flashes that revealed HMS *Stag,* which was on a course of about Nor'east, now, sailing to interpose herself between the convoy and the intruder. Moments later, far-distant HMS *Horatius* lit up the seas to the West with another full broadside of her own at something beyond her, silhouetting herself for several long seconds.

"Deck, there!" a main-mast lookout shouted down. "Th' enemy's goin' about! Tackin'! Two point off th' larb'rd *quar*-ter!"

"Thank God for small mercies," Lewrie whispered, no matter how ignominious it was to be "rescued" by a sister ship. It felt much like playing the role of a breeding bull being saved from the terror of a vicious, marauding terrier by the arrival of a cow from his own herd!

Sure, I'll never hear the end of it, Lewrie bemoaned.

"Pardon, sir," Lt. Langlie said, coming to his side and tapping the brim of his hat in salute. "The Bosun's Mate has been below, with the Carpenter, Mister Garroway. Mister Towpenny reports that all the steering tackle is taut and sound, with no shot holes near the tiller head. He fears 'tis the rudder itself, sir."

"Mast-head!" Lewrie barked aloft. "Where away that *corvette,* now?"

"*One* point off th' larb'rd *quar*-ter, *six* cable'r *more,* sir!" an anonymous cry came back. "Might jis' be past Stays, an' bound to th' *Sou'west*! Breakin' away, looks like, sir! Made a big, frothy patch!"

"Very well!" Lewrie shouted, then turned to his First Officer. "In that case, get the way off her, 'fore we rip what little's left clean off, Mister Langlie. Bosun and Carpenter to the quarterdeck at once, and I'll have a battle lanthorn fetched with 'em. Order Mister Catterall to secure his guns, and stand ready to assist where he can."

"Aye, sir."

When a ship tacked, she slowed, wheeled 90 degrees or more, created a large patch of disturbed water, and fell off the wind for a spell before firming up on a new course; that was what the lookout had seen, that pale phosphorescent half-acre of foam of a ship gone about, daunted from her desires by the presence of two frigates, and unready to trust her luck against the second one. This brief fight was over.

As the guns were levered back to right angles to the hull, and swabbed clean, tompioned, and bowsed to the bulwarks, as freed sailors went aloft to take in the royals and t'gallants, and once more reduce the tops'ls, Lewrie, Mr. Towpenny, and Mr. Garroway went aft with the lanthorn and a coil of light rope to inspect the rudder.

"Sonofabitch . . . sorry, sir," Towpenny gasped as the lanthorn bobbed, dangled, and swung, lowered halfway to the waterline under the frigate's counter. "No wonder she's yawin' like she's drunk as Davy's Sow . . . th' lower part o' th' main piece's swingin' like a barn door!"

"Upper stock of the main piece is nigh shot clean through, sir," the Carpenter also marvelled, " 'tween the second and third pintles and gudgeons, and, I suspect the lowermost's been torn completely away."

"Else she'd not sway like that, aye," Mr. Towpenny spat. "Fir baulks t'th' trailin' edge has been shot off, too. Hangin' on by less than a fingernail, she is, sir."

He shifted the lanthorn lower, and then slowly raised it, bumping up along the sternpost. "Ah, 'tis bad. Horrid bad, that," Towpenny sorrowfully commented with a wince, and a sucking hiss. "Nigh shot through 'twixt the second an' third pintles, an' *both* fourth an' fifth torn free, too, sir. An' wot's left o' th' sternpost below th' waterline's anybody's guess. Bronze gudgeons, an' pintle arms . . ."

"Seasoned oak for a replacement . . ." Carpenter Garroway mourned. "Fir's no problem, perhaps, but . . . there's no oak in Africa, is there?"

"Good, dense English elm f'r sole an' back, an' wot them balls did t'th' fayed triangle strips o' th' sternpost an' rudder, both . . ." Mr. Towpenny added.

"Could it be 'fished,' like a broken yardarm, Mister Towpenny?" Lewrie hopefully enquired, ready to all but cross his fingers behind his back. "Some *vertical* iron strips, bolted through, 'stead of fore-and-aft strapping like the tiller head?"

"Might could *try*, Cap'm, but I'd not trust it in anythin' more than calm seas," Towpenny said with a sad sigh. "Do it get boist'rous, th' rollin' gits too heavy, she might snap like a fresh carrot, an *then* where'd we be, sir? Nossir, we need a whole new main piece."

"Any other wood besides English oak that might serve?" Lewrie asked him. Towpenny hoisted the lanthorn up to the taffrails, with a distant look on his grizzled face, waiting 'til the lamp was in-board before he spoke.

"Mahogany or teak, sir," Towpenny speculated. "'Tis dense an' stiff enough, but th' *findin'* o' such, long an' broad enough . . . an' *seasoned* enough, not green, wellsir. That'd be a real poser, Cap'm."

"Damn!" Lewrie spat, clapping his hands behind his back, pacing forward and away. There were Cuban-built Spanish ships fashioned from truck to keel of mahogany, and the envy of anyone who captured them, for they were incredibly strong and long-lasting. He'd seen merchant vessels in the Far East, "country ships" in the local trade, made from teak, and they bore reputations for strength, too, but . . . India was a long way off, and without a rudder, they'd never get there to find the material necessary to *fashion* a new rudder! And, Lewrie rather doubted there were any Spaniards still in the Far East trade, who might put in at Cape Town and just *happen* to have a spare rudder gathering cob-webs in their bosuns' lockers!

He spun back around. "I take it we've not enough seasoned oak of the proper size to fashion a new'un, either, Mister Towpenny?"

"Nossir, we've not," the Bosun's Mate replied, after sharing a quick, silent conference with the Carpenter. "Nothin' thick or long enough t'make new, Cap'm."

"Well, damn my eyes," Lewrie growled.

One good *point,* he thought, taking what wee scrap of fortune he could from *mis*-fortune; *'thout a rudder, surely to* God, *we'll not have t'go on to Bombay or Canton in Sir Tobias-bloody-Treghues's company!*

Assuming they survived 'til dawn, for Lewrie was reminded that *Proteus,* with the way now almost completely off her to save what was left of her shattered rudder, was still prey to the West wind and the Eastward-setting current. Mr. Winwood had thought them about twenty sea-miles offshore when the action had begun, and they had worn away to leeward and steered Nor'east for a time before coming back to Due North to follow the convoy, which might have resulted in their losing a mile or better shoreward . . . a high-cliffed, rocky shore where the bottom rose up steeply and quickly, and the waves crashed with a fury, even on the best days. There would be no chance to come to anchor as they drifted ashore with the sea-bottom so far below.

Neither could they come up to the wind close enough to attempt a tack, or even fetch-to, for God's sake! Such a swing might rip the tatters right off the sternpost. Besides, it took a sound rudder for fetching-to, to maintain her head when the fore-and-aft sails and the back-braced sails on the yards countered each other in a constantly-shifting balancing act!

Are we fucked, or what? Lewrie miserably thought.

"Mister Langlie," Lewrie called out.

"Aye, sir?"

"I think it's time we fired some more of those signal rockets," Lewrie said, admitting to himself that he could think of nothing else to do, for once. "What is the number to convey 'Need Assistance'?"

"Five at once, sir," Lt. Langlie quickly replied.

"Make up a sea-anchor, get it over the side; and we'll hope for the best, Mister Langlie," Lewrie said, glad that no one could see him blushing with embarrassment in the dark.

"At once, sir."

About a half-hour later, HMS *Stag* came looming up in the gloom, surging alongside under reduced sail, but still going a lot faster than *Proteus,* within a long musket shot of her larboard, seaward, beam.

"Hoy, *Proteus*!" Capt. Philpott cried through a brass speaking trumpet. "You there, Captain Lewrie? Something amiss, is there?"

"Hoy, Captain Philpott!" Lewrie shouted back. "I'm still here, but we've a wee problem with our rudder. Shot halfway off!"

"That's what happens when you let a bad'un sneak up and spank you on the arse, aye!" Philpott cried, sounding like he was chortling.

God, I didn't know how much *I despise him, 'til now!* Lewrie took a moment to think.

"Do you request a tow, Lewrie?" Philpott offered.

"Aye . . . we need a tow into harbour, Philpott!" Lewrie shouted, figuring that if Philpott would drop the honourifics, he would, too, no matter did he outrank him on the Captain's List.

"Be ready when we come round, again, sir!" Philpott ordered. "I'll fetch-to off your bows, do you reduce to bare poles, and lower a boat to transfer the towing cable. Your cable, or mine, ha ha?"

"I will supply!" Lewrie replied.

"Good-ho! Mind, Lewrie . . . towing you in, I'll *not* demand that you fly my flag over yours, as my 'prize'!"

Choke on it, an' damn *yer sense of humour, ye bastard!* Lewrie furiously thought, wondering if it could *get* any more humiliating.

After a moment, Lewrie took evil glee in the comforting thought that whilst *Proteus* swung to her anchors at Cape Town, making repairs, it would be Philpott who would have the utter delight in accompanying *Grafton* and *Horatius* 'cross the Indian Ocean, with not a jot of shore liberty . . . and Lewrie would have free access to the Cape, "the tavern of the seas"!

Do I thank that Frenchman for that? Lewrie wondered; *Mine arse on a bandbox if I will!*

BOOK IV

"Contemnere, miser! Vitanda est improba Siren desidia, aut quidquid vita meliore parasti ponendum aequo animo."

"You will earn contempt, poor wretch.
You must shun the wicked Siren, Sloth,
or be content to drop whatever honour
you have gained in nobler hours."

HORACE, *SATIRES* II, III, 14-16

CHAPTER TWENTY

Oh, 'twas a splendid little victory, the saving of the convoy, on paper, at least! Nine helpless merchantmen (*eight* of them worthy) assaulted by a French squadron, which *might* have been consisted of *two* frigates, *and* a brace of *corvettes*, the foes' fell purposes countered by English Pluck and Daring, superb Seamanship, and Argus-eyed gunnery, all most shrewdly directed and concentrated in a trice by rapid application of a unique night-signalling system invented by the escorts' commander, a system the Fleet would *surely* find superior to any other!

And, had the Frogs been possessed of *real* "bottom," it could've been a *spectacularly* conclusive fight, resulting in the capture or the utter destruction of a significant number of the French raiders who preyed on British trade in this part of the world's oceans, adding even brighter laurels to the Royal Navy's fame, and their Sovereign's honour.

But, the shivering cowards had done as much as they dared, then scampered away in the face of overwhelming strength, well-peppered and "much cut up" by good British iron, whilst their own sea-gunnery fared as poorly as it usually did . . . except for *sneaking* most unfairly and knavishly (but what could one expect of Frogs?) up on HMS *Proteus*, and whose fault was *that*, certainly *not* the "Victorious Squadron's" alert commander, who was at that instant busy directing the activities of his own flagship, and his squadron's ships, *miles* away, so there!

Lewrie looked up from a copy of that report, after gathering the gist of it, and bestowed upon the Flag-Captain to Vice-Adm. Sir Roger Curtis, commanding officer of the Cape Station, a most dubious expression, all but rolling his eyes.

"Indeed, sir," the Flag-Captain derisively simpered after Lewrie handed it back to him. "Captain Sir Tobias Treghues may make of your encounter with the French what he will, but 'tis doubtful if *Admiralty* will find his account much of a success. We shall, of course, despatch it to London. . . ."

"Of course, sir," Lewrie replied with a knowing nod.

"With an account of our own, of course, anent this odd affair," the Flag-Captain further said, with a mocking brow raised.

Lewrie had already seen a thumbnail sketch of this report, in a scathing personal letter that Treghues had sent aboard, a letter replete with "Lewrie, how could you spoil such potential glory by your inattentiveness!" by *allowing* himself to be taken so unawares, salted with "I have always felt uneasy in my mind over your lamentable lack of assiduousness," and with several "Tsk-Tsks" over his utterly *casual* and tongue-in-cheek and lack-a-day and dilettantish approach to such a serious and demanding profession as the Navy required, and *et cetera* and *et cetera*, in much the same vein, concluding with the supposition "that one could suspect that, to avoid a long and depriving voyage to the Far East, you *finagled* a way out by letting your ship be damaged by a mere *corvette*," along with a closing warning that should any part of the convoy suffer loss due to further French action, with the escort so reduced, then he, Capt. Sir Tobias Treghues, would personally hold Capt. Alan Lewrie responsible for it, and make sure that Admiralty did, too!

Lewrie had not expected to see the *official* version, though . . . junior officers were *never* allowed such a luxury; but, this *was* Sir Roger Curtis he was dealing with, he had to recall.

They had met, briefly, in the aftermath of the battle that had famously become known as The Glorious First of June, in 1794, on the decks of HMS *Queen Charlotte*, when Capt. Sir Roger Curtis was Flag-Captain to Adm. Sir Richard "Black Dick" Howe. Lewrie had spent a whole day being pursued by two scouting French frigates, ending penned up against the unengaged side of the entire French line of battle, and had gotten round the end of their line and into the shelter of Howe's battle line by the skin of his teeth. That exploit had not been mentioned in despatches by Sir Roger, gaining Lewrie no fame of it. And, playing favourites most shamefully, then-Capt. Sir Roger Curtis had also omitted the names of captains and ships that had not been able to come to close grips with the French on the light winds that prevailed that day, denying them Admiralty recognition—and the gold medals!—given to those in the van of the snake-bent line of battle; or, as some spitefully suspected, omitting the names of people with whom he'd served in the past, and still disliked!

Adm. Duncan at Camperdown, Adm. Jervis at the Battle of Cape St. Vincent, certainly Adm. Nelson at the Nile, made sure that *all* captains were cited for their efforts, for all the world to see in the *Gazette* and the *Marine Chronicle*, but, evidently, Sir Roger Curtis, Baronet, still had no truck with the new-fangled idea of "We Few, We Happy Few, We Band of Brothers"!

Treghues is fucked, Lewrie told himself; *poor, desperate bastard*.

"Ye say your ship was damaged aft, Captain Lewrie?"

"Our rudder was nigh shot off, sir, aye," Lewrie replied. "Four guns dismounted, two with divots the size of dinner plates shot out of them, and I'm leery of firing full charges from them in future. I have six dead and thirteen wounded, as well, with three of those not long for this world, or so my Surgeon informs me, sir."

Lewrie unconsciously fingered the St. Vincent and Camperdown medals that hung round his neck for this full-dress interview, as if to reassure himself, and the Flag-Captain, that he had done much better in the past, and that the French ambush had been a rare fluke.

"You may enquire of our stores ship for replacement timber with which to mend, or replace, your rudder, Captain Lewrie," the man off-handedly allowed. "As to guns, there *may* be some captured Dutch twelve-pounders with the local Prize-Court. The Court's warehouses may also hold bosuns' stores from prizes taken by the ships of this station in past," he concluded with a preening smile.

What bloody prizes? Lewrie sourly thought; *Don't tell me that Elphinstone's are still here, five years later.*

In '95, Sir George Keith Elphinstone had led a squadron to the Cape; three 74s, two older 64s, and a pair of 16-gunned Sloops of War, along with transports carrying the 78th Regiment of Foot to take over the Dutch colony, which he had done, right handily. Now, the squadron assigned here was little larger—minus the transports—with older and lighter frigates replacing the Sloops of War, a force not much bigger than Treghues's escort force! Table Bay, treacherous as it could be, was huge, but fairly empty, at present, and once the East India trade sailed onwards, it would be even emptier. For the moment, there were only a pair of 74s, a lone 64, and one old 28-gun Sixth Rate at anchor, besides the stores ship. And . . . crippled HMS *Proteus*.

And, neither Cape Town nor Simon's Town on the other side of the peninsula owned a graving dock or dry dock, where serious repairs *could* be made. *What had the Dutch done before we got here?* Lewrie had to wonder.

"I must own surprise, sir, that such an important station, bestride one of our most vital trade routes, does not have an official dockyard establishment," Lewrie stated. That seemed safer than asking what prizes the Cape Squadron had managed to reel in.

"One'd *think* so, wouldn't one," the Flag-Captain breezily answered, "but, there *is* a war on, and the Cape is rather far removed from *major* French naval ports such as Rochefort, Brest, or Toulon. With the Dutch, French, and Spanish round-the-Cape trade nigh-completely ended, and the much smaller neutral countries' trade so lightly-armed, there is no real threat to Crown interests. Gad, can you imagine the Americans, or the *Roosians,* coming in on the French side, then mounting expeditions to come *here,* ha ha?"

"Though the French *do* hold Mauritius and the Seychelles with a strong force of lighter ships, sir," Lewrie carefully pointed out; he would get *no* help if he irritated the local squadron. "And, wasn't it a rather firm rumour that they have also fortified the old pirate hole on the northern tip of Madagascar? Fort de France on Mauritius is, so I was told, as large and nigh-impregnable as any of their home ports."

"But *rather* far from here, sir," the Flag-Captain replied, with a bit *less* casualness, as if awaiting criticism.

But, ain't that what warships are for? Lewrie cynically thought; *Go play silly buggers* thousands *of miles away, t'keep you awake nights?*

"I also must own that neither I, nor Captain Treghues, had warning of the French operating on *this* side of the Cape of Good Hope, sir," Lewrie added, keeping his face serious, perhaps play-acting perplexity, so the Flag-Captain wouldn't take affront and kick him in the "nutmegs." "Is this something new since we left England, sir? I thought their best hunting grounds would be 'twixt Ceylon and here, not in the Atlantic."

"Well, despite the tight blockade of the French home ports, *some* re-enforcements *do* slip through the net," the Flag-Captain dismissively—and rather grumpily—answered. "And, though Fort de France on Mauritius has its own dockyard facilities, there are times when ships have need of serious repair . . . such as is your case, hmm?" he added with a prissy sarcasm. "And, they must sail for France, or *replacing* warships and privateers must sail out to Mauritius. In the face of a strong Royal Navy presence, it would only make sense for them to sail together, rather than risk a 'singleton.' Sir Roger and I are of an opinion that what your Captain Treghues encountered the other night was such a mutually-protective group, on its way to France, that ran across you all by accident, and could not resist the opportunity to sail home with some additional prizes, d'ye see, sir."

"Well . . ." Lewrie began to say, deeming that wishful thinking.

"We've three frigates at sea, this instant, sir, hunting just that sort of movement," the Flag-Captain insisted. "In your case, it was a fluke. Treghues *still* retains a strong escort force, so I doubt he'll have *another* encounter like that in the Indian Ocean, more's the pity for his aspirations to glory, what? And, by the time he is back, you might be repaired and ready to re-join his command."

"But, that'd be *months,* sir!" Lewrie protested. "With no yard, and no replacement timber . . . !"

"No more than six to eight weeks, most-like," the Flag-Captain said with a shrug, doing nothing to reassure him. "Our esteemed 'John Company' convoy service is now a monthly business. Put in a request to the yards at Bombay, and you could have a spanking-new rudder shipped here for installation. Request goes with the India-half of Treghues's trade, the rudder arrives . . . sooner or later." To make things worse, the senior officer added, with what felt like a malicious little grin, "Assuming that there would *be* a homebound Indiaman who'd break their passage at the Cape. They usually don't, even the trades out-bound from China." Evidently, Lewrie *had* rankled the man, even with a pose of innocent perplexity plastered on.

"Dear Lord," he breathed, his shoulders slumping.

"For the nonce, allow me to advert to you the services of the local Dutch chandlers, sir," the Flag-Captain cheerfully blathered on, making it sound as if he'd gladly foist all responsibility for repairs and stores well-wide of the Cape Station's limited funds, and place it all squarely on Lewrie, and *his* purse. "Have you been ashore, yet?"

"Only briefly, sir," Lewrie said. "Funeral arrangements."

"They're most capable, and passably well-stocked. From the very first days of Dutch settlement, they've brought in farmers, servants, and slaves from their Far East colonies. 'Tis an 'all-nations,' like a dram shop, ha ha!" the Flag-Captain chuckled. "Javanese, Sumatrans, Malays, Hindoos, Lascars, even Chinamen. Some of whom are fishermen, boatmen, and pearl and oyster divers, d'ye see, sir? The local Dutch *myhneers* could put you in the way of some who could survey the damage to your ship, do the preparatory work for you, without need to careen your ship on some beach, what?"

"Well, that's a grand idea, sir!" Lewrie said, perking up considerably. "I'll, ah . . . take no more of your busy time, then, sir."

"Anything needful, send word, once you conduct your initial survey, and we'll see what we might possibly do for you, Captain Lewrie."

"Shore liberty for my people, sir?" Lewrie off-handedly asked, hoping that the Cape Squadron had not yet gotten word of what had happened on St. Helena.

"Within reason," was the Flag-Captain's reply. "Cape Province is the Land of The Lotus Eaters, so be wary of allowing your tars any freedom beyond the immediate town environs. 'Tis all too possible for a man to live well off the back-country. More than half the Dutch are what they call *trekboers,* who live semi-nomadic . . . herds, waggons, and kinfolk, native slaves and all, stopping just long enough to plant the staple crops, then moving on when the land plays out . . . or, they get bored, I expect," the Flag-Captain said, rising to indicate that their interview was over. "There's more than a few sailors, *well-paid* hands off Indiamen and passing traders, who run no risk of battle such as we do, have 'run' and taken up the life. Damned fools."

"Thankee for the warning, sir," Lewrie told him, gathering up his hat and such. "I will caution my officers and warrants t'be wary."

" 'Tis such a pity, though . . . that so much of the beguiling wildlife can kill you."

"Kill, sir?" Lewrie asked, trying not to gawp. The two times he had broken his passage at Kaapstad, as the Dutch called it, in '84 and '86 between the wars, he hadn't gotten into the back-country; taverns, restaurants, and rich-gentlemen's brothels had been more beguiling to *his* tastes. A spirited horseback ride on a hired "prad" from Kaapstad and Table Bay to Simon's Town on Simon's and False Bay represented his best effort at "exploration" . . . and there'd been clean posting-houses and taverns all along the way, too.

"Oh, *God* yes!" the Flag-Captain exclaimed with a *moue*. "Snakes and scorpions, spiders, biting ants, biting flies, and such? They are as vicious and deadly as a pack of hungry lions. Wild beasts running in herds so vast they blanket the land, miles across. Not to mention a large assortment of fierce native tribes, simply *keen* on poisoning their spears and arrows.

"God only knows what the Dutch hoped to make of a toe-hold in Africa, other than a way station on the way to the riches of the Far East. And, now *we* have possession of it, God only knows of what avail 'twill prove to be to us, hah?"

"Well, at one time, one might've said much the same of North America, sir," Lewrie drolly pointed out.

"Oh, quite right!" the Flag-Captain hooted, in much mirth over Lewrie's quip. "Quite right, indeed! Ah, *empire*! What a grand and glorious thing for Britons to own . . .'til one must actually go take a squint at it, close up, and be confronted with its sweaty, itchy, and uncomfortably fatal nature. Look at India, for God's sake! Best of luck with your repairs, Captain Lewrie. Any difficulties, don't hesitate to ask," he vowed, though how much aid he'd actually be was a moot question. Beyond the stores ship, it would be up to them, alone.

⚓

At least armed with some more-than-credible things for his crew to dread when they went ashore, preventing mass desertion, Lewrie went back aboard his frigate. Once the ritual salute was done, he went aft to the taffrails to stare long and hard at the inviting shore, leaning on the cap-rails on his elbows, most lubberly.

Two guns short, even if there *was* enough seasoned timber ashore or in stores to re-mount them on new truck-carriages; unless the Prize Court really *had* captured 12-pounders, he would have to accept sailing with a weaker gun battery. Assuming Bombay had a slab of seasoned oak big enough for a new rudder, the stores ship had it, and would really give it up!, the Dutch chandlers had it, well . . . *sailing* might be a moot point, too. Six, possibly *nine*, hands short, if Mr. Hodson's sad diagnoses proved correct, with nigh a dozen more prime sailors recuperating from wounds, and on light duties for weeks more, to boot. There wasn't even an official naval hospital ashore, not yet, and Admiralty seemed loath to spend ha'pence more on the Cape Town Station than absolutely necessary, so Lewrie supposed that he would have to rent a place in the town, something airy, clean, and shady where his wounded sailors could recover, for the small sick-bay near the forecastle aboard ship was the worst sort of make-shift sick-berth.

One comfort: the long-settled Dutch, no matter how much rancour existed 'twixt them and the English, were also Protestant Christians, with none of the intolerance for other faiths that obtained in Spanish, or Catholic, lands. There had already been an established, but small, Church of England parish to serve the needs of transient British sailors in Cape Town, and the church's rector had most-kindly offered his services, and his graveyard, where Lewrie's dead were now buried. With a *real* churchman to officiate, a hand-pumped organ and organist to accompany the heartfelt hymns, and altar boys to both assist the rector in his duties and form the core of a tiny choir which had turned out to honour fellow Englishmen as they went under the earth, the service had been much more satisfying to one and all than anything that Lewrie could have done, with his battered Book of Common Prayer in one hand, and equally tattered hymn book in the other, awkwardly reciting ritual by the starboard entry-port as the dead were tipped over the side, one by one, sewn into a canvas shroud with round-shot at their feet, a last stitch through their noses, sliding from the carrying board from under the Ensign to plunge into the unfathomable, abyssal depths.

It was best, though, that his dead had come ashore already sewn into their sail-canvas shrouds, for two of the six had come from among his "Black Jamaican volunteers"—Landsman George Anson and Ordinary Seaman Jemmy

Hawke—and Lewrie was mortal-certain that the vigourous youngish rector, kindly as he'd seemed, would have raised a torrent of objections had he seen Blacks going into the ground beside Whites!

"They were related to those august gentlemen, were they?" he had comfortingly enquired in a private moment. "How horrible 'twill be for such famous naval families to learn of such early demises for kin, who had their promising careers ended so tragically early. Should I write letters of condolence, perhaps . . . ?"

"No kin to former admirals, nossir," Lewrie had had to say with a straight and mournful face, suddenly amused nigh to titters with the astonishment everyone would evince were the shrouds opened, or letters sent to the Anson and Hawke families back in England. "In fact, they were but common sailors, good men, but without any ties to gentlemanly families, I fear. Men volunteer, or declare themselves when 'pressed,' under false names. *Take* false names to avoid being taken up by civil authorities, were they wrongdoers before, d'ye see."

"Ah, I understand, Captain Lewrie," the rector had said, "and I feel certain that, no matter their sins were scarlet, dying in service to King and Country, they were washed as white as snow by their dedication to Duty, and by the true Valour they evinced in their last instants. Heaven will be their reward, no matter how humbly born."

"Truly said, sir," Lewrie had replied. "As for notifying their kin, I have already composed letters. 'Tis *my* sad duty."

Half the morning gone, kicking his cooling heels waiting to be seen by that Flag-Captain, whilst Mr. Pendarves, Mr. Towpenny, and Mr. Garroway had been over the side on a catamaran, a floating work stage, surveying what they could above the waterline, the damaged gun-trucks being repaired with what stocks of seasoned timber they had in stores aboard *Proteus,* and the "divotted" artillery pieces dis-mounted, ready to be slung into the cutter and rowed ashore for exchange, should there actually be Dutch 12-pounders to exchange them for. Lewrie would not be picky; they could be tiger-mouthed Hindoo or Chinese guns, for all it would signify to him at that point!

So much to do to put *Proteus* to rights, to care for his maimed sailors, one of whom, "Sam Whitbread," was also Black, and what Dutch renters thought of that when he sought shore lodgings for them, well!

Six, eight weeks, he said? Lewrie thought with a dismayed moan; *Longer? Land of The Lotus Eaters, bedamned! And, the French. Could they have gotten strong, or bold, enough, to haunt Table Bay,* despite *what the local Navy officers think? I* can't *sit idle, swingin round the anchors, if the Frogs think they can raid this close to home.* For a bleak moment, he pictured that French squadron sailing right into the bay for a night raid on shipping, and with *Proteus* so lamed . . . !

He thrust himself erect, determined to get a way on, to achieve something productive before sundown; though, what that was, he hadn't a clue, at present. He paced back forward, but caught sight of *Festival,* anchored about a mile off, and now swarmed with barges and boats to unload her menagerie, scenery, and such for a long "run" of performances. Her main yardarm was dipping to sway out a sling which held a horse, a *white* horse, Eudoxia's well-trained gelding.

Hmm, he speculated; *eight weeks or more, in a Paradise, even if it's a* deadly *sort. With her ashore? Lord, give me strength!*

CHAPTER TWENTY-ONE

Two days later, and the prospects for his frigate didn't look so bleak. Requests for material assistance from the Indiamen that they'd convoyed this far had resulted in enough oak from their own, civilian, bosuns' stores for new truck-carriages to replace the ones too smashed up to be repaired, and for repairs on those that could be salvaged.

Out of gratitude that one, or all, of them hadn't been taken by the French, perhaps, there had also come enough dried and seasoned fir or pine with which to fay the face of the sternpost and the lead edge of the rudder, enough elm for faying and soling, as well. With timber had come a few iron pigs that could become reinforcing strapping bands, enough bronze in-pig for a shoreside blacksmith to forge new gudgeons or pintles, and bolts. A personal meeting with salty old Capt. Cowles, the convoy commodore, and he'd sponsored a whip-round from the other Indiamen that had resulted in a flood of offerings worthy of a Cornucopia, a veritable Horn of Plenty.

Had seven of his brave sailors now passed over? Were ten still lying wounded? For each man, mates and passengers had made up a small purse to cover their sick-berth fees, which Ships' Surgeons and Mates would deduct from their pay, even if the Spithead Mutiny had ended the practice of wounded men's pay being stopped 'til they were healed, so they would not suffer financially. Dead men's grave fees were paid to the parish, and a tolerable amount had been contributed to send on to their families, to augment the miserly pensions Admiralty granted. More was to go to providing fresh victuals for those who lingered in the rented cottage high up on the windy bluffs of the Lion's Rump!

Artillery, well . . . neither the stores ship nor the Prize Court storehouses had 12-pounders for exchange. They had some few 6-pounders and a pair of 9-pounders taken off Dutch merchantmen captured in port when Elphinstone had landed, and a pair of Dutch 18-pounders that had never been installed in the sea forts built to protect Cape Town; but, Lewrie was slavering, but wary, of how much recoil and weight that his decks, his bulwarks and his breeching cables could withstand, should he dare install those monsters and touch them off, fully charged!

In the face of such freely-offered bounty, Lewrie had no choice but to reciprocate by dining-in Capt. Cowles, the masters and mates off the other Indiamen, and those passengers who had contributed. He had dreaded the expense, but, a local inn had done him proud off the local viands, and at a fairly decent price, too.

It had turned out to be a "game supper." The soup had been egg and guinea fowl, mainly, with some rice and fresh peas. Crisply fresh salad greens came next, then the vast assortment of meats brought in as removes, more guinea fowl or pheasant, even *ostrich*!; for venison there had been springbok or gemsbok, antelope and impala, even *giraffe*, for God's sake! Then had come wild boar with mushrooms, followed by fish courses such as Cape salmon, thumb-thick shrimp as long as one's whole *hand* done in olive oil, lemon juice, garlic, chilies, bay leaves, and cloves! There had even been a kick-shaw made of crocodile!

Local made-dishes such as *bredies* and *boboties* had made their appearance, the *bredie* a mutton stew stiff with pot vegetables, and the *bobotie* nearly the best mild curry of shredded lamb, fruit, and rice Lewrie had eaten in his life. Fresh breads, local wines, mounded rice pilafs or *satays* showing Javanese influences, and, to top all of that off (should anyone have had a cubic inch of stomach left for them), the desserts (besides fresh, whole fruits) had consisted of rich, cinnamon-laced milk tarts, a steamed brandy pudding as good as any to be found in England, or *koeksisters*, which were wee braided, doughy confections sopping with honey, spices, and heavy fruit syrups.

Port, sweet biscuit, and nuts had seemed superfluous, and Lewrie was still belching, two days later.

Now, though, Lewrie paused midships of the larboard gangway as the sound of cannon fire caught his attention. The convoy of Indiamen was setting sail to complete their long journeys to India or China, and HMS *Grafton*, *Horatius*, and the unfortunate HMS *Stag*, with the equally disappointed Capt. Philpott, were getting under way with them, the flagship firing a proper salute to Vice-Adm. Curtis's flag as it went.

I made the effort, Lewrie told himself, for he had sent an invitation to his shore supper to his fellow captains, and Treghues, too, but only Philpott and Graves had attended, Treghues had sent a stiff note of regret that Stern Duty would not allow for such idle socialising at such a moment. *Poor, stiff-necked bastard*, Lewrie bemoaned.

Sir Roger being Sir Roger, that worthy had laughed that report Capt. Treghues had submitted, and sent on to London, to scorn, eagerly *sharing* his scorn among his coterie. It actually made Lewrie wince to see Treghues grasping at such a slender straw, to turn what had been a half-blind shambles into a signal victory . . . or, at least a thumping-good repelling of a back-stabbing French attempt on his convoy. What a misery Treghues might find his wartime career, of plodding to India and back with his guns rusting for want of use, and with never a foe strong enough to challenge him, Lewrie could not imagine. Didn't *want* to imagine, for by comparison, he'd already had more than his share of a lively war, with the medals, rank, and "post" to prove it.

Did Treghues hope that a report of *any* sort of action involving gunpowder, *any* sort of success against the French, might bring him to the Admiralty's notice in a fresh, new light, which might earn him his promotion to *real* Commodore rank, command of a squadron in more active and important seas? Or, might a release from boresome convoy duties be the excuse he craved to land his dour wife ashore whilst he sailed "in harm's way," as that American pest John Paul Jones had termed it? No one, in Lewrie's jaded experience, could tolerate such a tart and termagant mort like her for very long, not even if she came with access to the rents of an entire *shire*!

"Fa-are-well, and *adieu*, you-ou *sour* English sai-lor, fa-are-well, and *adieu*, you-ou arse-load of *pain* . . . !" Lewrie softly sang under his breath as he watched HMS *Grafton* curtsy and heel as she manned her yards to make more sail.

Oh, a host *of foreign "bye-byes"!* Lewrie gleefully thought, as he tried to dredge up half-forgotten phrases from his experiences.

Adios . . . came to mind, quickly followed by *Vamanos!*, which was more *apropos*. *Auf Wiedersehen* . . . *au revoir*, both of which he thought too polite by half; the catch-all Hindoo *Namasté*, good for welcome and departing; what had he heard at Naples, Genoa, and Leghorn in the Med? Ah, *arrivederci!*, that was it!

Ave atque vale, from his schooldays Latin. He would have tried the Greek, but there was a language he never *could* get his wits about, for which failure his bottom had suffered at a whole host of schools.

There was Eudoxia's *dosvidanya;* there was what he had read in Captain Bligh's book following the *Bounty* mutiny, that the Sandwich Islanders said . . . *Aloha Oh-Eh;* what the first explorers to the colony of New South Wales had heard the Aborigines shout at them on the beach of Sydney Cove . . . *Warra-Warra!* Later settlers—the willing, not the convicts—had learned that it was *not* a cry of welcome, but a wish for the strange new tribe to "Go Away!" How *very* apt!

"*Warra-Warra!*" Lewrie softly called out, lifting one hand as if bestowing a blessing on HMS *Grafton*, though, did one look closely, one *might* have noticed that Lewrie's index and middle finger of that hand were raised a bit higher than the rest, that hand slowly rotated, palm inwards, towards the end.

Rudder, Lewrie reminded himself, turning away to deal with his greatest problem. He went to the starboard entry-port, clad in an old shirt with the sleeves rolled to the elbows, his rattiest, oldest pair of slop-trousers rolled to his knees above bare shins and shoes about to crack apart with age, mildew, and damp. Bareheaded, he tossed off a sketchy salute to the side-party and scampered down the battens and man-ropes to his gig, where Cox'n Andrews and only a pair of oarsmen awaited. They would not bear him far, just down the starboard quarter, then round the square-ish stern, where other people were already occupied.

"Good morning, Mister Goosen," Lewrie said to the Dutch ship chandler, who had contracted to do the survey. He was a square-built fellow in his early fifties, heavily bearded contrary to current fashion elsewhere, garbed much as Lewrie was, but for a wide straw hat on his pink and balding head. Reddish cheeks and nose, the sign of the serious toper . . . or, one who spent his days in the harsher African sun, and on the water, to boot.

"*Gut* morning, *Kaptein*!" Goosen jovially replied from his boat, an eight-oared thing nearly fourty feet long, with both a false forecastle and imitation poop, that had once been as grand as an admiral's barge, but had gone downhill rapidly in civilian hands. Goosen waved a wooden piggin at Lewrie, by way of greeting, then emitted a belch at him, which required a fist against his chest. "Cold, sweet lime water. Ver' *gut* on hot days, Kaptein, but making die bilious," he explained.

"What have your divers discovered so far, sir?" Lewrie asked as he shared a look with the Bosun, Mr. Pendarves, who was sitting on the edge of his catamaran with his feet and shins in the water, alongside the damaged rudder.

"Rudder iss fucked, Kaptein," Goosen replied with an expression halfway 'twixt a scowl and a grin. "Sacrificial fir baulks shattered, die main piece, uhm . . . iss die green-twig broke. Not clean broke but hang by shreds? Thin end, oop dahr, iss strained at both tiller-head holes, it flop too much after break happen. Be bitch to fix, oh *ja*."

"Come from too much helm effort, sir, th' tiller-head holes," Mr. Pendarves added, flapping his feet and shins in the harbour water. "Gudgeons an' pintles 'bove th' waterline *seem* sound, but, th' way she she were swingin' so free, I've low hopes 'bout the two lower-most."

A pair of Oriental-looking sprogs came bursting to the surface in welters of foam, bobbing like corks for a moment before starting to paddle with their legs and wave their arms sideways to stay afloat. One swabbed water from his face and long hair, then kicked a few feet over to Goosen's barge, took hold of the gunwale, and began a palaver in a tongue that was most-likely half-Dutch and half-Javanese, neither of which Lewrie could follow.

Goosen listened, nodded here and there over the choicer bits, sucked his teeth and winced, then translated. "*Kaffir* say gudgeon at bottom of sternpost iss *open*. Iss bolted to sternpost, but die hole-for-pintle-part iss not hole, but like diss!" Goosen said, frowning, and holding up one hand, thumb and fingers forming a cylinder, before snapping them apart to make a wide U-shape.

"And the lower-most pintle?" Lewrie prompted.

"Iss half tore loose, Kaptein, wit' pintle pin *bent*," Goosen further translated, bending his forefinger into a crook to describe it. "Die bolts heff tore up rudder, too. Next-est to sternpost, be gone. Pintle fitting hang by last bolt, next-est to aft end."

"What in God's name *hit* us, then?" Lewrie wondered aloud. "If the lower-most of the five sets of pintles and gudgeons are the thickest and heaviest-forged of all?"

"Ah, but deepest part of main piece rudder taper thinnest, die wood be planed slimmest, *Kaptein*," Goosen pointed out, with too much heartiness to suit Lewrie. "Bronze thickest, but bolts shortest, for die upper four pintles and gudgeons be *expect* to bear die most weight."

"And the fourth set?" Lewrie further enquired, his hopes for a quick repair sinking.

"Bent," Goosen told him, making as if to wring out a wet towel. "Bad *wrench*, when rudder be shot. Pintle and gudgeon there *both* are wrench. When Frenchman dammitch rudder oop dahr, whole weight go on die next-est oop set. Gudgeon dahr be wrench almost out. Gon' need whole *new* rudder, oh *ja*! New pintles, gudgeons, bolts, nuts, top to bottom, *ja*!"

Tell me something we didn't *know!* Lewrie sourly thought, musing on that sad news and looking away, up the shattered sternpost and the rudder to the square overhang of the transom. He had to smile, nonetheless, for the sash-windows of his great-cabins were open, and both of his cats were posed in them, paws resting on the sills, intrigued by such a rare sight below.

"We've received enough iron and bronze to have new pintles and gudgeons fashioned ashore," Lewrie stated, looking back at the sweaty Dutchman. "If our own armourer cannot do the work, that is. New oak, of this size . . . ? Or, is there some sturdy local tree that might serve just as well, hereabouts, Mister Goosen?"

"Local timber? Pah!" Goosen countered with a humourless laugh. "Die *verdammte* African termite eat *gut* timber, quick as goat eat paper, *Kaptein!* Unt oop in mountains . . . die Cederburg, Hex Mountains, die Drakensberg, iss only *pine* grow tall unt straight," he said, waving a hand at the far distant blue ranges surrounding Table Bay. "Termite, he bad as ship-worm. All rotten, in a few year, oh *ja*."

"Well, damme," Lewrie sourly said.

"Other African tree," Goosen morosely went on, "*if* sound, *not* full of termite, not grow thick unt straight, unt iss only good for die knees, fashion pieces. Before you *rooineks* come, I can get *fine,* big wood from Rotterdam . . . Hamburg oak, *English* oak, compass oak, unt Americanischer *white* oak, *gut* for ship repairs, but now . . ." he said with a fatalistic shrug. "Ashore, heff *many* blacksmither, carpenter, but . . . little to work wit', you see."

"Then we're stuck here 'til an Indiaman comes back with a hunk of teak or mahogany," Lewrie spat. As he mused over *that,* even more of Goosen's Javanese divers bobbed to the surface from their mysterious work below the hull, gasping for air and laughing together, which did little for Lewrie's sour mood, either.

How long can *they hold their breath?* he asked himself, for he was sure that they'd been down long before he'd been rowed round the stern. "We can't wait *that* long, Mister Goosen," he said, trying not to sound like he was pleading. "Surely, there must be something . . ."

Lewrie rather doubted he and his officers could *invent* enough make-work aboard an idled, crippled ship for two whole months of dull thumb-twiddling to keep the crew from going dull or querulous. And, if their last shore liberty was anything to judge by, his only other option was to keep them penned aboard ship, else Cape Town would end in splintered ruins long before a replacement rudder turned up!

"Wahl . . ." Goosen drawled, with a cagey stroking of his beard. "Table Bay iss bad anchoring, *Kaptein* Leew . . . Loo . . . *myhneer*. Unt, worser iss False Bay, other side of peninsula, below Simon's Town. I know of a fresh wreck, dahr. One of your *rooinek* Indiamen, drove in by bad wind to first-est shelter. Her *kaptein* mistake Cape Hanglip as Good Hope, at last see Simon's Town, unt try steer there, but hit die Whittle Rocks, for iss too far North of best-est course to round die Noah's Ark Point. Drive ashore to save what he can before she sinks? *Ver' gut* work, dat, for he miss Roman's Rock unt hard shoal, then go aground on sand beach *North* end of Simon's Bay."

"A wreck," Lewrie said, most dubiously.

"Drive ashore bows *first-est, Kaptein*!" Goosen hooted in glee. "Stern, sternpost, unt *rudder* still in six, eight feet of water, oh *ja*! Was three, four month ago, middle of winter. Die *burghers* down dahr get much work for to salvage . . . much *booty*, for it three days before *rooinek* soldiers, or your navy, get there to stop them, haw haw haw! Almost nobody drown, for *rooinek kaptein* iss *die slim kerel* . . . crafty fellow, see? But, ship is total loss."

"God A'mighty, Cap'm sir," Mr. Pendarves exclaimed, "her rudder must be s' big, ye could whittle a *barge* out'n it! There's *some* o' it still sound oak, sure!"

"But, you say she's been salvaged over, looted . . . ?" Lewrie said, unwilling to raise false hopes too soon.

"Other chandlers unt me been strip her over," Goosen admitted. "Mast, spar, sail canvas, unt cordage . . . upper bulwarks, deck planks, unt blocks. Locals take boats, cabin goods, straightest oak timbers for houses, unt I *was* going to go down dahr unt burn what is left for her nails unt metal, *butt* . . ." he drawled, brightening. "Stripped so far only halfway, to midships, so far. Hoisting rings still standing. You hire my *kaffir* divers to undo bolts unt t'ings, rig hoisting line wit' kedge capstan unt shear-legs . . . ! I sell you *big* rudder for *gut* price, *Kaptein* Loo . . . *myhneer*!"

"Well, I'm damned!" Lewrie said with a happy *whoosh* of wind. "We could sail down round the Cape, take your barge, our launch and cutter, and . . ."

"Iss *big* rudder, big sternpost, too, *Kaptein*," Goosen cautioned. "Get offshore in heavy Cape swell, wit' that aboard, you swamp, sure. *Nie*, best-est, you hire timber waggon. *Volk* at Simon's Bay, dey heff *many* boats, all sizes. I speak to my cousin, Andries de Witt, he heff timber waggons, heff *big*, strong dray horses. You, me, my *kaffirs* unt two-dozen men of yours for heavy pulley-hauley. Well, maybe take *more* waggons, for shear-legs, heavy cables, tents, food unt water, rum unt beer . . . your men ride in waggons, not walk so far, too, *ja*! One day down, two, three day work like Trojans, one day back, unt you heff new rudder, quick as *wink*, haw haw!"

"You're *sure* it's still there, not looted, yet," Lewrie pressed. "Word of honour, it's in good shape!"

"On Holy Bible, on my *vertroue* in God, it is so, *Kaptein*!" the stout older fellow vowed, one hand in the air pointing to Heaven, with a suddenly solemn air.

"And . . . just how much d'ye expect this expedition of ours will cost, Mister Goosen?" Lewrie asked him, satisfied that the Indiaman's rudder and sternpost was still there, but suddenly leery when it came to talk of "cousin Andries" and his magically available waggons.

"Wreck now belong to me, rudder unt sternpost belong to me unt other chandlers, but . . . I give you *gut* price, word on that, too! My cousin Andries, well . . . I am sure *something* be worked out, to mutual satisfaction, *Kaptein* Leer . . . *myhneer*," Goosen swore, his face going as cherubic, and as innocent, as the veriest babe at Sunday school.

That's what I was afraid of, Lewrie thought with a well-hidden sigh, but . . . reached out and shook hands with the cagey bastard. If he played his hand well enough, there was a good possibility that the Navy might sport him the cost, entire!

CHAPTER TWENTY-TWO

"*Kapitan* Lewrie!" a tantalisingly familiar voice interrupted a foul musing as Lewrie's little train of waggons reached the Southern outskirts of tidy little Cape Town, almost into the first of the farms and vineyards, on the dusty road to Simon's Town. *"Zdrasvutyeh!"*

Oh, shit, and where's her papa? Lewrie thought with a twinge of alarm as he reined his hired mare and wheeled her slowly about, to see the equally familiar spirited white gelding loping to catch up with his caravan. Eudoxia Durschenko was beaming fit to bust as she easily and athletically "posted" in her stirrups, heels well down, and back just as straight and erect as a fence-post as she came near.

"Is good be seeink you, again, *Kapitan* Lewrie!" Eudoxia gaily called out as she reined in her horse to a walk, patting his neck as he tossed his proud head and snorted in frustration that his fun was over. "Ve have not see you at circus or theatre, since comink here, pooh, fine *Engliski kapitan*. Where you are goink wit' ox and waggon?"

That had been the first surprise; "cousin" Andries de Witt had refused to risk his precious dray horses, as big as English Punches, to haul that much weight, and had supplied six oxen to each long and narrow, pink-ended waggon, that rose up so high at "bow and stern" that they resembled Yankee dorys, and a round dozen oxen as the team for the timber waggon, which was little more than two sets of wheels as tall as a man, and a stout frame linking them together.

"Mistress Eudoxia . . . *enchante!*" Lewrie responded in an equal gayness, and doffed his newly-purchased wide-brimmed farmer's hat to her. "You keep well . . . you and your father?" he asked, not taking it for granted that the surly bastard wasn't lurking somewhere over the next rise, or skulking behind the last house but one to spy on her. "As to where I'm going, we're off to salvage a new rudder for my frigate, to replace the one the French shot up."

"*Da,* and it was so *brave* of you, *Kapitan,* to save us from the *Fransooskie,* las' week!" Eudoxia quite prettily gushed as her gelding came up alongside his mare, 'til they were riding knee-to-knee. And a rather slim and attractive knee it was, for Eudoxia, paying no heed to prim Dutch Boer proprieties, was wearing a pair of green moleskin breeches, only slightly less snug than the skin-tight ones she wore in her performances, black-and-tan knee-high riding boots, and was, *gasp!,* shamelessly *astride* her saddle. And if Eudoxia *had* made an attempt at "propriety" by wearing a loose linen shirt tucked into those breeches, with a loose and unbuttoned tan suede waist-coat over it, the shirt's collar was unbuttoned nearly all the way down the placket. To top off her *outré ensemble,* she had chosen a light grey, wide-brimmed hat with perhaps her one and only gesture towards proper femininity, for it was flounced with long, trailing ribands, one brim pinned up over her right eye, with a long, locally-obtained ostrich plume caught in the fold.

"Our peoples is *karasho, Kapitan* Lewrie," she beamed. "Everythink good, everyone good, but for Poppa's best lion. He is die, *eta tak groozni . . . prasteenyah.* Sorry, it is too sad, am meanink to say. Vanya, we are thinkink he eat somethink bad for him at Saint Helena . . . find head of little dog in cage, then he lose appetite."

That'd explain the last *complaint Treghues got from the governor's wife, aye!* Lewrie thought with a wince; *Exit one former lap dog, stage left!*

"Find collar in throat, after Vanya die . . ." Eudoxia explained.

"Choked t'death on a pug and his collar, hmm," Lewrie opined.

"Vanya is oldest, grown when Poppa get him from old trainer," Eudoxia sadly continued, "not like Ilya, who is not to be trusted wit' head in mouth . . . 'less he is very well-feed . . . fed? *Da,* fed. Even then, Ilya is . . . how you say, uhm . . . frisky! Now, Poppa not havink lion to swallow his head!"

Well, 'twas a forlorn hope, at best, Lewrie thought, grinning.

"So now, Poppa is goink hunt for *new* lions," Eudoxia breezily said on, "for is best, raisink from cubs. Mister Vigmore, he is hunt for new beasts, too! Want *real* zebra . . . maybe feed donkeys to lions, at last. Ostrich, giraffee, even ele . . . ?"

"Elephants?" Lewrie supplied, turning in surprise.

"*Da,* ele-funts, *spasiba*!" Eudoxia happily exclaimed. "Thankink you for right word. Mister Vigmore, he say 'ele-funts,' it soundink so funny . . . *hell*-ee-finks!" she told him, tossing back her head to give out a rich laugh. "Mister Vigmore beink *Engliski,* like you, *Kapitan* Lewrie, but *God!* He havink such *stranyi* accent!"

"Hallo, miss!" Some of the sailors in Lewrie's party, lolling at their sublime ease in his gear-waggons for a rare once, recognised her from her circus and theatrical performances . . . and from the kiss she'd planted on their captain, that last night at St. Helena. They waved their tarred straw sailors' hats and gave her a cheer. "Gonna ride t'Simon's Bay wif us, missis?"

"Simon's Bay?" Exdoxia asked.

"Down the Cape, t'other side of it, on another bay, my dear," Lewrie informed her. "There's a wrecked ship there, where we hope to obtain a new rudder, and timbers, to repair *Proteus*. And what of you? You're rather well-armed, I must say. Doing a spot of hunting as well, are you, Mistress Eudoxia?"

She looked down at the brace of single-barrelled pistols jammed into dragoon holsters either side of her saddle's front, the long and slim firelock in a leather scabbard under her right leg, and the bow case and tube that held at least two-dozen of her arrows. "Oh, pooh, is only to practice. A quiet place in country, where I am practicink not to disturb peoples in town. For wild beast, if one come. For the wild *man,* if one come, too! Corn merchant in town who sellink us feed for beasts say many dangers in Africa, must always be ware. *Rifled*, see, *Kapitan*?" she declared, drawing her musket from its scabbard. "I buyink musket and pistols in Ph . . . Philadelphia, in tour in America. *Mnoga . . . much* better even than Poppa's old ones. Lighter, too. See? *Try, Kapitan,*" she said, thrusting the rifled musket into his hands.

He swung it up and sighted down the barrel, hand well clear of the trigger or lock, for he was sure that she'd loaded it before leaving town; that would be mere caution for a young woman out riding all by herself in the wilds of Africa . . . which, like inland settlements in North America, began about fifty yards past the last truck garden.

It was light, and pointed well, though the comb of the stock was tailored to a slighter form, custom-made by a talented Yankee gunsmith. Glossy burled wood, lots of brass, with brass or silver inlay, about as fine as the Pennsylvania rifles that his ship had captured from an American smuggling brig in the Danish Virgins in the Caribbean, all of them top-grade presentation models sent as gifts or bribes to the rebel ex-slave leader Toussaint L'Ouverture and his senior generals.

"Magnificent!" Lewrie told her, handing it back. "A match to a rifle I took in the Caribbean. And, I've a breech-loading Ferguson as well, ever seen one? We should have a shoot, so you may try them . . . though I'm certain you'd out-shoot me without even trying."

"I would *like* that, *Kapitan* Lewrie! You thinkink you are good shot?" she teased as she slid the rifle back into the scabbard.

"Uhm . . . passing fair, I s'pose," Lewrie said with a grin, and some false modesty. "Potted pirates in the China Seas at two hundred yards with my Ferguson."

"Wing-shot?"

"Give me a decent fowling piece, and I can fetch home a decent bag," Lewrie chuckled. "Though, up the Mississippi, I *did* manage to knock down ducks and geese on the wing, with an *air* rifle!"

"Schto?" Eudoxia gaped, leaning away in her saddle. "Wit' *air* rifle? I am seeink one, in gunshop in Portugal, but never am *shoot*!"

"I'd let you," Lewrie teased back.

"Ooorah!" she whooped, startling both horses. "Uhm, *skolka vremene*, pardon . . . how long it take you to be goink to this Simon's Bay?"

"Two days each way," Lewrie said, unconsciously gritting teeth at the thought that horses would have been much faster. "Perhaps two or three more to fetch what we're after, so . . . call it almost a week, together. Oh, but you'll be off hunting, by then, I'd expect."

"Nyet," Eudoxia said with a silvery laugh. "No, *Kapitan*. *Men* go hunt, but sailors and girls stay in Cape Town. We do circus, but soldiers have seen, *Gallandya* . . . Dutch peoples have seen, and plays in *Engliski* make no sense to them, so . . . we are finish performances. Mister Vigmore puttink hunt t'gether. *Kapitan* Veed lookink after us 'til they come back, *ponyemayu*? See? Poppa say huntink lion in wild Africa no place for girl, hah! Say I stay on *ship* wit' *Kapitan* Veed, but *Moinya*, big sweety," she said, patting her gelding's neck in affection, "mus' not go stale, mus' ride him, every day. *Moinya* is for to say in *Engliski* 'Lightning,' *da*?"

"And a cracking-fine horse I'm sure he is," Lewrie praised her, "one worthy of his name. So . . . when *does* the hunting party leave?"

"Oh, not for week, at least, *Kapitan* Lewrie," Eudoxia told him, with a mischievious glint in her large amber eyes almost as playful as his own, and prettily lowering her lashes at him. "Vigmore is talk to . . . Boers, what you call them . . . *trekboers*, who are knowink country, ev'ry stitch! Havink waggon trains like yours, wit' ox teams, wit' a band of Black drivers, like yours, too! Mister van der Merwe, one is called, he havink *cutest* little Black fellows who drive his oxes! I am thinkink they call them . . . Hottentots! Like *doll* peoples!"

"Well, we *should* be back, by then," Lewrie off-handedly said. "Perhaps we could . . . once my ship is repaired, o' course, ride out to the back-country and have ourselves a shooting contest."

"Oh, would be *bolshoi*! Would be *grand*, *Kapitan* Lewrie! And . . . *may-be* . . ." Eudoxia posed girlishly, shyly, all but biting her lower lip and drawing out that tentative, suggestive word, "you showink me grand *Engliski* frigate, *da*? *Then*, we have shootinks. Race horses or hunt *little* beasts, not lions! Take picnic basket. . . ."

"Why, what a delightful idea, and thankee for suggestin' that!" Lewrie cried, his baser humours well-stirred, by then. *And, with yer pesky poppa off gettin' bit half t'death by flies, too!* he thought in glee; *And, damn my eyes, but, for play-acting so doe-eyed innocent, I* swear *there's an eager vixen in her nature!*

"We're to 'break our passage' at an inn that our guide, Mister Goosen, knows, up ahead, Mistress Eudoxia," Lewrie further suggested. "Care to ride with us and dine with us?"

"Oh, so sorry, *Kapitan*," Eudoxia said with sudden pout, "but, I am promisink Poppa I not ride far, give hour I must return. *Spasiba*, for invitation, but I mus' go. I makink it *up* to you, in a few days?" she hinted with an enticing chuckle, in a throaty, *promising* way.

"Then I will be looking forward to that most eagerly, Mistress!"

"Pooh, *Kapitan*." Eudoxia pouted some more. "*Mistress* Eudoxia, always Mistress. So stuffy, *da*? Is *Eudoxia*, please? You are *Alan*, not *Kapitan*. Beink *very* good, maybe I sayink '*tiy*,' not '*viy*.' How you say . . . *un*-formal? Unner-stan'?"

"Completely," Lewrie told her with glad leer, stunned by that allowance, and half-strangled by the implication.

"*Dosvidanya*, Alan," she cooed, leaning over from her saddle to plant a chaste kiss on his cheek and put a hand in the small of his back. Before he could respond in kind, though, she gave out a whoop and put spurs to her horse. She whipped away, to go cantering down the length of Lewrie's motley caravan to its very head, spin round before the ox team of the first waggon, and come gal-loping back along the far side of it towards town. "*Sh-chastleevava pooti! Paka!* Have good trip, Alan! See you!"

God in Heaven! Lewrie thought; *And just how long'll it take for Wigmore and her poppa t'hunt down their lions, elephants, and such?*

CHAPTER TWENTY-THREE

"Well, h'it's a *big* bugger . . . h'ain't it?" one of the sailors commented with a scowl on his face as they contemplated the wreck of the Indiaman.

"Big as a bloody three-decker," Bosun Pendarves agreed, looking up at her from a few yards away, hands on his hips and goggling at her ruined hull which towered over them. "Bigger'n a Third Rate, anyways."

The East Indiaman, once named the *Lord Clive*, lay rolled over on her starboard side, with her bows driven into the knee-deep shallows and her forefoot, cutwater, and bluff bows now half-sunken into the soft sand of the beach, while the rest of her extended out into the water of the bay, her stern underwater up to the counter under the stern walks that her best-paying passengers had enjoyed. Local scavengers had salvaged most of her forward hull planks already, those they could reach without a boat, so her ribs, frames, knees, and carline posts showed in the gaps they'd torn, clear from her larboard side to starboard, where crushed frames could be seen, after her grounding on the Whittle Rocks.

Even as Mr. Andries de Witt's caravan was unpacking and setting up camp on the low bluffs above the beach, die-hard local Boers sawed and pried on her forward half, even redoubling their efforts before the new-come "interlopers" could decide to run them off.

"Damned shame," Lewrie said to the Bosun as he joined him beside the wreck, looking up at her great bulk. "What d'ye make her, Mister Pendarves? One hundred eighty feet on the range of the deck? Perhaps fourty-eight feet abeam?"

"Summat near that, aye, Cap'm," Pendarves said with a sage nod. "Big as an eighty-gunner, or a Sir William Slade–designed seventy-four o' th' Large Class. Bigger'n th' Common Class for certain, sir."

"She'll have one hell of a rudder and sternpost, then," Lewrie surmised. "Might take a deal of cutting and trimming down."

"Aye, sir, but we'll do 'er, long as it's in decent condition."

"Ah, here come our boats, I believe," Lewrie pointed out, as a group of three rather large cutters came near them, from the docks at Simon's Town. Mr. Goosen stood in the bows of the lead boat, waving.

Talk about your book-ends, Lewrie thought with a scowl of his own, as he walked down to the hard-packed sand of the lower beach; *Both of 'em bad bargains . . . crooked as a dog's hind leg*. Still, reminding himself that beggars can't be choosers, he waved and smiled in similar enthusiastic fashion to greet Goosen's arrival.

"*Ach*, dere be Goosen!" Andries de Witt cried from his left side.

Book-ends, indeed; both were squat, solid, and stout, both florid of face and balding, and both sported beards so thick they looked like a brace of "owls in an ivy bush." All Lewrie could normally make out of their features were thick and meaty lips—which they licked with sly relish whenever he enquired about costs—and pale blue eyes.

"*Gut* morning, *Kaptein* Lewrie!" Goosen bellowed ashore, flapping his wide-brimmed hat in the air. "You see, we heff boats! And, I am speaking vit' de leading *burghers* of Simon's Town, to assure them all you vish is de rudder, and they can keep the rest of the wreck, oh *ja*!"

"Very good, Mister Goosen!" Lewrie shouted back, cupping hands to his mouth. "Can we board your boat and take a look at the rudder right away, sir?"

"Ah, *ja*, climb aboard!"

" 'Tis big, aye," Bosun Pendarves commented again, minutes later after the cutter had been secured under the *Lord Clive*'s stern counter. The locally-hired Dutch crew—owner and helmsman, and two younger lads who seemed to bear an *uncanny* resemblance to Goosen and de Witt—found a quiet spot right-aft by the tiller and took themselves a well-earned nap, the doings of *rooinek* British sailors no concern of theirs.

Mr. Pendarves got out his long wooden ruler, and Mr. Garroway, *Proteus*'s Carpenter, produced a long hank of knot-marked and ink-ruled twine. For long minutes they hemmed and ahummed over the great rudder, which hung as far over as its gudgeons and faying pieces would allow, as if the last helm order had been to put it hard-over. Thankfully, it still seemed to be in one piece, above-water at least, and all pintles and gudgeons in reach had held firm through the grounding, and still supported the rudder without evident strain.

"Four foot even, I make it," Bosun Pendarves announced, at last. "Four foot even allow th' hances, fore-and-aft. Oak main piece, fir sacrifice boards, an' all, Garroway. Did her builders follow ol' Navy fashion, that'd mean she'd widen t'five foot, seven inch at th' sole."

"What d'ye make it, Buckley?" Garroway asked one of his junior mates, who had shinnied up the green-slimed main piece to the gallery above, where the upper stock entered the overhanging counter.

"Two foot, two inches wide, Mister Garroway," the Carpenter's Mate called down. "Two foot, four inch, fore-and-aft. An' th' tiller mortices look sound, too. Nothin' sprung, f'um wot I kin see."

"Means the main piece would taper to four inches wide, at the sole, then," Garroway said with a satisfied grunt and nod. "We need a stock t'be one foot, six inches, the sole t'be three inches wide. We can plane that down, easy enough, hey?"

"Aye," Pendarves agreed, lost in their own little arcane world. "We carry a stock o' one foot, eight inch, front t'back, an' planes an' adzes'll take care o' that. Whether she's wormed, though . . ." he said, finding a new fret to frown over, and digging into a canvas bucket full of odds and ends, then produced a small drill-auger with which to take a few sample bores from the exposed portion of the rudder's main piece.

"Taller than we need," the Carpenter pointed out. "Shorten the stock, that's easy. . . ."

"Cut new mortices for th' tiller bars, aye," Pendarves agreed, "a'low th' old'uns. Make me calmer in mind, d'we do that. Stronger," the Bosun muttered, happily drilling away. "Ship this size fits seven sets o' pintles an' gudgeons . . . *Proteus* fits five . . . so we'll haveta bore fresh bolt-holes, too, an' that makes me even gladder."

"Strip the fir trailing-edge timber off, plane the main piece to a taper," Garroway speculated, "and might lop a bit off the sole as well, so she's even with our sternpost."

"Uhum," Pendarves dreamily replied.

"Salvage the copper disks 'tween pintles and gudgeon holes. . . ."

"Goes without sayin' . . ."

"Our old sternpost, though . . ."

"Aye, there's yer bugger."

"Take a morticed block from this'un, and shiv it into ours, or . . . rip this bigger post clean off, trim it down, and replace ours, do ye think?" Garroway asked.

"Be a bitch, that, but . . . might be stronger, all in all! Aha!" Pendarves cried, sounding very pleased. He withdrew his drill-auger and carefully cupped a palm-ful of oak shavings . . . as bright, fresh, and worm-free as the best "seasoned in-frame" timber from an English dockyard. "Cap'm sir . . . I do allow we got ourselves a sound rudder!"

"Marvellous!" Lewrie crowed, all but ready to swing his hat in the air and cry, "Huzzah!" Though, after a long look up the rudder . . .

"How heavy d'ye think it is, though, Mister Pendarves?" he asked in a soberer voice. "And, how the Devil do we get the damned thing off in one piece?"

"Well, hmmm . . ." from both Pendarves and Garroway.

I knew *it couldn't be this easy!* Lewrie told himself.

Indeed, it wasn't. First off, Mr. Goosen's Javanese divers had to swim down to survey that part of the rudder that lay underwater, and in what condition the unseen pintles and gudgeons were. The locals had already taken the long, straight tillers, so temporary new ones had to be cut so they could *turn* the rudder while it hung at its precarious angle. Uncontrolled, when they attempted to hoist it free of the gudgeons, its great weight could crush or kill someone.

Hoisting chains had to be rigged from above, thick cables run from the chains to the after capstan, and new bars fashioned to insert into it, for the local Boers had taken those, as well.

The sacrificial trailing-edge pieces of fir had to be stripped off to lighten it, the hard and water-resistant elm dowel pins saved for later use, and that took many dives by the Javanese, too, so they could hammer them out while several feet down and holding their breath.

The triangular strips of "bearding" elm from the centreline of the sternpost, and the forward edge of the rudder, also had to be removed with care, so they could employ them on *Proteus*, too.

Involving even more diving (and Lewrie's money), a hole had to be drilled through both the leading edge and trailing edge of the rudder's sole, and ropes threaded through them, led up either side of the stern to the jeer bitts, and belayed. When that massive weight was hoisted free, there had to be some way of controlling its swinging, and half of Lewrie's working-party would be tailing onto those lines while another half would be breasting to the new capstan bars. And, as Mr. Goosen explained, trying to drill underwater was a long, laborious process, where one turn on a drill-auger could rotate the worker off his feet, unless anchored with a weight on the bottom, and loops of line where he could snag his toes.

Naturally, all that took *days* longer than Goosen had estimated, with a resultant increase in the final cost, as did the cost of keeping Mr. de Witt's waggons, beasts, and *kaffir* workers idly waiting for the rudder to be recovered, and trekked back to Cape Town.

As frustrating as the delay was, Lewrie found that camping out on the bluffs could be enjoyable . . . so long as precautions were made against snakes, spiders, scorpions, and other nasty native buggers. Simon's Bay and False Bay were wide and yawningly empty and the surf was calm on all but the worst days. A firm, stiff wind swirled in, cooling even the hottest part of the day, and, all-in-all, Lewrie found the climate near the 40th Latitude so mild and invigourating, the sound of the surf raling on the beach so pacific, and the dawns so cool and bracing, that Lewrie began to think of the Cape as a prickly sort of Paradise.

Late each afternoon, after the Javanese divers were exhausted, and the sunlight on the waters slanted at too great an angle for them to see what they were doing, all work ceased but for camp chores, and experiments by sailors off *Proteus* at fishing, halving off in watch-versus-watch to stage a football match on the hard-packed lower beach, or lounging about like the aforesaid "Lotus Eaters" after a refreshing dip in the surf, themselves . . . careful to keep an eye out for sharks, which were reputed to teem in southern African waters, and were of an especially vicious, man-eating nature . . . or snoozing in the shade of a tent fly 'til mess chores summoned them.

Lewrie had his horse, and had fetched along his lighter fusil musket. For a "piddling fee," Andries de Witt offered him the loan of a young Boer by name of Piet duToit as a hunting guide, and Lewrie got into the habit of riding out into the countryside each afternoon with the lanky thatch-haired Boer, in search of game.

Settled as the lower Cape below the Cederburgs and Drakensburgs were, as neatly Dutch-orderly as the farmland appeared, game was still plentiful, and with the larger predators driven out by years of "pest" or trophy hunting, decent-sized herds of ungulants had prospered with the lions' absence, and every day ended with something for the pot.

Piet duToit wasn't the most talkative fellow, but he did enjoy pointing out a few cautions on their rides: how to spot puff adders or black mambas; how to scan trees very warily for the slim, green, tree-dwelling *boomslang* that was so poisonous; both versions of cobras to avoid, the Cape cobra that bit and chewed its venom into a wound, and the *rinkhals* that could spit death into one's eyes a goodly distance.

They ran across a bewildering array of beasts, such as rhebok, reedbok, red hartebeest, steenbok, and klipspringer, wee duikers, and grysbok, larger elands, and impalas, and God only knew what-all. Piet duToit boasted that this was nothing, for north beyond the Cederburg Range, out in the Great Karoo savannahs and *vlies,* there were *bigger* creatures: kudu and wildebeest, Cape buffalo, giraffes, hippos, and rhinoceros, warthogs, zebras, and elephants, and, the kings of all, the lions! DuToit would go there, he swore, once he found a properly sweet wife, and amassed enough money for waggons, oxen, horses, guns, and *kaffir* slaves. He'd find a well-watered spot, break ground with the plough, and start raising his herds and flocks, and if that land played out, or he got bored, there'd always be something even grander to see, a week's trek farther along. Town life was *so* boresome, and confining! No place to raise a brood of a dozen children.

The bird life was equally fascinating to Lewrie, both the ones worth shooting and those too grand to eat, for the countryside teemed with them, too. Ostriches and tall, dignified secretary birds, Kori bustards that looked too big to fly, but did, cattle egrets, and red oxpeckers, hornbills, storks, ibises, a dozen varieties of eagles, hawks and owls, kites, buzzards, falcons, kestrels, and goshawks.

On the gentler side, there were hoopoes and louries, the lilac-breasted rollers, bee eaters, glossy and plum-coloured starlings, the waxbills that came in either yellow, blue, or violet, red bishops and jewel-like sunbirds, and the maricos that came in their own palette of vivid colours.

For shooting, there were red-eyed doves, laughing doves, ring-necked Cape turtledoves, and Namaqua doves; helmeted guinea fowl, crested francolins, and sandgrouse, moorhens, Egyptian geese, yellow-bill or white-faced ducks, Cape teals, even flamingos (which only the richest ancient Romans had eaten) that ended on Lewrie's plate, though young duToit was the better shot with a double-barreled fowling gun, nailing three for each one that Lewrie brought down.

There were anteaters and honey badgers, or *ratels* as the Boers called them, mongooses, and four kinds of smaller hunting cats: civets and genets, which were closer to mongooses than true cats; servals, and caracals . . . and jackals and Cape foxes, and bat-eared foxes, and if Lewrie ever wished to take a *real* hunting trip, he could bring back pelts and masks from leopards, cheetahs, and lions . . . for a reasonable fee, of course. Piet duToit swore he could outfit him with anything he wished . . . tentage, bearers and cooks, body-servants, waggons, spirits, and gunpowder. Even a string quartet, if he wished!

"Some people I know have hired a guide, and gone on an inland hunt," Lewrie remarked one afternoon as they watered their horses by a small stream. "Those circus folk who staged those shows."

"Those stupid *rooineks*?" duToit harshly laughed, between bites off a strip of *biltong*, a sun-dried meat of unknown source. "The *gut* God help them, *myhneer*, for they go vit' Jan van der Merwe."

"B'lieve that was the name they mentioned, aye," Lewrie slowly allowed, his curiosity up and stirring. "Why? What's wrong with this . . . van der Merwe?"

"*Machtig, myhneer* . . . what is *right*?" duToit scoffed back with sour mirth.

"A sham, is he? A 'Captain Sharp'?" Lewrie asked further.

"Don't know this *Kaptein* Sharp *kerel* you speak of, *myhneer*, A sham? Oh, *ja*. Jan van der Merwe is, what you call, a *joke*? He could get lost in a field of mealies . . . cannot trail smoke back to a campfire! Once, he think he tame hyenas, thinking they are just another kind of big puppy-dog, haw haw! Those circus people mean to hunt out in the *vlies*, they have no need of guide to *find* game. Just ride far enough, they will see *thousands* of beasts an *hour*! Only need *kaffirs* to butcher and skin, drove oxen to bring back pelt and ivory, set up the camps, and cook, you see? *Any* fool can boss camp *kaffirs* . . . know just enough Bantu to tell them what to do. Ha! Van der Merwe cannot speak proper *Dutch*, much less . . ."

"They were, ah . . . more of a mind to *capture* animals than hunt for trophies," Lewrie explained. "To add to their menagerie and such? Real zebras, 'stead o' tarted-up donkeys, elephants to ride and train to do tricks, lion cubs to raise . . ."

"*African* elephant?" duToit gasped in true shock, raising his voice higher than his usual cautious field-mutter. "African elephant is not like the Indian, *myhneer*! Try to train them, they stomp you in ground, then mash you to *soup*! *Bad*-tempered beasts, good only for the shooting, and ivory. And, anyone think to steal cubs from a pride of *lions*, they end up eaten to the bone, and their bones *cracked*! Bones end as play-things for those *cubs*!"

"*Thought* it sounded a touch daft," Lewrie replied.

"*Machtig* God," duToit exclaimed, "those people tell that fool van der Merwe that is what they plan? They pay him good money for him as guide? You never see *them* again, *Kaptein* Lewrie. *Rooinek* idiots . . . even so, I feel sorry for them."

"What *is* a *rooinek,* Mister duToit?" Lewrie felt pressed to ask, though the picture of Arslan Durschenko being gnawed down to splinters *was* intriguing.

"Ah . . . *rooineck* in Cape Dutch means 'red neck,' *Kaptein,*" his guide matter-of-factly decyphered, well, perhaps with a tiny touch of arch amusement in his eyes. "Your British soldiers come here, we see their tight red collars . . . the colour they turn in the sun, too, you see? What we say, instead of British. More *biltong*?"

"No thankee, I've eat sufficient," Lewrie replied, thinking it odd that he wasn't offended. "Uhm, what is *biltong* made of, then? It puts me in mind of venison or beef 'jerky,' as the American Indians I met called it, but . . ."

"*Ja,* it is any kind of game meat," duToit told him, though he seemed suddenly distracted, moved very slowly and carefully, and felt behind him for his musket, his eyes fixed on something beyond. "Cape buffalo, old cow, anything."

"Smoked?" Lewrie asked.

"Dried in the sun, maybe with nets to keep the bugs off. Get your musket ready, *myhneer* . . . slowly," duToit instructed in a harsh whisper. "Take the reins of your horse, too . . . gently, and do not spook him before the crocodiles do, if you wish to *ride* back to camp."

"Croc . . . ?" Lewrie gawped, fighting the urge to whirl about and shout something nigh to "Holy Shit!"

His horse had drunk its fill, and had grazed over to some green grass, so it never even noticed the crocodile, as big as a Louisianan's cypress-log *pirogue,* that had stealthily slunk off the far bank of the stream about a musket-shot above them, and had let itself be wafted by the faint current to close pistol-shot, only its horny-scaled head and eyes visible.

"Rub 'em with spices?" Lewrie asked, once they were saddled up and paced out of snapping distance.

"Crocodile?" duToit gawped, turning to look quizzically at him.

"*Biltong,*" Lewrie said.

"Some do."

"Cheap, is it?"

"Very cheap, *myhneer*", duToit replied.

"Might make a nice change from salt-meat junk aboard my ship," Lewrie speculated. "And, I've my two cats to feed. Does it keep long?"

"Months, *Kaptein*."

"Better and better!" Lewrie enthused. "But it by the bale, I'd expect. By the hundredweight. Soak it in water. . . ."

"You can add it to *bredies*, soups, stews . . ." duToit suggested. "But, *myhneer* . . . why buy, when you can shoot your own, and I can dry it for you . . . for a very cheap price, that is," he added, with an avariciously sly grin. "We start now, *Kaptein*. Small herd of steenbok . . . there," he whispered, pointing at something only he could see, at about half a mile or so, for Lewrie couldn't spot them at all. "Get up close, leave the horses, and . . . creep up *there*," duToit decided, after licking a finger to determine the direction of the wind. "Take one each, we will have a nice small roast, tonight, and cousin Andries's *kaffirs* can prepare you the rest as *biltong* in two days. Hundredweight, as you say, between the pair. And steenbok doe is *tender*. *Ja?*"

I knew *he was another damn' "cousin"!* Lewrie told himself.

"Might need a third for the hands' supper," Lewrie speculated.

"I have second musket," duToit smugly told him, patting a scabbard under his saddle. "Three steenbok it could be. We try?"

"Aye, let's!" Lewrie agreed with a feral grin.

The brace of steenbok didn't cause the sensation in camp, that evening—surprisingly. duToit had missed with his second shot, once the steenbok had been startled into great springing bounds and leaps, and darting evasions at the crack of musket fire—rather it was the crocodile tail-meat that they'd fetched in, once they'd decided to go back and bag it, after all.

Lewrie and his guide had both shot it in the head at the same time, within two inches of each other, so the skull was ruined for a trophy, but the largest teeth were still impressive, as was the still-moist hide. The black waggoners, bearers, and cooks had sprung on it, to stake it out for drying in the sun, along with the steenboks they had field-dressed, and one of them swore he could string those teeth into a quite nice necklace, if *baas* Lewrie wished . . . heathen, savage but nice.

Along with the slices of roast steenbok, there were treats that the *burghers* and women of Simon's Town had come to sell, now that they were over their "sulks" at *uitlanders* camping out too near their proper and tidy Boer settlement, and helping themselves to part of the wreck that was theirs by right.

They vended more *bredies* and mutton *boboties*, more Sumatran or Javanese *satays*, along with piping-hot fresh breads and syrupy sweet baked *koeksisters* or pies. Along with the viands, though, so Lewrie learned, there had come strong and hearty Dutch beer, some local rum, some of the rawer sort of Cape wines, and that gin-clear Dutch peril, that "tangle-tongue" *akavit*.

"Sound a tad *too* me-hearty, Mister Pendarves?" Lewrie scoffed, once he got the Bosun off to one side for a heart-to-heart. The last thing he needed, with the ship's hands off ashore and given much ease from their unremitting daily schedule, was too much drink. Riot and mutiny were the worst he could expect; the *least* would be people kept on such strict spirit rations drinking themselves into insensibility, and uselessness on the morrow, given the slightest opportunity.

"That Mister Goosen, and Mister de Witt, told the locals that they'd best not get 'em *too* hot, sir," Pendarves cautiously laid out in his own defence. "Small bottles an' such, an' Mister Gamble an' I been keepin' a wary eye on th' trade, too, sir."

"God above, Mister Pendarves," Lewrie spat, "to the Dutch, it's a patriotic *duty* t'fuddle their occupiers! Without the Master-At-Arms and Ship's Corporals, the Marines, they'll go witless if they get even a *touch* drunk!"

"Can't keep th' men from all spirits, sir," Pendarves pointed out, "beggin' yer pardon, an' all. Half a pint o' beer with supper, a tot o' wine 'stead o' their reg'lar rum issue . . . well, maybe *along* with th' rum, but . . . me an' Mister Gamble warned 'em, stern, Cap'm. Anybody gets rowdy, 'tis my good right fist he'll be eatin'. Along with 'is teeth! They don't have much coin, sir, an' th' Dutch don't give credit, so they couldn't buy all that much. Besides, what little the Dutchies brung, they're chargin' an arm and a leg for, so most o' our lads can't *afford* a good drunk, An' the Dutchies camped out near us ain't of a mind t'share, like, Cap'm."

"You've had no trouble, then?" Lewrie wondered aloud, dubious, but slightly relieved by what he'd heard so far.

"Well, we did have a couple o' fights, sir," Pendarves admitted, looking cutty-eyed, "but . . . Mister Gamble jumped 'tween 'em before it got outta hand, an' said, did they want t'fight, do it proper, an' form a ring for 'em. Referee an' all, and wagers laid, so it turned more a . . . *sportin'* show, sir."

"How did the fights turn out, then?" Lewrie asked, snickering, and revising his already-good opinion of his oldest Midshipman a little higher.

"Both ended in draws, sir," Pendarves told him, with a twinkle in his eyes. "Not much damage done, and I gave 'em all a good duckin' in th' surf, after. Then swore to 'em they'd be doin' th' most work, come mornin', an' the same'd go for anyone who got so drunk that I took notice, sir."

"My compliments to Mister Gamble, and to you, Mister Pendarves," Lewrie said, satisfied by their bare-knuckled solution. "Just be sure you prowl about before 'Lights Out,' and see them bedded down properly . . . and *mostly* sober, hear me?"

"Aye aye, sir!"

"Carry on, then, Mister Pendarves," Lewrie said, before heading off to his own tent for a scrub-down, and a hot supper.

CHAPTER TWENTY-FOUR

It took far longer than anyone's rosy estimates, but the work at last was done. The massive rudder and sternpost of the *Lord Clive* was off, the bronze fittings, bolts, elm dowels, and bearding strips labelled with paint and itemised for later use, and everything packed up in the waggons. It was a well-fed, sun-bronzed, and much-refreshed working-party of tars that slowly trundled back into the outskirts of Kaapstad, the unsprung waggons clattering, axles squealing, and ox teams farting and lowing.

Goosen's chandlery would receive the reclaimed materials into a beachfront works yard, where both Lewrie's specialist petty officers, and their crews, and *yet another* set of cousins—Paul Riebeck, who was reputed to be a skilled carpenter, and his metal-working brother Hendrik—would set up their forges, anvils, and tools to assist the hands off *Proteus* in cutting down, shaping, and planing the *Lord Clive* rudder down, and manufacturing new bronze and iron fittings.

All that for a "most reasonable fee," it went without saying!

Lewrie turned things over to Midshipman Gamble and Mr. Pendarves, sure that "cousin" Andries de Witt knew the way to that works yard with his eyes shut, and for them to send word to the ship that they were now back. Turning his horse aside, Lewrie rode up the steep, curving road of the Lion's Rump to the tidy farm cottage where his wounded men were recuperating.

"All's well?" he asked their *émigré* French Surgeon's Mate, Mr. Maurice Durant, who came out to greet him on the windswept slopes.

"Three hands are still poorly, Captain," Durant said with a most Gallic shrug as they stepped into the shade of the deep galleries that fronted each side of the rented farmhouse. "Suppuration from the oiled oak splinters that caused their wounds, I am sorry to say. The rest are still too stiff for even light duties, I am also sorry to relate, sir, but they are healing."

"And Whitbread?" Lewrie enquired about one of his Black sailors.

"*Quel dommage*, he has gone away from us, Captain," Durant sadly related, reverting to the old French expression for death. "Lieutenant Langlie was informed, and saw to his burying . . . well-wrapped in a canvas shroud, *n'est-ce pas*?" he said with a conspiratorial wink and nod. "That young English rector suspected nozzing, and now Samuel Whitbread is interr-ed beside his shipmates and fellow escapees, poor fellow. A great pity, though . . . now, there are only seven of the Black fellows left from your humanitarian gesture, Captain."

"Nine," Lewrie insisted as Durant helped him dip an oak bucket of water from a butt on the gallery porch for his horse.

"*Non*, Captain . . . seven," Durant corrected, as if it was of no matter. "The lean, young marksman who calls himself Rodney? And, the one who calls himself Groome, who tried to ride the sham zebras? They have run, Lieutenant Langlie tells me."

"Run?" Lewrie snapped. "Deserted? Mine arse on a. . . . !"

"The *cirque* . . . the circus people who go into the wilds," Durant calmly went on, offering Lewrie a copper dipper of water, too. "Groome and Rodney were ashore on liberty when the circus party departed, but they never return to the ship. I gather, from what Lieutenant Langlie learn, that they had hung about the circus menagerie, and talk often to *M'sieur* Wigmore and their guide, a local Boer. . . ."

"Van der Merwe!" Lewrie spat.

"Ship's cook, he tell Lieutenant Langlie that several wish-ed to be in circus, Captain," Durant said with another fatalistic shrug. "Groome believe-ed he could be elephant tamer or rider, handle horses and *real* zebras . . . even be an actor, if they do Shakespeare's *Othello*. Rodney, he say he is the crack shot, good as any, and wish to shoot the great beasts of Africa, his native land, after all. Perhaps perform in circus with guns, like Mistress Eudoxia. Lion tamer, Durschenko . . . ?"

"*Him!* Aye?" Lewrie growled, drinking off half of the dipper and swirling the rest to rinse it, before heaving the rest over the railing.

"Before he injure his eye, *he* was the crack shot, *aussi*, he tell me," Durant went on, as if desertion was an everyday occurrence, nothing to get exercised about, for it had nothing to do with his specialties. "He come to me, when he learn I was once the physician trained in Paris, to see if his eye was hopeless. *Quel dommage*, there is nozzing anyone may do to restore his sight, but . . ."

"That flap-eyed bastard! What'd he tell you?" Lewrie demanded, instantly suspecting that luring some of his sailors to desert was the man's way of getting back at him, if putting one of his daggers in his heart was not in the immediate offing.

"He *does* say, when I treat him, that such a hunt will be one of life's grand adventures, Captain, though the danger is *aussi* the great, so, as many guns who go along will be welcome. He suggest, I think, I might enjoy such with him, *hawn hawn*!" Durant said with the nasal sort of laugh of which only the French seemed capable.

"He rode up here?" Lewrie pressed, hoping that Durschenko had no idea, being a foreigner, that Black sailors weren't all that common in the Royal Navy, not in such numbers aboard a single ship, or that burying them alongside Whites was heavily frowned upon. *Else, he'd be crowing it from the rooftops, t'spite me!* Lewrie fretfully thought; *Or, if Groome, Rodney, one of the others, blabbed about how I* got *'em . . . !*

"Lured 'em away, did he?" Lewrie griped.

"That is very possible, Captain," Durant agreed, with the calm of a saint, which, to Lewrie, was becoming maddening.

"Mine arse on a band-box!" Lewrie exclaimed, stomping about the gallery, all but ready to flap his arms in anger. "Didn't the idiots *know* that the Dutch keep slaves here, same as Jamaica . . . that they're trading one set o' chains for another, once they're far enough away in the wilds where the *trekboers* can do anything they like with 'em?"

"Perhaps they assum-ed that they were under the protection of that *M'sieur* Wigmore," Durant said, and if he performed just one more of his damned shrugs, Lewrie would not be responsible for his actions! "Or, that *M'sieur* Durschenko would prevent that . . . if they were going as free Black men, employ-ed by the circus, Captain."

"Damn, damn, *hell* and damn!" Lewrie cried, in a stew, for there was no way, short of organising a hunting trip of his own, to get them back, and he was already several hands short; and, what guarantee was there that galloping a press-gang to go after them might not result in even *more* free-spirited hands . . . even Marines! . . . thinking that the merry life of the *trekboers* was infinitely better than that of an overworked, underfed, and underpaid Jolly British Jack?

"There was no way to prevent it, Captain," Durant tried to console. "You were away, and could not have known. Lieutenant Langlie or the ozzer officers could not have known their intentions beforehand, lizz . . . either."

"Doesn't *matter*, dammit," Lewrie gravelled. It *was* his fault. Whatever occurred, for good or ill, was *always* the captain's responsibility! "Hereof nor you nor any of you may fail as you will answer the contrary at your peril!" it said near the bottom of his Commission, a phrase the Navy was rather *keen* on. Bleakly, Lewrie thought that the best he could do for the next week or so would be to see to the ship's repair, no matter how tempting it would be to hare after his deserters and haul them back in irons.

"Do they survive, Captain," Durant continued in his maddeningly serene voice, "you may arrest them on their return, *n'est-ce pas*?"

"Well, there is that," Lewrie bitterly allowed, slouching, with his hands resting on the gallery railing, and staring out at Table Bay. "Not that their present absence does the rest of our people any good. I might have to cancel shore liberty 'til we have 'em back, before any *more* of our hands think to emulate 'em. Replacing the rudder and the sternpost'll keep 'em busy enough, for a while, but . . ."

Much as I find it loathsome, I'll have to have those two at the gratings, he thought; *Give 'em both* four-*dozen lashes apiece, just to drive the lesson home t'one and all!*

"You will see the wounded, Captain?" Durant asked.

"Aye, I will. What I rode up for . . ." Lewrie began to say, but took closer notice of Table Bay before he swung back to face Durant. There was a new ship anchored near Green Point, inside the encircling peninsula. And, even more ships were entering the bay, just starting to round Green Point. Even without a telescope, he could make out a few identifying details in the clear air, so far up above the haze of Cape Town's hearth and workshop fires.

The arriving ships appeared to be five East Indiamen, escorted by a lone two-decker. And the anchored ship seemed to be flying the distinctive "Post-Boy" flag of a mail-packet, a Red Ensign sporting a Union flag in the canton, with the horn-blowing rider on a horse that filled the rest of the fly.

"A convoy coming in," Lewrie muttered.

"Ah, *oui*?" Durant replied, cheering up as he came to Lewrie's side by the gallery overlooking the wide bay. "Too soon, I am told, for ships from England, so this must be a convoy from China or India. I hope *M'sieur* Hodson or I may go aboard them while they are here . . . to ask of ingredients for fresh medicines. Oil of cloves is . . ."

"And the mail-packet?" Lewrie asked. "What of her?"

"Oh, she came in yesterday," Durant answered. "I trust there are letters from Madelaine and our babes. For a time, both Hodson and I had to be up here to tend our wounded, but, now their care is not so urgent, *M'sieur* Hodson return-ed aboard *Proteus*, leaving me with only three loblolly boys," he gently complained, his old plaint of being a better-educated and trained physician serving under a "saw-bones" surgeon. "I would ask, should you discover any mail for me . . . ?"

"Done, and done," Lewrie assured him, half his attention still on the incoming ships. "Well, let us go and visit our hurt men. Once that's done, I'll sort through our mail and send a Midshipman up here with anything for you, or our patients, sir."

"*Merci*, Captain. *Merci beaucoup*."

I think *I can trust a Midshipman not t'run off with the circus!* Lewrie grimly told himself.

CHAPTER TWENTY-FIVE

"Welcome back aboard, sir," Lt. Langlie said, once the salutes of the side-party and officers were done. "Might I enqire if the hunt went well?"

"It did, indeed, Mister Langlie," Lewrie gleefully told him as they began to walk aft together. "The rudder and sternpost are sound as the pound, and now in the local contractors' yard. A week or three more, and we'll be completely ready for sea, again."

"Excellent news, sir!" Langlie enthused.

"What's happened aboard, now two of our Black sailors have run?" Lewrie asked him. "And, how did *that* happen?"

"I stopped all shore liberty since, sir," Langlie reported, turning sombre. "My fault, sir . . . should have seen it coming, what with that mountebank, Wigmore, beguiling them. Perhaps as early as our stop at Saint Helena, I now gather. . . ."

"When they return, *if* they return, we'll have to make examples of 'em, Mister Langlie," Lewrie grimly announced. "Was Wigmore after any of the others?"

"The more exotic, the better, I believe, sir," Langlie replied. "Play-act as Hindoo *mahouts*, should they get themselves some elephants . . . trick them out as eunuchs or Turk swordsmen for one of his plays, or the circus parades, but, I also have ascertained that the rest of our sailors thought it a daft idea, and rightly reckoned the consequences of desertion. Especially in a land that keeps native Blacks as slaves, and makes war on the rest, sir."

"Good!" Lewrie declared, relieved to hear it. "Mister Durant tells me a mail-packet has come in. Was there anything for us?"

"Scads, sir!" Lt. Langlie said, brightening. "And, may I convey my congratulations, Captain."

I've quickened another *babe somewhere in the world?* he thought in confusion; *I've inherited all of Surrey?*

"You have me at a loss, sir," Lewrie said to that.

"The latest Captain's List, sir!" Langlie gushed. "Your name now appears among those of *More* than Three Years' Seniority. You may 'board' your second epaulet!"

"Well, damn my eyes," Lewrie replied, after a stunned moment, then began to chuckle. "With all that's occurred lately, the date that I was 'posted' quite slipped my mind. Thankee for that news, Mister Langlie. A ream of officialese from Admiralty, too, I s'pose."

"All your letters are in your clerk's possession, sir, awaiting you in your cabins," Langlie told him.

"Very well, sir," Lewrie said, eager to be at them, for, with a slew of official documents, there might be personal letters from home *as* well, word from Twigg or that gaggle of earnest do-gooders who had sworn to defend his good name. "I'll be aft and below. Do you, in the meantime, see to victualling arrangements for our shore working-party, and send a Lieutenant along to supervise the work, when it begins, on the morrow."

"Aye aye, sir."

"Hello, lads!" Lewrie cooed as Toulon and Chalky swarmed him. "Miss me, did ye? Yes, I smell exotic, don't I? African dirt, blood, and meat . . . ain't it *tasty*? Yes, love you, too, Toulon," Lewrie told the black-and-white ram-cat as he knelt down, allowing both of them to sniff him, raise up on their hind legs to rub chins on his clothes, and make snoring noises over such blissful new scents.

"Welcome back, sir," Aspinall happily said. "Will ye be havin' a sip o' somethin' . . . a scrub-up? There's lashin's o' fresh water comes aboard every mornin', enough for a hip-bath, do ye care for it. And, I've your workin'-rig uniform fresh as a daisy, when ye call for it. Cool tea'll take no more than half an hour, too, sir."

"Should have taken you along, Aspinall," Lewrie said, as Chalky swarmed up his thigh to scrub the side of his little head on his chin, and start to snuffle his hair. "I could have *used* a bit of civilised seeing-to. Ah . . . a sponge-down, first, aye. A gallon of water, if that much is aboard . . . *two* gallons, and I'll wash

Africa out of my scalp, too. Ow, Chalky! Here, lad . . . *biltong*!" he beguiled, as the newest cat's affection turned "nippish." Lewrie reached into a pocket of his slop trousers and pulled out two strips of dried springbok wrapped in a handkerchief. "Wild game meat, lads. *Could* have brought it down yourselves, I'm certain, but you can pretend. Smell good, hmm? Taste it, Toulon, ooh yes!"

He tore a strip into wee bites, feeding both cats a bit or two from his fingertips as they swished their tails, rose up on their hind legs again, and went frantic, meowing loudly for more.

"I've two hundredweight coming aboard, Aspinall," Lewrie said, still on his knees. "We'll have to find a safe place to store it, else they might founder on it, the first dark night."

"I'll think o' somethin', sir. Hot water's on the way."

Lewrie rose at last and went to his desk, where he discovered a fair-sized mound of correspondence, sorted out by his clerk, Padgett, into official Must-Read-First, personal and newspapers, bills, and a slush-pile of Who-Cares and Future-Toilet-Necessities.

Surprisingly, the official pile was rather small, the most of it those sort of directives sent out at quarterly or half-year intervals to every warship in active commission, and yes, it *was* delightful to pore over the Captain's List to see his own name among those who'd lived long enough, and hadn't come a cropper, with the beginnings of real seniority; down at the *bottom* of that list, even so, but his name was finally there. And, Lewrie could smugly note, about a quarter of the names above his did not command ships or hold *active* commissions.

He had to stop and play some more with the cats, reach into the larboard pocket of his trousers, and dig out another strip of *biltong* with which to placate them before he could pore over the list for the names of friends or foes.

Keith Ashburn, a fellow Midshipman in 1780, was listed in the lower third, in command of a frigate; Francis Forrester, that fubsy fart with all the "interest" and patronage, was above Keith, now pestering the crew of his own Fifth Rate. His old captain in the Far East, Ayscough, was near the top of the list, with a two-decker 74.

Dropping down to Commanders, he found that Midshipman Hogue of those Far East adventures under Ayscough had just taken command of one of those new-fangled Brig-Sloops, and even more pleasingly, his First Officer into HMS *Jester*, Lt. Knolles, had been promoted into a Sloop of War with an epaulet on his shoulder, too. Far down, though, there was Kenyon . . . damn his blood! That "windward passage" bugger was now a Commander, too.

" 'Ere's your hot water, sir," Aspinall announced as he and Seaman Bannister staggered into the great-cabins, each bearing two gallon buckets, and Lewrie's reveries ended for a time.

It was only after he was squeaky clean, his hair trimmed and still slightly damp, and clad in a fresh-smelling uniform, that Lewrie started in on his personal correspondence. There was a nice selection from which to choose; a thick letter from Theoni Kavares Connor, the mother of his bastard son in London; even one from his half-Cherokee bastard son, who was now a Midshipman in the fledging United States Navy. His *actual* offspring, Sewallis, Hugh, and Charlotte, had written him, too. There was one from the Trencher family he had met in London, one from his wife Caroline, wonder of wonders, one from Sir Malcolm Shockley, one of his patrons in the House of Commons, but . . . there was a very thick packet from Zachariah Twigg, and, despite his desire for news of his family . . . his real family . . . he felt himself drawn to it despite himself.

Lewrie undid the bindings, letting the travel-stained covering fall open to reveal a stack of newspapers bound in twine, with a folded letter atop it all. He opened the letter very carefully, using only the tips of his fingers, as if handling a dud exploding shell.

"Sir," Twigg's letter began, "our Cause advances most promisingly, though I must, in good Conscience, confess that the Enthusiasm of your Abolitionist Allies quite took me by surprise, and that I greatly under-estimated just how much Notice . . . favourable Notice, mind . . . that the Publick has taken of your Exploit. I daresay, as you may see from the enclosed papers, that Revd. Wilberforce and his associates have made of you quite the Nine-Day Wonder, and your freeing of slaves in the Caribbean the talk of the city. As the odious French might say, you and your Cause are become a *cause célèbre*!"

"Oh . . . my . . . God!" Lewrie groaned aloud. "*Damn* their. . . ."

"It is possible that General Napoleon Bonaparte's recent escape from his failed Egyptian expedition and his most recent accession to power once back in Paris *may* be the greater news, at present, but, you do run him a close second," Twigg went on.

"You are lauded, should that be the correct way to put it, by the sobriquet which I supplied them, of 'Ram-Cat' Lewrie, the Publick and the newspaper scribblers making the obvious mistake of imagining that 'Ram-Cat' represents your belligerent Nature when confronting our foes at sea, instead of what we both know as more representative of your Lascivious proclivities. You will find from the Abolitionists' tracts which I included, however, that you are now equally spoken of as 'Black Alan' Lewrie, or 'Emancipation' Lewrie, and the Hero of the hour!"

"Mine arse on a band-box if I am!" Lewrie shakily growled; he had no idea it would come to this! What happened to subtle defence?

"All this was prompted," Twigg continued, "by a letter which I received from Mister Peel on Jamaica. Peel continues to thrive, by the by, and expressed to me that I should convey to you his utmost respect and best wishes. It would seem that the Beauman family, from whom you stole those dozen slaves for seamen, had finally coerced, or beaten, enough evidence from the other Slaves remaining on their Plantation on Portland Bight to discover the Hows and Whens, and, most especially, the Identity of their Thief. Peel warned that the Beaumans intend to pursue the Matter in a Court of Law, and are not to be dissuaded from their Purpose by any means at Peel's disposal. He *would* stand ready to initiate extra-legal means to thwart them, though he fears any such action on his part might not redound to your Discredit should word of it reach England. They have engaged a prominent colonial Barrister in Kingston who is, I learn, soon to be despatched to London, where he is to lay charges on his own, or further engage lawyers who deal in King's Bench cases to either assist him, or take upon themselves the Matter, entire. By the time you are in receipt of this letter, he may already be there."

"I'm ruined, I'm done for," Lewrie felt like shrieking. "I'm . . . hung!"

"Publick Opinion in your Favour, though, has most likely prejudiced their Suit before the case may be laid," Twigg further wrote to reassure him. "A legal friend of mine, and old schoolmate, who sits on King's Bench cases, explained to me that you have the right under English Common Law to be confronted by your Accusers in the Flesh, and not by dry Affidavit, as well as by Witnesses, which will require the Beaumans, perhaps their whole odious Clan, to sail to England for the Proceedings, a requirement they should have been told by their legal representative on Jamaica in the first place, or shall soon learn, to their further distress. Equally, Witnesses to testify to your perfidy must include Slaves from that Plantation, and, what a cunning Defence Council may make of their living Conditions, Punishments, Victuals, and the Means the Beaumans applied to force Confessions from them will be the finest Grist for the Abolitionists' mill! Were I a Beauman bent upon Revenge against you, I should think twice before appearing such a despicable Ogre for all the world to see!"

Lewrie raised one eyebrow as he fantasised Hugh Beauman in the dock, squirming in anger and arrogance as a sharp barrister took him to task, whilst the gallery, perhaps the judges, too, openly wept over the slaves' testimonies, all England swayed to freeing every . . .

I've been had . . . again! Lewrie suddenly thought with a gasp.

The Abolitionists *could* have mounted a silent, subtle defence, but, had they really looked upon him, that morning he had walked into the Trenchers' parlour, as a test case, the very sort of *cause célèbre* which *would* sway public opinion to *demand* emancipation for slaves in the British Empire?

Have I been their "Bread Cast Upon The Waters"? he had to ask himself; *Their sacrificial baa-lamb? It works, I'm a hero, not hung. If it fails, they'll weep a bit, then try again with someone else, and I'm a martyr to their cause! Christ, shit on a . . . !*

And why, Lewrie suddenly wondered, feeling that such erudition on his part had come much too late; *did Zachariah Twigg write to me so quickly? Am I his damned cat's-paw . . . again? He knew just* exactly *whom to approach, the conniving, devious old . . . secret Abolitionist! Why, he might've been one of 'em for years! In on it from the first!*

Now glowing with anger, Lewrie returned to Twigg's letter.

"Conversely, you may not be tried in Absentia, which will require your presence, a Circumstance subject to the whim of Admiralty, and an advantage greatly in your Favour so long as the Navy needs you at sea in command of a frigate, delaying the Confrontation for years, during which your allies the Reformers and Abolitionists may continue to beat the drum and keep the matter of Emancipation in Publick notice."

"I knew it!" Lewrie growled. "I just knew . . . well, no, dammit. Not 'til now I didn't, but . . . damme!" he spat, sopping sweat off his forehead.

"This has, of course, required us to engage legal representation for you, and, with the aid of your Solicitor, Mister Matthew Mountjoy, and his good advice, succeeded in engaging one Mister Andrew MacDougall, Esquire, one of the finest up-and-coming legal minds in England. He is one of those canny Edinborough Scots, usually thought to be just too clever by half, but, in your Cause, such sharp and clever wit may prove to be vital," Twigg continued. "Do not dread the costs, for I am assured by Reverend Wilberforce, the Trenchers, and others, that a campaign will be launched to gather donations towards your defence, so this Necessity might not touch your purse too dearly."

"Not *too* dear, for God's sake?" Lewrie bleakly croaked, with a cringe, imagining all his prize-money being shovelled down a rat-hole, of ending penniless, homeless, and on half-pay . . . and that was if he *prevailed.* The scandal would be too great, as if it already *wasn't!,* and the hour after his vindication, the Navy would chuck him out the servants' entrance like a drunk at closing time, and did they feel a *keen* vindictiveness, a Court-Martial for "Conduct Unbecoming" would make even half-pay moot!

Unless . . .

For a mad moment, Lewrie contemplated Wigmore's circus. Three of his Black hands were now dead and gone, already, and two more now "run." He wondered what sort of deal he could strike with Wigmore to hire-on the rest, so when he sailed back to England, he could respond with "*What* stolen slaves? You see any?"

Maybe he could learn to ride horses standing up on their backs, and jump through flaming hoops, juggle, or portray naval characters in dramas. No, comedies would be better. More apt!

There was more to come in Twigg's long letter, and he returned to it, though by now he dreaded what *else* the man might have arranged.

"Support for our Cause in Parliament is building quite nicely, too, I assure you. No matter the *seeming* Criminality of your Actions, your chiefest Patron in the Commons, Sir Malcolm Shockley, has spoken most eloquently for you, and has gathered round him not only some of the leading lights from his own growing faction, but many of the up-and-coming Reformist sorts, such as Sir Samuel Whitbread, and many of the Crown's own faction. Given the best face official government has put upon our recent *debacle* on Saint-Domingue, in which you played a part, and the Publick pronouncements of Congratulations to the former slaves of that colony who rose up and rebelled against the cruel state in which their former French masters kept them—cynical and false though such pronouncements were!—the ruling faction cannot appear the two-faced Janus and condemn one of their Sea Officers who freed a dozen slaves, no matter how ilegally, or be called down as hypocrites. Those voices in Commons condemning you, therefore, are mostly from the Shipping and Sugar interests, whose only god is Mammon, and rest assured that Sir Malcolm and others have made certain that everyone in Great Britain knows their Venality for what it is. A great many who might condemn your actions and call for your immediate return to face charges have muted themselves, else they are tarred the same. Even in Lord's, a body usually much more conservative and hide-bound than the Commons, you have found remarkably supportive Voices speaking to the Justification of your deed, rather than to the cut-and-dried facts of common thievery, among them your old schoolmate, Lord Peter Rushton, of all hen-headed wonders. Your deed has been interpreted as a bold *geste*, a blow struck for Human Freedom, as you will note when you see the newspaper articles, and the many letters written upholding your actions. . . . I'm told that homilies and sermons have been preached . . ."

He'd had enough of Twigg for the moment, so he turned to that pile of newspapers and tracts, and, if he thought things were horrid *then*, he rapidly discovered what "horrid" really was.

The *Times*, the *Gazette*, even the *Marine Chronicle*'s latest numbers featured articles about him, not one of which actually got the facts right, or made things up out of whole cloth, though they weren't *that* condemnatory, and most of the letters to the editors *sounded* like the bulk of the writers somehow approved. England, after all, didn't much care for slavery; if "Britons never, never, never shall be slaves" then why should anyone else, and only "foreigners," meaning Spaniards and other assorted evil types, did it, didn't they? Slave labour was something that happened far overseas, and even if Englishmen *did* keep slaves in the Sugar Isles, "our" sort of slavery couldn't be all *that* bad, could it, compared to Dons, Dagoes, and Frogs?

The lesser papers, though, and the tracts . . . Good God!

Every one of them splashed a copy of a large wood-cut drawing on its front, a fantastic picture of a bare-headed Lewrie in full uniform storming a *minor* fort of Utter Evil, with a huge sword, much like fabled King Arthur's Excalibur, in one hand, and a knight-crusader shield on his other arm bearing a shining Christian cross and the word "Freedom" on its face! The bloated and knobby-faced villains atop the ramparts were as ogreish as anyone could wish, cringing and tearing at their hair as they directed a legion of skeletons garbed most remarkably like French grenadiers to oppose him as he (the artistic Lewrie!) actually was depicted leading a band of winged *angels*, for God's sake!

Little ribbons of captions led from the villains' mouths, with " 'Tis only Business, ye Meddlesome Upstart!" and "Curses on him who'd come 'tween us and our Money!" and other statements sure to rile the average reader.

At Lewrie's feet knelt several "grateful" Blacks—those not impaled on the evil minions' bayonets!—expressing the most pitiful expressions of thankfulness for even a few of them being liberated, a selection of phrases that made Lewrie cringe in embarrassment and squirm in his chair!

"God above, they got Cruikshank t'do it!" Lewrie gawped aloud, when he took note of the wee signature beneath the artwork. No wonder the villains resembled the worst aspects of that artist's depictions of his stock-character "John Bull"!

No one had loaned Cruikshank a portrait to copy, though, thank God, so "Saint Alan, the Immaculate" (or so the scribbles on his coat stated) bore an uncanny likeness to Horatio Nelson kicking Bonaparte's fundament . . . though Lewrie thought that Cruikshank *had* made him both taller and more manly than that slim little minnikin!

"Must not've paid him all *that* much!" he muttered. "Damn!"

He pushed all that aside, skimmed over the last few sentences of Twigg's letter, which didn't amount to much, and sat back in utter misery. A trip to his wine-cabinet was in order, he decided, badly! Re-armed with a glass of brandy, he returned to his desk to see what *else* there was to plague him.

Well, there were letters from Sewallis and Hugh. Both of them almost made him feel much better, for they were frankly *proud* of him, all eager to leave their stultifying school, and go fight the French, *and* the evil "blackbirders"!

His father, Sir Hugo, was also complimentary, noting that his and their ward Sophie's social invitations had increased since word of what he'd done had first appeared in the newspapers, though the old fart *did* complain that he'd have to sell off his shares in a Liverpool slave ship on the *quiet* side, since the price had suddenly sunk so low, and he might not have profitted from it, anyway, and how dare his son associate with such a "wild-eyed and rabid pack of hounds," sure to be exposed in future in secret league with the most Jacobite and Levelling wing of the Foxites and "French-Lovers" who had lost all credence after King Louis and his Queen had been beheaded in '92! Besides, an English gentleman should *not* appear in the papers unless he did something glorious or noteworthy; else, only his birth, his wedding, and his demise should be grist for common reading by the lower sorts!

His daughter, Charlotte, sent a one-page letter, which stated that "Mama told me you did something Heroic, though extremely Foolish and Reckless, over some Black People, but that is your Nature, as Mama has ever said. Thank you for the dolls from heathen Brazil, they are very pretty, though the package contained a large, black, and hairy Spider as big as my hand. Before Governess squished it, it was most awfully good fun to chase about! Mama says the Admiralty told her you are now in Africa or India. If you can find another spider, I would love it. If not a spider, I would very much like a Monkey!"

And, Caroline, herself, well . . .

Long-suffering, God-only-knows-what-you-have-done-to-shame-us-this-time, though she did note that the vicar of St. George's in Anglesgreen had delivered a rather impassioned (for him) homily about slavery, and why it should be abolished throughout the realm, as it was already in Great Britain. She also noted that her brother, Governour Chiswick, a former slave-owner himself in the Carolinas before the American Revolution, had nearly stormed out in anger, had not his sweet wife, Millicent, restrained him, and that the two of them were now at-loggerheads over the subject. The vicar had praised their own local "Emancipator," had almost (but not quite!) called him a "True Christian Gentleman" (which might have set off inappropriate laughter, and driven *Caroline* to storm out, Lewrie suspected) so that almost everyone in Anglesgreen now thought him a fine fellow, even the local squire, Sir Romney Embleton. What his otter-faced son, Harry, thought was not recorded, but then, who cared a damn what Harry Embleton thought!

"... though our lands in the Cape Fear, of such sweet Memory, were, indeed, worked by Negro Labour, never in my mind can I recall an *instant* of such Brutality as the papers describe in the Sugar Islands of the Caribbean, Alan. Why else would Old Mammy and a few others of our household clew to us so fiercely, and kindly, and my old Mammy to Emigrate with us to England, where, 'til her Passing, she served Mama and Papa and me so Faithfully and Cheerfully, even after Manumission?

"I can only pray that the accounts of the Reformers and Abolitionists are greatly exaggerated to foment their Cause's success, or, should they prove True, that the Reformers *succeed,* for no one of our former acqaintance in North Carolina, a most genteel and refined Society, could ever have even conceived of such fiendishness. Evidently, the planter class in the Sugar Isles are an utterly Depraved lot, bad as the tobacco-chewing dregs who are now, I am told, populating lower portions of the old Georgia colony!"

Am I too cynical, or is she too naive? he had to wonder at her well-edited remembrances.

"Alan, you have ever been a Puzzlement. Worthy of cursing for an inveterate Rogue and Rake-Hell, a jocular and slothful Lack-A-Day, where an Upright Man would shew Sobriety, Diligence, and Rectitude in his doings. For a man grown, you evince such a Boyish, Indolent face to Life. Surely, such should preclude your Advancement in such a demanding profession as Seafaring, and the Navy, yet, you not only thrive, you are become a great Success, and a Hero.

"I also pray that this recent *beau geste* of yours is a sign of you turning from Folderol to Rectitude, that the Navy has forced you to so Discipline yourself in your professional and publick Life that some wee bit of that Discipline has, at last, trickled over into your private life, as well. Had you the ability to apply but a Tithe towards mastering your Amatory Nature, our Marriage would have remained a most Happy One, no matter now many years apart, nor how many thousand miles separate us. If only such were True I could own to Complete Approval and Adoration of an heroic Husband! Though, until such is proven to me, you will understand you have won but a Portion of my Praise, you Incomprehensible, Paradoxical, Ever-Amazing Man!"

Which was certainly a lot more warmth than he'd gotten from her past letters, Lewrie decided. Did all England hail him as "Saint Alan the Emancipator"—and they forgot that horrid "Black Alan" quickly, pray God!—Caroline *might* deign to accept him back, in public, at least. Were they cheered in the London theatres like Horatio Nelson, she *might* stand beside him in their private box, and even go so far as to wave and smile in appreciation with him . . . though Lewrie doubted if she'd be gazing up at him in mute adoration, exactly.

Most-like she'd keep her eyes out for the flirty orange-seller wenches, Lewrie grimly thought; *and rip the lungs out of the first'un who tried t'hug me! Not that I can act'lly* blame *her . . .*

Still, it was a start towards *some* sort of reconciliation, but only the iciest sort, and only if he came out his troubles smelling like Hungary Water. There *was* a chance they might reside under the same roof, again. In the same bed-chamber, the same bed, well . . . he might have to hire-on a food-taster, and sleep with one eye open for a time.

". . . Mother Charlotte is failing, Alan, and we despair that we may see her with us by Autumn," Caroline related by long-distance, in her "homebody" *persona*. "We do hear, though, that, in Response to our informations sent to Burgess in India, he is now of a clear mind to throw up his Commission with the East India Company Army, now that he has achieved a Majority with the 19th Native Infantry, your father's old Bengali regiment, and, with the last remnants of the Tippoo Sultan Uprising quelled, in which Burgess informs us he has amassed quite the "Chicken Nabob" fortune, it his greatest Wish to be home with our Dear Mother whilst she is still well. Who knows, perhaps his Fortune will prove even greater than the one you reaped in the . . ."

Beyond that news, there was only a formal close, and an *almost* jocular plea that he closely inspect any packages of gifts he sent for the children in future, and under no circumstances was he to send them anything *living*. A formal set-piece of a final sentence, worthy of a letter to a corn-merchant of long, but arm's-length, standing, and she signed herself rather *coolly* simply as "Your Wife, Caroline."

Lewrie determined to write her back, instanter, to strike while the iron was at least luke-warm. And, he'd write Sir Malcolm Shockley, too, and ask him to delve around Twigg's and the Abolitionists', true motives, and whether he really had been set up as a sacrificable cat's-paw!

CHAPTER TWENTY-SIX

"It is sinkink?" Eudoxia asked with a puzzled look as she used his telescope to study *Proteus* as she sat at her anchors out in Table Bay.

"Everything we could shift is moved forrud," Lewrie explained, "to lift her stern as high out of the water as possible. The divers have hammered new gudgeons in place, underwater, and we've 'spliced' the sternpost above the waterline with the timber we fetched back from Simon's Bay. It just *looks* precarious."

Precarious, indeed, for with all her artillery, round-shot, and victuals casks shifted up near the cable tiers, the frigate sat like a badly-anchored duck decoy on the water. Her bows were immersed as far as her lower gunwale timbers, the sea up almost as high as her hawse-holes and the lowermost beakhead rails, whilst *Proteus*'s stern was up as if she was a live duck, ready to bob and feed off the bottom weeds of a pond. It even made Lewrie sweat to see it. But, without a dockyard and a graving dock, this was the best they could do.

Andries de Witt's multiple oxen team and his timber waggon had rumbled down to the piers with the new rudder, where Lt. Catterall and the Bosun, Mr. Pendarves, had erected a shear-legs to hoist it off the timber waggon's supports, then sway it out and down into a large barge . . . *another* of Mr. Goosen's "quite reasonable" hirings. It was as ungainly and squat as a fat-bellied Dutch coaster in the Scheldte or the canals, nearly fifty-four feet long and over sixteen feet in beam, the scruffy sort of thing that usually bore cargo or an entire six months' supply of water in vast casks in her belly; low freeboard, fitted with a dozen sweeps . . . a cockroach scuttling 'cross a harbour in full daylight, and just about as handsome.

"Once under our counter, we'll moor the barge snug against the stern," Lewrie went on with his explanation, wishing he could cross a finger or two, for the reality could *not* go as easily as his breezily glib exposition. "The long, thinner part is the upper stock, and that will slide up through a large hole under the transom. The bottom end will swing, even *float*, but, with the kedge capstan and the hoisting chains, we'll lift her 'til she's almost hangin' right, then use brute force, aloft and a'low, to get the bronze pins of the pintle fittings into the holes of the gudgeon fittings, and she'll ride all her weight on 'em, once we've let out slack on the hoisting chains and cables."

"You *do* speak *Engliski*, Alan?" Eudoxia asked with a crease in her forehead as she lowered the heavy glass. "Half of what you say is . . . *shumashetshi* . . . how you are sayink . . . ?"

"Daft? Mad babbling?" Lewrie supplied with a snicker. "That's sailors for you. Our own language, even our own dictionary."

"*Da* . . . daft," Eudoxia said with a giggle, testing the word a few more times, and finding "daft" right pleasing.

"Lower away . . . handsomely!" Lt. Catterall bawled to the work-party, as the massive, and heavy, new rudder finally was swayed off the side of the pier, above the barge. He was echoed by Goosens, spouting a flood of Dutch, the local variety some called Afrikaans, Javanese, or Hottentot, for all Lewrie knew. Now and then came an English phrase having to do with "damn your eyes, don't sink my boat!" or some such.

"So . . ." Eudoxia further said, with a playful, teasing note to her voice as she stepped closer to hand him his telescope back. "You get the . . . rudder . . . on, you sail for England right away, Alan?"

"That'd be up to Vice-Admiral Sir Roger Curtis, Eudoxia. Once we're seaworthy again, he may tell us to escort that new-come convoy to Saint Helena, or all the way to the Pool of London, I truly don't know. It may take days to get us set-to-rights, proper, and they may sail without us, and we'll have to do a short patrol cruise round the Cape, instead, 'til Captain Treghues comes in with another homebound trade," he told her.

"Hmmm," was her pleased, purring comment to that news. "If you wait that long, we go shootink together? You give me tour on frigate?"

"Be delighted to, m'dear," Lewrie vowed, taking a second of his attention from watching the rudder being lowered into the barge, and, yes, with his cack-hand fingers crossed along the seam of his breeches. "A shore supper, what the Frogs call a '*pique-nique*' . . . a basket of food and wine one eats outdoors, that is. . . ."

"We *shoot* food, roast on sticks!" Eudoxia cheerfully enthused, all but bouncing on the toes of her moccesins. "Build fire, take big blanket . . . cut poles, and put up *palatka*, uhm, dammit . . . *tent*! Hunt springbok, duck, and grouse . . . ! Eat wit' fingers, get greasy . . . !"

Damme, but it does *sound temptin'!* Lewrie thought, one eye on the swaying rudder, one ear cast for Eudoxia's patter, the other ear cocked for pierside sounds, like snapping or groaning ropes, squeaky or jammed blocks in the hoisting tackle, trying to sort them out of a constant intrusion from the comings-and-goings of rowing boats along the pier from the newly-arrived Indiamen, and the clatter of coaches and carriages either dropping off passengers or arriving to pick them up. *A tent. Hell yes! Night in the wilds,* he fervidly imagined; *one of those* bomas *duToit mentioned, ring the camp with thornbush to keep lions out of the . . . what was it?* Kraal, *that's it!* Kraal! *Just me and her?* He almost had to shake himself to stay focussed. *Well, some natives t'hew an' tote, but off in their own little . . .* kraal, *once the sun goes down, and . . .*

"My word! Lewrie! It *is* you!" a sharp voice intruded.

"Uhm? Hah?" Lewrie gawped, whipping his head about to find a source, irked that his urgent attention on the doings with his rudder, and his fantasies, were so rudely interrupted at possibly the most inopportune instant. He espied a quartet of people just attaining a firm footing on the pier from the wooden stairs that led from the floating landing stage on the south side of the pier. There was an older Reverend in the all-black "ditto" and white bands that were Church "uniform" the world over, a stout woman of equal age in dark and drab grey silk, sporting a grim little bonnet atop her tautly drawn-back hair under a parasol worthy of a *rainy* funeral, a young lady gowned much the same who bore a fair sort of resemblance to the older people, though quite pretty, in a *prim* way, and a sun-darkened man in the red and scarlet of an officer of the East India Company army, right down to the bright silver chain-mail epaulets on each shoulder, aiding the girl.

"Burgess Chiswick?" Lewrie yelped in glad surprise. "Damn my eyes, Burgess. Caroline just wrote me you were on yer way home! Give ye joy, lad! Give ye joy!" he whooped, forgetting everything else for a moment to step forward and offer his hand. "Ye'll pardon me, but I have a wee situation here, Burgess. M'new rudder. The Frogs shot the old'un off, a couple of weeks ago, just out yonder," he added, waving a hand seaward.

"Mother hasn't . . . ?" Burgess uneasily asked him as he not only shook hands with him, but threw his arms about him, too.

"Caroline wrote that Mother Charlotte's poorly, but as of four months ago, was still with us, though as for autumn . . ." Lewrie told him, pounding him on the back. The diffident lad that Lewrie had met during the siege of Yorktown so long ago, who had seemed so ill-suited and sometimes naive for a soldier's life in the harshness of India, had turned into a well-weathered man, and a confident and seasoned veteran of nearly fourteen years of command in the field.

"*Hellish*-good t'see you, Burge!" Lewrie loudly told him.

"Ah, hum . . ." Burgess cautioned, with a subdued cough to remind Lewrie that he wasn't on his quarterdeck, that a churchman was nearby.

"Yer pardons," Lewrie said, blushing. "Oops! I'll see to the last of our lowering away, then . . ."

"Vast, the God-damned larboard snub-lines, ye idle duck-fuckers!" Lt. Catterall bellowed, all unknowing, fully into his task, and in ripe Catterall form. "Belay ev'ry inch of that shite!"

Eudoxia found that outburst hilarious, even if such Billingsgate language made her blush. She laughed right out loud, obliviously, and repeated the "duck-fucker" part to herself several times, savouring it in wicked glee. Lewrie could practically *hear* scandalised heads snapping from him, to the unseen Catterall below the edge of the pier, and to Eudoxia, could hear stiff faces crackling into scowls!

"Uhm, hah . . ." Lewrie mumbled, going to the edge of the pier to stand by the shear-legs. "Rev'rend on deck, Mister Catterall!" he said in warning.

"Arr, *fook* th' preacher!" Ordinary Seaman Slocombe growled back in a voice just loud enough to be heard.

"I've a'ready done that, 'usband," Landsman Sugden cackled in a female *falsetto*, providing the end of the old jape about the habits of some circuit-riding ministers, and their doings. "Now, 'e warnts ye t' kill 'im a chicken!"

Can it get any *worse?* Lewrie sadly asked himself.

"God Almighty!" he yelled down to the barge without thinking, in his quarterdeck voice. "Belay that language, or there'll be people at the gratings, come morning!"

"Vaht is meanink 'to kill him a chicken,' *pajalsta*?" a giggly Eudoxia just *had* to enquire, stalking up to Lewrie's side. It didn't help matters that today she sported a new pair of buff breeches as snug as a second skin, her knee-length moccasins with all the fringes, a tan linen shirt unbuttoned halfway to her navel, a bright yellow sash tied about her waist, and that damned hat with the long egret feather plume, to boot, and most-like looked about as outlandish and savage to the Reverend and his family as a Muskogee war chief.

"I'll explain later," Lewrie muttered from the side of his mouth, and trying to shush her with a hidden gesture.

"Alan, you knowink this fine soldier, *da*?" she blithely asked.

He *couldn't* snub her, could he? Well, he *considered* giving her a shove off the pier into the water, *or* the barge, but by then, every eye, every brow lifted in prim expectation, was on him, and her, just ready to pounce, and Lewrie *had* to follow through.

"Burgess, allow me to name to you Mistress Eudoxia Durschenko," Lewrie managed to get out, just knowing it would all turn to shit, no matter what he did. "Mistress Eudoxia, this is Major Burgess Chiswick of the East India Company Army, an old comrade of mine from the American Revolution, and my . . . brother-in-law."

"Mistress Eudoxia," Burgess smoothly replied, as if such things happened every day; perhaps he'd seen odder in India. He doffed his hat to her and made a presentable "leg." Eudoxia stuck out a hand, at first, before remembering the finer customs, and dipped him a shallow curtsy, which, in boots and breeches, looked perfectly scandalous, as she murmured, "Your servant, Major Cheese . . . sir!"

"You are, ah . . . of local Cape Dutch extraction, Miss Eudoxia?" Burgess brightly enquired, in hopes of explaining her *outré* clothing to his travelling companions, perhaps to himself, as well.

"*Nyet*, Major Cheese . . . Week," Eudoxia proudly stated. "I am *Russki*! Russian. Vith Vigmore's Travellink Extravaganaa. I do bareback ridink, expert archery 'turn,' *and* some acting in comedies, and dramas! Is pity we finish our run of shows before you arrive. Now, Vigmore and Papa, who is beink lion tamer, are away on hunt for new beasts, but I learn African elephant is *not* good for performink. But, you come from *India*?" she gushed, all agog and feckless. "Land of tiger and ridink elephant? You *see* them? *Hunt* them? Oh, you must tell me all, Major Ch . . . sir! Your friends? Family?" Eudoxia asked, *pointing* to the churchman and his brood, unaware of how gauche it was. "They see elephant and tiger, too? You introduce me, *da*?"

"Uhm, ah . . ." Burgess dithered, caught in Lewrie's trap, after all. From the instant Eudoxia had opened her mouth, there had come a *series* of prim gasps; *circus* person! Bareback *anything*! And, horror of horrors, *actress*? If she'd said she rode a broomstick, boiled up potions to cast spells, ate children, and stuck hat-pins through *all* her cheeks whilst bussing Satan's fundament, she couldn't have given them a worse case of the "fantods"!

"Reverend Brothers, allow me to name to you Mistress Eudoxia . . . uhm, Durschenko. Mistress Eudoxia, may I name to you the Reverend Brothers . . . his wife, Mistress Brothers, and their daughter, Mistress Alicia Brothers. My fellow passengers on the *Lord Stormont*."

I don't know which of us is worse-fucked! Lewrie grimly thought as he watched the Brotherses' reaction to *that*! *Him, or me, 'tis about equal shares!*

I could *trot out knowing Wilberforce, Clarkson, and old Hannah More, but I doubt it'd cosset 'em. No, they'd never believe it!*

"Your servant, sir . . . madam . . . miss," Eudoxia said, smiling in anticipation of tales of India, her curtsies to each deeper, and more graceful, as if she was finally catching on. Then . . .

"Oh, but you are so *pretty,* Mistress Alicia!" she exclaimed, all but clapping her hands. "You comink from India, too? Did you ever ride elephant? Hunt tiger vith noble *rajahs?*"

"Why, thank you, but . . . !" the young lady stammered.

"Certainly not!" and "Never!" her parents huffed.

"I'd also like to name to you my brother-in-law, sir, ma'am . . . Miss Alicia," Burgess interjected, about ready to tug at his shirt collar and suddenly too-tight neck-stock. "Captain Alan Lewrie, of the Royal Navy."

"Reverend Brothers . . . Mistress Brothers . . . Miss Brothers," Lewrie purred, doffing his cocked hat and dipping a formal "leg." "Your servant."

"Sir!" from the husband. "Hmmph!" from the stodgy wife.

"Brother-in-law?" from Eudoxia, in a hellish-sharp tone.

Oh, shit! Lewrie miserably thought; *I'm in the quag, now!*

"Alan, you not tell me *tiy jenati zamujem*! You are *married?*"

"Aah . . ." was Lewrie's "spiffy" reply.

"Schto?" Eudoxia snapped, her colour up and her breasts heaving. "*Chort!* Hell-and-damn! *Tiy gryazni sikkim siyn!* Lying . . . *peesa*!"*

And where've I heard that *before?* Lewrie sadly asked himself as she glowered at him, hands on her hips, and probably wondering where she'd left her horsewhip, or her papa's daggers. A stamp of a boot on the pier, a gesture that involved flicking her thumb off her upper teeth (perfectly white and lovely, he noted!), followed by a last one she must have picked up in her travels, her forearm thrust at him, bent skyward, and a hand slapped into the crook of her elbow.

"Dosvidanya . . . viy sabaka!"† and she stomped off, gathered the reins of her waiting white gelding, and swung up into the saddle with a lithe spring and roll. She sawed the reins to turn "Lightning," and gave him her heels, drumming him into an instant mad gallop into town.

"Well, hmm," Burgess commented in the stricken silence that ensued. "Perhaps we'll see each other about town, before we sail, Alan, old fellow. For now, though . . ."

*"What? . . . Damn! . . . you [intimate case] dirty sonofabitch Lying . . . prick!"

†"Goodbye you [formal case] dog!"

"Aye, before we sail, of a certainty," Lewrie gloomily replied. "Reverend . . . ma'am . . . miss," he intoned, doffing his hat again. The Brothers family gave him the "cut sublime" in return, suddenly intent on the clouds, the bay, and tidy little Cape Town.

Well . . . that's torn it. Lewrie bleakly thought as he watched them toddle off . . . rather more rapidly than properly languid; *And here I didn't think it could* get *any worse. Fool, me! If Caroline hears o' this . . . which sure-to-God she will, 'less I can bribe Burgess t'keep mum! . . . I'm back sleepin' in the stables. Lord, is that "dominee do-little" in with Wilberforce an' his crowd, I'm in the quag up t'my eyebrows with them, too!*

He ambled (an impartial observer might have said stumbled!) over to the pier edge once more, to a stout combination piling and bollard against which he could lean (or slump, depending on your outlook) just by the stern of the ungainly barge.

"All done, sir!" Lt. Catterall proudly shouted up at him. "It is finished!"

"And ain't it, just," Lewrie wryly commented. "Very well done, Mister Catterall, lads!" he congratulated. "Secure all, ready to get under way. Ready, Mister Goosens? No time like the present."

And, with a spryness he did not feel, he scuttled down a steep ladderway to the north-side landing stage and into the barge. At the least, he could sail home to "pay the piper" aboard a *sound* ship.

CHAPTER TWENTY-SEVEN

"And, what about those eighteen-pounders, Mister Catterall?" he asked, the morning after HMS *Proteus* had completed her repairs, with a sound rudder and sternpost firmly attached, and a short test sail about Table Bay done to assure them that it was a *permanent* repair.

"Guns and carriages fully found, sir," Catterall gruffly replied. "Though, any eighteen-pounder frigate or older ship of the line calling at Cape Town has already carried off most of the round-shot. I doubt if there are a dozen rounds remaining in stores, and none of the warships on the station at present mount eighteens, sir."

"And if they did, they'd be extremely loath to share with us," Lewrie glumly decided. He paced about his newly-pristine quarterdeck, now free of piled cable, shear-legs, heaps of hoisting chain, and the carpentry or metal-working implements needed for last-minute tinkering to make the rudder and sternpost fit properly. "It appears that we'll be forced to sail a brace of guns short, then. Dammit."

HMS *Proteus* was a 32-gunned frigate of the Fifth Rate, a classification that could be misleading to the uninitiated, who might think that thirty-two guns meant thirty-two heavy guns, sixteen mounted on each beam. She had only mounted twenty-six 12-pounders, and the grand total included six 6-pounders; four on the quarterdeck, and two forward on the forecastle for chase-guns, and carronades didn't *count*.

Now, Lewrie had only twenty-four 12-pounders he could trust, the two "dinged" ones stored on the lower-most hold with the ballast, with the two midships gun-ports yawning empty.

"We could shift two carronades to fill in," Lewrie mused aloud. "But, then we'd also have to shift stores aft, again, to compensate, so our new rudder has its proper 'bite.' "

"Well, sir," the burly Lt. Catterall suggested, "the new rudder is actually broader than our old'un, fore-and-aft, and that with only one fir sacrificial strip on the trailing edge, 'stead of two or three as the old'un did. Might not be completely necessary to push her stern down to the old seventeen-and-a-half-feet draught we had before, sir."

"Seventeen'd do it, then, Mister Catterall?" Lewrie asked. "Or slightly less? Hmm."

Lewrie paced a bit more, all the way aft to the taffrails for a peek over the stern, with Lt. Catterall following a few feet "astern" of him whilst he did some mental calculations.

Four "long twelves" in my cabins, now, he thought, *Shift two of 'em to the midships ports, that'd lighten her astern by better than four tons, right there. Ah, but ships are* meant *t'be stern-heavy. Makes 'em quicker on the helm, does the rudder have a deeper bite. Though, with a broader rudder, like a Dutch coaster . . . ?*

He turned and peered forward along the freshly-washed and "holystoned" length of the quarterdeck, now restored to almost a paper-white neatness. There were two 6-pounders on each beam, and two carronades, the short, stubby "Smashers," not very long-ranged pieces, but capable of throwing a heavy 24-pounder solid shot, or be loaded like a fowling gun with grapeshot, langridge, sacks of musket balls, scrap crockery, or any sort of hard objects to maim and kill when up close alongside a foe. They weren't meant to take the powerful powder charges needed in a "long" artillery piece, so they, and their slide-carriages, weighed less than conventional artillery.

"Any carronades in stores, Mister Catterall?" Lewrie asked the Second Officer. "And twenty-four-pounder shot?"

"Oh, *aye*, sir!" Lt. Catterall said, brightening. "The Indiaman, *Lord Clive*, mounted twenty-four-pounder long guns *and* carronades. Vice Admiral Curtis's people salvaged her guns, but little else, after she went aground."

"I want two of 'em, Mister Catterall!" Lewrie declared. "We'll shift two twelve-pounders from my cabins to amidships, the after-most pair, and replace 'em with a pair of 'Smashers.' They'll *almost* make up the weight and balance diff'rence. Get 'em for us, sir, no matter what it takes . . . beg, borrow, or steal!"

"Aye aye, sir!" Catterall cheered. "Er . . . how, sir? If they won't give 'em up, that is," he asked, more soberly a second later.

"You know where they are?" Lewrie pressed. "You've seen 'em?"

"Aye, sir, 'board the stores ship, but . . ."

"Just go *ask* for 'em, Mister Catterall!" Lewrie exclaimed with a sly grin. "With my chit in hand, o' course. Take our largest boats and sufficient crews. By now, our people should know all about shiftin' heavy loads, as should you. In the meantime, I'll go aboard the flagship and request 'em, formally. With the list of expenditures to date t'repair our ship. We've not made much demand 'pon naval stores, yet, and, 'a penny saved is a penny earned,' as the old Rebel Benjamin Franklin used t'say. Salvaged guns goin' t'waste, free and clear of Prize-Court folderol, well . . . ! Muster your boat crews, sir, but spare me my gig's hands and Cox'n. I'll have you a note for the stores ship in two shakes of a sheep's tail! Get me those guns, and as much round-shot as you can manage, another fifty or sixty, do they have 'em. Cartridge flannel, gun tools. . . . Hell, take the Master Gunner with you and let him 'shop' to his heart's content. Slide-carriages, new breeching ropes, he'll know what's needful. Go, get ready!"

You steal or borrow, old son, Lewrie told himself as he trotted below to his desk for pen and paper; I'll *do the begging*!

"My word, sir," the Flag-Captain said, rolling his eyes over a neatly-penned list of out-of-pocket expenses to put *Proteus* right. "As much as that, what?"

"The local Dutch, as they say, sir, 'saw me coming,' and made the most of our predicament," Lewrie uneasily explained, shifting one leg over the other as he sat before the senior officer's desk, thankful that the flagship's transom windows didn't face the stores ship, so that worthy couldn't see his boats scuttling 'cross Table Bay with the first of the requested goods. "Not so much in materials, mind, but in labour, and hires, sir. The waggons and ox teams and su . . ."

"And you contracted all this without consulting me as to which part of it Sir Roger might *authorise*, sir?"

"I fully intend to present my sums to Admiralty, in London, as soon as we return to England, sir," Lewrie purred back with a blandly reassuring smile. "*Proteus* sailed under orders from Captain *Treghues,* sir, and is not, strictly, the responsibility of the Cape Station, so, I did not wish to impose my monetary needs upon Sir Roger, d'ye see."

"Ah, well," the Flag-Captain mused. "Hmm. Not under *our* flag, as it were. A *transient* in need of repair, aha! Aye, it'd be proper to submit your expenditures to the Navy Board, 'stead of us."

"Which'll be my problem, sir, since so much of the costs came from my own purse," Lewrie told him, shifting uneasily once more; the very idea of how much his personal funds had been depleted was enough to break a sweat; a local bank now held a *hefty* note-of-hand that they would draw from his account at Coutts' Bank in London, a hefty sum he *prayed* Admiralty would reimburse . . . someday *this* century.

"Well, I must own to a sense of relief, Captain Lewrie, that we are not bound to offer recompense to you . . . or foot the bill, entire, to the local chandlers and such, ha ha!"

"Never even crossed my mind, sir," Lewrie assured him, tossing in another disarming "shit-eating" grin.

"So, *Proteus* is now ready for sea, in all respects?"

"Well, sir, there is the problem of my two damaged guns," Lewrie casually allowed, crossing his legs the other way round. "I have been informed the stores ship has no twelve-pounders available, so I *could* sail two pieces short, but . . . I am also told that she holds several twenty-four-pounder carronades salvaged most swiftly from the wrecked *Lord Clive*, and I had a thought to mount two of them in lieu of great-guns, temporarily. To be turned over to Gun Wharf, soon as we're back home. Other than that lack, we are, indeed, ready for sea, and for an engagement with any lurking French raider or privateer, sir. Unless a greater need exists here on the Cape Station for 'em, that is."

He crossed the fingers of his left hand, down below the edge of the desk where the Flag-Captain couldn't see them.

"I'd be very much obliged, eternally *grateful*, really, to have your permission to indent for two of them, sir, along with sufficient round-shot for a *brief* engagement, should that occur."

"Hmmm . . ." the Flag-Captain said, thoughtfully rubbing his chin.

"With the rest of Captain Treghues's ships now halfway to India or China, *Proteus* must either become part of the Cape Squadron, or be assigned to bolster the escort of one of the other 'John Company' convoys, I'd suppose, so . . ." Lewrie suggested. "Perhaps the one waiting to depart in harbour now, sir?"

"Aye, Captain Leatherwood *would* find you useful, Lewrie," the Flag-Captain informed him with a smile of his own. "Some trouble with the previous escorting frigate reefing down too late in a squall just off Ceylon. A squall, and a heavy roll that put her on her beam ends, and rolled her masts right out of her. She put back to Calcutta, or the nearest port with a yard, under jury masts, and Captain Wheeler had to request the assistance of a warship from the Bombay Marine, which saw his convoy as far as the Southern tip of Madagascar. Not allowed to operate West of Good Hope, the Bombay Marine, and, not much of a sea-force, either. A few British officers of doubtful abilities, and the crews made up of God knows *what* sort of natives. Low-caste Hindoos at the best . . ."

"Who can cross the 'great black water' without breaking their caste, aye, sir," Lewrie happily supplied.

"Been in Indian waters yourself, sir?" the Flag-Captain asked.

" 'Tween the wars, sir, aye."

"Under the circumstances, then, I do believe that Leatherwood will find you more than welcome, Captain Lewrie," the Flag-Captain said with a beamish smile, as if that settled the matter. "Bad run of luck, all round, has Captain Leatherwood. Three of his charges took bad water aboard when they victualled, and there's been sickness among passengers and crew."

"*Cholera*, sir?" Lewrie asked with a shudder of dread. Cholera was to blame for most of the untimely deaths among Britons who sailed East to make their fortunes.

"No, thank the Lord," the Flag-Captain told him with a shudder of his own, and a rap of his knuckles for luck on his desktop. "A bit of 'gippy-tummy,' *mal de mer*, and 'the runs' but no deaths. It'll be a day or two more, before they scrap their water casks and load fresh ones, then fill them with safe Cape Town water."

"My brother-in-law's a passenger aboard the *Lord Stormont*, sir," Lewrie said. "He said nothing of it when we met, and looked healthy as a horse."

"Don't believe she was one of the affected ships."

"Uhm . . . about those carronades, sir," Lewrie reminded him one more time. "Might I have your permission to indent for them, if this Captain Wheeler is in immediate need of a frigate, sir?"

"Don't see why not, Captain Lewrie," the Flag-Captain allowed with an easy chuckle. "It's not as if short-ranged carronades will be doing us much good here. 'Tis proper *fortress* guns we need. Thirty-two-pounders and fourty-twos, but will Admiralty, or even the *Army's* Artillery Board at Woolwich, respond to our needs? Can't hold this harbour without, should the French stir themselves, but . . ." He dug into his desk for paper and pen, a steel-nib much like Lewrie's, and opened his brass inkwell to begin scribbling a formal indenture.

Thank bloody Christ! was Lewrie's thought; That *was easy!*

"There ye are, Lewrie," the Flag-Captain said, handing over the note to the stores ship. "Put them to good use, if needs be."

"Hopefully, sir, we'll *yawn* our way to Channel Soundings, but I am indeed grateful to you, no matter," Lewrie declared as he got to his feet. For a quick exit, before the Flag-Captain could change his mind! "I'll be going, then, sir, and thank you once again for all you have done for us."

"A good voyage, Captain Lewrie," that worthy replied as he rose as well, and offered his hand in parting. "Fair winds, calm seas . . . all that, what?"

His gig came alongside the starboard entry-port just about the same time that the first carronade's slide-carriage was being hoisted aloft from the ship's cutter in a sling hung off the main course yardarm. All the gun-ports gaped open, the port lids raised to show their red interior paint, and Lewrie was delighted to see that the two aftermost in his great-cabins already were yawning empty, and the red tompions stuck in the muzzles of the 12-pounders which had occupied those ports were now brooding in the amidships gun-ports.

"Got 'em, sir!" Lt. Catterall hooted from the cutter, where he was overseeing the hoisting. "Fifty rounds of shot apiece, to boot!"

"Next trip, Mister Catterall, I'll have the formal permission for you to give to the stores ship's captain!" Lewrie shouted back.

"Right-ho, sir!"

A scamper up the boarding battens and man-ropes to the gangway and the ceremony of welcoming a captain back aboard, and Lewrie could beam with pleasure to see that both slide-carriages for his new carronades squatted in the waist, ready to be hauled aft.

"The 'Smashers' will take two more trips, sir," Lt. Langlie told him, after he had paced to the centre of the hammock netting overlooking the waist. "A further trip for the shot, with the launch to bear all that Mister Carling requested, and it's done, Captain."

"Very good, Mister Langlie. Excellent!" Lewrie declared.

"This note came aboard for you, in your absence, sir," Langlie told him, offering a folded-over sheet of paper.

"Ah, hmm," Lewrie said, breaking the seal, which did not bear any stamp or signet mark. "Ah! My brother-in-law, Burgess, is ashore, and asks me to dine with him."

He dug out his pocket watch and checked the time, frowning as he realised that the hour appointed was fast approaching for dinner at a shore establishment, the very place, in point of fact, where he'd fed those generous Indiaman passengers and captains. There was no time to send a reply; he would just have to show up.

"My compliments, Mister Langlie, but I'm off ashore, at once," he told the First Officer. "Here . . . give Mister Catterall this note from the flag, so the stores ship captain won't think we bilked him out of anything. Call away my boat crew . . . no, Cox'n Andrews, but a fresh set of oarsmen, and I'm away."

"Aye, sir."

Burgess surely has gotten sour letters about me from Caroline, Lewrie fretfully thought, no matter the casually-pleased face he put on it as he waited for his gig to be readied. *Is he t'give me a good cobbing 'bout my "sinful" ways, I wonder?*

CHAPTER TWENTY-EIGHT

"So nice of you to invite me," Lewrie said as they were seated on a deep side veranda at the travellers' inn, where jewel-bright birds in cages flitted and chirped, and a cool breeze blew stirring hanging-baskets of local flowers.

"Well, I saw that your ship was no longer in danger of sinking," Burgess Chiswick snickered, "and supposed that you'd be off as soon as the next tide, or something, and meant to see you before you departed."

"Won't sail 'til you do," Lewrie told him. "I gather that we're to escort your ships to Saint Helena, to help that lone sixty-four-gun that brought you in. Perhaps all the way to the Thames."

"Why, that'd be splendid, Alan!" Burgess cried. "Then, with any luck at all, you could even coach me all the way to Anglesgreen!"

"Haven't been home myself in quite a while, aye," Lewrie said.

Hang it, might as well broach the subject myself, he thought.

"Not been exactly *welcome* round the homeplace, actually," Alan added. "Bit of a dither . . . ?"

"Oh, that," Burgess deprecated with a snort as their first wine arrived. "Women simply *won't* understand the realities, Alan, old son," Burgess scoffed with a worldly-wise air that he'd not had before he'd headed for India. "Caroline's written me all about it, several times, as has Governour. *He's* quite wroth with you, though before he wedded Millicent, Governour was quite the Buck-of-The-First-Head when we were back in the Carolinas. Tell me, has he *really* gotten as stout as they say? Mother was concerned for his health, in her letters."

"A proper John Bull stoutness," Lewrie replied, chuckling.

"Comes of good living, and living under Millicent's thumb, I'd expect," Burgess said with a frown. "Quite good wine, this. In India, we came to like Cape wines. Their reds don't travel well, but whites keep main-well. Well, Governour . . . as the eldest, he always *did* see himself the arbiter of just about everything."

"Threatened to shoot, or horsewhip, me." Lewrie admitted.

"What a fatuous arse!" Burgess exclaimed. "Just 'cause *he* can't caterwaul or take a mistress, now he's a down on you. Most-like will take *me* to task, does he ever learn of my *bibikhana*."

As a Major in the East India Company Army, Burgess *would* have lived in a private *bungalow*, apart from the ensigns, lieutenants, and captains who would share quarters off the collegial mess building for his regiment's officers, nearly as grand as a Colonel. And a man with private quarters *had* to have his own cook, manservant, butler, cleaning maids, *punkah* boy to keep the fans or suspended mats swinging for cool air, and no one would think a thing wrong of him did he furnish a women's quarters out back, where he could keep a brace of fetching *bibis* to ease a man's essential needs, without running the risk of a brothel or street prostitute in such a disease-ridden country.

"Impressive, were they?" Lewrie asked with a grin.

"Only the two, but yes, Alan." Burgess beamed back with a wink. "Most delightful. Now, most English ladies who come out to India *see* that their husbands have needs, and when in the field, are presented with opportunities galore. From what Caroline wrote me, I don't think you ever actually dallied with any wench when you were *home*?"

"No, I didn't," Lewrie quickly said, immensely pleased that his brother-in-law was being so sane and reasonable about it. "Well . . . I did spend some time at Sheerness with, ah . . ."

"The Greek widow, yes," Burgess supplied with another wink and a snicker as the waiter approached their table. "Other than her . . ."

" 'Twas all *far* from home, Burge," Lewrie swore. "With bloody *years*, and thousands of miles, between homecomings."

"And, you were always careful," Burgess blithely assumed. "Ah! *Satays* and *boboties*, ye say? Like Hindoo cooking? Splendid. I will essay the 'country captain,' and be sure to set out a pot of *chautney*."

"I'll have the Cape salmon," Lewrie decided, looking over their chalked menu slate. "Salad, egg-drop soup, and let us share a platter of eland strips in the plum sauce between us, first off. Fresh-sliced, is it, or are they soaked *biltong*? Fresh is best, thankee, and a glass of your best burgundy each with it."

"Biltong?"

"What you'd call jerky," Lewrie explained. "My cats adore it. I have nigh three hundredweight in stores for 'em."

"Oh, you and your cats!" Burgess laughed. "I'll see your eland, and raise you the fresh lobster *remoulade*, and make it a *bottle* of the burgundy . . . my treat, after all, and we might as well make a feast of it whilst we may. Ship victuals are passing-fair, but . . . ! God, your cats. Two of 'em, now? I recall that hulking old ram-cat of yours you left with Caroline when we sailed for India. William Pitt, wasn't it? Didn't take to *me,* I'll tell you, though he adored Caroline."

"They're good company at sea," Lewrie told him as their waiter topped up their glasses before heading off for the kitchens. "So, you became a 'chicken *nabob,*' Burge? Lashings of a *rajah*'s *loot*?"

"Loot," itself, was a Hindi word.

"I've come away with better than sixty *thousand,* Alan!" Burgess imparted in a careful, but gleeful, whisper cross the table. "Note-of-hand drawn on Army agents, some in *rouleaus* of guineas for easy access, and some jewelry I scooped up when we broke into rebel *rajahs'* palaces, to boot. Haven't even had them assayed, yet, and *still* have no idea of their value. Emeralds and rubies, big as pigeons' eggs, nigh a *pound* of strung pearls and such . . ."

"Good Lord, you fortunate young dog!" Lewrie congratulated with a hoisted glass. "And, you're looking to buy yourself a British Army commission? Why not a whole regiment while you're at it?"

"Oh, I'll end with a regiment of mine own," Burgess casually rejoined. "Do I not make brigadier, I'd be more than happy commanding a regiment of regulars. This will be a long war, Alan, longer than any of us expect, and sooner or later, we *must* beard the Frogs on their own ground. A naval blockade won't defeat them, begging your salty pardon. Have to kick them in the teeth, make them howl in anguish, and parade down the streets of Paris before they cry 'Uncle.'

"I expect to find an opening as a Major, at the least," Burgess boasted, "even are 'John Company' officers sneered at by the loftier sorts round Horse Guards. 'Tis not so much my experience, which *has* to be much greater than theirs, but the *money* I can bid for my 'colours,' after all. Is there need for a Lieutenant-Colonel in a *middling* regiment, well, I could afford that, too. Then, with what I've learned of *real* soldiering, not 'square-bashing' and Church Parades, I could turn that middling regiment into one of the finest in the Army. You watch and see if I don't . . . just like you expect to turn any new ship you're given into the best, as well!"

Lewrie could not remember Burgess being so confident, or so loquacious, but he thought it a grand improvement on the boy he'd known.

"After a proper spell of leave, o' course," Lewrie chuckled. "A quick run through civilised Society, at least."

"Aye, that, too," Burgess agreed. "And, perhaps marry."

"Well . . . certainly," Lewrie said, surprised.

"D'ye know the old Army saying?" Burgess asked with a puckish expression. "Might be King's Regulations, for all I know . . . ensigns or cornets *must not* marry . . . captains *may* marry . . . majors *should* marry, and colonels absolutely *must* wed! A good woman, with the proper taste and manners, sets the right tone in the mess. Seen it, when it's good. And, seen the results when the Colonel's wife wasn't up to snuff."

"The adorable Miss Brothers, perhaps?" Lewrie japingly hinted.

"Oh, Lord!" Burgess exclaimed, all but writhing in his chair.

"No?" Lewrie teased. "*She* seems a prim, mannerly sort."

"The good Reverend and his wife have been all but shoving her at me, Alan, soon as word got round the ship that I'd made a fair pile of 'tin,'" Chiswick scoffed. "After all my time in India, I'm not sure what a good woman *looks* like, but, for all *her* time in India, Mistress Alicia is still the 'shrinking violet' sort, *so* prim and sheltered she might as well be new-come from the Moon!

"Besides," Burgess grumbled, "she and her family are as 'skint' as . . . church-mice. I doubt the girl would fetch me fourty pounds per annum for a dowry, and her paraphernalia might not extend beyond poor Hindi-made furniture and bedding. Like . . . calls to like, what?"

"Definitely not 'landed,' either, I'd s'pose?" Lewrie asked.

"Spent their whole time traipsing from one poor glebe to a next, doing 'good works' and ministering to pagans and 'rice Christians' in the Bengali slums," Burgess told him with a mocking shudder. "Reverend Brothers may be the *only* man ever took Holy Orders who *believed* in a vow of poverty. Either that, or he's a disguised Catholic monk with a weakness for dour bed-partners, haw haw! Aha! This is our eland?" he exulted as the waiter fetched their first course. Chiswick forked some onto his plate, slathered a bite with the spicy-hot plum sauce, and sampled it. "Marvellous!" he cried after a sip of the local wine. "This Cape burgundy's better than any they sent *us*, too, I'll tell you. That . . . *biltong* of yours. It's as good as this? Might I be able to purchase some for the voyage home? 'John Company' victuals are decent, but I'd relish some game meat, now and again."

"Purchase-able, aye," Lewrie told him, "though, I shot most of mine. A little hunting down the peninsula to Simon's Town, and back."

"I'd *adore* an African *shikar*," Burgess declared, between bites. "Didn't get much chance, our first voyage out East. Hunted all over India, of course, even bagged a tolerable tiger once, but, there might not be time enough, even with the bad water problem. Comes from relying too much on local suppliers, who filled their casks *close* to Calcutta, 'stead of inland."

"Hooghly River sewage, no *wonder* they had sickness aboard. 'Tis a wonder no one died," Lewrie commented, raking several strips of hot eland meat onto his plate before the ravenous Burgess Chiswick gobbled them all. "I'm told they'll be ready to sail in two days."

"Not enough time, then," Burgess said with a disappointed sigh. "Look here, then, Alan . . . do you recall anyone round Anglesgreen who might be a suitable mate? I intend to heed Millicent's and Caroline's advice in seeking a good match. . . ."

"Well, Caroline might be a touch prejudiced on wedded bliss," Lewrie admitted with a wee grimace. "Not much local 'talent' . . ."

"Always did have her head in the clouds," Burgess scoffed, "all those horrid romance novels she's read. As you allude, Millicent may be my best advisor."

"You could call on my father in London," Lewrie teased, again.

"Not *him*!" Burgess hooted. "Well, perhaps London, but not with *his* advice. A wider 'market,' what? In fact, Alan . . . I've received letters from Sir Hugo, 'bout once a year or so, and, frankly, had I my druthers, I'm much intrigued to be introduced to your ward, *Comptesse* Sophie de Maubeuge."

"She's no 'dot,' no dowry worth mentioning, Burge," Lewrie had to caution him. "Though, she is become a fine and fetching, mannerly young lady, of the best accomplishments. Beyond the usual parlour and musical doings, she's an excellent horsewoman."

"Fine as your Russian Cossack wench?" It was Chiswick's turn to tease. "My *word*, but your Mistress Eudoxia was impressive."

"Not *my* wench," Lewrie was quick to correct him. Just in case he got home and spoke to Caroline before *he* could. "Never laid a hand on her. *Really!*" he added, at seeing Chiswick's extremely leery expression. "Might have given it a *thought*, but . . ."

"And I didn't help matters. Ah, well," Burgess said, sighing again. "Wroth as the mort is with *you*, I doubt a stab at her on my part would go down well, either. *Seemed* taken with you . . . a while."

"Probably not," Lewrie replied, busying himself with knife and fork and plum sauce, secretly relieved that Burgess had no chance with her, even he didn't, either. *Jealous, am I?* he thought; *Whyever?*

"A harmless flirtation on her part," Lewrie dismissively said. "Here's a thought, though. When you take leave and go up to London, I *am* acquainted with a very rich tradesman's family with a daughter you might wish to meet. The Trenchers, whose daughter Theodora is about as angelic as ever I did see. Elfin and wee, about nineteen or twenty . . . perhaps *too* young, but she seemed sensible, and comported herself well. Enthusiastic, and outgoing, not your run-of-the-mill languidly-bored and too-elegant-for-words missy. Slews of spirit."

"Hmmm?" Burgess prompted, sounding intrigued.

"Very dark, curly brown hair, almost black, and the most *amazing* violet eyes," Lewrie further tempted. "Soberly dressed, when I met her, since the family's on the newly-fashionable 'respectable' side, but with excellent taste. The hints of a fine form . . . though I wasn't exactly *looking*. Met her with the Reverend Wilberforce, Clarkson, and Mistress Hannah More, that crowd. . . ."

"You!" Burgess exclaimed, rather loudly, in point of fact. "In with Wilberforce and the Clapham Sect . . . that slavery abolition pack?"

" 'Twas the reason for our meeting," Lewrie confessed, turning a touch guarded as he recalled that the Chiswicks had been slave-owners once and his brother Governour Chiswick was still fervidly in favour of the practice. "I've a dozen Black hands in my crew, some of them, ah . . . *might* be runaway slaves who volunteered aboard on Jamaica. . . ."

"Well, good for you!" Burgess told him. "Horrid thing, that."

"*You* think so? I'd have thought . . ."

" 'Tis one thing to *hire* Hindoo labour and such, and yes, you get a slacker now and then who needs a touch-up with your quirt to keep him on the hop, but actual slavery is just . . . despicable," Chiswick swore. " 'Twas my parents in North Carolina who thought slaves necessary for a plantation. Mother Charlotte was born there, and used to it. Father, God rest his soul, adopted it after he emigrated to the Cape Fear, no matter what he really thought of it. And, yes . . . I suppose I took it for granted, as well, but . . ."

"You rather surprise me, Burgess," Lewrie had to confess.

"Well, times change . . . people change," Chiswick shrugged off. "You remember at Yorktown, those runaway slaves who served with us to earn their freedom, should we have defeated the Rebels? They served your artillery, and stood with us ready to march and volley, though I doubt they knew the first *thing* of soldiering, and there wasn't enough time for them to learn. God forgive me, but that was the first time I saw slaves as *men,* not useful animals! They'd have gladly *died* under arms than be taken, and returned to lashes, manacles, and slavery."

"Aye, I do recall them," Lewrie agreed. "Though, at the end, we abandoned 'em, and made our own escape."

"And, God forgive us for not even thinking of taking a single one with us," Burgess spat, turning soberly stern, after all his previous *bonhomie*. "Met more of them when what was left of our regiment skirmished round New York, before the surrender, and evacuation, and not one of our generals thought to include them in the terms before we sailed away, either. Then, India . . .

"Serving under your father, Alan, in the Nineteenth Native Infantry, commanding *sepoys* as dark as Negroes, most of them, learning to be the next best thing to a *father* to the ones in my company, on campaign elbow-to-elbow for months on end, well . . . it changes your way of thinking 'bout the so-called 'lesser races.' Makes you see them just as human as *us*, by God. Worry 'bout their wives and children, just as we do, get into debt, gamble, drink too much, fight like tigers, be as idle or industrious as any White man . . . 'eat our salt' and prove themselves even better soldiers than *British* regiments in India! Now, what is a fellow to make of a lesson like that, but to realise that they're our *equals*, but for their lack of being *like* us."

"Governour's going t'dislike you as much as he does me," Lewrie told him with a chuckle, and a sigh of relief.

"Well, he never had that great a love for you, anyway," Burgess teased him. "The subject comes up, I expect Mother will go off into a fit of the 'vapours,' and Governour will puff up like an adder and spit fire. Don't know what Caroline will think of me. Don't signify to me, really, for I've come to believe that real chattel slavery's a degrading evil which Britons should expunge wherever we hold sway, not just in Great Britain, and *damn* the Sugar Interest! And yes, Alan . . . once I've worked out the kinks back home, I'd admire could you arrange me an introduction to some of Reverend Wilberforce's people. Can't buy *all* the tomfoolery they spout, but I *can* side with them on ending slavery. And," he added with a droll expression, "being introduced to the girl you mentioned wouldn't go amiss, either."

"God bless you for that, Burgess, and, aye, I shall . . ." Lewrie began to promise, almost ready to confess that he'd *stolen* his Black "volunteers," warn him that the subject of emancipation *would* come up about five minutes after the welcoming hugs and kisses, but was stopped by a sudden rising commotion in the dusty street beyond, a din that got all their attention.

"What the Devil . . . ?" Burgess Chiswick wondered aloud, removing his napkin from his collar and tossing it into his empty plate as he got to his feet.

There came the usual sounds of *trekboer* waggons, the lowing and grunting of huge oxen, and the steady clop of unshod hooves. Mingled with that were the squeals of ungreased axles, the timber-on-timber thuds of unsprung waggon bodies, and the squeak of jostled joinery, as a train of pink-ended waggons slowly rumbled into town. Under all the expected sounds, though, was the hum-um of pedestrians and shoppers on the sidewalks, taken by the novelty, some even tittering laughter, as the waggon train heaved into sight. And, there were unusual sounds as well . . . some squealing "meows," hisses, and growls, some loon-like and silly brays, some nasal . . . trumpeting?

Lewrie joined Burgess by the railing of the deep veranda facing the street, up above the sidewalk and the strollers who had stopped in their tracks to witness this oddity.

"Aha!" Lewrie cried. "The circus is back in town! The 'mighty Nimrods' are back from a successful hunt!"

"Someone been on *shikar*?" Burgess had to ask.

"To bring them back alive, aye," Lewrie told him, chuckling.

For there was Mr. Daniel Wigmore, mounted on a decent mare, in the lead. He sat his saddle like a sack of heart-broken turnips, head down and grumbling to himself, it looked like. Next came a local Boer on a much better horse, but a man with as poor a "seat" as Wigmore, a lanky, heavily-bearded, and thoroughly dispreputable-looking bean-pole of a man who looked so filthy it might be possible to shake him hard, and reclaim ten pounds of topsoil. He bristled with weapons: a musket laid crosswise of his saddle before him, two *more* in scabbards hung on either side, and a brace of fowling pieces bound behind him. One arm hung in a sling, and fresh, bright-red scratches crisscrossed his bare arms and what one could see of his craggy face. As soon as he came in view, people on the street began to hoot, point, and laugh out loud.

"Van der Merwe . . . gobble-gobble!" in Dutch Lewrie heard some of them cry out; he couldn't follow anything past the fellow's name, but was sure that he was clapping eyes on the very idiot whom his guide, Piet duToit, had disparaged. After seeing the fellow, he could see the why.

Then, up came Arslan Durschenko on an even better horse, riding stiff-backed, erect, and easy, as a proper Cossack should. He looked a bit worse for wear, too, but when he caught sight of Lewrie, he scowled with fresh anger, his eyes brightening, and his long whip cracking.

Then came the waggons, ox teams driven by near-naked Blacks with goads or lance-long thin wood poles which bore short whips at the ends. Some were the fabled little Hottentots, some stouter and taller. Some between waggons bore crates on their shoulders, or atop their heads.

"Well, I'm damned!" Burgess cried. "Look at that!"

Behind the second waggon was a menagerie. There were two baby African elephants, at least half a dozen *actual* zebras, the source for those inane brays they'd heard earlier. The next huge waggon carried a stout wooden cage containing a pair of cheetahs, who didn't look very happy to be Cape Town's latest Nine-Day Wonder, either. Atop the next waggon's pile of camp gear and tentage stood a smaller cage filled with three *lion* cubs, who hissed and spat, and uttered raspy little growls of displeasure at each jounce, though tumbling all over each other as clumsily as domestic kittens to take in all the strangeness of a town.

There were four ostriches leashed together into a kicking and outraged coffle. There was a middling-sized crocodile in a cage, and other cages borne by Black bearers contained a half-dozen wee baboons; a brace of spotted panthers, and some young wildebeests, or *gnus*!

"Looks as if they were successful," Burgess commented.

"But not very happy about it," Lewrie pointed out the many who looked utterly exhausted and hang-dog, the many who sported bandages, or limped on make-shift crutches.

Lewrie had been scanning each face of the new arrivals, looking for his runaway sailors, Groome and Rodney. He expected them to be on horseback, if they'd been promised freedman's treatment by the circus, but could not spot them. Finally . . . !

He recognised little Rodney, standing inside the last waggon of the train, clinging to the sideboards and the wood hoops that held up the partially-furled canvas cover . . . barely, for Rodney was swathed in blood-spotted bandages bound round his left shoulder and chest, and another set wound about his scalp.

"Hoy, there!" Lewrie yelled, agilely springing over the railing of the inn's veranda to the sidewalk, and jostling his way through those jeering spectators. He trotted up to the waggon, and scrambled up on the lowered tail-board to 'front his deserter. Rodney had turned grey-skinned with shock to see Lewrie, and shrank back as if the cat-o'-nine-tails was already cutting the air as Lewrie got to his feet before him.

"Damn your eyes, Rodney! You deserted!" Lewrie accused. "You'll come with me, lad!"

"S . . . sorry, suh!" Rodney cringed. "Ah *know* ah done bad, suh, runnin' off, but please *God*, suh, don' whip me! I *paid* for it, surely t'God I did! Oh, Law, but ah done paid!"

"Where's Groome?" Lewrie snapped, grabbing hold of the waggon's hoops to stay upright.

"He *daid*, suh!" Rodney stammered, tears running from his eyes. "Dot damnfool Dutch feller git 'im kilt, got a whole *bunch* o' fellers kilt, an' dey woz gon' leave *me* art there t'die, too, I didn' git on mah feets, aftah de lion maul me. Groome, he daid, suh, ain' lyin' 'bout dot. Damnfool Dutch feller say we take some o' dem buffaloes wif de *big* horns, an' *dey* kill 'im. Chase 'im up a tree, but it warn't tall 'nough, dey butt it down an' trample Groome to a puddin'. Nuttin' we could do 'bout it, neither, Cap'm suh."

"*Cape* buffalo?" Lewrie asked, gawping at the very idea. He had been warned by his guide, duToit, that they were probably the most dangerous beasts in the wilds, and almost impossible to shoot and kill if one hit the boss of their massive horns.

"Lick de skin raght orf 'is feets, 'fo' dey knock de tree down, suh, 'coz Groome couldn' shin up no higher," Rodney told him in misery. "God A'mighty, but ya shoulda heard 'is screams, when . . ." Rodney could not go on, but broke down into blubbing, wiping fresh tears with the back of his hand.

"Stop this waggon!" Lewrie shouted to the ox-tenders. "Now!"

They turned their heads to look at him, but could only shrug in confusion, for they knew no English, only their tribal tongues, or the *pidgin* of local Dutchmen. "Can somebody tell these bastards to stop this damned waggon?" Lewrie cried to the onlookers.

It was a lounging Piet duToit who sprang off a hitching rail to the street and waved a hand at the drovers, grunting out commands that thankfully brought the ox team to a plodding halt.

"A problem, *Kaptein* Lewrie?" the young man asked, looking up at him with his hands on his hips, and a smile on his face. "What I tell you about Jan van der Merwe? A fool, *ja*! You wish help down?"

"Down, aye. I've a hurt man in this waggon," Lewrie told him.

"A *kaffir*?" duToit scoffed, espying Rodney and his bandages.

"One of my sailors," Lewrie answered. "Got mauled by a lion, he says. Van der Merwe's fault, I'd imagine."

"Hah," was duToit's dismissive sneer; what care he for a Sambo.

"A deserter from my ship," Lewrie added, thinking that would be more to the Boer's liking. It was, for duToit came round to the tail-board and actually laid hands on Rodney to help Lewrie lower him to the dusty street. Burgess Chiswick was there, too, of a sudden, offering to assist the hobbling and wincing sailor to the sidewalk in front of the inn, into a bit of shade, for once Rodney was on his own feet, the young Dutch hunting guide lost all interest in him, loath to touch him any more than he had to. Surreptitiously, duToit wiped his hands along the sides of his canvas trousers.

A shadow loomed over them.

"Is hurt, him?"

Lewrie looked up and almost gasped to see Eudoxia astride of her white gelding, her face a mixture of disdain for Lewrie but, beneath that stiffness, a concern for Rodney's injuries. There was a sadness in the cast of her large, hazel eyes, too, Lewrie thought.

"Lion mauled him," Lewrie answered her. "You know that tavern by the piers . . . the one with the red shutters?"

"*Da,* knowink," a very subdued Eudoxia replied.

"Ride there for me, if you please," Lewrie bade her. "Ask for Coxswain Andrews. That's where my boat crew was eating, waiting for me to go back to the ship. Tell Andrews to come quick. Rodney here needs to see our Surgeon."

"Is *many* needink surgeon," Eudoxia said, her face working into a grimace. "Is some circus men *dead,* Papa tell me. Antonio, best clown and mime, who tended camels and donkeys . . ."

Oh, Lewrie thought sarcastically and impatiently; hellish *loss, a mime!*

"Will you?" Lewrie pressed. "Please, Eudoxia?"

"*Da,* I go," she promised, already sawing at her reins. "I ask for C . . . Coxs . . . sailor Andrews." And she did, putting her gelding into a lope for the harbour.

"Fetch me some water, will you, Burgess?" Lewrie asked, kneeling at Rodney's side. "Better yet, a watered brandy."

"Right-ho," Burgess agreed, springing back over the rail of the veranda and calling for their waiter.

"You're a God-damned fool, Rodney," Lewrie sternly told him.

"Amen t'dot, suh," Rodney said with a grimace of pain.

Within minutes, Andrews and the gig's crew were back in a sweaty trot. Burgess had organised the gathering of long poles and canvas off the stalled waggon with which to fashion a stretcher, with the help of some lingering Boers who had stayed to gawk over the drama, once the comedy and the circus parade was done.

"Back to the ship and Mister Hodson with him, Andrews," Lewrie ordered. "I'll be along later, soon as I'm able, in a hired boat. No need t'make a long row for me."

"Aye, sah," Andrews replied as the boat crew picked up the ends of the poles, with Rodney stretched out atop the canvas.

"Be easy with him, deserter or no," Lewrie told him. "He's one hellacious tale t'tell, I'd expect. We lost Groome . . . out yonder."

"See 'im safe aboard, sah," Cox'n Andrews vowed. "Heave 'im up, an' haul away, lads. Easy, now. . . ."

"Well," Chiswick said as the sailors and their burden began to head down the street to the piers. "Don't we have a lobster course to come . . . before all the excitement, happened, that is?"

"Aye, we did." Lewrie brightened, though still plagued by what in the Hell he would do with Rodney. "Let's finish our dinner. Since you're payin' so generously for it, as I remember?"

Using the steps this time, they went through the inn, then out onto the veranda to their table the usual way. Under the big, square covered outdoor veranda though, there was another intrusion, Daniel Wigmore, to the life, still swabbing sweat and trail muck from his brow with a handkerchief. Two empty steins sat before him, soon to be joined by a third, the way he was chugging his fresh one down.

"Cap'm Lewrie, 'ow do," Wigmore said with a shame-faced grin.

"We need t'*talk*, Mister Wigmore," Lewrie sternly replied, " 'bout you luring two of my sailors to desert, maiming one, and killing the other," he said, turning a chair back-side-round to sit down at Daniel Wigmore's table, lean close over the chair back, and glower at him.

"Ah, them laddies woz *mad* fer joinin' me circus, Cap'm Lewrie!" Wigmore blustered, eyes widened and his smile broader. "Nivver knew a thing *h'about* h'it 'til we woz '*ours* down th' trail, and I *couldn't've* turned 'em back t'town, 'thout a gun or 'orse, wif night comin' on, an' all *sortsa* beasts lookin' fer supper? Cruel, that'da been, sir! *Cruel!* An' 'oo's this fine gennelman wif ye, Cap'm Lewrie?"

"My brother-in-law, Major Burgess Chiswick, of the Nineteenth Native Infantry, in India . . . Mister Daniel Wigmore, owner of Wigmore's Travelling Extravaganza," Lewrie sarcastically did the honours, "one of England's *notable* liars and 'sharps.' Admit it . . . you really tempted something horrid, promised 'em the Moon if they'd make your shows more exotic. Told Groome he could play *Othello* in your dramas, hey?"

"Well, I mighta mentioned a *minor* turn on stage, but . . ."

"Hah!" Lewrie scoffed.

Burgess quietly came back to the circus owner's table with the rest of their burgundy left on theirs, pouring them both a goodly measure. Lewrie took the offered glass and sipped slowly, his eyes boring into Wigmore, who was now squirming in anxiety that Lewrie, or the Indian Army Major, had the authority to bring him up on charges . . . or could find someone who could, right quick. Dan Wigmore uncomfortably noted that Lewrie's eyes, usually a merry blue when at the circus, sniffing round Eudoxia, had gone a chilly Arctic grey, and most vulture-like, making him wilt and look away in dread as he chugged down his beer and waved for another.

"Roight, so I *woz* of a mind, not *much* o' one, d'ye see," Wigmore croaked, "allus on th' lookout fer talent, so . . ." He shrugged with a weak and sickly defeated grin plastered on his sweaty face.

"What happened to Groome? What happened with Rodney?" Lewrie demanded. His voice was level, his tone almost mild, but there was a steel to it, and Wigmore knew he was a long way from being out of the woods.

"Now, alla that were van der Merwe's doin', 'at feeble *idjit*!" Wigmore exclaimed, all but wringing his hands. "Lord, Cap'm Lewrie, ye don't know wot a *trial* we been through, worse'n th' wand'rin's o' th' h'Israelites h'in th' Wilderness . . . worse'n me namesake, Daniel, h'in th' Lion's Den, oh yes! 'Twoz *Biblical*, 'ow we suffered h'out there, I tell ye gennulmen . . . *Biblical*!"

"Do tell," Lewrie dubiously said. "No, really . . . *tell*."

Wigmore's litany of woe was long and plaintive. First, one of his shave-pated strongmen who posed as a Hindoo *jetti* had been bitten by a *boomslang* and died within minutes. The second night out, their *kraal* hadn't been properly ringed with enough thornbush, and had been invaded by a pack of warthogs, which had spooked the horses, requiring a whole day to round them up again . . . minus the one that got pulled into a stream by crocodiles, less one that a pack of lions had eaten!

Then, there were the termite mounds and man-tall ant hills that van der Merwe had led them to, praising the unique oddity of aardvarks and aardwolves, which they captured . . . though not without being swarmed by an army of biting ants after they'd used too large a keg of gunpowder to spread the "treats" as bait for the aardvarks and aardwolves, and everyone had dashed off to the nearest waterhole to bathe them off, shedding clothing as they went, not noticing the half-dozen crocodiles lurking in said waterhole, first, who ran them back onto dry ground . . . rather a long way, and *that* change of clothing was lost to hyenas.

Under van der Merwe's knacky guidance again, they had ringed a tree in which a pair of spotted panthers were sleeping, banging on pots and ox-bells, yelling to daunt the cats as they brought up stout nets. Unfortunately, the panthers *hadn't* felt much like joining the circus, and had leaped down at the worst possible moment and ganged up on the circle of beaters, who just had to *shoot* their way wide of disaster, but had ended up shooting mostly at each other, the tree, and anything inside their circle . . . excepting the panthers, of course, and they'd lost a Black bearer, which, considering the firepower at hand, and the level of terror and chaos, could have been a lot worse. It resulted in Panthers: 1, Nimrods: 0, though they did manage to take another pair of panther *cubs* they got up another tree, later.

Then, when van der Merwe had suggested that hyenas just *might* be able to be tamed, one night, the dawn had revealed that three more of their native helpers had decamped, and they, thankfully, gave up on *that* idea.

Groome, well . . . van der Merwe told them that Cape buffalo were immensely strong beasts, never got *rinderpest* like domestic cattle and oxen, so vital to the Boers, did, and wouldn't they be a novelty when trotted into the ring towing circus waggons, once broken to the goad, and the yoke! And, what a boon to Boer mobility!

They had stalked a herd of them, thinking to corral a few with another ring of noisy beaters, and fleet horsemen with rope nooses to capture the ones they wished. The queston had turned out to be who was herding whom, though. The herd *had* milled tight together, flowed round as one for a bit, then whirled into formation and *charged*, with Wigmore likening it to an evolution of a brigade of British dragoons or lancers, perfectly *bristling* with hundreds of *horns,* not sabres or lance-tips! That pretty-much put paid to the circle idea, and everyone had run or galloped for their lives. Groome had run to a flimsy flame tree and scaled it, but hadn't lasted two minutes once the Cape buffs had circled below him and butted the damned thing down.

More natives had realised they'd been hired on by a nit-wit, by then, and, uttering the Bantu equivalent of "Bugger *this* for a game of soldiers!," had melted away into the bush.

Wigmore's second false *jetti* had followed van der Merwe's sage lore that zebras calm down just sweet as anything if one pulled a jute sack over their heads, and somewhere in the braying stampede, *jetti* #2 had gotten kicked in the head, then trampled to death.

They'd captured Durschenko's trio of lion cubs with yet *another* encirclement of beaters, but had had to shoot the male and three females to part them from the cubs. That's where Rodney had been mauled, when the adults in the pride had bowled through jittery gunners and beaters.

"We found h'elephinks," Wigmore sorrowfully related. "Sorta 'ard not to, wot wif s'bloody many of 'em bellerin' an' trumpetin' so mad, when we camped by th' water'ole they warnted h'at. H'at's where we lost pore ol' h'Antonio."

"The mime," Lewrie commented, now nibbling on cold lobster with his fingers, their dinner re-directed to Wigmore's table.

"An' a good'un 'e were, too, Cap'm Lewrie, an' din't th' lit'l chil'ren love 'im," Wigmore wistfully replied, piping at his eyes with his handkerchief. "Ne'er 'ad th' voice t'be a good h'actor, d'ye see, but that man knew 'is way wif a pig bladder or a dummy chicken like 'e was *born* t' th' craft. An' I allus knew me camels an' such woz in good 'ands . . .'less h'Antonio were in drink, or feelin' h'amourous."

"He . . . with livestock, d'ye mean t'say?" Burgess gasped.

"Well, now an' h'agin, but 'e ne'er meant nought by h'it," Dan Wigmore said with a mournful sigh. "Butt h'ugly'z h'Antonio woz, not a woman h'in th' world woulda . . ."

"Male, or female?" Burgess asked, lips quivering rather oddly.

"Oh, females h'only, sir!" Wigmore primly declared, tugging at his waistcoat as if insulted. " 'Twoz nought queer 'bout h'Antonio!"

Burgess shot to his feet as if outraged beyond all countenance, and crossed quickly to the veranda railing facing the street. Wigmore fretted with his coat lapels, shrinking into it as if embarrassed . . . 'til Burgess Chiswick erupted in laughter, great heaves of laughter that sounded something very much like "Bwooharharhar!" along with the odd snort, cackle, and wheeze.

"Well, h'it 'appen, Cap'm Lewrie," Wigmore explained. "Now, I'm 'at sorry we lost one o' yer sailor boys, an' 'at lit'l Rodney feller like t'got *et* by 'at mama lion, but 'e'll *most-like* 'eal up an' serve ye good'z h'ever, oncet . . ."

"But that isn't the point, is it, Mister Wigmore?" Lewrie said with a wintry crackle to his voice. "You had your way, how many *more* of my hands would you have lured away? By God, sir! I should string you to a hatch-grating and have you flogged 'til your *backbone* is exposed! A fubsy such as you, the 'cat' would pare your flesh like it'd cut fresh, soft *cheese*! Mine arse on a *band-box,* I should!"

Wigmore paled, blinking rapidly in dread; unable to look Lewrie in the eye, he turned to heed Burgess Chiswick, who was rattling that veranda railing with his laughs. Wigmore *tried* to smile it away.

"Nivver do h'it h'agin, sir, swear h'it!" Wigmore tumbled out. "Point taken, Cap'm Lewrie. Make h'it up t'ye, h'if I could. *Blood*-money! I could pay . . . I'm told yer fond o' playful, furry critters, sir. 'Ow 'bout a *mongoose*! 'Ey's Hell on rats, an' cute as anythin'!"

To which offer, Lewrie could not help but hide a grin, try to maintain fierceness, but said, his own lips quivering with amusement, "No thankee . . . *have* one!" He stood, suddenly, scaring the man. "Oh, drink yer damned beer, Wigmore. But, do you come sniffing round any of my sailors, again, I'll come after you myself with a cat-o'-nine-tails!" he warned.

Leaving the man in a speechless, hang-jawed sweat, Lewrie went to join Burgess Chiswick at the railings, about ready to cackle, too.

"Nothin' queer 'bout Antonio, my Lord!" Burgess was still weakly wheezing to himself. "Oh, Alan, did ye ever hear the like?"

"Oh, probably," Lewrie muttered, still fuming. "One gets about. Who knows . . . worse things happen at *sea*. Burgess, my apologies, but I must cut things short. Things t'see to aboard ship, you understand."

"And we didn't even get to the main courses, ah well," Burgess replied, sobering at last as he sprang back from the rail to face him. "In point of fact, here comes your soup and such."

"Hate t'waste good victuals, but I must," Lewrie told him, digging for his purse to repay him in part, but Burgess waved his offer away.

"I'll sample a bit of everything, and call it a feast," Burgess told him. "Perhaps we'll find time enough for a drink or two, before we sail?"

"Of course we shall," Lewrie promised him, gathering up his hat and sword from their own abandoned table. "Failing that, though, allow me to offer to treat *you* to yer first English supper, once we're back home. We'll go up to London and make a whole night of it, hey?"

"Come to think of it, we'll do both," Burgess brightened. "And, we may bore each other to tears with our war-stories."

"Looking forward to it," Lewrie promised as he clapped his hat on his head and squared it away. "For now, though . . . *adieu*."

He got to the red-shuttered tavern by the piers and began hunting for a rowboat to hire to take him out to *Proteus*, but, to his utter astonishment, found not one but two gigs waiting at the foot of the wooden stairs that led down to the floating landing stage: a strange gig painted green and picked out with white stripes with a Midshipman just debarking from it, and . . . his own gig, with his tars and Cox'n Andrews in it. The sight of it made him pause halfway down the narrow stairs as the Midshipman was coming up.

"Pardons, sir," the lad said, backing down to the landing stage to make way for a senior officer. He doffed his hat as Lewrie finished his descent. "Uhm . . . might you be Captain Lewrie, of the *Proteus* frigate, sir?"

"I am," Lewrie replied, at which discovery the strange Midshipman beamed, and reached into his coat to an inner pocket, from which he withdrew a folded-over sheet of paper. "Midshipman Hedgepeth, Captain Lewrie, of HMS *Jamaica*, out yonder?" the boy added, with a sweep of his hat towards the bay, and the anchored 64-gunner. "Captain Leatherwood extends to you his utmost respects, sir, and requests that you attend him aboard, at your earliest convenience. I gather, sir, that *Proteus* will join our ship to escort the East India convoy homeward? And . . ."

"Thank you, Mister Hedgepeth," Lewrie replied as he took hold of the letter, swallowing the impatience he felt with another intrusion into what was already a tempestuous day. "Since my own gig seems so readily available . . . *surprise*, that . . ." he added, lifting a leery eyebrow at Andrews, who stood beside the boat, "it seems I may manage mine own conveyance to see your captain, this minute. Do you wait a moment, though."

"Of course, sir," Hedgepeth said, doffing his hat once more as Lewrie brushed past him.

"You made quick work of it, Andrews," Lewrie said, standing at his gig's side. "Out to *Proteus* and back so soon. I *said* I'd engage a bumboatman. . . ."

"Ah, beggin' yah pardon, Cap'm sah, but . . . we didn't go out to th' ship, sah, not egg-*zackly* . . ." Andrews waffled.

"And whyever did you net?" Lewrie harshly snapped.

"Dat Mizz Yew . . . de Russian gal, sah?" Andrews tried to explain, all but wringing his doffed straw hat in his hands. "She tell us it'd be bettah fuh Rodney was de *circus* surgeon t'see to 'im, Cap'm sah. We got 'im heah to de piers, but she an' dhem circus people jus' 'bout *took* Rodney, sayin' Navy Surgeons don' know nothin' 'bout men who got clawed up so bad, an' *dheir* 'saw-bones' handle such ever' day, sah."

"And you just . . . *let 'em*?" Lewrie barked. "Mine arse on a . . . !"

A good rant would have felt so *damned* fine, but right after he drew in a deep breath for his first "broadside," Lewrie shut his lips with an audible "plop."

When they had handed little Rodney down from that Boer waggon, the lad had been shirtless, for the first time in Lewrie's memory, and he had *seen* the old whip scars that his former masters, the Beaumans on Jamaica, had cut into him. And Lewrie had felt queasy to think that he would have had to, under the rigid requirements of the Articles of War when dealing with recaptured deserters, put Rodney to the gratings for several dozen lashes. He would have had no other choice, else his men would have gotten the idea that he was softer on his "Black Pets" than his other crewmen; that he could wink at desertion; that he was turning into a "Popularity Dick," or a soft touch! Lewrie couldn't think of a *better* way to split his crew into grumbling factions, and destroy what *esprit* they had. Without fear of consequences . . . without fear of *him* . . . he would lose *all* his authority, and his officers, warrants, petty officers, and midshipmen would lose theirs along with him.

Might be best, after all, Lewrie grimly told himself, knowing that allowing this to stand only *delayed* what he'd *have* to do.

"Uhm . . ." Lewrie grunted, instead. "Might be something *to* that, Andrews. I doubt either Mister Hodson, or Mister Durant, has ever run across a lion's clawing . . . and the sepsis sure to follow such. Very well, we'll leave him aboard the *Festival* . . . for a short time at the least . . . to see what their surgeon may do for him."

"Aye, sah," his Cox'n cried with both relief and pleasure, and Lewrie could *hear* the tension whooshing out of his tense boat crew.

"Return to the ship," Lewrie ordered. "*Jamaica*'s gig may bear me out to her, and back aboard *Proteus* once we're done. My respects to Mister Langlie, and he is to see that our injured men in the cottage up above the bay, along with Mister Durant and his sick-berth attendants, are fetched back aboard."

"I tell him, sah," Andrews replied, knuckling his brow.

"Mister Hedgepeth?" Lewrie called, whirling about. "Might you indulge me with a boat ride out to your ship?"

CHAPTER TWENTY-NINE

HMS *Jamaica* was a hard-worked ship and looked it as Lewrie was rowed to her starboard entry-port, noting the much-faded paintwork on her side, the dribbles of tar and oakum showing between the outermost planking of her gunwales and bulwarks. A laconic rural American would have said of her that "she'd been rode hard, and put up wet," Lewrie could imagine. If there had been shiny gilt to brighten her, it had been worn off long before; and it appeared that there wasn't enough of a supply of linseed oil, tar, or pitch to spruce up her hull to Navy standards, especially the standards of admirals closer to Europe. But, Lewrie also noted that *Jamaica*'s yards were mathematically squared, her standing and running rigging well set up and tautly blocked or belayed. Her gun-ports stood open for a cooling breeze on both decks, red paint faded, too, on the inboard faces, but the cannon muzzles' tompions were still bright, and every piece squatted in the same exact position as its mate. Up alongside, *Jamaica*'s boarding battens, main-chain platform, and dead-eyes for the main-stays were sound, and her man-ropes strung shallowly through the outboard ends of the batten steps were white and fresh, served with Turk's Head knots. The battens were clean, sanded, though the two-decker's waterline was a gently waving garden of weed, despite her coppering.

And, despite her obvious long and hard service, Lewrie could, on his way up to the starboard gangway, note that the smell of her that wafted from those opened gun-ports on both decks wasn't the reeky fug that one could expect aboard such a small line-of-battle ship, crewed by several hundred men pent in such close quarters for so long, either. Her captain surely put a great stock in cleanliness, Lewrie imagined.

He attained the gangway, taking the salute from clean and well-dressed Marines and sailors, from hands scattered about her decks who doffed shiny black tarred hats, pausing from their labours for a bit.

"Lewrie, of the *Proteus* frigate," he said to a sober, gangly officer. "Your captain requested me to attend him, and why waste time on notes back and forth."

"Of course, Captain Lewrie," the man replied. "Welcome aboard, sir. Allow me to name myself. Suddarth . . . First Lieutenant."

"Glad t'make your acquaintance, Lieutenant Suddarth."

"I will inform Captain Leatherwood you've come aboard, sir. He is aft, at the moment . . ." Lt. Suddarth offered, but such task was not necessary, for his own captain emerged from his great-cabins beneath the poop to the aft end of the quarterdeck, still shrugging his way into a rather shabby undress coat and hat, without summons. Suddarth made the introductions as Leatherwood approached.

"Yer servant, sir," Lewrie said, doffing his hat in salute.

"And welcome you are, Captain Lewrie," Leatherwood genially said in reply, waving an arm aft in invitation. "Do join me in my cabins, where we may get down to business, sir."

Capt. Leatherwood's private quarters were a lot more spacious than Lewrie's, the painted canvas deck chequer as bright as the true tile that it imitated. Only 6-pounders marred its interior to give it a martial air. And, whilst his deal partitions and panelling gleamed with paint or polish, Leatherwood's furnishings were rather plain and spartan, and well-used. Instead of a formal interview with Leatherwood seated behind his desk, and Lewrie in a chair before it, he was led to a folding settee on the larboard side of the day-cabin, with Capt. Leatherwood taking a padded wood-frame chair on the other side of the ivory-inlaid low table between, which rested on a brass-trimmed ebony folding frame. The small carpets which livened both the day-cabin and the dining-coach were of a set, both of Hindoo manufacture, and most-likely bargains obtained in Bombay or Calcutta. Within a few breaths, a cabin servant in nattily tailored sailors' togs appeared with a tray that held a bottle of hock, and two short-stemmed glasses.

"I trust you don't mind hock, Captain Lewrie," Leatherwood said with an easy smile on his weathered face, "but I've always been partial to white wines, 'stead of claret. This one's what the Germans call the *spaetlese* variety. A touch sweet, but spicy. And, we will *not* ask how it was exported past the French, hmm?"

"Honoured, sir," Lewrie replied as he accepted a glass and took an appreciative sip, liking it rather well. Appreciative, too, of Capt. Leatherwood's welcome. Many captains senior to him, he'd found, *would* play their little games of self-importance, forcing him to wait on the quarterdeck in foul weather, or stand and stew before their desks while they pretended to frown sternly over charts or paperwork, kneading their brows as if the war's turning hinged completely on them, alone. Others, Lewrie thought with a hidden grimace, who knew him, would act much the same, but their motive was mostly personal dislike!

Leatherwood *looked* to be a pleasant sort. He was about an inch taller than Lewrie, in his early fourties or so, sunburned to a mellow colour by years under tropic skies, care-worn and over-worked, but with merry brown eyes. He wore his own hair, with a short beribboned queue atop his collar, his hair salt-and-pepper and receding at his temples; slimly framed, and perhaps the victim of some tropic illness, for his uniform fit rather looser than his tailor might have originally sewed it.

"Quite good, *and* spicy," Lewrie adjudged.

"The Cape Squadron informs me that your frigate is free to join me," Leatherwood began, after a few sips of his own, and a shift in his chair to a more comfortable nigh-slouch. "Haven't much to spare, else. They also told me you've just finished some repairs? Ready for sea?"

"In all respects, sir," Lewrie assured him, giving Leatherwood a thumbnail sketch of the convoy battle, his rudder problems, his reduced and altered gun battery, along with being a few hands short.

"Sounds about as good as we can expect," Capt. Leatherwood said with a resigned grunt and nod. "I should have six hundred and fifty-odd aboard *Jamaica,* but what with sickness, accidents, and desertions, we're about fifty people short, as well. And, badly in need of refit. You noted my 'decorative water garden' as you came alongside, sir?"

"Your, ah . . . weed, sir?" Lewrie agreeably said.

"Damned tropics," Leatherwood said with a sigh. "The seas are so rich with marine growth, and whatever they feed upon, that I might as well have dunged and fertilised, deliberately. Four years, we have spent out here, Captain Lewrie. Saint Helena to Calcutta or Bombay, and back again, with but two careenings when we could be spared to fire and scrape her clean in all that time. Too few warships, too much of a threat from the French, too many convoys, and never enough time off.

"But, that's about to change!" Leatherwood perked up. "We are bound for *home,* at long last, to pay off. 'Twill be a *slow* passage, I fear . . . slow, but steady, as they say. *Jamaica* might attain a knot or two more than our Indiamen, and that on a *stout* wind, mind. Your own quickwork, sir. You said you re-coppered at Halifax?"

"Last year, sir, that," Lewrie had to tell him, "so my one weed has grown apace, but, on our short test sail after the new rudder was in place, *Proteus* seems fairly fast, still. And, that new rudder is a *tad* broader than an English yard might install, so she's very quick on the helm . . . more manoeuvrable."

"Good," Leatherwood declared, sounding relieved. "For our slow plod North, I'll place you astern of the convoy, and will take the van position myself, do I not work out on a flank, now and again. You'll bear the onus, should the French have a go at us. With the winds from the Sou'east, and with the Agulhas Current shoving us along, even the Indiamen could make enough sail to out-foot a beam approach. . . ."

"And, t'would be the rare Frog working far enough North to intercept us, or lie in wait, sir," Lewrie pointed out.

"Exactly, so the main threat will come from astern," Leatherwood said with a vigourous nod of his head. "The convoy Commodore tells me another ship will sail with us. What do you know of this *Festival*?"

"She will?" Lewrie exclaimed in surprise. "Makes sense, I do suppose, now they've rounded up their new menagerie of beasts. She's a *circus* ship, sir. Mister Daniel Wigmore's Travelling Extravaganza. Circus, theatrical troupe, fire-eaters, sword-swallowers, acrobats, and clowns . . . ? We escorted her here as part of my former convoy. Not the swiftest old tub, I fear, sir. *Slower* than an Indiaman by day, under all plain sail, and even slower at night. Lots of visiting aboard her on the way to the Cape—"

"Not in *my* convoy, Captain Lewrie," Leatherwood interjected. "I want us as far North as we can manage, as quickly as we can manage, and there'll be no shilly-shally. I'll place her at the stern of the trade, and you can play whipper-in to keep her up with the rest."

The Frogs come after us, she'd be no loss? Lewrie thought; *Just like the Russians . . . throw somebody off the back of the sled to delay the wolves? S'pose so . . . compared to the wealth in the Indiamen, the* Festival*'s not worth a groat. An* amusin' *prize, but . . . !*

"I didn't much care to hear of the French having a go at your former convoy, so close to Cape Town, Captain Lewrie, 'deed I didn't," Capt. Leatherwood told him, looking pensive, and a bit fretful, setting his glass on the table between them to rub his horny hands together, a very sandpapery sound.

"The local commanders are of the opinion it was a fluke, sir," Lewrie told him, outlining the Flag-Captain's explanation that it might have been a clutch of warships on-passage simply "stumbling" on them.

"Told me much the same," Leatherwood grumbled. "And what did you think of that, Captain Lewrie?" he demanded right-sharp.

"Complete and utter horse-apples, sir," Lewrie deemed it with a derisive snort. "No one knows how many warships and privateers working out of Mauritius the French now possess. Don't *know* what's happening past Good Hope, but, if the Frogs have amassed enough strength, they could be thinking of raiding further afield. I believe that attack on my convoy was a test, sir. They know our monthly convoy schedules, by now. They most-like know how few ships we have on station, too. That has worried me, I'll tell you, Captain Leatherwood. And, I understand that you had a rough passage. Did you encounter any French ships?"

"Captain Lewrie, I was *hunted* here," Leatherwood declared with a fierce scowl, his first sign of displeasure. "It wasn't too bad at first, 'til I lost the services of my companion frigate off Ceylon to a 'blow.' I was almost of a mind to turn back, since we were still in Indian waters, for we began to see strange tops'ls on the horizon, as far North as within an hundred leagues of Cape Comorin. Avoided them, or they avoided us, then crossed hawses with a Bombay Marine brig, and thank the Good Lord her captain agreed to see us below Madagascar, even if that was far from his usual cruising grounds.

"Should have turned back, for certain, when three of our Indiamen got into their foul water casks, and sickness broke out aboard them. That'll be the *last* time 'John Company' masters try pocketing the few pence difference 'twixt the prices British chandlers, and native chandlers, charge for fresh water!" Leatherwood told Lewrie with a humourless bark. "Not that *Hooghly*, the Bombay Marine brig-o' war, would've been much real help, if the French had been determined. Her guns were only six-pounders, and half-rusted, at that. Half a dozen British officers and senior hands aboard, her crew but two-thirds' normal complement, and most of them exiled European drunks, ne'er-do-wells, some low-caste Hindoos, or Lascars from God knows where. Might daunt the local native pirates in scabby *dhows* and such, but not quite the thing to go against a French National Ship, or privateer. Stayed with us to about five hundred miles East of Cape Agulhas, then *had* to turn back, and we had to supply shot and powder in the first place, then water and foodstuffs, the second, so they could make it back to India without starving!"

"And you saw *more* strange sail, sir?" Lewrie worriedly asked.

"Almost *daily*, Captain Lewrie," Leatherwood told him, summoning his cabin-servant for a refill of their glasses. "I thought to employ a ruse. The master of the *Lord Stormont* agreed to hoist a Navy Ensign and play-act the part of a Third Rate seventy-four at the convoy's van, whilst I brought up the rear, and put *Hooghly* to work on the seaward side. On the down-wind run, *Jamaica* had a *bit* of 'dash.' "

"Perhaps *Lord Stormont* could play the same part for us, sir," Lewrie suggested. "My brother-in-law is one of her passengers, and he might even like it."

"I count on it, though, towards the end, after *Hooghly* departed, the strange sail pressed closer," Leatherwood explained, "and I'm not sanguine that they didn't finally get close enough for a good look, and saw through my ruse, so it might not work a second time, if the French that haunted us decide to lurk off Cape Town, waiting for us to continue our passage.

"Frankly, Captain Lewrie," Leatherwood gravelled, "I doubt I'll get a wink of sleep 'til we're above the Tropic of Capricorn."

"We've had no *fresh* reports of any French cruising this side of the Cape, sir. Not *lately*, at least," Lewrie told him, about ready to chew on a thumbnail in fret. "Aye, did they follow you . . . Was Vice-Admiral Curtis's staff any more forthcoming?"

"Lewrie, I very much doubt those worthies would know where, and in what strength, the French are 'til they sail round Green Point some night, and sink, take, or burn all the shipping in Table Bay!" Capt. Leatherwood exclaimed. "We've a hellish task ahead of us. Yet, from what I've learned of you from the old newspapers, with *Proteus* aiding me, I *might* manage at least a *cat-nap* or two before we come to anchor in James's Valley on Saint Helena."

"You do me too much honour, sir," Lewrie rejoined, torn 'twixt the expected modesty and the desire to preen, which he hadn't had much a chance for, lately. "*Proteus* and I shall hold up our end, sir. And, after the shameful way the French mauled us, my people will relish a chance for a slugging match against them, should it come to that."

"All I may ask," Leatherwood said, pleased with the answer and looking relieved. "Well, then! 'John Company's' Commodore is meeting on the *Earl Cheshire* with all captains and masters, tomorrow morning, at Four Bells. With any luck, they'll *feed* us . . . though I'm not sure I would *yet* drink their water, hey, Captain Lewrie? Following that, do you look for me to hoist the 'Blue Peter' . . . the day after I expect, is the weather fair, and the winds sufficient."

"Very well, sir," Lewrie agreed. "Just one thing, sir?"

"Aye?"

"Is it possible you bought this excellent German wine here at Cape Town, sir, I'd be much obliged did you give me a course to steer by, so I could lay in some for myself."

BOOK V

"Quocirca vivite fortes,
fortiaque adversis opponite pectora rebus."

"Live, then, as brave men,
and with brave hearts confront
the strokes of Fate."

HORACE, *SATIRES* II, II, 135-136

CHAPTER THIRTY

Slanting West-by-North on larboard tack, HMS *Proteus* was making a goodly way, swanning from the starboard quarter of the convoy to the larboard quarter, and beyond, and it was joyous. Had she been steered directly Nor'west, with the steady Sou'east Trades right up her skirts, the warm African day might have felt stifling, for she would have been sailing about the same speed as the Trades, and the apparent wind would have been negligible. Now, though, the rush of the Sou'east Trades almost could be heard in the miles of rigging, and loose clothing could be fluttered by it, bare heads and long hair disturbed by it, and perspiration evaporated before one could even imagine one was sweltering, like the crews and passengers aboard the Indiamen that plodded, despite the strength of the Trades, in two columns off *Proteus*'s starboard bows.

Marine M. Cocky, the sea-soldiers' champion rat-killing mongoose, scuttled down the windward gangway in a sinuous, arcing series of bounces between brace-tenders' bare feet, pausing now and then to take a play-nip at a particularly tasty-looking toe, before scampering onto the quarterdeck. Toulon and Chalky, who had been sunning atop the hammock nettings with their forelegs tucked in and their eyes half-slit in drowsiness, got to their feet, put their backs up, and began to hiss at him. The mongoose stopped, rose up on his hind legs, and wiggled his nose at them, one paw on the nettings and one poised like a pointer on a scent. For ha'pence, he'd scramble up and pester them, grinning.

"*Mister* Larkin!" Lewrie drawled in a loud voice. "No 'private Marines' on the quarterdeck except in battle, remember?"

"I'll see to him, sor . . . sir," their youngest Mid replied, as he came forward to doff his hat quickly, then scoop up the offending mongoose, clatter down the larboard ladderway to the waist, and shout for Sgt. Skipwith to come get his errant beastie. Again. Once it was safe to do so, Toulon and Chalky settled down on their haunches to judder their little jaws and utter "I'm-Going-To-Kill-It" mews.

"Such *brave* catlings," Lewrie muttered with a smile as he clung to the larboard mizen stays to enjoy the refreshing breeze, his uniform coat discarded, along with his formal cocked hat, and waist-coat undone and flapping either side of his shirt.

"Thus!" Lt. Langlie cried as *Proteus* settled on a course a full point more Westerly, now they were clear of the larboardmost column of ships, and could begin to range outwards to scent for trouble skulking over the horizon in the West or Nor'west. Lewrie planned to stand out nearly six miles, before wearing and slanting back to the convoy. He paced down the slightly-slanting deck to amidships, by the binnacle and compass cabinet, and the double helm.

"Damn my eyes, Mister Langlie," Lewrie exulted, "but it feels so good t'be back at sea, does it not?"

"Indeed it does, sir," his First Officer happily agreed; and on the faces of the two Quartermasters manning the helm, brief smiles alit to say that it felt good to them, too, after so many weeks of drudgery in Table Bay, and too few chances for ease.

Making the Quartermasters smile, too, was the last full day of shore liberty that Lewrie had granted the crew after the Commodore's conference aboard the *Earl Cheshire*, before Capt. Leatherwood had put up the "Blue Peter" pendant, now two days past. Everyone had gotten a last chance for some deep drinking in Dutch Boer taverns, a last shot of "putting the leg over" some willing, or commercial, wench, and buying remembrances of Cape Town. That had resulted in rather a lot of small, jewel-like birds in woven cages, one grey parrot with a "salty" vocabulary, an odd, fox-faced little creature called a bushbaby that was already proving himself to be a very noisy pest, and a "gen-yoo-ine" *African* mongoose, adverted to its new owners as quicker, fiercer, and a lot cleverer than any Indian mongrel the Marines had. There would be a new contender for champion, in a few weeks, it seemed. At least Lt. Catterall and Bosun Pendarves had prevented the boarding of an entire troop of baby monkeys! The ship was crowded enough with new livestock for later consumption, up forward in the ship's manger; a whole new set of piglets, chickens, goats, and two small, scruffy, locally-obtained cattle, no bigger than some shaggy Scottish breeds.

Two days North of Cape Town, they were out of the Variables and fully into the Sou'east Trades, skirting the edge of the great counter-clockwise swirl of the South Atlantic Current, which fed like a river into the Agulhas Current to whisk the convoy along. It was just about two thousand miles to St. Helena, but the Northward passage would be much quicker than the passage it had taken to get to the Cape of Good Hope; and every hour took them farther from threat of French raiders. Hopefully. Leatherwood had ordered *Proteus* out to sea with him, fully twelve hours before the convoy was to up-anchor on the next tide, for a good look-see over the waters near Cape Town, searching for a single scrap of suspicious sail on the horizons, and had found none, yet . . . like Capt. Leatherwood, Lewrie was now so infected by his nervousness that he felt as if *he* would not have an untroubled night's sleep 'til they anchored in James's Valley Harbour, either.

Where *Proteus* went from there, well . . . on a monthly rotation of homebound and out-bound trades, there would be a convoy of Indiamen waiting at St. Helena; that convoy's escort force would split up, as his own had on the outward journey—the bulk of it sailing back to England to re-enforce the small escort that had fetched the homebound convoy that far. If there *was* a greater French threat on the Atlantic side of the Cape of Good Hope, there was a very good possibility that *Proteus* would be conscripted by the outbound convoy Commodore as part of his escort force. Just because Treghues had sailed away on his own did not mean that Lewrie and his frigate could consider themselves as "Independent," free to toddle back to Great Britain. There was no formal squadron or fleet assigned to convoy duties; warships got assigned that task "catch-as-catch-can," and Lewrie and *Proteus* had been caught! In truth, once repaired, should Lewrie cross hawses with Treghues, he'd still be under his orders, 'til officially reassigned by a Flag-Officer senior to Treghues.

And, should *Proteus* be forced to bolster an out-bound convoy, it was very likely that such a meeting *would* occur off the Southern coast of Africa, and *Proteus* would be forced to soldier on under that tetchy man's eye for years, much as Capt. Leatherwood and HMS *Jamaica* had been stuck on grueling convoy work, 'til the bottom threatened to fall off his ship!

For now, though, free of the land (where Lewrie just naturally found himself in trouble, more often than not) and with a single and specific task to perform, he could be happy enough. Twenty years he'd spent wearing "King's Coat," at sea and holding an "active" commission much longer than most of his contemporaries, and he'd always felt this way, this sense of relief and of new beginnings, these first few days after sailing, when the shoreline sank away, and there was nothing but the immensity of the oceans, and limitless horizons.

Boredom could come later, as it always did, but, for now, Lewrie was . . .

happy. And would be happier still, if they attained harbour at St. Helena without incident!

"Is that *gunfire*?" the Sailing Master, Mr. Winwood, mused aloud, pausing in his perambulations along the starboard bulwarks. He lifted his nose as if he could *smell* the source of gunpowder. "My word . . . !"

All eyes swung to the convoy, the only ships in sight.

"Mister Larkin," Lewrie bade the Midshipman of the Watch. "Do you lay a glass on *Jamaica*, and tell us what you make out."

"Aye, sir!" Larkin responded, clambering up the starboard ratlines of the mizen stays with a telescope. "Signal, sir! 'Gun-Drill,' sir! She's workin' her great-guns, and so're th' *Indiamen*!"

"Ah!" Mr. Winwood said with a whoosh of a sigh.

"Why, those poor skinflints!" Lewrie chortled. "Forcin' 'John Company' captains t'blow away money! Tsk, tsk."

"Cut into their profits something sinful, that, sir," the First Officer snickered, along with the rest of the quarterdeck staff. "Do they keep at it much longer, there will be angry letters sent to Admiralty about it."

"Upset the passengers something sinful, too, sir," Mr. Winwood stated. "Imagine being shaken from their indolent torpors, the middle of their morning naps."

"Mister Langlie!" Lewrie called out. "*Jamaica*'s signal applies to us, as well. Let us hold live firing, from this instant to Seven Bells of the Forenoon. Our own guns, and crews, need the rust blown off."

"Aye aye, sir! Bosun, pipe 'All Hands'! Beat to Quarters!"

What a perfectly fine morning! Lewrie gladly thought as silver bosuns' calls piped, as a Marine drummer began a long roll, and hands came scampering up from below to man the guns, cast off, and begin to serve their pieces, as sea-chests and mess-tables were slung below to the orlop, deal and canvas partitions came slamming down, and hundreds of feet pounded on decks and ladderways.

The wind was fresh, the South Atlantic was a sparkling blue under an azure sky framed by high-piled white clouds, and soon, the guns would be bellowing.

The reek, the roar, the hull-shaking explosions, and the squeal of recoiling carriages, the gushes of spent powder, all of it pleased Capt. Alan Lewrie. The live firing would make him happy, too. Even more so . . .

At least Admiralty lets me have powder and shot for free! he could gloat.

CHAPTER THIRTY-ONE

Oh, it had been a grand day at sea! Even after gun-drill, the rum issue, and the crew's noonday mess, Lewrie had ordered an hour and a half of small arms practice with boarding pikes and cutlasses to whet the rust off those skills, too, after so much harbour sloth. By the end of the First Dog Watch, as the sun was sinking into the West in a spectacular red, amber, and pink glory, *Proteus*'s people were spent—wearily, but garrulously happily so, if the lack of horn-pipe dancing, but the cheerful songs and music, were anything to go by. Even if the horizon to the East and Sou'east gloomed up darker than the usual sunset greys, down-sun. The farther one sailed North along the coast of Africa, once past the arid regions that bordered the Dutch settlements, the more often rain squalls were commonplace. A passage close to shore took a vessel through a zone termed "The Rains," after all.

Mr. Winwood stood on the quarterdeck at the change of watch at six of the evening, hands clasped behind his back, and sniffing at the air again, much as he had at mid-morning when seeking the source for gunpowder, and frowning sternly.

"A squally night, Captain," Winwood slowly pronounced, at last. "A rising wind, and heavy rain, this evening. Rains which might continue through mid-morning, tomorrow, I do avow, sir. Can you not get a whiff of it on the wind?"

"It is muggier, and cooler," Lewrie agreed, noticing a hint of fresh water in his own nostrils as the Trades gusted slightly. As it grew dark, *Proteus* had ceased her wearing from one flank of the trade to the next, and had fallen in three miles astern of the convoy, with the two columns of ships equidistant from each bow, and steering Nor'west with the wind right astern; yet even with her sailing no faster than those winds could blow, now and then a stronger gust caught up with them to presage a stormy night. Just as well, Lewrie decided, that it was the convoy's practice to reduce so much sail at dusk, this particular dusk especially, for it could be a rough night.

"Deck, there!" a foremast lookout shrilled. "Flagship's lightin' 'er lanthorns! Convoy's lightin' 'eir lanthorns!"

"Thankee, aloft!" Lt. Adair shouted back through his brass speaking-trumpet.

"Mister Adair," Lewrie said, "light our own taffrail lanthorns, foc's'le lanthorns, and binnacle cabinet. Be sure all masthead fusees and signal rockets are near to hand, as well."

"Very well, sir. Permission to call masthead lookouts down to the deck, Captain?" Adair responded.

"Not 'til we've reefed down for the night," Lewrie told him as he paced aft to take a peek into the binnacle cabinet, to see that the proper course was being steered. "Pipe 'All Hands On Deck' to reduce sail." Even as he ordered that, another much cooler gust came sweeping up from astern and to the starboard quarter. "Additionally, sir, I'll have 'quick-savers' rigged on the fore course, and all three tops'ls, and . . . should any lurking Frog upset things, make certain that 'quick-savers' are borne aloft to the tops for rigging on the main course, and the t'gallants. Just in case," he said with a shrug.

"Aye aye, sir."

Quick-savers "crow-footed" over the faces of the squares'ls to keep them from blowing out into tatters in a hard blow were a last-ditch re-enforcement of ropes to gird the sails' canvas.

With "growl ye may, but go ye must" groans, *Proteus*'s achy crew went aloft to perform their duties, knowing that soon, once this last hard chore was over, they'd be piped below to their suppers; a little after that, "Down Hammocks" would be piped, and half of them could turn in for a few hours of sleep.

"Aye, t'will be a wet and windy night," Mr. Winwood prophecied.

By the time sail was taken in for the night, and the precaution of the "quick-savers" had been rigged or stored aloft for future use, it was already raining, and the evening had gotten darker. Squalls of rain swept like curtains over the convoy from the East-Sou'east to the West-Nor'west, even blotting out HMS

Jamaica and the lead ships of the short columns for brief moments. The seas were rapidly making up, and *Proteus* began to ride them in a more lively manner, performing a long, slow pitching motion, along with a leeward roll. The nearest ship to them, the *Festival* off their starboard bows, was pitching as well, and heeling her larboard shoulder to the seas; they could witness her taffrail lights swing down left from horizontal in slow arcs, and see her forecastle belfry lamp rise up above the taffrail lanthorns for a bit, then sink ponderously below them and out of sight as the old merchantman made heavy work of the night. Beyond her, other pairs of taffrail lights wanly glimmered, as the other six Indiamen struggled to remain on course to the Nor'west, and in line-astern of each other, trusting to "follow the leader" like sheep following the bellwether, and hoping that the lead ships knew what they were about.

Another half-hour and it would be the end of the Second Dog, and the watch would change once more, this time for a full four hours, which would let Lewrie go aft and below to his own supper. For now, he stood in tarred tarpaulins on the quarterdeck, stifling inside the supposedly impermeable hooded canvas coat, with wetness trickling down the back of his neck, and his old slop trousers soaked from mid-thigh down to his boots. He would dine alone this night, saving himself a few shillings by not entertaining officers, warrants, or midshipmen. Meagre though a typical solitary supper usually was—reconstituted "portable" soup, the last of his fresh shore greens for a salad, toasted stale rolls of what had been fresh bread, and a rice-and-*biltong* stew—he found it hard to wait that long. He wanted to be *dry,* to open a bottle of that *spaetlese* German hock he'd found at the last minute in Cape Town, then soak those stale rolls into the soup and slurp up something *warm,* for the rain was a chill soaker, when it was whipping 'cross the decks!

And it did not help that the last savoury smoke from the galley funnel got swirled as far aft as the quarterdeck, bringing lip-smacking aromas of boiled pork to him, along with the sound of fiddle, fife, or Liam Desmond's uillean lap-pipes, and the rough good humour of sailors hunched over mess-tables, half "groggy" from the last rum issue.

"What in the name o' God is that?" Lewrie yelped, like to leap out of his boots as an unholy, piercing wail arose from below.

"Ah, that'd be our bushbaby, sir," Lt. Langlie told him with a wince of his own as the high-pitched caterwauling continued. "I wish we'd known what a racket it could make, before allowing it aboard. A member of the Lemur family, I'm now told. And able to hoot, cry, and screech half like a howler monkey, half like a human infant. Eerie!"

"Eerie, *and* irritating," Lewrie growled, already miserable, and that damned thing wasn't helping. "It keeps that up, it'll end up in a pie, 'fore the *next* Dog Watch. Eerie, aye, and . . . ominous."

T'Hell with this, Lewrie thought; *suff'rin' like this is what lieutenants are* for! "Mister Langlie, you have the deck 'til the end of the Dog. I'll be below."

"Aye, sir. I have the deck," Langlie crisply responded.

He clattered down the larboard ladderyway to the main deck just as the bushbaby's cries set off the parrot, which began to squawk, and then scream its few English words, which consisted mostly of curses or blasphemies, which squawking frightened the other caged birds atwitter, which tumult made the goats, lambs, cattle, and piglets bleat, bawl, or squeal. And, it really couldn't be, not with *Proteus* up to windward of *Festival,* but Lewrie could almost swear that he heard a lion's roar and some baby elephant trumpets in answer!

Ain't a warship, it's a bloody Ark! he fumed as he got near his sopping-wet Marine sentry by the doors to his great-cabins. To punctuate his escape from foul weather, there was a first flash of lightning, and a not-so-far-off roll of thunder. The storm was getting worse, and Lewrie resigned himself to a quick meal, then a whole sleepless evening on deck, sodden to the skin.

"D'ye hear, there!" came a thin cry from one of the on-deck lookouts on the quarterdeck that he had just quit. "Dark ship on th' starb'd quarter, mile'r two off! Off'cer o' th' Watch, they's . . . !"

"Deck, there!" the lookout atop the main mast cross-trees added with the same urgency. "Three-masted ship, four points orf th' starboard quarter! Looks t'be a *frigate*!"

"Beat to Quarters, Mister Langlie!" Lewrie bellowed after he had slammed to a stop, and whirled about to swarm back to his quarterdeck. "Now!" he added, as he got to the top of the ladderway by the uselessly-empty hammock nettings. "Night signals, quick as you can, to warn the convoy. Someone lay aloft and light the fusee on the main truck!"

He jogged over to the starboard bulwarks, stoicism and a serene demeanour bedamned, to add his own eyes to the frantic search as harsh voices and bosun's calls shrilled. A curtain of heavier rain blotted out the sea for a long and frustrating minute, then . . . *there*! In the split-second flash of another lightning bolt, several lookouts yelped discovery, just as the Marine drummer began a long roll, and the ship began to drum as well to the stamping of running feet, inspiring that bushbaby to even louder cries.

The lightning bolt struck up to windward in the East-Sou'east, a sizzling, actinic blue and writhing fork of fire that silhouetted a lean three-masted ship so thoroughly that her sails momentarily turned ghostly white.

Not a mile off, more like three, Lewrie thought with a shuddery feeling of relief, and fear, under his heart; *Big enough a bugger, but we just may have enough time, thank God!*

"Topmen aloft, Mister Langlie," Lewrie said over his shoulder, sure that the reliable First Officer would be nearby. "Trice up, and lay out t'loose tops'ls, *with* 'quick-savers,' then shake out the main course to the third reefs. Let's get some speed in hand."

A second, closer, lightning flash lit up the enemy warship, letting them all see that she was flying full tops'ls, a full fore course and main course, and what looked to be three-reefed t'gallants, along with almost her full set of heads'ls.

"How the Devil did she *find* us in all this, sir?" Langlie asked in puzzlement, once the requisite orders had been passed, and the crew had thrown themselves into well-drilled action.

"Inshore of us, round dusk," Lewrie rasped, shrugging his own puzzlement. "Stalked us as the weather made up in late afternoon, on the front edge of the storm, perhaps? Came closer as the visibility reduced, figuring the convoy would hold the same course all day and all night. Second lookout aloft, Mister Langlie, on the mizen. The last time we met these shits, they were working in pairs. He's t'keep his eyes peeled astern, so we don't get buggered a *second* time."

"Aye, sir!"

Even as the peal of thunder from the last lightning strike was dying like a titanic game of bowls, a third bolt far to the South lit up the sea. A quick measurement against *Proteus*'s stays and stanchions told Lewrie that the enemy ship had only out-footed them a trifle, and he frowned and pursed his lips in furious scheming.

The convoy had been making about four or five knots in typical Indiaman night fashion, but were now spreading more sail, and might be up to six knots, by now. The enemy frigate *might* have two knots more in-hand, and could catch them up on her present course, eventually . . . but—another lightning flash!—she seemed to be steering with the gusting, rising winds directly astern, not hauling off a point to fall down on them, not yet. As if the French captain over there *wished* to dash in and wade into the merchantmen, but might plan to race up abeam of the starboard column before hauling his wind. To alter course two points to the West would put the wind fine on her larboard quarter, so . . . why hadn't her captain already done so? That could boost her rate of advance two more knots, easily, and *still* place her alongside that starboard column of Indiamen without losing the weather gage.

Lewrie swivelled about to peer forward, over *Proteus*'s bows, to see what he could espy of the convoy whose safety he was supposed to be guarding. He could still make out the dark bulk of *Festival* and a pair of taffrail lanthorns, now with a fusee alit atop her main mast. Other tiny glims of amber oil or blue pyrotechnic lights looked all a'gaggle, in no particular order as individual merchant masters swooped about to either flank to put the storm's wind fine on *their* quarters so freshly-spread sail could snap and strain completely full to give them just a knot or two more speed, free of the wind-shadows cast by the Indiamen behind them, up to weather. It was like peering through a filthy pane of pebbly glass, in a driving night rain, to try and count the number of cigar smokers on a hill a mile off.

Small red-amber-yellow signal rockets went soaring up, from the lead ships or HMS *Jamaica* Lewrie surmised, too many to count, or make a conjecture as to what signal Capt. Leatherwood's 64-gunner had meant to convey. Lewrie thought that Leatherwood was a sensible sort; once he'd seen *Proteus*'s alert rockets, relayed to him by even more rockets, that doughty fellow *should* be trying to order all ships to bear off to the West, wind fine on their quarters to try and outrun the French 'til the storm passed, or the dawn came. With any luck, the worst of the storm was still to come, and the convoy could break away as visibility shrank to nothing, never to be found again. HMS *Jamaica* should also be coming about to deal with the threat out of the East-Sou'east and Sou'east, to bolster *Proteus* and daunt the French, but Lewrie saw no sign of that, either. And, on these winds, and butting against the making seas, HMS *Jamaica*, already admitted to be a slow sailer, would make but a snail's progress, steering Full And By. *No help there,* Lewrie sourly thought; *And, in this gloom, one of the Indiamen pretendin' t'be a seventy-four won't work worth a tinker's dam, either . . . if it ever did. If Froggie didn't see through it all along! Just thankee Jesus!*

"A point to starboard, Mister Langlie," Lewrie ordered after he swung back about to catch another eye-blink lightning flash of the foe. "Crowd her a little, and let's see what 'Jean Crapaud' will do."

"Aye aye, sir." Langlie replied, sounding all business-like, now that the initial shock had worn off.

"And somebody strangle that damn' bushbaby," Lewrie griped as the beast began a new "aria." He peered upwards in satisfaction to note that his frigate now sported more sail, that the fusee was lit and burning, and that the topmen were already shuffling inwards along the foot-ropes to the cross-trees and tops.

"Guns manned and ready, sir!" Lt. Catterall reported from below in the waist, in his usual eager bawl. "The ship is at Quarters!"

"Very well, Mister Catterall!" Lewrie called back, stepping up to the hammock nettings, which were once more stuffed with the sailors' rolled up bedding and hammocks, not only on the quarterdeck, but along the bulwarks, as well. Perhaps not as tightly-rolled as they might be to pass through the ring-measure each morning in the crew's haste, but there was now some level of protection for waisters and brace-tenders on the gangways, the Marines prepared to volley behind the thick oaken bulwarks, and for the vital command group on the quarterdeck. Lewrie had been so absorbed with his own concerns that he hadn't paid attention to the slams, bangs, and thuds of a warship being stripped for action. The red glows of battle-lanthorns between the guns, and the weak sparks of lengths of slow-match, coiled about the tubs of swab-water that would be used to douse any lingering embers in gun barrels before re-loading, gave him a momentary reassurance that, this time, they'd be ready for whatever came at them, from whichever quarter. And if the rain slicked the flints so they did not spark-off the igniting quills stuck down through the touch-holes to the powder bags, the slow-match could be jammed onto them, and his artillery most likely would still fire.

A stillness fell over the frigate, now that the din of preparation was over, and the only sounds to be heard were the keening of the wind in the miles of rigging, and the snuffly thunder of the hull that butted its bows through the long-rolling, white-flecked, waves; that, and the crack and rumble from the storm, of course.

"The French, out yonder!" Lewrie bellowed down to his crew, his hands gripping the cap-rails of the hammock nettings. "Mean to screw up their courage, and try a second time to finish what failed, before! They might've given us a *little* dusting, then . . . but, now it's *their* turn t'taste iron! If they dare! Are ye ready t'kill some Frenchmen, lads? Ye ready t'get some of your own back?"

The snarling, vengeful cheer that arose told him all he wished to know of the mettle of his crew. Lewrie looked over towards the foe to judge her distance, and how long they had before they came to grips.

"Fiddler, fifer! Desmond! Give us a tune, a lively one!" he roared, and the ship's finest musicians got with the Marine drummer, and launched into "The Stool of Repentance," then "Lord Dunmore"!

"Yah sword an' pistols, Cap'm," Cox'n Andrews said at his side, and helped him jam his pair of double-barreled Mantons into pockets in his uniform coat, beneath the tarpaulin foul-weather coat, where their primings might stay dry. "Cats is below on th' orlop with Aspinall, sah, an' he said t'send ya dis," Andrews added, once he'd also helped Lewrie strap on his hanger. Andrews held out a large tin mug of soup and stew combined, with some stale, toasted rolls crumbled up and sopping juices in it. A cheap, older horn spoon jutted upwards from one side, both mug and spoon no loss if Lewrie had to throw them overside or let them fall to the deck to get trampled.

"Thankee, Andrews," Lewrie said, looking him square in the eyes. "And, give me thanks to Aspinall, should you see him first when this is done. And, I expect t'see your ugly phyz amongst the living, then, hear me? Have a care with yourself."

"An' don' ya go bein' too bold yahself, sah," Andrews replied with a shrug and a sketchy smile. "Beggin' ya pahd'n fo' sayin' such, Cap'm Lewrie, sah." Andrews knuckled his forehead in salute, then he was off along the weather gangway with both Lewrie's breech-loading Ferguson rifle and the Girandoni air rifle he'd gotten in New Orleans for a little "man-hunting" should the French come within near shot.

"Cast of the log, Mister Langlie," Lewrie snapped, coming back to proper concern. Lightning flash, and a crash of thunder! Lewrie snapped his attention to the French frigate, the sea astern, the sea abeam, for all that he could glean from that finger-snap of revelation.

Might be as fast as she is, or soon will be, he told himself; *I could stay ahead of her a bit, block her direct approach. Looked t'be no more than a mile off our starboard quarter, that time. Do I slow, let her rush up abeam?*

Were *Proteus* a bit slower over the ground, it might be possible to get to grips quicker, then wheel a point or two more to starboard, and *force* the enemy frigate to accept battle, broadside to broadside.

Or, the bugger ducks under our stern and goes for the merchantmen, Lewrie thought with a scowl; *shoots right up our transom, again, then dashes past with the wind right up his own arse, and I'd have to wear t'catch him up. Have the* weather *gage, but . . . No. By the time we got worn about, we'd be lucky to* spot *her again in all this. Chase the gun flashes half the night, same as we did before.*

Proteus was out on the starboard quarter of the convoy, after her turn up more Northerly. And the convoy was doing something right, wearing off slowly and cautiously more Westerly, out into the open Atlantic. With their much smaller civilian crews, and so much sail, the Indiamen were taking a hell of a risk of dismasting to alter course, even so slightly, to take the hard wind on their larboard quarters; a single mistake, and one of them could end up lying crippled, and lost to the French. To broach, get shoved on their beam-ends . . . would be even worse, for then they'd be lost to the sea, and the storm!

We wear on this wind, we could suffer the same fate, he thought with a sudden chill, yet; *So could the French! Could I* make *her do it?*

The musicians were now staggering up and down between the tiers of guns in the waist, well into a medley of "Banish Misfortune," "Go to the De'il and

Shake Yourself," and "The Rakes of Mallow," and the crew stamped their feet, and their gun-tools, on the deck in time, with the Marine drummer jauntily plying his sticks as if on Sunday parade on the ramparts of Southsea Castle in Portsmouth.

A loud crack, and a lightning flash!

"Mister Langlie, does she look t'be hauling her wind a half a point?" Lewrie demanded. "Putting the wind squarer on her stern?"

"About that, sir," the First Lieutenant replied, trying to keep a fretful tone from his voice. "Might she be readying to wear?"

"Possibly," Lewrie said, rubbing his chin and looking aloft at his sails and yards. "Helm up a point, Mister Langlie, bring us back to our original course of Nor'west."

A look alee showed their merchantmen now off *Proteus*'s bows to larboard, after her jog outwards, and their own slight turn away from the threat of the enemy warship. Very disappointingly far off, there was a taffrail light and a masthead fusee to the right of the fleeing Indiamen; HMS *Jamaica* evidently had worn about to the Nor'east and was most likely trying to come up to the wind for a tack, which in such a stiff wind and a rough sea would be nigh-miraculous, should Leatherwood pull it off without getting the "sticks" ripped right out of her.

The French frigate was closing with them, now within less than a mile, but foreshortening, her profile aspect turning more bows-on, just a tantalising bit. To follow the convoy, even if her first attempt had been mis-judged, and her captain now would settle for a stern-chase, *if* he could just get past this pestiferous "Bloodies'" frigate? Would she wear about, shift the winds onto her larboard quarters, duck under HMS *Proteus*, and force Lewrie to chase *her*?

"Prepare to come about to larboard, Mister Langlie. I think we will attempt to wear," Lewrie decided of a sudden. "And, when we do I will have the tops'ls clewed up for the heavy haul, bat-wing them, in 'Spanish reefs' for a bit, 'til we're round. That'll ease the strain on the masts and spars, *and* the brace-tenders. That Frog yonder wears, so do we. Hands to stations, and stand ready."

"Aye, sir," Langlie replied, though there was a leery squint to his eyes; it *could* have been the driving rain that caused it. "Bosun! Pipe 'Hands To Stations To Wear'!"

Yet, they stood on for about a minute more, straining for sight of each other, waiting for the lightning to illuminate what their respective foes were doing. Nature obliged with another crackling bolt of lightning, one that seemed to leap *from* the sea, not from the low and racing clouds, a triple forked bolt that jerked across the sky like the flailing arms of a marionette.

"Heads'ls are shivering!" Lt. Langlie yelled, pointing his useless night telescope at the French frigate. "She's going about, sir!"

Sure enough, the enemy was swinging nearly bows-on to *Proteus*'s starboard quarter, jib-boom and bowsprit pitching upwards as she rose, fore-and-aft heads'ls getting smothered for air as her fore course came directly downwind and stole the force of the wind. Just as an impenetrable squall of rain swept over her from astern and blotted her out!

"Helm up, Mister Langlie!" Lewrie shouted. "Get us about, quick as dammit! Clew up tops'ls, there!"

And the wear *was* quick, for with so little pressure aloft, the brace-tenders could swing the yardarms just that more easily, despite the gale of wind. And, that new, broader rudder helped her get round, too. "Quartermasters . . . make your new course Due West!" Lewrie cried.

It was still a staggering, thrashing muddle for hands tending to the freed running rigging, for the gun crews, whose brutally heavy pieces along the larboard side strained breeching ropes and handling tackle 'til they groaned, with the frigate laid over nearly fourty degrees on her starboard side for a long minute. *Proteus*'s hull groaned and creaked, the masts gave out ominous moans, but, there were none of the crackling, popping, or snapping sounds of imminent disaster. The music stopped, of course, with everyone slid over to leeward, and the distraught bushbaby and the rest of the livestock found something new to wail about.

And, as she slowly rolled back upright, as the tumbled waisters, brace-tenders, and gunners got back on their feet and regained control, the curtain-like rain of the squall passed, and the stiff wind lowered its pitch and volume for a moment.

"Let fall the tops'ls!" Lt. Langlie shouted through his speaking trumpet. "Sheet home, sheet home!"

Then, there was the French frigate, now also steering Due West on larboard tack, about a half a mile up to weather and three points off *Proteus*'s larboard quarter, sailing parallel with them.

"What d'ye plan t'do, *now*, ye snail-eatin' sonofabitch?" Lewrie roared, cupping his hands to his mouth as if his voice could carry all that way in the storm. "We've dry priming up forrud, Mister Langlie?"

"One would hope, sir!" the First Officer replied, laughing like a hyena to see the French countered.

"Fire a challenge shot from one of the six-pounder chase-guns," Lewrie demanded, chortling himself. "The only way he gets to the merchant ships is through us, by God! Let's see if 'Monsieur Crapaud' has the 'nutmegs' for a stand-up fight!"

"Mis-ter A-Dair!" Langlie shouted over the din of the weather, and the rush of the sea against the hull as *Proteus* began to step out right-lively under her re-spread sails. "Fire . . . chase-gun . . . to . . . windward!"

The bows dipped in a steady hobby-horse fashion, spray flying up over the beakhead rails, over the top of the roundhouse and forecastle platform, but a 6-pounder's flintlock striker was cocked, then the trigger string tugged, and the chase-gun erupted with a sharpish noise, almost lost against the drum of rain, with a bright red flash, a spurt of grey-white gunpowder, and a shower of bright cloth embers from the cartridge flannel, and the crew cheered some more to know a formal challenge had been made, and the French could not pretend that they hadn't seen it, or the puny feather of ricochet that leaped from the sea before the enemy frigate's bows. Had they *any* honour, combat, warship to warship, broadside to broadside, must be accepted, now.

"She's reducing her main course, sir," Lt. Langlie pointed out, "and shaking out a reef in her tops'ls."

"Wants a bit more speed in-hand, aye," Lewrie agreed, "though she'll not pass ahead of us, and on this wind, there'll be no clever manoeuvring. Being on her lee will work in our favour. Hard as both of us are pressed, she'll not be able to fire on our masts and sails, as they usually do. Can't lower the breeches low enough for that."

"Whilst we, heeled at this angle, have our choice of shooting at *hers*," Langlie realised with a smile, "or jamming the quoins fully under *our* guns' breeches, and hull her 'twixt wind and water, aha! It is quite advantageous for us, sir. My congratulations. The old adage of *always* seizing the weather gage doesn't always avail, it'd seem."

"Well . . ." Lewrie replied, shrugging in perplexity for how best to answer, for the tactic truly *hadn't* occurred to him; he merely wished to get to grips, and put himself 'twixt the enemy and the convoy. And, Langlie "pissing down his back" with praise . . . that wasn't his typical demeanour. False modesty wouldn't suit; neither would polishing nails on the lapel of his coat to preen, were he baldly honest about it.

Do I owe him money? Lewrie wondered, in a hard-snatched moment of idleness.

There came another flash of lightning, another peal of thunder, and with it, the burst of a cloud of white smoke on the enemy warship's starboard bow; the challenge had been noted, and accepted.

"D'ye *hear,* there!" yelped the lone lookout who had been sent to the mizen cross-trees to watch their stern, who, 'til that moment, had little to do except cling like a leech to the swaying mast and hang on for dear life. "Hoy, th' deck! *Second* enemy frigate, two points offa th' starb'd quarter!"

Oh . . . My . . . Christ! Lewrie thought in sudden shivers of dread.

CHAPTER THIRTY-TWO

It took a further lightning strike on the sea, one more of those lingering, flickering monsters, to espy the second Frenchman from their decks. Smaller than the first, perhaps, or just farther off? She was running "both sheets aft" with the wind right up her stern, to the Nor'west, or a touch West-Nor'west, bounding, pitching, and slithering over the blue-black, white-flecked sea . . . for the convoy!

"Nothing we can do about it," Lewrie spat through gritted teeth, his jaw ruefully clenched. "They *do* work in pairs, and in all this excitement, I forgot that, damn my eyes! Nothin' t'be done but shoot the shit out o' this'un, and Devil take the hindmost."

Which would be Festival, *the slowest,* Lewrie thought; *the poor, old cow!* For the only taffrail lights still anywhere near enough to be made out clearly were certainly the circus ship's. *Eudoxia!* He cringed, fearful for her in French hands . . . even if she *had* come within a hair of clawing his eyes out.

"First honours to Mister Adair, and his chase-guns!" Lewrie felt need to shout, to keep his crew's spirit up, and put his own impending fight ahead of anything else. "Let's have tunes more to *his* liking!" he ordered, turning to face the enemy frigate, which was now surging up closer to abeam of *Proteus,* and slowly falling down onto her. Desmond and the other musicians launched into livelier, more Scottish airs—"Campbell's Farewell to Red Castle," "Hey, Johnny Cope," "The Flowers of Edinburgh," and one of Lewrie's old favourites, "The High Road to Linton."

He stood at the larboard bulwarks, the windward side that was a captain's proper post, clinging against *Proteus*'s motion with his left hand on the mizen stays, his right hand beating the tempo of the music . . . waiting, and shamming utter serenity for his officers and sailors, which was about the hardest thing to do before the iron began to fly.

"Run out the larboard batt'ry, Mister Catterall!" he shouted as the range diminished, and gun-port lids swung up and out of the way to bare their blood-red painted inner faces, stark against the lighter colour of the gunwale hull paint. Black iron muzzles slowly juddered forward as the blocks of the run-out tackles skreakily sang, and everyone could hear Lt. Catterall bellowing at his gun crews in a harsh and loud voice full of blasphemies and good-natured curses for one and all, and their foe, rising to new heights of his burly, rumble-tumble style that had even old salts grinning over his inventiveness.

The Frenchman's gun-ports also opened, her own muzzles seeming to waver as their crews fiddled with their aiming . . . most likely trying to slide the thick wooden quoins out from under the breeches, with their usual intent to fire high and cripple *Proteus* with chain-shot or star-shot, to take down her masts and sails, and allow their frigate to dash past, and get at the convoy.

He really have his heart in this? Lewrie had to ask himself, as he steeled himself for the first crashing broadsides. A long slugging match was not what most raider captains had in mind, he knew; the point was to take merchantmen, to pummel a convoy with a rapid strike, cutting out a few before the escorts could intervene and deal out real, cruise-ending damage. Rake in prize-money, and loot, punish the hated *Anglais*, "The Bloodies," frighten their ships' husbands and sponsors, their insurance cartels, captains, and crews, alarm Admiralty in London, and stop overseas trade, which the British had, but the French did not.

Just a bit closer, Lewrie silently urged the French frigate; *just a tad. A cable's distance, or less . . . double-shotted guns can't miss, that close. Can't waste the first, and best, broadside!*

"Quartermasters, put your helm down half a point . . . easy!" he snapped over his shoulder. Take the wind a bit more abeam, put *Proteus* on a broad reach and ease the angle of heel, provide a flatter, firmer deck for the guns . . . ! "Thus!" he cried, now satisfied with the course. "Mister Catterall, at *half* a cable, you may open upon her!"

"Take aim, you rowdy bastards!" Lt. Catterall barked. "On the up-roll . . . by *broadside* . . . wait for it! By broadside . . . FIRE!"

Twelve 12-pounders, three 6-pounders, and four monstrous 24-pounder carronades roared, almost as one, the great gouts of spent gunpowder smoke caught by the wind, turned into a solid bank of choking fog for a second or two, before the wind rapidly whisked it over the decks and alee. And, that quick-keening wind brought to them the glad sound of solid shot, aimed " 'twixt wind and water," crashing and crunching into the French ship's side, the parroty *Rwawrk!* screech of shattered planking, the thuds of heavier timbers as her frames were battered . . . and, the thin, terrified cries of frightened, wounded, or quick-slain men. Just seconds before a matching great bank of gunpowder sprang to life as her own guns stabbed long reddish tongues of flames, and the thunder of artillery bellowed, almost lost in the cracks and roars of Nature's fury!

"Christ A'mighty, aw Christ A'mighty," Daniel Wigmore whinnied, wringing his hands in despair as rain poured down his face like tears from a whole clan upon the death of its laird, plastering long strands of hair to his cheeks. "Me silver, me gold, Cap'm Weed! Me *h'animals*! 'Em fookin' Frogs'll most-like *h'eat* 'em, or toss 'em h'over th' side, an' we'll all be ruint! Busted! Tents, scen'ry, costumes, performers all gone . . . th' girls raped'r worse! H'an't 'ere *summat* ye can do, I akses ye, man? Christ, we'll lose th' ship, t'boot, iff'n . . . !"

"Nothing to be done, 'gainst a frigate, Mister Wigmore," Captain Weed told him, looking equally despairing of the loss of his livelihood. "We got all the sail she'll carry aloft, already, and she *still* wallows like a hog in mud. Might be we could bear away more Westerly, turn it into a *long* stern-chase, but that'd only gain us two more hours, maybe less. 'Less we could put up some sort o' resistance . . . which we can't, not with these puny old guns of ours, and no trained gunners, who *you* wouldn't let me hire on, if ye'll remem . . ."

" 'Wishes were fishes, h'ever'body'd h'eat'!" Wigmore snapped.

" 'For want of a nail . . .' " Capt. Weed cited right back. He had himself a gloomy squint aloft for inspiration, for an Act of God, or a Sign, but all he saw was dark sails and black rigging, masts, and spars, now and then going ghostly in the lightning flashes. The blue fusee at the truck-cap of the main mast had finally burned out, inspiring him to order the twin taffrail lanthorns to be extinguished, too, hoping that it might make *Festival* harder for the French to chase in the darkness.

As if to scoff at that forlorn hope, another long, flea-flicking fork of lightning lit up the sea like a full moon, revealing the French frigate pursuing them as clear as broad daylight, revealing *Festival* to them just as clearly.

"Damn 'em!" Capt. Weed gravelled as he peered about for the rest of the convoy. No matter how deeply loaded with the untold riches from the Far East, the East India Company ships were sleeker, faster, their bottoms cleaner, and carried much larger crews that could make the most of their acres of sail. They'd scarpered for the far horizons, and damn their black souls to Hell for running off and leaving them. Though, in all honesty, were their places switched, Weed would have been halfway to St. Helena by then, and "hard cheese" for the laggards!

Capt. Weed also spotted one lone blue fusee still burning over a pair of stern lights, off to the Nor'east. Another bolt of lightning revealed HMS *Jamaica,* all too far away to be of any immediate aid, but she *had* managed to come about in the storm, and was butting, pitching, and crashing as close to the wind's eye as she might lay, almost bows-on to *Festival* on what Weed thought was a course of South by West, six points off the storm's keening winds.

"Could we but hold them off a *few* minutes, Mister Wigmore!" the desperate Capt. Weed shouted almost into Wigmore's ear. "Offer up *some* resistance, there's *Jamaica,* coming to our . . . !"

"*Wot!*" Wigmore barked back, leaning away in shock. "Are ye daft, Weed? *R'sistance!* Why, 'ey'd shoot us t'kindlin', 'en come swarmin' h'aboard an' slaughter us all, men, wimmen, an' babes; ye great ninny! Said yerself, we can't fight a bloody *frigate*!"

"The Frogs don't want to sink us, or slaughter us, sir," Capt. Weed urgently insisted. "They want a prize, a *whole* prize. . . ."

"O' *course* 'ey do, puddin' brains!" Wigmore screeched in alarm. "Sure t'God, 'ey h'an't come fer a *matinee*!"

"To *board* us!" Weed snapped, going so far as to seize Wigmore by his sopping-wet lapels, wishing he could go for his throat instead, and who *needed* this job and why had he *ever* signed on this bloody Ark? "Up close, *alongside,* d'ye see! Hard enough to do in a storm, already. We have nets to catch your acrobats, do they slip and fall. We could rig them along the starboard side for *boarding* nets, to slow them down! I know your people have guns, swords, knives, and such, besides our pikes, cutlasses, and muskets. I dasn't trust our rusty old artillery with a full powder charge and solid shot, but I *can* load 'em light, with scrap iron and langridge. *Man*-killin' stuff, lit off right into their Froggy *teeth,* man! The bears? The lion? Bloody bows and arrows? Your knife-thrower, your fire-eater and his oils? Free the God-damn' *baboons* if . . . !"

"You wish *Fransooski* man killed, *Kapitan* Veed?" a harsh voice at their elbows rasped, and there was Arslan Durschenko, so loaded down in weaponry that he had trouble standing, his precious rifled *jaegers,* and at least a full dozen of his long-barreled rifled pistols jammed in any pocket, sash, or belt handy, strapped over with powder horns, cartouche pouches, and accoutrements from his days as an expert marksman, before a flash in a pan had seared out his right eye. "*Fransooski* not lay one hand on my Eudoxia, *yob tvoyemat*. *I* fight the *sikkim siyns*. Other men, girls, they shoot, too, if you do not. I die *Cossack*!" he boasted with a free hand pounding his chest. "Not prisoner, and not *poor*! Rodney!" he called over his shoulder, and up limped little Rodney, swathed in his bandages, which turned eerie blue whenever a bolt of lightning struck. "*Malyenki Chorn malcheek* . . . little Black boy, is *bolshoi* shot and he kill many *Fransooski*, too! Almos' good as me, *yob tvoyemat*."

"Ain' no *boy*, Mistah," Rodney soberly corrected, though without much anger. "I'z a Ord'nary Sea-*man* in th' Royal Navy, an' a *free man*. An' I *is* a damn' good shot, e'en wif muskets. Somebody he'p me upta th' mizen top, an' gimme somebody t'load fo' me, an' I keeps 'em on de hop. Gimme a half-dozen muskets an' I kill as many French as ya wants, sah."

Rodney took a look around as another series of lightning bolts played about them, and raised his unwounded arm to point at the struggling 64-gun *Jamaica*. "We keeps on a bit mo', dat sixty-fo' be up wit' us, lookin' fo' a fight, an' dat French'un might take a big skeer, Cap'm. Might sheer offa us," he opined with a shrug, and a wince from the pain that cost him. "Be wot my Cap'm Lewrie'd do, count on it."

"The lad's right, Mister Wigmore," Capt. Weed cried, more than ready to grasp even the slimmest straw of hope. "Get guns, everyone!"

"Not go up mast," Arslan Durschenko told Rodney. "Little man he shoot from . . . poop, *da*? High enough, and he cannot climb, *kanyeshna*. I shoot here, close, where I still can see. Eudoxia . . . *nyet*!" Arslan exclaimed, to see his daughter on the deck with sheafs of arrows, and her recurved horn bow. "I forbid! *Dohadeetyeh*, go away, you!"

"God helpink them who help selves, Poppa," Eudoxia serenely said, wearing a stiff but brave smile, giving her father a fatalistic shrug. "*Fransooski peesas* no have *me*, over dead body, *da*? *Neeksgda!* Never! You die Cossack, Poppa, *I* die Cossack! Urrah!" she whooped.

"*Bootyeh zdarovi, kraseeva doch*," Durschenko said with a hitch in his voice, and stroked her rain-wet cheek. "I bless you, beautiful daughter. *Ya lyubeet tiy*. I love you. And, I am proud."

"*Ya lyubeet tiy*, Poppa," Eudoxia more-sombrely replied, tears welling in her eyes. "*Dosvidanya*."

"Arr, fook h'it," Wigmore weakly griped. "Mad as 'atters, th' 'ole lot o' ye. H'ever'body, h'arm yerselves, th' law's comin'! I'll go b'low an' git me pistols.

Mind now . . . ye git me robbed an' ruined, an' I'll haint h'ever' last one o' ye t'yer dyin' days!"

"Keep on with double-shot, Mister Catterall!" Lewrie howled to the waist, and the guns. "Keep on hullin' her!" To the four helmsmen manning the double wheel spokes, he added, "Pinch up a'weather, lads. Another half-point to weather. Crowd up to her to shorten the range!"

He paced, feeling every rumbling, squealing movement of the gun-carriages as they were run out, the shock and buffeting muzzle blasts from each fired gun, and the rapid horse-clopping of gun-truck wheels over the main deck planks, sanded that morning to a pristine paleness, but now rapidly turning smutty grey. Each piece that slammed against the extreme lengths of the breeching ropes, he felt that, too, and he could hear the groan of iron ring-bolts in the bulwarks and decks crying out as tons of artillery slammed back, some of them now so hot that they *leaped* a foot off the deck before stuttering back down in recoil.

Twenty years in"King's Coat," most of that at sea, and Lewrie could sense the rush of the hull, its staggers, reels, and heel through his toes—could wince, too, at each crashing arrival of round shot from the French guns, and was staggered whenever a high-elevated shot chewed large pieces from the larboard bulwarks and gangway. Staggered, too, by shot that missed completely, and went screaming low over the deck, the French guns unable to be cocked up high enough to dismast his frigate. It was only on a lucky up-roll, when the French warship wallowed to nearly level decks, that bar-shot, chain-shot, or expanding star-shot could punch ragged holes in *Proteus*'s sails, or carry away a stay or brace. Frustrated, the French were changing over to solid shot, accepting the unfairness of fighting hull-to-hull as the British Navy did, and attempting to out-shoot and smash up *Proteus* in like manner.

It was a bit too dangerous to remain by the gnawed-up bulwarks, so Lewrie sidled over to amidships, and paced between the binnacle and helm to the hammock nettings overlooking the ship's frenetically busy waist. Six-pounder quarterdeck guns barked, spewing both round-shot and bags of grapeshot or musket balls as the range decreased, despite the Frenchman altering course to weather a bit to keep away. Twenty-four-pounder carronades belched with titanic roars from fully-charged muzzles, hurling double-shotted loads from their stubby muzzles, then came slamming back on their greased wooden pressure slides.

Lightning flickered, so fast that sweaty gunners were frozen in a jittery series of *tableaus* as they thumb-stalled the vents, swabbed hot barrels, inserted the flannel powder charges, and rammed them home, once removed from the wood or leather cannisters that the youngest and quickest lads, the powder monkeys, brought in scampers from the magazine. Balls were snatched up from the shot-garlands, gun-captains no longer concerned with perfect roundness or freedom from rust or scales, just *load*! A solid thump from a flexible rope ramrod to seat them, a quick shove to tamp down wet wadding, perhaps a final chore by a ram-merman to seat a sack of grapeshot, musket balls, or langridge, atop ball, and it was time to pulley-haul, again.

Up to the port sills, an overhaul of the run-out tackle and the breeching ropes, then a leap for the train-tackle, maybe the employment of crow-levers and handspikes to shift the whole gun and carriage just a bit to left or right. Some fiddling with the elevating quoin block under the heavy breech to make sure that the piece pointed true at the blackness of the enemy's hull, as low as possible, and a leap away from the gun, feet well clear of tackle and ring-bolts on the deck, lest the men lose their feet as if scythed away, the gun-captain off to one side with his left arm high to show ready, right hand grasping the trigger line to the cocked flint striker, the priming powder in the touch-hole, and . . . BLAM! to begin it all over, again, quick as panting, and bare-chested, men could serve their brutal pieces.

Fuck proper aim, at this range, *fuck* drill and showiness; just fire, load, and *keep* firing, no matter what was happening around them.

A hard strike, low on the waterline it felt like, with *Proteus* shuddering as if gut-punched, and almost a human groan forced from her timbers. Another slamming hit, and more larboard bulwark went flying in tatters, a yard's length of oak turned into arm-long, prickly splinters like gigantic, well-chewed tooth-picks that whirred and fluttered with the sound of frantic birds' wings, some lashing and spearing men's bodies as they went, and raising a chorus of dis-believing screams.

A sudden lull, a horrified, hushed second, before Lt. Catterall could be heard screeching raspy for them to "by broadside . . . *fire*, and *murder* the bastards!" and *Proteus* shuffled to starboard to that shove of directed explosions a few feet alee.

And all Lewrie could do, by that point, was pace, observe, and behave sto-ically, for now that both warships were close-aboard of each other on the same course, their jib-booms and bowsprits almost level with the other, and the range down to less than sixty yards, it was up to his trusted warrants and petty offi-cers, the steadiness of his gun-captains, the stolid courage of officers and mid-shipmen, the speed and stamina of his crew, despite the horrors they could see on every hand. Did he die, the next minute, it would make no matter. This was what a captain *had* to do, and no amount of hopping about, waving sword, and crying, "Damn my eyes!" could change a thing 'til it was concluded.

And there were horrors.

A decapitated Marine hanging half off the chewed-up gangway, to spurt, then ooze, his blood onto the gunners below, making the deck so slippery that a second bucket of sand had to be cast. The young Marine drummer boy's corpse, and his shattered drum, was slung against the main mast trunk, soon to be disposed of overside through a lee gun-port, to make fighting room. Half the crew of a quarterdeck 6-pounder was gone, strewn like bloody piles of laundry amidships. Another sailor from one of the engaged-side carronades was being carted below on a mess table by the Surgeon's loblolly boys, gasping like a landed fish with a two-foot length of bulwark splinter in his chest.

Somewhere, in all the bedlam, Lewrie could hear the sawing of a fiddle, a mad rush of improbable sound that soared now and again above the deafening, ear-hammering din; but then, all ships' fiddlers were as mad as hatters, as daft as March Hares. Lewrie looked forward, down the main deck between the guns, and saw their fiddler capering a horn-pipe or jig to his own urgent music . . . over and over, he played, what sounded like "Pigeon on the Gate," and beaming and cackling fit to bust!

Another hard hit! Another flickering, whining, keening flight of wood splinters, and Lewrie staggered, again, pausing in his pacing. God, but he wished to draw his sword, bark orders, shout encouragement, do something useful! Instead, he pulled out his watch and opened the ornately-engraved lid, grunting in utter surprise to see that the fight had gone on for over half an hour since the first broadsides were fired! He clicked the lid shut, carefully put the watch back into the pocket of his waist-coat, then paced over to the compass binnacle.

Due West, and away from the convoy, which, the last he had seen, had been steering Nor'west by West, escaping as he delayed the frigate. A quick look over at the French, and he walked the few feet aft to the Quartermasters on the helm. "Another half-point to weather, lads. Get us up closer, still."

"Aye aye, sir!" stoic older Austen agreed, shifting a dry quid of tobacco to his other cheek. Zip-zip-zip! A musket ball thudded off the forward wheel, taking a divot of ash with it, and sudden splintery quills arose from the deck as other musket shots missed. Mr. Motte, on the after wheel, gave out a sudden shriek and dropped as if pole-axed, with a musket ball in his neck.

"Another helmsman, here, Mister Langlie!" Lewrie barked, gulping down nausea, and shock, then turning away, *as he must*! "By God, those people are beginnin' t'make me angry! Still with us, Mister Langlie?"

"Aye, sir. 'Nother helmsman on the way."

"Swivel-guns in the tops t'open on theirs, as we get closer!" Lewrie snapped, wishing he had his Ferguson, his fusil musket, or even his Girandoni air rifle.

Hell with this stoic *shite*, he determined; *I'm gonna kill some of those bastards, myself!* as he drew out his first double-barreled pistol to check the dryness of its priming.

"We've been hulled, several times, sir," Lt. Langlie said, after he had done as Lewrie directed. "The Carpenter reports better than one foot of water in the bilges, so far, and at least five shot-holes, that he can see near the waterline. He also found an intact round-shot, sir. An eighteen-pounder, wedged in a starboard timber."

"I *thought* yon Frog was hitting rather hard," Lewrie said, with a wince; he'd been sure that *Proteus* and the foe were of equal calibre and weight of broadside. But, perhaps the slowness of the French gun crews had given him that impression. "Making fast, is the water, sir?" he asked Langlie.

"Not *too* quickly, sir . . . not yet," Langlie said with a shrug.

"Have to live with it, for a while, then," Lewrie decided. "No hands may be spared for the pumps, 'til it gets a lot worse. Have any more joy for me, Mister Langlie?"

"Mister Adair reports that the larboard six-pounder on the forecastle is dismounted, too, sir," Langlie added, looking grim and quite grey from head to foot with powder residues. "As is Number Two twelve-pounder, and Number Eleven in your cabins, from our larboard battery."

"I'll take joy from thinking that the Frogs are having a worse night than we are, Mister Langlie," Lewrie had to shout in his ear, as several guns below their feet erupted together. "Must have not had an impressive raiding cruise . . . if they felt the need to toe up and slug it out! Honour and glory, 'stead o' loot? Not their, ha! . . . *forte*!"

Lewrie said it with a fatalistic shrug of his own, to think they would continue to batter each other, perhaps for hours, but Lt. Langlie could see the feral rictus of a smile on his captain's face, take note in a flash of lighting that Lewrie's usually merry blue eyes were gone cold, Arctic grey, and *snapping* with battle joy.

"Carry on, Mister Langlie," Lewrie said, clapping his First Officer on the shoulder. "Pour it to 'em. The French aren't much good at this sort of yardarm-to-yardarm fight. Give it time enough, and they will lose their nerve, long before us. *Hammer* 'em, lads!" he shouted to the gunners, all that stern stoicism the Navy required gone at last. "Hammer 'em, and shatter their bloody *bones*! Pour it on, pour it on!"

"And damned be he who first cries, 'Hold, Enough!'" he thought, becoming

gun-drunk on the bitter powder fog, and the heart-stopping, lung-shaking roar from his beloved artillery.

"*Damned be* he," "*damned be* him"? *Never* could *keep that straight,* he told himself with a deprecating chuckle and a faint grin, which, in the ruddy Hell-fire flashes of *Proteus*'s guns, looked positively wolfish. *Whichever's right, by* God *it won't be us!*

CHAPTER THIRTY-THREE

Oh, Jaysus, oh, Jaysus!" an Irish sailor whispered as he stood behind the starboard bulwark, a bare-bladed cutlass jammed into a wide belt, a clumsy-looking pistol stuck into a pocket of his slop-trousers, and gripping a Brown Bess Sea Pattern musket. In addition to all that, a keen-pointed boarding pike rested upright against the rack of belaying pins near the main mast's stays. He looked up and down the rainy gangway at his mates, similarly armed, who crouched down out of sight, and felt the need to cross himself. "Mither Mary, comfort me . . . !"

"Arr, stop yer gob, Paddy," one of the hidden chid him. "Where away, now?"

"M . . . musket-shot, Oi thinks," the Irishman said with a shudder as lightning crashed bright ghoul-blue and lit up the sea, showing the dark frigate closing rapidly. Sailors stood atop her bulwarks, up her larboard shrouds, with even more crowding elbow-to-elbow along her sail-tending gangway . . . every mother-son of them waving cutlasses, hooting, jeering, and whooping fit to bust. Like Beelzebub's demon army!

"Fook if they are!" the hidden sailor spat, after a quick peek. "Still 'arf a cable off. No wonder th' doxies don't fancy ye, Paddy. Cain't judge distance worth a tinker's dam. Tells 'em 'e's got seven inches, an' th' hoors kin only mark three, har har!"

"Wait fer it!" the First Mate was intoning from the quarterdeck. "Wait fer it! Ever'body stay hid, 'til th' cap'm says 'leap,' there."

"Gonna kill us all," Paddy whispered, his lips trembling, and a hand clawing inside his sodden shirt for his rosary. "Gonna . . . !"

"Hesh, lad!" an older shipmate hissed. "Buck up, laddy."

The frigate sidled down upon them, no matter the futile alteration of course, the dangerous release of reefed sails. But, her gun-ports were still closed, and did not flap open to her rolling motion; they weren't even freed . . . yet. It would be a boarding, hull pressed and grinding against hull.

"Wait for it . . . almost there!" the First Mate shouted, again.

"Heu!" a harsh voice came down to them on the noisy wind, from the foe. "*Voici le frigate* Vesuve, *à Marine Français*! 'Eave to, z'ere, *et surrendre. Vous* not, ve fire on *vous, comprendre*?"

"We cannot heave-to in this weather, you no-sailor, you!" Capt. Weed could be heard shouting back through a speaking-trumpet. "We *must* keep a way on, downwind. *Comprendre?"*

"Surrendre, vite vite!" came the harsh answer as the *Vesuve* continued to close. "Take in *votre voiles* . . . you damn' sails!" And, in seeming obedience, *some* free sailors began to clew up tops'ls, as the French frigate shuffled down within mere yards of them. And, the gun-ports were *still* shut! French sailors at bow, stern, and amidships on her bulwarks appeared with heaving lines and grapnels to bind the two ships together.

"We're all gonna die, damn yer blood!" Daniel Wigmore said from chattering jaws, snuffled, and wiped his nose on his coat sleeve.

"Aw, you lived too long, anyway, you old fraud," Weed told him. "*Jamaica*'s but five miles off, and coming hard. Who knows? With any luck at all, you'll live, and reap a year's free advertisements from this. Wait for it . . . !"

"Thousands o' th' buggers, though. . . ."

"*Hundreds,* anyways," Capt. Weed professionally noted; he'd had his own start in the Royal Navy during the American Revolution. "And, I do think I see half her crew or better still below her gangways, on her *starboard* guns, and such. They mean to send a *fair*-sized boarding party to us, yet keep enough men in-hand to stall *Jamaica* whilst they make off with *us*. This just might work, after all!"

The heavy grapnels flew, biting into *Festival*'s timbers as the *Vesuve* came to within hand-shaking distance.

"Now, by God!" Capt. Weed howled. "Now! Up, and repel boarders! Gunners . . . fire!"

French sailors were leaping across the empty air between ships, howling in glee, or swinging in piratical fashion on freed lines, but were countered by the acrobats' and aerialists' nets hung from the tips of the yardarms, pinning themselves against them like flies glued to a spider's web, and their victory cries turned ugly and harsh.

But, then the muskets began to bark and flash, as pistols were emptied right in their faces, as cutlasses and small-swords and sabres were thrust into the bellies of those clambering upon the nets . . . as the puny old cast-off artillery pieces, double-shotted with scrap metal, musket balls, and grape, erupted, quoins fully out and aimed up high to scythe the French frigate's bulwarks and gangway. Rusty swivel-guns in the tops yapped, pointing down at acute angles at the gangway, as well, and French sailors were suddenly screaming in pain and terror as they were plucked from the rails, caught in mid-swing, and dropped in the foaming mill-race between the hulls, to be crushed or drowned!

"Tarakans!" Whoosh. *"Nasyekomayeh!"* Whoosh. *"Peesas!"* Whoosh. "Cockroaches! Insects! *Pricks!*" Eudoxia Durschenko shrilly hallooed, each curse a punctuation to a loosed arrow. *"Chyepooha!"* Whoosh, and *that* for *rubbish*! as another broad-point hunting arrow skewered a well-dressed man, with a fore-and-aft bicorne hat and a costly sword, who'd gained *Festival*'s bulwark and was chopping at the nets. He screamed as he looked down to the doom buried deep in his chest, eyes widened by utter astonishment that he'd be slain by such an ancient thing, just before he tottered backwards and disappeared between the grinding hulls!

"*Snova*, girl!" her father bellowed. "Again, and again!"

"Bast'rd, yew *mine*!" Rodney swore as he took careful aim from behind the poop deck's bulwarks, alongside the clowns firing one of the swivel-guns. His target was an older man, maybe a petty officer, who was shoving French sailors forward. The musket shoved him in his good shoulder as he fired, and that petty officer died so quick he didn't even have time to clap a hand to his chest, where a .75-calibre ball smashed his heart, and fell off the gangway to sprawl atop one of the cannon. The clowns, in full white-face—their war-paint, they said!—whooped over his accuracy as they charged their rail-mounted shot-gun for another round. "*Got* you, yeah!" Rodney cheered, too, as he tossed the musket to the rear, and flapped his right hand to demand a fresh weapon from the little blond acrobat girl who was loading for him. This weapon was one of Durschenko's Pennsylvania rifles, like the ones that he and *Proteus*'s Marine marksmen used from the tops in action, and he smiled an evil little smile as he brought it forward, over his injured left forearm for a rest, and drew the dog's-jaws back to full cock. There, on the quarterdeck! That was an officer, for sure, he reckoned, all bellow, gilt-and-beshit. "You *mine*, butt fuckah!"

⚓

Lashed together, hulls grinding paint, tar, and linseed oil off, the French were but briefly daunted. The unexpected check was like a red flag waved at a bull, enflaming their blood lust. Swords chopped through nets, slashing suspending ropes, and parts of the netting came down at last, allowing a small flood of boarders to gain footing along *Festival*'s gangway.

"*Vaya con Dios, amigos,*" Jose whispered as he removed muzzles from his bears, and cuffed them hard on their snouts to enrage them. "Go, *hasta luego, niños*! Eat Frenchmen!" he directed, pointing, then shoving them in the right direction. Fredo and Paulo might not have been all that hungry, or all that enraged, either, perhaps imagined a time free of their constricting muzzles was a time to *play*. Whatever *they* made of it, the pair of brothers, usually as gentle as baa-lambs as Jose had promised, made a *distinct* impression on the French sailors who had gained the gangway as they loped towards them on all fours with their mouths open, their fangs flickering in the back-flashes of the lightning, and their claws skittering rather loudly on the oak planks!

It didn't help that Jose, in his second role as knife-thrower, was whickering butcher-knives at the French as he ran behind his bears, and shrieking curses, aiming to *hit* for a change, not outline the girl who spun on his large wooden wheel with near-misses!

"Ilya, mean old son of bitch," Arslan Durschenko cooed into one ear of his lone adult lion after he had led him up from his cage down in the upper hold. "*Ya lyubeet tiy, syegda*. Lovink you, always, even if you no damn' good. Chase there, *da*? Want *head* for bitink? *There*, Ilya, *there*! Sweet meat, *Fransooski* bastards!"

The lion whuffed at the din of combat, of clashing swords, and howling men, his mane shivering at every discharge of musket or pistol. Ilya was old, as old as poor, dead Vanya, and he had never had what one might call a sweet disposition. His rheumy eyes lit up with an ancient joy, though, and, free for once of a controlling leash and collar after Durschenko removed it and gave him an encouraging slap on his rump, the lion just had to do what a lion had to do. He leaped from the weather deck to the gangway with the spryness of a young male, huge hind paws not even having to scrabble at its edge, found himself a victim on the gangway, and rose up to drape his front paws on a man's shoulders, his gaping, fang-filled mouth inches from his nose as he let out a roar!

Thankfully for *Festival*'s crew, Ilya's first choice *was* French, though nothing about lions was gilt-edged guaranteed. The French tar shrieked, sword clattering to the deck in terror, and fainted away, a good thing for him, for Ilya didn't think that was very much fun, nor was it even tasty, so he rose up again and began slapping those plate-sized, sharp-taloned paws about to right and left, this time draping himself on the sole remaining trio of Frenchmen who *hadn't* been swatted into bloody tatters, and took himself a lovely mouthful of face!

"Stay th' Divil away f'um me, ye bastards!" Paddy was shouting, musket emptied into one man, pistol emptied into another, then used as a club to shatter a third's skull. His boarding pike had been lost in a Frenchman's belly, a man who had joined his shipmates in the sluice between the hulls, and he was now reduced to whirling his cutlass like a frantic St. Catherine's Wheel, and he was holding off two sword-armed enemies by creating a steel fan in front of him, but his arms were now growing lead-heavy and weak. "I don't *wanna* die, Jaysus, Mary, an' Joseph! Don't hurt me, or Oi'll *kill* ye! Go-od *damn*!" he gawped.

Ilya had come to his rescue, pouncing, rather playfully kitten-like it *could* be described, onto their backs, and naturally going for the tried-and-true neck-bite on one of them, jostling the other to his knees with his cutlass down, and Paddy whisked his blade like an axe, cleaving right down through the crown of his foe's skull, deep into his brain. "Oi told ye, Oi warned ye! Oh, shite!" *His foe* bleated out a death-scream, *Ilya*'s prey shrieked his own as long fangs met together in the unfortunate sailor's throat. Ilya gave him a good shake, then looked at Paddy with his eyes glowing in eager green chatoyance.

"*Gooood* kitty!" Paddy whinnied, leaping rather spryly, himself, for the main mast shrouds and rat-lines. "*Noice* kitty!" he whimpered as he shot up the stays past the cat-harpings in an eye-blink, hoping that lions didn't much care for nigh-vertical ascents on shaky ropes, and swearing that if he survived, he'd *never* sign aboard a ship which carried *any* sort of critters! "Mither?" he cried to the main truck as the lion took a moment to look up at *him* and ponder his chances.

"What are you fools . . . ?" a French Lieutenant bellowed as sailors came tumbling back aboard the frigate *Vesuve*. "Attack, I say, go back and *attack* . . . Eeekk!" as a lion—a shaggy-maned *lion*!—sprang from one bulwark to the next, balanced for a short second on all four paws like a domestic cat on a balcony railing, then sprang for *him* and took him down with his massive weight. The bloody-mawed beast landed atop him, embraced him with gigantic front paws, and clawed his torso from breastbone to groin with his hind paws, roaring in his face, and fine broadcloth wool and clean white silk—always to be worn when in combat, for it was easier to withdraw from wounds!—went flying like a rag-picker's rejected quilt pieces! His sailors shot, stabbed, and bayoneted the beast, but it was far too late for the Lieutenant, and Ilya actually managed to claw a *matelot* to ribbons before he died, managing to shatter the night with one last, prideful roar that sounded like utter satisfaction, and the total domination of all Africa that he had been denied when captured as a cub so many years before.

"I not cry," Arslan Durschenko muttered as he heard his lion's last victory roar. Even so, he had to pipe at his good left eye for a second, before turning to receive a fresh-loaded rifled musket from a wee red-headed "actress," and brought it to his left shoulder to take careful aim. The French were still so close that Durschenko could aim, then shut his left eye before he pulled the trigger to prevent the loss of his remaining sight. A lifetime of marksmanship assured him that he would strike his man, and even before he opened his eyes, the shout of pain that followed the snap of the lock and the flash in the pan, then the bark and recoil of the rifled weapon, told him he had scored.

"A pity," the brazenly pert little redhead told him as she took the rifle back, and handed him a pair of double-barreled pistols. "'E were a good lion . . . mostly."

"Ilya was *Devil* son of bitch," Arslan Durschenko snarled as he cocked all four locks. "But, he die good, I give him one last chance. Those two pistols, too, *kraseeya dyevooshka*, and I showink somethink. Keep down, *dyevooshka*. Too pretty to fight. Watchink this!"

The girl ducked down behind the compass binnacle as Durschenko strode forward towards the starboard gangway with a pistol in each of his hands. The French were retreating, flowing back to their frigate, but Durschenko's blood was up. Off-handed, shooting from the hip with his left eye squinted, he volleyed off, first from the right hand, and then from the left, alternating right-side and left-side barrels from both guns, and four Frenchmen slumped to the deck! He dropped both of his empty pistols and drew his last pair of single-barreled duellers, raising the right one to shoulder level.

The other foemen spotted the threat at last, some raising their cutlasses, or swinging muskets towards him, but not before Durschenko blasted one of them backwards to slam into the gangway bulwark with a ball in his heart, folded over himself. Durschenko raised his other pistol, just as the Frenchman who had levelled his musket right at him yelped in agony as an arrow drove deep into his right side, and pulled the trigger as the muzzle dropped, to drive the ball deep into the oak deck. Before the French could react to this new threat, yet another arrow went into the left eye socket of the man who had swung to find the source, and his death-scream was as un-nerving as a dying woman's.

Then, the bears arrived from up forward, both Fredo and Paulo clumsily stalking aft on their hind feet, rolling their massive heads and roaring with their mouths open and their upper lips laid back from long, though un-bloodied, fangs. Durschenko fired his last pistol and found his mark, and the French at last broke and ran, scrambling from *Festival* to the relative safety of their frigate, abandoning weapons to free their hands for the desperate and dangerous crossing. Men on both ships, with good reason, were hacking at the grapnel lines with boarding axes and swords.

Astern of them, Capt. Weed was shouting orders for brace-tenders and sheet-handlers as he spun the spokes of the wheel to a blur to get his ship away into the darkness as quickly as he could. Her own battle lust not yet slaked, Eudoxia smoothly plucked a shaft from the sheaf on her back, notched it, and drew to her cheek in one slick motion, firing four more arrows in as few seconds, it seemed, and tumbling all four of her marks into the widening gap between the hulls, or making them drop onto the frigate's gangways where their shouts and cries and confusion-causing bodies kept the recent shock and terror redly alive.

"Urrah!" Arslan Durschenko shouted, both arms and empty pistols thrust at the stormy night sky in triumph. "We win! Urrah!" he cried, looking up at the poop deck, where a bandaged Black man stood with his hunting rifle in one hand, and cheering, too.

"Urrah!" Eudoxia seconded, coming to hug her father, to dance in place and bounce on her toes in victory.

"Cossack *forever*, *Fransooski* bastards!" her poppa howled.

"Damned h'if we didn't!" Daniel Wigmore marvelled in complete astonishment, ready to feel himself over for wounds as he rose from a handy hiding place near the break of the poop. He had an un-fired pistol and an un-bloodied sword, but he waved them aloft with as much exuberance as the rest. "Damme h'if h'it didn't work, ha ha! Eeek!" he added, as Fredo and Paulo, their "play-pretties" now gone, came loping aft, looking for more excitement. "Jose, come git yer damn' bears, I say! P . . . please? Jose!"

"Hoy, th' deck!" came a forlorn voice from the main mast truck, astride the furled and gasketed sail and yard. "Kin I come down, now? Is 'at lion gone, arrah?"

CHAPTER THIRTY-FOUR

HMS *Proteus* shuddered to another hit, thick oak scantlings crying as they were punctured, and a framing timber under the Number Five larboard gun-port gave out a great groan of pain as the 18-pdr. round-shot *thonked* into it inches deep and lodged there.

"Two feet or more in the bilges, now, sir," Lt. Langlie had to report, his cocked hat gone, and his face smeared with grey gun-grit.

"Their rate of fire's slackin'," Lewrie commented, giving that dire news but half an ear. The storm was finally blowing itself out, the winds moderating, and the rain coming down in sullen, vertical showers, instead of being whipped horizontally into their faces. The worst of the weather had scudded off Nor'west with its heavy lightning, so if a bolt now struck, it was no longer close-aboard, and there were several seconds between the crack and the rumbling thunder roll.

"There!" Lewrie snapped, pointing at their foe in a weaker glimmer of a distant lightning strike. "See *there,* Mister Langlie! Hands to the braces, and we'll make up a bit closer to her, still. Quartermasters . . . another half-point to weather!"

The enemy frigate, in that blink-of-an-eye flash, stood revealed as a battered shell, her hull planking stove in, and riddled with star-shaped shot-holes, several of her gun-ports hammered into one, and her starboard bulwarks gnawed away in places, from abaft her cat-heads and swung-up anchors to abeam of her mizen-mast.

Lewrie grimly supposed that *Proteus* probably didn't look a whit better, after more than a full hour of trading shot, but . . . his masts still stood, whilst the Frenchman's lower main and mizen *seemed* canted from the proper angle of rake; *Proteus*'s sails still drew, with only a few holes punched through them, and her yards, standing rigging, and running rigging were still mostly intact.

She's fallen astern a tad, too, Lewrie took satisfying note; *a bit. Not enough for us t'draw ahead and bow-rake her, but . . . time to end this.*

"Mister Catterall! Quoins fully out, and aim for her rigging!" Lewrie shouted down to the waist. "Mister Langlie, brace and sheet men will haul in *too* taut, and get us heeled *far* over!"

The French frigate, was it starting to brace up, as well, going more South of West . . . to break off the action and run? Lewrie speculated. "Mister Catterall, a *controlled* broadside! Shot *and* grape!"

"Aye, sir! Load, load, load, ye miserable cripples, or I . . . !" Lt. Catterall chortled in a voice gone creaky with over-use, stamping about the deck in blood-lusty glee.

Proteus fell silent for about a full minute, as fresh 12-pdr. shot was fetched up from below, the hatchway shot racks and the thick rope shot-garlands between the guns nigh expended. Lewrie noted a gun here and there being charged with powder with wooden *ladles,* for, their over-ample store of pre-made powder cartridges, and empty flannel *bags* for filling in the magazine, had already been shot away. For certain, they had most-like used up the upper tier of powder casks, as well, and were into the older stuff from the second tier.

The French warship continued *her* fire, and *Proteus* had to stand and take it, but Lewrie could count only eight discharges from her battery, and those were fired independently, haltingly, with better than two minutes between explosions from those gun-ports.

"Ready, sir!" Catterall bellowed, his voice cracking raspily.

"*Thus,* Quartermasters!" Lewrie cried, chopping his hand to show the alteration of course desired. "Sheet home, brace up *sharp*! Stand ready . . . !"

Proteus seemed to gather a bit more speed, a quarter-knot or so, like a good hunter bunching its hindquarter muscles to take a hedge. As she did so, amid the loud squealing of blocks as the square sails were drawn at right angles to the wind, and the fore-and-aft sails were put flat to it, she began to heel over onto her starboard shoulders. Rose, then paused, pent atop a passing beam wave, as well, steadied, and . . .

"*Fire,* Mister Catterall!"

The brief gap between the frigates lit up harsh and orange, for a second, and the range was still so close that *Proteus*'s weary gunners could see the results of their handiwork, for once, before the bank of powder fog rolled back down on them and over the lee side, giving them a cause to cheer and howl in pleasure, no matter how dry-mouthed, weak, or tired.

The Frenchman's main mast shivered as a great rat-bite appeared in it halfway 'twixt her bulwark and main top. Clouds of grape ravaged her upper and lower shrouds, blasting away the dead-eyes that kept her top-mast erect, by the edge of the main top, shattering her slender top-mast, and bringing the whole thing, from truck and cap to halfway up above the main top, swinging down in ruin, the furled and gasketed royal, half-reefed t'gallant, and tops'l, with all their mile of rigging, collapsed alee to drape utter chaos, and highly flammable sails, over her engaged side!

"*Ease* her, Mister Langlie!" Lewrie shouted, so pleased that he just-about started to caper in delight. "Mister Catterall! Secure, arm your people, and prepare t'board her! Close reach for a bit, sir, and fetch us alongside, Mister Langlie! Mister Devereux, are you with us?"

"Aye, sir!" his Marine officer shouted from the larboard side.

"Ready to volley and clear the way for us!" Lewrie directed as he tore off his foul-weather coat, at last, and patted his pockets to assure himself that his pistols were still there, then drew his hanger an inch or two to determine that it would draw easily when needed, but was snug enough to stay in its scabbard during his clamber across.

With an upper mast and sails dragging over her lee side, and a catastrophic loss of sail area with which to maintain her speed and her agility, the French warship sagged down on *Proteus*, even as the British frigate swung up to meet her.

"Ready grapnels, there!" Bosun Pendarves was shouting.

Proteus had not rigged boarding nets, and the French ship, with the intent of a rapid assault on a captured merchantman, had not rigged hers, either. There would only be wreckage to hack away . . . or use as a handy footbridge for the quicker and more agile.

Proteus drew ahead, angling to windward, the French ship's foremast falling astern of abeam before the hulls met with a titanic thud, rebounded a foot or two, then clashed back together as grapnels flew.

"Ready, sir!" Lt. Catterall rasped, his teeth white in a wild and wide smile.

"Aye aye, sir!" Lt. Adair up on the forecastle cried as well, his smaller party of gunners and sail-handlers gathered round him by the larboard cat-head.

"Boarders!" Lewrie ordered in a quarterdeck roar. "Away!"

Swivel-guns yapped from both ships, from the bulwarks and tops, though British guns vastly out-numbered the French. Lt. Devereux and his Marines levelled their muskets, volleyed as one, and nigh a dozen Frenchmen waiting with cutlasses and axes in hand to repel them reeled away from sight, shot dead in their tracks!

"Let's go, Proteuses! Kill me some Frogs, ha ha!" Lt. Catterall encouraged as he stood atop their bulwarks, shrouds in one hand, and a glittering sword in the other. His gunners began to surge forward, in obedience to his urging, leaping and scrabbling across the gap between the tumble-home of hulls, though both frigates' waterlines were inches apart.

A swivel-gun coughed, and Catterall grunted in agony, his right arm torn completely off, and his shoulder shredded. "Well, just damn my eyes, if I . . ." he loudly cursed, before swaying backwards to fall dead on the gangway.

"Come on, lads!" Midshipman Larkin, their little Bog-Irish imp, shrilled as he swung across on a freed line. He gained the Frenchman's gangway, atop that pile of wreckage, dirk in one hand and a pistol in the other. He shot down one French sailor, and hopelessly clashed his short and slim dirk against another's cutlass, slyly kicking his opponent in the teeth to drive him back. But, a boarding pike came driving upwards, taking him deep in the stomach. A twist of the long and slim pikehead to make it even crueller, then the French pikeman lifted him like a forkful of reaped hay to fling him in-board to the enemy's gun-deck!

Lewrie slid down the larboard mizen-mast shrouds to the channel and dead-eyes, leaped onto the French ship's main mast chain platform, and began to scramble up, praying that his left arm, slightly weakened after being broken by a Dutch musket ball at the Battle of Camperdown, would serve him, for he already held one of his double-barreled pistols in his right. British sailors followed his path alongside him, others made the risky leap over his head. Muskets, pistols, and swivels made a minute-long fusillade, before hard-pressed men on both sides ran out of time for re-loading, and the clatter of blades replaced them. Up to the level of a French gun-port, the hint of a shadowy figure within . . . *Bang!* went his first shot, rewarded by a throaty, gobbling scream, and Lewrie clambered higher, cursing his left arm for its slowness, wishing that he didn't have to *do* this, just this once, for every now and then, the hulls rebounded off each other, despite the taut grapnel lines, and the mill-race below his feet sounded as loud as a rain-choked Scottish river.

Up to level with the bulwarks, into a snarl of rigging, broken spars, and sailcloth, but a wide gap had been blown through it, and it was with a great sense of relief that he flung his right arm, then his right leg, over the splintery timbers, and crawled to his feet, on the enemy's decks, at last!

Shoot *that* bugger, close enough for his pistol to set his shirt on fire, before he could skewer him with a pike! Drop empty pistol . . . draw sword . . . fill his left hand with the other pistol, and draw back to half-cock on both barrels with his right forearm! Look about, and discover his own sailors and Marines either side of him, thank God!

"Take it to 'em, lads! *Skin* the bastards!" he shouted, taking a tentative step forward to peer over the inner edge of the gangway to see . . . a butcher's yard! Guns were dis-mounted, massive barrels and truck-carriages overturned on squashed men, splintered, dis-emboweled, half-charred gunners betrayed by their pieces when they burst, or the powder cartridges had blown up, turning flesh the colour of rare roast beef! And a *sheet* of gore on the main deck, reflecting battle-lanthorn light like a reddish full moon on a calm lake! *Mounds* of bodies about the main and foremast trunks, smaller piles of arms, legs, and bits of men, as well . . . and two ragged rows of screaming, writhing wounded by the unengaged larboard side, still waiting to be carried below to their Surgeons, the French cockpit surgery already filled to bursting with the *worst*-off.

Triage, the Frogs call it? Lewrie numbly recalled, appalled and about to retch. If these men were the better-off, he did not want to see what an urgent case looked like!

"Reddition, m'sieur!" a young, wide-eyed French officer in the ship's waist called out, taking Lewrie, in his cocked hat with a pair of epaulets on his shoulders, as in command. "*Nous surrendre,* please? *Nous amener* . . . strike, *oui*? Quarter, *m'sieur capitaine.*" He tossed away a pistol and let his sword dangle from his right wrist by a strap of leather. *"Ze fregat* L'Uranie *surrendre, m'sieur!"*

"Tell them!" Lewrie roared, pointing his hanger at the officer, then at the melee still going on from bow to stern. "Order your men, *votre matelots,* to . . . *désarmer*! Lay down their arms . . . *vite, vite*!"

Lewrie looked aft, to where his own sailors had swept the quarterdeck clean of resistance, and were even then hauling down the French Tricolour, without their foes' approval.

"Quarter!" Lewrie bellowed, hands cupped to his mouth, to fore, aft, and amidships. "*Quarter,* lads, they've struck! Their ship is ours!" And, to the shuddery young French officer, he added, "Best ye sheath that damned sword o' yours, *m'sieur,* 'fore one o' my men takes ye for a die-hard, *comprendre*?"

Guns, pikes, and edged weapons clattered from numb hands to the decks, and physically and spiritually exhausted sailors sagged to their knees . . . some completely spent and wheezing, some in shame, with tears streaking clean channels through powder-smut on their faces, and some ready to weep with joy for being alive and whole. Only a rare few remained on their feet, glaring defiance—wisely *dis-armed* defiance, as British tars, sore losers, and spiteful victors, jeered them and spat curses that they *could* have killed all of them, if allowed.

"Mister Langlie?" Lewrie called out in the relatively peaceful silence, his ears still ringing from an hour and a half of cannon fire, and with the fingers of his left hand crossed for luck.

"Sir?" came the First Officer's weary voice.

"Parties to secure the on-deck prisoners, Mister Langlie. Then, Leftenant Devereux, his Marines, and a party of our Jacks to go below, and chivvy any skulkers on deck. Make sure they're all dis-armed, not even a pen-knife on 'em, and no arms near them, should some have a sudden change of heart. And *drink*, Mister Langlie! Don't care it it's a vintage bottle, you discover spirits, drain 'em into the bilges. Keep a keen eye on *our* people, keen as you will on the French, right?"

"Aye aye, sir!"

Lewrie had seen defeat and victory before, both shivering losers and strutting winners, aloft and a'low, who'd use the chaos of the aftermath to guzzle themselves senseless and did *Proteus*'s sailors get in drink, the French could turn the tables on them and cut *their* throats!

"Mister Carter . . . no," Lewrie began to call out, before remembering that he'd seen him fall. "Mister Adair?" Another crossing of his fingers. To his relief, Lt. Adair piped up, too, and came to his side.

"Get with the Bosun and Carpenter, Mister Adair," Lewrie ordered. "Any spare hands, you may now put them to the chain-pumps to keep our own ship afloat 'til morning. A survey below of this'un, as well, sir. I'd admire could we get her to a Prize-Court, after all the trouble we went through t'win her."

"Aye aye, sir," Lt. Adair replied, performing a shaky doffing of his hat in salute.

"And, Mister Adair . . . you are now our Second Lieutenant," he added in a sombre tone as he sheathed his hanger and un-cocked his pistol.

"Very well, sir," Adair gravely answered.

He felt it, then, that shuddery weakness and lassitude that he had suffered at the end of every sea-fight. There were an hundred details to be seen to before dawn, a myriad of repairs to be made aboard both frigates before he could feel sanguine, but *God*, he felt spent! What he most craved, that moment, was a bracing drink, a pint of water to put moisture back into his tongue and gums, then a brimming bumper of brandy or Yankee-Doodle corn-whisky . . . followed by a lie-down and perhaps a nap, maybe a long one since he wasn't getting any younger, but . . . "Um, *m'sieur capitaine*?" It was the wide-eyed young officer below him on the main deck, who still stood there, looking up at him, looking a bit embarassed to bother him. "*Mon épée* . . . sword, *m'sieur*," he said, offering up his small-sword, now sheathed in its scabbard, in formal sign of personal surrender.

It was "bad form," and un-gentlemanly, for Lewrie to accept it. The proper form would be to wave it off, tell the man whose throat one wished to slit and bowels one tried to spill what an heroic defence he had put up, so "honourably," but, Lewrie wasn't feeling especially charitable that evening, so he took hold of it and gave the young fellow a grave nod. Damned if he'd let *any* armed Frog ponce about with a sword . . . he might relent and give it back, once sure that both ships would float and sail. "*Merci,*" he said, its hilt to his face in salute.

He stumbled aft along the enemy warship's starboard gangway, a tangle of dead and wounded, of splintered wood, sails, rigging, and hidden ring-bolts, to the enemy's quarterdeck, where some of his sailors were capering and laughing that particular uproarious good humour that only whole survivors could laugh, atop slain foes.

"Cap'm, sir!" Ordinary Seaman Martyn chortled, handing him yet another sheathed sword. " 'Ere's 'er cap'm's blade, sir. Won't 'ave a need f 'r it in *'is* life no more, Cap'm, nosirree!"

"Mus' be worth fifty guineas, sor!" Able Seaman Clancey hooted, producing yet another. "An' thayr First Off 'cer's sword, 'ere, 'tis a fine'un, too, sor. Poor feller's not long f 'r this world, neither, we reckon," Clancey callously snickered, pointing back towards the wheel, where an officer who'd had a leg shot off at the hip, and the other one bent at an un-natural angle, was being tended by two French sailors.

"A guinea for each of you, lads," Lewrie told them, "but, let's not be makin' a career of lootin' the dead . . . even Frenchmen."

"Thankee, sor!"

"And, let's stay cold sober, too, 'fore I have ye all at 'Mast,' " Lewrie sternly reminded them.

Lewrie took a tour of the quarterdeck, taking in the heavy damage, the strewn corpses and dis-mounted guns, with his lips pursed in a silent whistle. Unlike most combats reported in the *Marine Chronicle*, where the French fired a few broadsides to salve their captain's conscience and uphold honour before striking, this ship had fought to win . . . and had paid the price. It was a slaughterhouse!

French frigates carried over-large complements compared to English warships, sometimes as many as 350 or more. For raiders such as this *L'Uranie,* intent on prize-taking and long cruises, they carried more officers, petty officers, and sailors to man and safeguard those ships they took, leaving enough aboard to maintain the raider at full strength if she was required to fight to keep possession of her prizes.

But, with so many men aboard, it was no wonder that every shot through her hull or bulwarks had reaped *L'Uranie*'s over-manned crew as thickly as a farmer's scythe would cut down a field of grain. Excess hands could replace gunners and sail-tenders for a time, but if battle lasted long enough . . .

To Lewrie, gazing down into the waist, it looked as if half of those 350 Frenchmen lay on deck where they fell, or whimpered their lives away in those two long rows of savagely mutilated! A few more lanthorns bobbed about, fetched from *Proteus*, so his own petty officers could survey their own frigate's damage from out-board, or rig thick rope mats as fenders to protect both ships as their hulls thudded together, or . . . to pick and hunt among the dead and wounded for their shipmates, leaving the French where they were, for now. *Triage*, but of a different form. From the French quarterdeck, Lewrie could look over at his own ship and shake his head at how many shot-holes and shattered planks he could count in the feeble, bobbing hand-lanthorn lights.

And what's me own "butcher's bill"? he sourly wondered, feeling sick at his stomach, in addition to bone-tired; *What'd Twigg tell me, back in London? Save mine arse from the gallows whilst far overseas by doin' somethin' . . . glorious!* He felt like spitting a foul taste from his mouth. *This "glorious" enough for 'em, hey? I slay enough Frogs, sacrifice enough o'* my people, *t'keep me neck un-stretched? Price is too damned high!*

Surgeon Mr. Hodson and Surgeon's Mate Mr. Durant would tell him the cost, soon enough, Lewrie was sure.

He *shoved* himself erect from his slump on shot-gnawed railings, all but shook himself like a hound to wake himself from his lassitude. With three captured swords under his left arm, Lewrie descended an un-damaged ladderway on the larboard side to pace the main deck and waist of the French frigate, looking up at the cross-deck beams and the boat-tier, where the ruins of cutter, launch, gig, and jolly-boat sat like a pile of gayly-painted scrap lumber.

"Sir . . ." a voice intruded, and Lewrie turned to face it. Mr. Midshipman Darcy Gamble stood there, tears in his eyes. Nearby, Mr. Midshipman Grace knelt by a still form, just rolling it over face-up. "'Tis Mister Larkin, sir," Gamble told him, and Lewrie looked down to see the rictus of agony on the poor lad's face, his final expression to the fact of his own hard death, so early in life. And the flickers of Midshipman Grace's cheap tin candle-lanthorn made the lad's wounds even more lurid. "Oh, damn," Lewrie softly muttered. "Poor, wee lad."

"Still has his pistol and dirk in his hands, sir," Grace added, snuffling as he looked up at his captain. "He went down fighting, sir."

"Honourable wounds to the front, aye," Gamble pointed out, striving for the stoicism the Navy demanded, but still on the ragged edge of open sorrow for a fallen mess-mate.

"We cannot let him just lie here, sir, perhaps . . ." Grace said.

"Time enough for Mister Larkin later, Mister Grace," Lewrie told him, after harumphing to clear his throat. "There's our ship, and our wounded, to see to, first. First, last, and always. Mister Gamble."

"Sir?"

"Pick one," Lewrie told him, extending the three sheathed swords to him, hilts first. "With Lieutenant Catterall fallen, you are now an Acting-Lieutenant, and Third Officer into *Proteus*. You, Mister Grace, are now our senior Midshipman . . . for now, our only Midshipman, though there may be a likely lad or two I may advance, later."

"I see, sir," Grace replied, sadly thoughtful.

"Up to you t'show 'em the ropes of table, duties, and cockpit," Lewrie further said, hoping new and demanding duties and responsibilities might take his mind off Larkin's loss.

"Hmm . . . a bit grand, these, sir," Gamble said, his mouth cocked into a shy *moue,* selecting the plainer sword, though one with a finer and more serviceable blade. Midshipman The Honourable D'arcy Gamble came from well-to-do parents, and could, when confirmed by Admiralty, easily afford better to wear on his hip, but for now, his choice gave Lewrie an even better estimation of him.

"Very well, Lieutenant Gamble. Seek out Lieutenant Langlie and tell him my decision," Lewrie ordered. "My respects to him, and he is to work you 'til you drop to make both ships fit to sail, again."

"Aye aye, sir," Acting-Lieutenant Gamble said, with sudden pride awakening in his eyes.

"I'll have Andrews see to Mister Larkin, Mister Grace," Lewrie added. "For now, we've need . . . what?" he asked, feeling a cold chill in his innards as Grace's face screwed up in fresh, shy grief.

"Sorry, sir," Grace all but wailed as he got to his feet. "We saw your man fall. Didn't wish t'be the one t'tell you, sir, but . . . I s'pose I must. He . . . was in the main top with the other marksmen and . . . was shot, and tumbled out, and hit the . . ." Grace had to pause, and gulp, "the edge of the gangway, sir, and . . . !"

"He's gone?" Lewrie croaked, suddenly much weaker, and wearier. "Andrews is gone?" *All these years, my right-hand man, Cox'n, and . . . ?* he thought, squinting his eyes in pain; *How many people must I get killed? Strangers, enemies . . . friends? For he was . . .*

"They . . . passed him out a starboard gun-port, sir, with the . . . other dead," Mr. Grace managed to relate. "Sorry, sir. Sorry."

Gone. "Fallen" was the euphemism of the age. It was what was done with Navy casualties in battle. The dead were put over the side, at once, to clear the decks for those who still fought, a brutal necessity to maintain their morale. In many cases, the hopelessly mangled and sure to die were "put out of their misery" by a petty officer with a heavy mallet, then shoved, un-conscious and un-knowing, out the ports, too, as a "mercy" for an old shipmate whom the surgeons couldn't save. It was why the inner sides of the hull, by the guns, were traditionally painted red, as red as fresh-spilled or fresh-splattered blood . . . in the heat of action, the living *might* not notice.

Lewrie looked down, not at Larkin, but at a bare patch of deck, willing himself not to weep. Andrews . . . *Matthew* Andrews! . . . a long-time companion, was dead and gone. No matter the gulf between common sailors and officers, how aloof and apart a captain must appear to his hands, Andrews and Aspinall had been his touchstones with reality, a pair of close *friends,* really, and his loss felt like an abyss, a part of his own years in-company with him, had been cut away and lost. In a way, perhaps it was best that Andrews had been put over the side . . . best that he was *physically* gone, for Lewrie didn't think he'd be able to bear to look on many more familiar dead faces. There would surely be enough of them, already.

Blaming himself, too, scathing himself, for Andrews had been the one to go ashore and lead his dozen "Free Black volunteers" aboard the night in Portland Bight on Jamaica when he'd stolen them from one of the Beauman family's plantations . . . as a cock-snooking lark!

Had he not, would Andrews still live? Without that act, *Proteus* might still be in the Caribbean, not *here,* in *this* hour, engaged with a French frigate of greater firepower. Groome and Rodney might not have run away, were there no circus to lure them, no Africa in which to die. Whitbread, the others, might not be buried at Cape Town.

Yet, had not Andrews run from his own master on Jamaica, first? Run from the softer chains of a house slave, better fed than the field hands, garbed in wealth-flaunting livery, yet run in spite of all? As the others had run, put everything at risk for a *whiff* of freedom, even the Royal Navy's harsh version. Andrews, and they, had endured sailors' poverty, plain victuals, and unending, back-breaking work in all sorts of weather, living with the constant risk of death or disablement, the sure coming of rheumatism or arthritis, the sicknesses that arose when hundreds of men were pent together so closely in a foul and reeking wet gun-deck, for . . . what? To be *free* men, to live a wild and adventurous life as free deep sea rovers; *paid* for their suffering, and worthy of their hire! Freely entered into, and, in the Navy, ready to fight the enemy, the ocean itself, to live, and maybe die, free!

"Damme," Lewrie softly spat, raising his head, at last, stiffening his spine after a long, sad sigh. Steeling himself to play-act a role of captain, second only to God. He had two ships to save, perhaps hundreds of men, his own and the enemy's, to succour and tend to, prisoners to keep a wary eye on, and, sometime after the sun rose, another French frigate to be alert for, and possibly fight.

And, he was mortal-certain, the first of many at-sea burials, as early as tomorrow's Forenoon Watch, with more to follow as they sailed into the equatorial heat. There was a convoy to re-join and round back up, should anything have happened to *Jamaica*. Duty, that grim, demanding bitch, come to call with all her nagsome sisters, would never give a man a moment of his own! There *would* be a time to grieve Andrews and all his dead . . . once anchored in a safe harbour.

"Very well, sirs," Lewrie forced himself to rasp, clapping both hands together in the small of his back. "Let's be about it, hmm?"

Stern, now, a facade of grim stoicism back on his face, Lewrie made the shaky crossing back aboard *Proteus*, though his shuddery limbs threatened to betray him. There was no formal welcome from side-party or bosun's calls, just a bone-weary man clumping awkwardly to the oak planks of the larboard gangway of a shot-to-pieces ship.

"Sir," Sailing Master Winwood said, doffing his hat as he came forward from the quarterdeck, limping from a leg wound upon his right thigh, his breeches cut away to reveal a thick, padded bandage.

"Mister Winwood," Lewrie acknowledged. "Oh. I know."

Mr. Winwood held in his hand a coin-silver bosun's call on its chain, *Andrews's* call, and mark of his post as Coxswain. Crushed . . . by the musket ball that slew him, or by his fall from high aloft?

"So many, sir," Mr. Winwood said in his usual mournful way. "I am told by Mister Hodson that we've nigh twenty fallen, and ten more in a bad way, with at least thirty others more-or-less lightly wounded."

"Admiralty will be *so* impressed," Lewrie sarcastically growled.

"Even so, it is a signal victory, sir," Mr. Winwood said in his gravest manner. "Off to the Nor'east, *Jamaica* has come to grips with the other Frenchman, or so it would appear. The lights of both ships are close-aboard each other, and all gunfire has ceased, so one might assume that she has conquered her foe, as well,

Captain. We have won. And, from what little I saw aboard our foe, before I sustained my own trifling wound," he proudly alluded to his leg, no matter how stoic *he* wished to appear, "they must have suffered over an hundred fallen, and a like number disabled. Aye, Captain Lewrie, Admiralty *should* be impressed. Perhaps a quarter, or a third, of the French squadron in the Indian and Southern Oceans eliminated at one blow, too, sir? Well"

"Forgive me, Mister Winwood, but, at the moment . . ." Lewrie attempted to apologise.

"I understand completely, sir," Winwood replied with a knowing nod, no matter how much he didn't really understand. "Andrews was your Cox'n for a long time. God save me, I shall even miss Mister Catterall, impious as he was, but . . . Andrews gave his all. As they all did. Did their best, and we shall miss them all, some more personally, d'ye see."

Lord, don't give me a sermon, *you . . . !* Lewrie silently fumed.

". . . up to us to do our best to honour their memories, and take comfort from the thought that they passed over doing what they freely agreed to endure," Mr. Winwood was prosing on. "In Andrews' case, and the other Black volunteers, perhaps it is also up to us to shew all of Britain that they could fight, and fall, as bravely as British tars, I do believe, sir. Prove to the world the truth of the tracts from the Evangelical and Abolitionist societies declare. . . ."

"Aye, we could," Lewrie suddenly decided, and not just to stop Winwood's mournful droning, either. "They did, didn't they. Andrews, and all our Blacks who ran away to . . . this. You have a point, Mister Winwood. We could . . . we *should* . . . and, we shall!"

Then you wouldn't have died for bloody nothing, Matthew! Lewrie told himself, feeling a weight depart his shoulders, a half-turn wrench of his heart tell him that it wasn't expedience, had nothing to do with saving his precious neck from a hanging, but might become a real cause! A noble cause!

"Ah, there ye are, sir!" his cabin-servant, Aspinall, exclaimed in great relief to see him, at last, as he came forward from where the great-cabins would be, once the deal and oak partitions were erected. "Sorry t'say, sir, but yer cabins're a total wreck, again, but soon to be put t'rights. The kitties are safe, 'long with the mongooses, an' that damn' bushbaby. He's took up with Toulon an' Chalky, an' hardly *don't* cry no more, long as he can snuggle up with 'em. No coffee—"

"Aspinall . . ." Lewrie interrupted.

"I know I'm babblin', sir, 'tis just *hard* t'know ol' Andrews is gone," Aspinall said, after a gulp, and a snuffle on his sleeve. "Him an' so many good lads. But, didn't we hammer th' French, though!"

"Aye, we did," Lewrie agreed, beginning to realise what they'd done, what a victory they'd accomplished, at last. And, beginning to feel that it had been worth it, no matter the price they'd paid. "Is that Irish rogue, Liam Desmond, aboard, do you know, Aspinall?"

"Aye, sir. On th' pumps, I think."

"Pass the word for him, then," Lewrie ordered. A minute later, Liam Desmond came cautiously up the ladderway to the quarterdeck; he'd been summoned before, usually to suffer for his antics. Lewrie noted that his long-time mate, Patrick Furfy, lurked within hearing distance at the foot of the steps.

"Aye, sor?" Desmond warily asked, hat in hand, looking fearful.

Lewrie held out the crushed bosun's call to him.

"Ah, I know, Cap'm," Desmond said with a sad sigh of his own at the sight of it, glittering ambery-silver in the glow of oil or candle lamps. "Andrews woz a foin feller, he woz, always fair an' kindly with us. Sorry we lost him, sor."

"You once said, during the Mutiny at the Nore, that you'd be my right-hand sword, if all others failed me," Lewrie gravely said. "I've lost my right-hand man, Desmond. Are ye still willing?"

"Be yer Cox'n, sor?" Desmond gaped in astonishment. "*Sure*, and I meant it, Cap'm! Faith, but ye do me honour, and aye, I'll be!"

"We'll get a better, when next in port, but . . ." Lewrie said as Desmond took the call from him and looped it round his neck on its silver chain. He took a moment to look down at it, battered though it was, sitting on the middle of his chest, and puffed up his satisfaction.

"Have to stay sober and ready at all hours, mind," Lewrie said, and could hear Furfy groan in pity on the main deck, even starting to snigger over his friend's new, more demanding, predicament. "And, we could do with Furfy in my boat crew, too, hmm? A strong oarsman. And, we wouldn't let him go adrift without your . . . influence."

"A right-good idea, that, sor," Desmond chuckled, looking over his shoulder and calling out, "Hear that, Pat?"

"Another favour, Desmond," Lewrie said. "Get your lap-pipes, a fifer, too, perhaps, and play something for us, now. For Andrews and those who won't get a proper burial sewn up in canvas, under the flag."

"Have ye a tune in mind, Cap'm?" Desmond asked.

"Play 'Johnnie Faa,'" Lewrie told him. It was sad, slow, Celtic, and poignant, sad enough for even the French survivors to feel what it spoke.

Sad enough a tune to excuse even a Post-Captain's quiet tears?

EPILOGUE

"Quid studiosa cohors operum struit? Hoc quoque curo.
Quis sibi res gestas Augusti scribere sumit?
Bella quis et paces longum diffundit in aevum?"

"What works is the learned staff composing? This, too, I want to know. Who takes upon him to record the exploits of Augustus? Who adown distant ages makes known his deeds in war and peace?"

HORACE, *EPISTLES* I, III, 6-8

CHAPTER THIRTY-FIVE

There was no need for a fire in the magnificently, and ornately, carved fireplace in the Board Room of Admiralty in London, for it was a fine summer day, and the tall windows had been thrown open to take the stuffiness and enclosed warmth from the room. The equally-showy chronometer on one gleaming panelled wall slowly ticked, and now and then a shift of wind off the Thames forced the large repeater of the wind vane on the roof to clack about to display whether the weather stood fair or foul for British warships and merchantmen to depart, or whether Nature might favour a sally by the French, or a combination of French, Dutch Batavian, and Spanish navies together.

The First Lord of the Admiralty, John, Earl Spencer, sat at the head of a highly-polished table. To his right sat the Controller of the Navy, Adm. Sir Andrew Snape Hammond. Down at the other end of the table, not so far away as to be out of ear-shot, for the Board Room was not so grand in scale as most imagined, Sir Evan Nepean, the First Secretary to Admiralty, sat and shuffled his notes and records brought by a junior clerk, a pen poised to record decisions.

"The man's not *worthy* of a knighthood, I tell you, sir! He is a scandal . . . a seagoing scandal," the youngish Earl Spencer declared in some heat. "A mountebank, more suited to the company of those scandalous, sordid . . . *circus* people Captain Leatherwood rescued."

"Do we not put his name forward, milord," Adm. Hammond mildly pointed out between sips of his tea, "then Leatherwood cannot be placed on the Honours List, either . . . and, in all, Captain Leatherwood had a *trifling* action 'gainst a panicked and 'rudderless' ship's company . . . once those horrid circus people had slain half their officers. It was *Proteus* that bore the brunt of it, fighting an action lasting one and a half hours, whilst *Jamaica* barely fired two full broadsides before her foe struck. I grant you, milord, that Captain Lewrie's, ah . . . repute is not completely of the best, beyond his fame as a pugnacious and sly Sea Officer. . . ."

"Fame, Sir Andrew?" the Earl Spencer scoffed. "Try notoriety."

"Even so, milord, he'd earned a bright name in the Fleet before this most recent exploit, and the newspapers, and the public, are falling over themselves in praise of him." To the Earl Spencer's distress, Sir Evan Nepean had been saving London papers, from the best publishers to the most scurrilous, and the many articles snipped out and piled on one corner of the table made an impressive stack. Alongside them was a second pile, mostly of Reformers' tracts, complete with wood-cut art of two frigates battling in what a lubberly artist portrayed as a hurricane. There were portraits of the aforesaid Capt. Alan Lewrie, RN, as well, even more imaginative, and saintly!, along with drawings of Black and White sailors—some labelled with the names of the heroically-fallen Blacks—with Lewrie leading them in the boarding of the French frigate, *L'Uranie*, as over-armed as an old depiction of a fearsome pirate . . . without the beard, and with better hair, of course.

"May I say so, milord," Sir Evan Nepean piped up from the bottom of the table, for many of Admiralty's day-to-day decisions were his to make, so that the responsible, and lucrative, post of First Secretary held much more influence than most outside the Navy thought. "But, the Reverend Wilberforce and his followers had made a public figure of him already, not *quite* on the level of an Admiral Nelson, but close. Do we *not* offer Captain Lewrie significant, and near-equal, rewards that any successful captain, and the public, has come to expect, there might be suspicions that His Majesty's Government, not just Admiralty, favours the side of slave-owners, colonial planters, and the sugar and shipping interests over what is quickly becoming a widespread sentiment against the institution of slavery."

"Preposterous!" the Earl Spencer snapped.

"Been a while since Nelson at the Nile, milord," Adm. Hammond softly stuck in from the other side. "The common folk and the Mob are starved for continued good news anent the war. Even what may be called a minor frigate action for the most part has quite elated them, and Sir Evan is correct, I believe. Lewrie must be awarded *something*, milord."

"Beyond the accolades he's gotten, already?" the Earl Spencer sourly rejoined, tugging the velvet pull-cord to summon them more tea. "Thanks of

Parliament, the usual presentation of a plate service, and an hundred-guinea sword from the East India Company for Leatherwood and Lewrie, both? Both officers granted the Freedoms of their towns or villages, along with the Freedoms of Portsmouth, London . . . the keys to *Hearne Bay*, for all I know!

"Both agreed that they were 'in-sight' of each other, and with *two* French National Ships brought in as prize," the Earl Spencer continued to carp, "so *Proteus* and *Jamaica* will reap a pretty penny from being bought into Navy service, as well. The next step *might* be presenting them at Saint James's palace, and knighthoods, but . . . as you say, Leatherwood didn't do all *that* much, and Lewrie is simply too . . . we might as well knight that Cockney, Wigmore, his actresses, and his *bears* into the bargain! No, Sir Andrew, I am extremely loath to place Captain Lewrie's name to the King. T'would be *too* embarrassing."

"His First Officer, Anthony Langlie," Sir Evan Nepean suggested more mildly, "promoted to Commander, of course, milord, and given an active commission into a suitable vessel?"

"The usual thing, aye," Adm. Hammond nodded with a smile on his face, "though I doubt Leatherwood's First earned the same thing. Or, should we? Right then, both of them promoted," he happily said after a resigned nod of assent from the First Lord. "A spell of shore leave for both Lewrie and Leatherwood, then, new active commissions for both . . . to better ships, hmm?" The First Lord cocked his head towards Nepean.

"*Jamaica* was due to be paid off and hulked, milord," Sir Evan quickly supplied, after a quick shuffle of his notes. "A very old and bluff-bowed sixty-four gunner, as slow as treacle even when new. Built just *before* the Seven Years' War. But, there *are* several Third Rates of seventy-four guns coming available, and Captain Leatherwood will be honoured to command one, I'm certain. As for Captain Lewrie . . . hmm."

He shuffled some more, as a steward in livery entered with tray and pot to replace the used cups and empty tea-pot, then silently went out like a zephyr of summer wind.

"*Proteus* is fairly new, but *has* seen rather more action than one may expect, milord. . . ."

"Lewrie was her first, and only, captain," Sir Andrew stated, as if trying to tweak the Earl Spencer, leaning towards him and grinning.

"The Surveyors think she will require a total refit," Sir Evan Nepean continued. "Four to six months' work. Might you wish Captain Lewrie to sit ashore on half-pay that long, milord?"

"By God I do not!" the First Lord barked. "There's no telling *what* Deviltry the man's capable of with that much idle time available him. And . . . there is the, ah . . . possibility of being tried for his theft of slaves on Jamaica. 'Out of sight, out of mind' seems apt, at this moment. I will not knight a man who stands a chance of being put in the dock a few months later. Nor will I allow the papers and public time to discover what sort of man he really is. A new ship, something larger and suitable, of a certainty. Preferably, one able to sail far from England, and possible embarrassment, Sir Evan."

Exactly what the Foreign Office appointee to the Privy Council suggested might be best for the Crown, Nepean thought, hiding his sly grin. "Ah. In two more months or so, milord, Sir Andrew, an eighteen-pounder gunned Fifth Rate frigate will be returned from the dockyards at Portsmouth, and ready for re-commissioning. She is the HMS *Savage,* originally built in '93, just after the start of the war, and in very good structural condition, barring the usual problems with her bottom, and such. Her former captain has already been re-assigned, so . . ."

"Two whole months with him ashore and unemployed, though," the First Lord mused with a suspicious frown. "Then, however long it will take him to gather a new crew. . . ."

"There would be no delay in it, either, milord," Nepean brightly added, "for we are in possession of a letter from both the officers and crew of *Proteus* . . . even the Marines and cabin steward lads, expressing their wish to remain under Captain Lewrie, entire."

"Remarkable," Adm. Sir Andrew Hammond allowed. He was Royal Navy, man and boy, and knew what sort of officer might elicit such loyalty, even if the First Lord, a civilian, did not appreciate it. "We could pay off *Proteus* into the Portsmouth yard . . . where she currently is anchored, I believe? Then turn over *Proteus*'s people into *Savage*. Quite neat, milord. And, with little reason for Lewrie to come up to London . . . into the clutches of the newspapers, hmm?"

"Oh my, yes!" the First Lord quickly, enthusiastically, agreed. "Make it so, Sir Evan. Now, as to the next matter on our agenda . . ."

The exotic beasts, the jugglers and acrobats, the fire-eater and his bursts of flame from his mouth, the capering clowns and their pig bladders and antics, and the clattering waggons painted in fresh bright red and yellow drew such a crowd as any that the Marine garrison from Portsmouth Dockyards had ever drawn. The circus's band, replenished by new musicians and outfitted in garishly-trimmed uniforms more imposing than the Army List of generals (including all retired ones), oom-pahhed, crashed, drummed, and tooted along at the head of the parade, children of the town deserting the kerbings for the cobblestones to prance and march along with them, goggle-eyed and shrieking with utter delight at such a wonder! H'elefinks, lions, dancing bears, zebras, and God knew *what-all,* and some of them, like the performers in their show costumes, had fought the filthy French, and won, for didn't all the newspapers say so, all the flyers printed by the circus, too, say it?

It wasn't just *any* tawdry old circus and theatrical troupe, it was *Wigmore's Travelling Extravaganza,* honoured with a proclamation by the Crown, with Thanks of Parliament to boot, back from deepest, darkest Africa, bigger and better than ever, and, "Oh, Mummy! We must see it! We must attend, *puh-lease?*"

Individual blossoms, whole nose-gays, were flung at the parading performers and beasts, even the hyena and the anteaters, and the red-arsed baboons in their waggon cage, the same sort of accolades given a regiment just back from a victorious campaign, and there was good old Daniel Wigmore on a fine horse, tipping his hat to one and all, a patch-eyed "foreign-looking cove" with a rifle-musket in one hand, and one of his squawling lion cubs on his saddle's pommel, a cove who could swing to face backwards, turn a flip on his horse's back, slide down to hang on the side of his mount like a wild Red American Indian, and gallop up the street like the very wind, huzzah!

And, that remarkably beautiful girl on the white horse, riding *astride,* in breeches and boots so snug you could see . . . ! and children's eyes were covered, and women tittered into handkerchiefs, but my!, but she was a horsewoman, too, and with that spiky crown, that flowing mane of curly black hair, and *that bow,* my Gawd! *She* was the lovely Eudoxia, slayer of a dozen, *two-*dozen, odious Frenchmen intent upon her ravishing, or worse, and when she stood on her mount's bare back, everyone cheered, whistled, and fell in love with her daring, and her bravery.

Then, she swerved from the parade's course, right to the doors of a venerable old posting house frequented by naval officers. Right onto the sidewalk she forced her horse.

"*Kapitan* Lewrie!" she gaily cried. "*Zdrasvutyeh!* Hello, again! Black fellow, Rodney, is healed up, *da?* Little shooter is well?"

"Mistress Eudoxia," Lewrie nervously replied, doffing his hat to her, though with one eye on her father, for Arslan Durschenko had brought his horse to a stop quite nearby, and he *did* hold a musket in his hand, and it *might* be loaded, and . . . ! "Seaman Rodney is now fine. Fit as a fiddle!" And the crowd about him began to whisper, then cry out, that that-there Navy man was "Black Alan" Lewrie, by Jingo, "The Emancipator," and "Hero of the South Atlantic," wot woz in all o' them tracts an' sich!

"I s'pose your circus will do well, now that . . ." Lewrie began to say, but Eudoxia got that impish look in her big, almond-shaped amber eyes, making Lewrie glance at her father, who was scowling *fiercely* by then, and starting to wheel his horse's head round, and . . . !

"Bravest man in all Navy!" Eudoxia loudly declared. "*Kapitan* is my *hero*!" A moment before she leaned down, took him by an epaulet, and kissed him smack on the mouth . . . with a sly bit of tongue to boot, it here must be noted, as the crowd went wild with amusement.

Oh, Christ, don't do that, *not* now, *not . . . !* Lewrie frantically thought, though (it here must be noted as well) he did not find the experience *completely* disagreeable.

"Mummy, who's that lady kissing Papa?" his daughter Charlotte crossly demanded as his children, and his wife Caroline, bustled from the inn's doors. "Why's she dressed like that? Is she *foreign* or . . . ?"

"Why, I do not know, dear, but I am certain we shall discover who she is, *soon*!" Caroline Lewrie drawled, fixing her husband with a very jaundiced glare. Middle son Hugh guffawed, his eyes alight with instant hero-worship of the famous Eudoxia, right before his eyes in the flesh (so to speak), whilst Lewrie's eldest, Sewallis, ever a cautious lad, merely gawked and turned red.

"Is *jena*? Wife?" Eudoxia asked, turning on her sugary charm. "Mistress Lewrie, wife of bravest *kapitan* in whole world, who savink us from *Fransooski* bas . . . bad peoples, *spasiba*. *Kapitan* Lewrie speak of you and *dyeti* . . . children so *often*! Is right word, 'often'? I am honour-ed to be meetink you!" she gushed. "You comink to circus, you and children? Will be *bolshoi* show!"

"We will see," Caroline coolly rejoined. "Honoured to meet you as well, since I've read so much about you, Mistress . . . Eudoxia?"

"Must go, now," Eudoxia said. "Wantink to say *bootyeh zdarovi* to Kapitan Lewrie one last time. Meanink 'bless you,' yes? For all he do for us. *Dosvidanya*, Kapitan. *Paka snova!*"

"Have a grand tour of Britain, Mistress Durschenko," Lewrie bade her in turn, doffing his hat and making a leg to keep it formal, and *innocent*. Eudoxia kneed her horse and made him perform a kneeling bow to Lewrie, to the further amazement of the crowd, as she swept something like a formal Eastern *salaam* while seated on his back, too.

"And *that* means . . . ?" Caroline warily enquired.

" 'Goodbye,' and 'see you' . . . I think, in Russian, my dear," he told her, thanking God that Caroline's only foreign tongue was a little French, for *"Paka snova"*—"See you, *again*!"—had been delivered with such a light in Eudoxia's eyes, laden with so much impish *promise*.

"And, *shall* we attend the circus, Alan?" Caroline icily posed.

"Well . . . I'm certain the *children* would enjoy it, dear," Lewrie replied with as much off-handed blitheness as he could muster, actually managing to look his wife in her eyes, 'stead of blinking too much.

"Oh, Mummy, could we?" Charlotte squealed, about to bounce out of her shoes, and her face as squinted as when she needed to pee; and Hugh and Sewallis clamoured for it, too. "We've never *seen* a circus!"

"We shall see, children," Caroline told them. "I'm sure that it would be *educational*. Though, perhaps it might prove too exciting for *some* of us," she added, a brow cocked in her husband's direction. "I believe your father has seen it several times, already, and, what with all that is needful to commission his new ship, might have no time to spare for *further* attendance."

"Well . . ." Lewrie glibly rejoined, shrugging again, higher.

And I never laid a finger *on the mort!* he thought; *Well, maybe a hand, a lip or two, but . . . damned if I did, damned if I didn't, and Caroline'll think the worst o' me, either way. Gawd, but this is going t'be a* long *reconciliation! Ain't I a bloody hero? Ain't that worth something, in my own house?*

"Come along, children," Caroline serenely instructed, gathering her brood, her regal air parting the press of the crowd before them as sure as Moses parted the Red Sea. "Come, Alan!" she bade her husband with a trifle *less* patience as he lagged behind a little, wondering for a second or two whether she meant him to be in their company, after all. "We're going to the chandlers' shops for your needs . . . dearest. Or so I thought," she said for the benefit of the close-pressed spectators.

"Oh, o' course, my dear," Lewrie replied, joining them at last. He linked arms with her, and plastered as much of an untroubled expression on his phyz as Caroline wore on hers.

"But, what about the *circus*, Mummy?" Little Charlotte whined.

"Oh, we shall attend, dears," Caroline vowed, turning to smile at her children. "Of course, we shall. Your father will take us . . . for are we not a family, after all?"

Thank bloody Christ! Lewrie thought with glad relief; *There* is *a thaw . . . maybe*. Then, began to contemplate how un-interested, aloof, and semi-bored he must act at the performance that night, and make his wife actually believe it!

AFTERWORD

At one time in the far-distant past, I rather naively assumed that I had Alan Lewrie's career in the Royal Navy plotted out with an appearance in a series of major events from his entry into the Fleet in 1780, all the way through to 1815.

Wrong, wrong, wrong! The more I associate with the rogue, the further afield I end up departing from that early stab at a *curriculum vitae*. It's as if my rubber bracelet, which bears the initials W.W.L.D.—What Would Lewrie Do—was ensorcelled by a cut-rate wizard down on Lower Broad here in Nashville, quite near Tootsie's Orchid Lounge and the Old Ryman Theatre, so that Lewrie's perverse streak of "Oh no, let's go *there*!" sometimes takes over. It could be worse; I could have been possessed by the ghost of Hank Williams, and drunk myself to an early death, years ago!

This all started quite innocently when I ran across a mention in a reference book about a British circus and theatrical troupe that had sailed to America in 1797, and had had a wildly successful year's tour down the coast of the United States, from New England to Savannah, and Lewrie, and I, both said, "Hmmm," about the same time. Him first, me first, I'm still not quite sure, but the thought of actresses, agile acrobats, bareback riders (which had a very sexual connotation in the eighteenth century—figure it out for yourself!), skimpily clad aerialists, breathy little "theatrical" *ingénues,* and actresses! Did I mention actresses? The only drawback was the clowns and mimes . . . along with the "Zoo-Doo" left by a menagerie of exotic beasts.

As for those slaves . . . the Rev. William Wilberforce and other people whom Lewrie met in London before his little Odyssey were actual people who were in the relentlessly grim process of reforming every wee bit of English Society . . . the word "Respectable" didn't even come into common usage 'til the late 1790s, after Wilberforce and Hannah More got their talons into things. Sarah Trimmer really wrote dismayingly "cute" children's books, damning all the old blood-and-guts and scare-them-to-sleep folk tales as too traumatic for such shrinking violets as British children. The first roots of the Politically Correct movement put out their first runners deep under the soil at that moment.

So successful were the Reformers, the Clapham Sect, the Evangelical Society, and the Society for the Abolition of Slavery that Britons became a *very* tight-assed people, just in time for the Victorian Age. To this day, you put up a sign demanding that Brits line up for something, and you'll get a queue the likes not seen outside ticket offices for Super Bowl seats. As Hannah More gleefully said, "Slowly we shall take away all the bad old influences, 'til the only thing they have to look upon is ourselves." Or something very much like that, but you may get the gist. They were social engineers so successful that they made Lenin weep with envy.

Slavery in the British Isles disappeared in the 1750s, though rich business interests fought tooth and nail to keep the sugar, teas, and coffee crops coming in from the Caribbean. It was not 'til 1807 that the slave trade was officially abolished throughout the British Empire, a ban honoured more with lip-service 'til 1815, when the Napoleonic Wars ended, and the government could pay attention to enforcing its laws. A peacetime Royal Navy became active in policing the African coasts with anti-slavery patrols to stop the continued export of slaves by other countries. Slavery itself was not abolished in all British colonies until 1833.

While Lewrie is not much of a real musician with his wee penny-whistle, and I have had my bad moments with bagpipe lessons and badly-done banjo playing, both he and I like music. In the last few books, readers will have run across the *titles* of eighteenth-century tunes, and for those who haven't been to the Smithville Old Time Fiddlers Jamboree, Uncle Dave Macon Days down in Murfreesboro, Tennessee, been to the Ryman and the Grand Ole Opry, or been fortunate enough to be my downstairs neighbours at one in the A.M. who just *adore* my CDs, let me cite a couple of them to put you in a "Lewrie state of mind." Drink, low companions, seedy dives, and "women no better than they ought to be" are up to you, though.

"Smash the Windows" is by a group called The Virginia Company, a collection of pre-Revolutionary tavern music on authentic instruments. Write The Virginia Company, Box 1853, Williamsburg, VA 23187, or call (757) 229-3677.

Another is "Nottingham Ale—Tavern Music from Colonial Williamsburg," recorded at the Raleigh Tavern. Contact the Williamsburg Foundation, Box 1776, Williamsburg, VA 23187-1776.

So, here's Lewrie, a national hero, and actually sorta-kinda reconciled with his *wife*? But, will it all end up aboard Tom Turdman's barge at Dung Wharf, as things involving Lewrie usually do? And, what is Zachariah Twigg *really* up to, and has Alan been set up as a ready-made martyr for the anti-slavery crowd, as Lewrie suspects? When *will* the Beaumans and their lawyers (boo, hiss!) arrive, and may Lewrie get his new frigate out to sea before they do? And, finally, just what *did* Eudoxia Durschenko have in mind when she bade him that enigmatic *"paka snova"*—"See you . . . again!"

"No, Lewrie, you can't go to the circus, again, damn yer eyes!"

Or . . . maybe he might.

W.W.L.D., y'all.